Alison Rober
live in the Sou
recently, but is
of New Zealan ~~ough to~~
write for the M~~ills & B~~oon Medical line. A
primary school teacher in a former life, she later
became a qualified paramedic. She loves to travel
and dance, drink champagne and spend time with
her daughter and her friends. Alison is the author
of over one hundred books!

Marion Lennox has written over one hundred
romance novels and is published in over one hundred
countries and thirty languages. Her international
awards include the prestigious RITA® award (twice!)
and the *RT Book Reviews* Career Achievement Award
for 'a body of work which makes us laugh and
teaches us about love'. Marion adores her family, her
kayak, her dog, and lying on the beach with a book
someone else has written. Heaven!

HEALED BY A MISTLETOE KISS

ALISON ROBERTS

BABY SHOCK FOR THE MILLIONAIRE DOC

MARION LENNOX

MILLS & BOON

First published in Great Britain 2023
by Mills & Boon, an imprint of HarperCollins*Publishers* Ltd,
1 London Bridge Street, London, SE1 9GF

www.harpercollins.co.uk

HarperCollins*Publishers* Macken House, 39/40 Mayor Street Upper,
Dublin 1, D01 C9W8, Ireland

ISBN: 978-0-263-30624-8

11/23

HEALED BY A MISTLETOE KISS

ALISON ROBERTS

MILLS & BOON

CHAPTER ONE

SHE DIDN'T WANT to go inside.

But she had to.

Nikita Wallace pulled her coat around her as the cold fog turned into more of a wintry drizzle that was verging on sleet. She stayed exactly where she was, however, well away from the shelter of the main entrance to Bristol's Central Infirmary—the hospital that she'd once believed she would be happy working in for the rest of her life as a trauma surgeon.

But she hadn't set foot through those doors in over a year.

Somebody's phone started ringing as they walked past her. They'd probably set the ringtone to a classic Christmas carol on the first day of December. Surely they were totally over it by now when they were almost halfway through the month?

A lyric from the carol sneaked into the back of Nikita's head and it was almost a taunt.

'Tis the season to be jolly...

Yeah...right... Nikita took a deep breath, feeling the chill of the air against the back of her throat. She'd thought she was more than ready to do this. She should have done it last week, in fact, when the approved duration of her leave of absence had expired. She knew she *had* to do it, if only to prove to herself that she had recovered enough to genuinely move on with her life. She just needed a moment, that was all. A moment to gather her courage to face something that was apparently going to be a little more difficult than she had anticipated.

It wasn't simply that she didn't want to be within the walls of this hospital. Or any hospital at all, for that matter. Or that it would be full of people—staff and patients, adults and children and probably babies as well—who would have no idea how much she didn't want to be too close to them. It wasn't that it was getting so close to Christmas Day either, and there would be decorations everywhere and people would be wearing silly headbands and jumpers and flashing jewellery, like the earrings of that woman she'd seen in the car park. There might even be carol singers gathered in the foyer or wandering through the corridors of the hospital to make sure that nobody missed out on a bit of seasonal jolliness.

It was all of those things.

Too many things that, even on their own, let alone when they coalesced, had been capable of triggering a flashback in the early days of this year. Nikita was confident that she had made a good recovery but…

…but that fear had never quite gone away, had it?

She took another slow, deep breath. In through her nose and out through her mouth, her breath making a puff of steam in the icy air. A shiver ran down her spine as well, but Nikita knew that was due to the cold, not fear.

She could do this.

It wouldn't take long.

And then she'd never have to do it again because that was why she was here.

To resign permanently from the job that had been held open for her for more than a year.

If there was a place Pedro Garcia loved to be in, other than an operating theatre, it was here—in the emergency department. And, as an orthopaedic surgeon with advanced qualifications in trauma, he got to spend as much time as he wanted in both places.

Right now, he was in the emergency department of Bristol's Central Infirmary in response to a call to a trauma case. A fourteen-year-old boy had come off his skateboard on the way home from school and had a dislocated shoulder. Pedro had ordered an initial X-ray to rule out any significant fracture and he was showing the image to his patient.

'See that, Thomas? That round bit there is the top of your humerus, which is the bone in your upper arm. It's what we call a ball and socket type of joint and that's the ball. The socket part, where it's supposed to be sitting, is that bit there...' Pedro pointed to the slightly blurred bony structure to one side of where it should have been. 'The good news is I can't see anything nasty in there so you probably won't need an operation to fix it. I just need to put the round bit back where it belongs. Is that okay with you, buddy?'

'It's going to hurt, isn't it?' Thomas increased the pressure he was using to hold his injured arm immobile against his body, even though it was already in a sling.

'We're going to make sure it doesn't hurt,' Pedro reassured him. He glanced up at the nurse standing beside the bed. 'Any idea of how far away Thomas's mother is?' It was certainly in the teen's best interest to have this dislocation reduced as quickly as possible but it was also preferable to have parental consent if possible.

As if in answer to his query, the curtain to the cubicle was pulled back and a stressed-looking woman was ushered in.

'Tommy, what on earth did you think you were doing? You *knew* that skateboard wasn't safe. You could have killed yourself.'

Pedro raised an eyebrow at Thomas, who avoided his gaze.

'It's got a dodgy wheel,' he muttered.

'And I promised him a new one for Christmas,' his mother sighed. 'Oh, Tommy...this is all we need at this time of the year. They tell me you might need an operation. I can't even stay here very long—my boss was less than happy I walked out and there's no one else to pick your sisters up from after-school care.'

Pedro caught the woman's gaze and held it. 'It's okay, Mamá,' he said. 'We've got this. I was just checking with Thomas that he was okay for me to try and put things back into place.'

'Of course it is. Please...just do whatever you need to do. I'll be ever so grateful if I can take Tommy home with me.' She wiped a tear streak from her face and smiled at her son. 'He's been the man of the house since his dad walked out on us a couple of years ago. I couldn't manage without him.'

Oh, man... Pedro knew a family's expectations could take a heavy toll. The kind of sacrifices that had to be made to meet them, like putting their needs so far above your own that you learned it was better not to want anything too much.

'Is it okay with you, Thomas?' he asked.

The teenager nodded but Pedro knew how scared the lad was. How brave he was trying to be. How determined he was to step up to responsibilities that, in an ideal world, should never be placed on the shoulders of someone this young.

'We got some good stuff to help,' he told Thomas in a confidential tone. 'I'm going to get you to suck on some Entonox, which is a mixture of nitrous oxide and oxygen. Some people call it laughing gas.'

Thomas was certainly not avoiding Pedro's gaze now. He was looking shocked. 'But that's NOS, isn't it? It's illegal. There are boys at my school who got into *big* trouble when they got busted behind the bike sheds using that.'

'It's not illegal in hospital,' Pedro told him. 'It's really good to stop things hurting, and that's when you're supposed to use it.'

The shock was turning into interest. 'Am I really allowed to have it?'

'As much as you need,' Pedro promised. 'Nurse Anna here is going to show you how to use it, but first, I'm going to put the back of your bed right up and I want you to sit on the side with your good arm against the end of the bed and your legs dangling over the edge.'

'Hold the plastic mouthpiece with your teeth and seal your lips around it,' Anna told Thomas a minute or two later. 'Just breathe normally through your mouth. You might feel a bit dizzy or get some tingling in your fingers but don't worry—that will disappear very fast once you stop breathing it.'

Pedro positioned himself behind Thomas as he was getting used to the Entonox. He undid the knot of the sling and supported the arm with one hand. When Thomas started giggling, he caught Anna's gaze.

'I think the Entonox is working,' he said. 'Can you take this arm, please? I'll let you know when to apply some gentle traction.'

He palpated Thomas's back and shoulder to locate the scapula and other anatomical landmarks he needed. Then he used his thumbs to push and rotate the bones, having given Anna the nod to apply traction. He could feel the moment the ball of the joint slid back into its correct position.

Thomas hadn't felt a thing.

'You can stop using this now.' Anna took the mouthpiece from his hand.

'Aww…' Thomas made a very comically sad face but then grinned up at Pedro.

'It's all done,' Pedro told him as he retied the knot of the sling. 'You were a champion. All that needs to happen now is another X-ray to make sure everything's as good as it can be and, if it is, you'll be able to go home.' He looked at Thomas's mother. 'He'll only need the sling for a week or two, and he can start some physiotherapy about the same time.' Turning back to his young patient, Pedro spoke seriously. 'The more effort you can put into strengthening the muscles around your shoulder, the less likely this is to happen again, okay?'

Thomas nodded. 'Okay.'

'Why does he need another X-ray?' his mother asked.

'Sometimes there are fractures that are hidden by the dislocation and, if they're not stable, they may need surgical intervention. I don't think we'll find any but we have to be sure, especially with someone of Thomas's age. We want to avoid any complications down the road with recurrent dislocations.'

He glanced at his watch and his tone was apologetic now.

'I have to run, I'm sorry. I've got a meeting I urgently need to be at, but I'll be available to check the X-ray if there's any problem. The radiologist will be able to give you an all-clear otherwise and Anna here will sort you out with a set of instructions of how to take care of that shoulder and an outpatient appointment for follow-up.'

Pedro walked from the emergency department to the nearest bank of lifts, which were in the main entranceway foyer. As usual, at this time of day, it was a busy place. Even busier at the moment, because there were people on ladders decorating a huge Christmas tree near the huge sliding glass doors. The gift shop was crowded and there was a queue in front of the café counter. Even the receptionists had more people than usual waiting for attention and the whole scene made Pedro smile.

He'd always loved Christmas. He loved the colour and brightness of the lights and decorations and the way people smiled at each other more often. He loved the excitement that hovered over the heads of children with increasing strength as the month progressed. He didn't even mind that he had to wait longer in queues at the supermarket or post office. He was relieved, however, that there didn't seem to be anyone else waiting for a lift right now. Pedro knew he should take the stairs but his meeting was on the fourth floor and he really didn't want to be late. He punched a button for the lift and watched the light start moving towards the ground floor.

Pedro was hoping, very much, that the rumour he'd heard was correct and that he was about to be offered a permanent position here at Bristol Central instead of losing the locum position he'd held for almost a year now.

He got into the lift as soon as the doors were open wide enough. He pushed the button for the fourth floor and then pushed it again, even though he knew perfectly well that it wouldn't make the doors shut any faster.

The hospital's foyer was more crowded than Nikita had expected.

There was a group of people wearing Santa hats, who were busy hanging lights and bright baubles on an over-sized Christmas tree. Someone was singing 'Jingle Bells' and they all looked delighted to be doing such a happy task.

Nikita tried not to look at the tree directly. She had to keep scanning the whole area, anyway, to be alert to anything that might be out of the ordinary.

Dangerous…

She could feel her adrenaline level rise as she processed the sounds of a child crying, a telephone ringing and laughter from a couple gossiping in front of the gift shop. Her senses were heightened enough that she could smell coffee and toasted cheese wafting from the café, but she was coping with a scenario that would have been unthinkable to go near not that long ago.

The noise of a glass decoration being dropped and shattering on the hard floor threatened to tip the balance, but Nikita simply increased the speed with which she was walking towards the lifts. She almost ran the last few steps, in fact, because she could see the doors of one of them starting to close and she didn't want to have to wait for another or try and get up four flights of stairs in a hurry. Mind you, she was already inexcusably late for her meeting with the Head of Surgery, John Barlow. He would probably be delighted to hear that she was planning to never come back to work here.

Nikita ducked through the gap in time for it not to sense an obstacle and slide open again. A glance at the control panel showed her that her destination button had already been pushed so there was nothing she needed to do. She didn't turn to acknowledge the only other person in this small space. Instead, she focused on the door in front of her and willed it to climb quickly and not stop at any other floors. She hadn't been in a confined space like this for months and, while claustrophobia wasn't one of her demons, it did feel like the steel walls had the potential to magnify unwanted thoughts by bouncing them back at her.

The lift gathered speed when there was no summons to stop at either the first or second floors. But then, with no warning whatsoever, there was a grinding crunch of machinery and the lift shuddered to a halt so violently that Nikita lost her balance. She would have fallen hard if the man behind her hadn't caught her arm but she didn't stay upright and that was by choice.

Something bad was happening and she needed to shelter. Without thinking, Nikita sat down in the corner of the lift, bringing her knees up to her chest and putting her head on top of them. She barely heard the man's voice assuring her that they were quite safe and the lift wasn't about to start falling, and his words became muffled anyway, as she crossed her arms over her head and waited for the worst to happen.

She knew it would. She felt the instant that it began to happen and could hear the agonised note in the breath that escaped her as the lift juddered again. The solid embrace of the man's arms around her could—*should*, even?—have made everything so much worse but, oddly, Nikita found it comforting. Like the rumble of his deep voice so close to her ear now.

'It's okay, Nikki. You're safe. Whatever went wrong has stopped and we're moving again, that's all. Look…we're stopping. The doors will open any second.'

Nikki?

He knew her name? Not just her name but the nickname that only people who had known her well, years ago, used?

The lift doors were still shut as Nikita dropped her arms and looked up at the man who was holding her.

'*Pedro?*'

He was smiling at her. A face from the past. Ten years in the past, when they'd both been in the same year at the same medical school. Pedro Garcia was someone who had known her when the world was a very different place for Nikita. Someone who had no idea what had happened since. She could see that he was only too aware that something had changed, however. The intense gaze from eyes that were so dark you couldn't see the pupils was disconcerting.

'Are you okay, Nikki?'

'I'm fine.' Nikita moved to scramble to her feet and

Pedro let go of her immediately. The doors had begun sliding open as she stood up.

She wasn't fine, of course, but Nikita wasn't about to start explaining what must seem like a ridiculous overreaction to a minor incident. She didn't want the reminder of how much her life had changed.

How much she'd lost...

Or that she had just failed in what she'd seen as a test of how far she'd come in her recovery. That felt like the worst aspect of this horrible situation and Nikita needed to get out of it as soon as possible.

'I'm fine,' she said again—as if she needed to convince herself as much as Pedro.

And then she escaped through the half-open doors of the lift and immediately turned to push open the swing door that led to the stairwell. She kept her hand on the banister rail for balance so she could run down those stairs as quickly as she could, given that she was wearing heels that she hadn't worn for a very long time and a skirt that was hampering her movement.

She was focusing hard to make sure she didn't fall, but that didn't stop her remembering the look of shock in Pedro's eyes.

Even after Nikita was out of the building—that Christmas tree no more than a blur in her peripheral vision as she raced through the main door—and she was heading for where she'd parked her car, she found herself looking over her shoulder, towards the hundreds of windows in the enormous hospital building.

It felt as if Pedro was still watching her.

CHAPTER TWO

HE COULD SEE her from the window of this fourth-floor office as easily as he'd recognised her when she'd rushed into the lift just before the doors finished closing.

Nikki Wallace…

'Sorry, did you just say Nikki Wallace? You mean Nikita Wallace?' The head of the surgical department at Bristol's Central Infirmary, John Barlow, sounded startled. He came to the window and looked down. 'Is that her going into the car park?'

'Yes. I just saw her in the lift so I know what she was wearing.'

John shook his head. 'Well, she's going in the wrong direction to be coming to see me and her appointment was nearly twenty minutes ago, anyway.'

'There was a bit of a hiccup with the lift. Some mechanical fault. It stopped rather suddenly between floors.'

'Oh…' There was a very different note in John's voice now. 'How did Nikita cope with that?'

Something in his tone put Pedro on alert. A sixth sense, like an instinct, made him feel suddenly protective of Nikki. Goodness only knew why, but there it was. Maybe it had something to do with how different she'd looked—a ghost of the woman he remembered rather too well from medical school days.

'It's always a bit concerning when an elevator malfunctions,' he said carefully. 'We've all seen those movies where people go plummeting to their doom.'

'Hmm…' John turned away from the window to drop a manila folder on his desk. 'We'll have to reschedule this meeting, Pedro. We can't do any paperwork concerning your position here when I haven't tidied up the position vacancy I thought we had. Nikita was supposed to be formalising her resignation before we had a chat about your future at Central.'

'Nikki? Resigning?' For the first time, Pedro could understand that odd expression of adding two and two and coming up with five. Surely he was wrong. 'Is it *her* trauma surgeon position I've been filling as a locum?'

'Yes.'

'How did I not know that?'

'Everything to do with Nikita has been kept under wraps for the last year.' John tapped the side of his nose. 'Privacy issues…'

'Oh…' Now Pedro was really curious. 'Has she been on maternity leave?' He knew that Nikki was thirty-six—the same age as he was. It was not an uncommon time of life to take leave and start a family.

'No.' John's huff of expelled breath made the word almost a chuckle of laughter. 'She'd need to make sure she could look after herself before she started looking after kids.'

The man's tone was patronising now. And Pedro didn't like it.

'Nikki and I were friends at medical school,' he said. 'Good friends.'

Okay, that was pushing the truth a little, given that they'd never been anywhere near as close as Pedro might have wanted, but they'd definitely been friends—until graduation day, when it had all gone so very sour. Imploded, even?

'We lost touch but…' Pedro cleared his throat. 'If I need to make a decision about stepping into her shoes in a surgical consultant's position, I think I should, at least, know the reason she's resigning. And why she's been on leave for the last year?'

The older man stared at him for a long moment and then he shrugged. 'PTSD,' he said. 'Nikita had an agreement to be released for three months of every year so that she could work with Médecins Sans Frontières. She took unpaid leave, which she can well afford, of course, but she was passionate about it.'

Pedro nodded. She always had been. Her desire to help others was one of the many things he'd admired about Nikki Wallace. She had planned her whole career to accumulate the kind of skills that would be the most useful in a Third World country or war zone. General surgery. Orthopaedics. A trauma specialty.

It was quite possible that Nikki's passion had influenced his own career choices.

'I thought I was replacing another orthopaedic surgeon,' he mused. 'One with the same leaning towards trauma that I have.'

'Nikita's skills were valuable with any orthopaedic trauma surgery,' John conceded. 'But she also had a subspecialty in the vascular field and her experience as a general surgeon often meant that extra resources of staff from other departments weren't needed in Theatre for a trauma patient.'

'You're talking in the past tense,' Pedro noted. 'Has she given up working as a surgeon?'

'Seems to have made that decision, yes. It's a shame, but there you go.' John didn't really sound as if he thought it was a shame. 'Can't say I blame her. You couldn't put your patients at risk if there was the possibility you were going to have a flashback at an inconvenient time, like in the middle of surgery.'

'A flashback to what, exactly?'

'There was an incident. A hospital she was working in got bombed a couple of weeks before Christmas last year. Absolute carnage, from what I've heard—from others, not from Nikita. It's not something she talks about.'

'I'm not surprised. She's lucky she survived.'

'Yes. But not entirely unscathed, as you would expect.'

'I wonder why I didn't hear anything about that?'

Pedro would have noticed her name in the papers. It wasn't as if he'd ever forgotten Nikki. Quite the opposite. It wasn't just his career choices she had influenced. The women he'd been attracted to when he gave himself time to think about finding a relationship had always reminded him in some way of her. Dark auburn hair, perhaps, or hazel eyes. A certain energy or smile. But the bar had been set too high and sometimes, in recent times, Pedro wondered if he actually knew exactly what he was looking for and, if not, it was pointless to keep looking, wasn't it?

Maybe he would have ended up being disappointed if he had got as close to Nikki as he'd wanted to. She had shown a rather different side to herself on graduation night, after all. Pedro could almost feel an echo of how hurtful her words had been. That harsh tone of her voice.

'You knew, didn't you? And you never told me. I thought you were my friend, but no real friend would have done that... I hate you, Pedro Garcia. I will never forgive you...'

Good grief...he hadn't thought about those parting words for years. Talk about opening a can of worms...

'Nobody did.' John's voice broke into Pedro's wandering thoughts. 'The actual bombing was reported and that MSF personnel were caught up in it, but nothing got released about the involvement of a British citizen. I didn't know that it was where Nikita had been posted until well after the event and I believe there was some high-level reason for it being covered up, but that information stays in this office, okay?'

'Of course.' Pedro had pushed aside any long-ago memories of Nikki now. Now he was thinking about the way she had curled herself into a ball in the corner of the lift when it came to that jarring halt. Had the movement or sounds taken her back to being somewhere a bomb had gone off? She must have been terrified. No wonder it had felt as if her muscles were coiled into something as solid as stone when he'd put his arms around her.

No wonder she'd fled as soon as she'd had the chance...

'So...we'll get it sorted ASAP. I'll give her a call and get her to make another appointment and we can jump through all the other necessary hoops after that. Hopefully by next week. Before the Christmas break and all the inevitable delays that will bring.'

Pedro tuned back into this conversation with his HoD.

'There's no rush,' he said. 'I wouldn't want Nikki to feel like she was under pressure to resign. I'm happy to carry on as a locum in the meantime.'

'It needs sorting.' John opened his office door as an invitation for Pedro to leave. 'We've given her every chance and she seems to be, quite literally, walking away from her responsibilities. I have to assume she's unlikely to recover from her PTSD.' He shrugged again, as if dismissing an unproductive topic. 'Are you heading away for the holidays? Back to Spain to visit family, perhaps?'

Pedro shook his head. 'No. I prefer not to travel with the chaos that Christmas creates. My mother is, sadly, now unaware of what time of year it is or who is visiting. She's very well cared for in her rest home and my siblings are scattered all over the world.'

As far as they could get from reminders of a tough upbringing in the slums of Barcelona?

'I prefer to be where I'm busy—and needed,' Pedro added. 'On call.'

'Good man.' John nodded approvingly. 'Just the kind of permanent staff member we need at Central. I'll see what I can do to speed up the formalities.'

It wasn't just random memories of Nikki Wallace that drifted into Pedro's head over the next couple of days. It was that conversation with the HoD.

Because it bothered him.

Not that he was about to analyse *why* it bothered him so much, other than it felt as if a member of staff was being treated with a disrespect they didn't deserve and he had to wonder if that might be as much part of the reason that Nikki was planning to permanently resign as the emotional repercussions of the traumatic experience she'd been through.

Pedro didn't want to think about it, because it was disturbing enough how many memories of Nikki were surfacing along with the emotions that came attached to them. Emotions that went hand in hand with attraction and admiration. Longing, even...

They might be fleeting enough to not interfere with the focus needed in order for him to do his job as well as he could, but they were also unpredictable and therefore disconcerting.

Like when he was under the bright lights of the operating theatre, doing a task that was automatic enough for an unrelated thought to surface at the back of his mind. Pedro's patient was a young man who'd come off his motorbike and had fractured his tibia, involving his knee joint. Internal fixation would be necessary but they had to wait for the swelling to reduce, so the first stage of treating the injury was to apply external fixation and stabilise the broken bones. Pedro had marked the position for the pins on the skin and was using a drill to make the holes in both the femur and the tibia for the pins that would anchor the bars to provide stability.

And there it was...a clear memory of the study group at medical school that had been where his life and that of Nikita Wallace had intersected most closely. They'd worked together that evening, drawing anatomical diagrams of bones, with the medullary canal containing bone marrow in the centre, the inner layers of cancellous bone and the hard outer layer of the cortical bone with the periosteum and endosteum on either side. Testing each other with rapid-fire questions and answers. Smiling at each other because they knew they shared a connection of being so passionate about what they were studying.

Pedro could feel the give of the drill bit as he got through the cortical bone and removed the drill to put a long pin in place. He applied pressure until he could feel purchase in the bone and then twisted the handle of the spanner to anchor the pin. Attaching the clamps and bars usually reminded him of playing with a favourite metal construction kit as a child, but not this time.

This time he was remembering how he and Nikki had competed to be at the top of their class. Fiercely on his part, but Nikki seemed to achieve her success with far less effort, still having time to enjoy an enviable social life. There was no such social life for Pedro. He had to excel—his family had sacrificed too much for him to have this opportunity to risk failure—so he'd made his own sacrifices to make sure he didn't disappoint them. And, yeah…maybe he'd wanted Nikki to notice him and perhaps even admire his achievements.

Not that it would have made any difference. The woman who'd captured his attention so completely was already in an apparently rock-solid relationship with Simon—who might not have been the most academically talented medical student in their year but he had certainly been the best-looking and most popular guy in school. Everybody had expected an engagement announcement might feature in graduation celebrations, not something that was so dramatically at the other end of the 'happily-ever-after' spectrum.

But Pedro wasn't going there. Even the split second it took for that memory and its associations to flick through his mind was too long. He focused hard enough to prevent it happening again and the job was done a short time later, with the last turn of the spanner to hold the bars tight in their clamps. He checked the placement of all his pins with fluoroscopy and nodded in satisfaction.

'Thanks, everybody. We're done. We'll wait for the inflammatory markers to get down to a normal range and then we can open the knee and do the internal fixation. Should be in seven to fourteen days.'

Pedro stripped off his gloves and pulled his mask to break the straps as he left Theatre. He had a full theatre list this morning, an outpatient clinic this afternoon and a ward round to do before he went home this evening. He was on call for the trauma team as well, so it could end up being a very long day.

The longer the better, as far as he was concerned. If he was busy enough and ended up being exhausted enough, perhaps he could stop thinking about Nikita? Why on earth did it seem to be so important, anyway? He'd got over her too many years ago to count. What was going on in her life at the moment was none of his business. He shouldn't be bothered by it.

But he was.

Because, like it or not, on some level, he still cared about her.

Enough to know he was never going to be comfortable with the way she was being treated by the people in charge of her employment in this hospital and, in particular, the HoD of orthopaedic surgery. So much so, that when he happened to see John Barlow in the corridor later that day he stopped to talk to him.

'I'm planning to visit Nikki Wallace,' he said.

The abrupt announcement surprised him as much as

John, but he couldn't admit that the thought had only just occurred to him. And maybe it was exactly what he needed to do. So he could check that she was okay and then stop thinking about her so much?

He found himself smiling then, as though he was looking forward to the visit. 'We've got a lot to catch up on,' he added. Which was true. They hadn't spoken a word to each other in the last ten years.

He'd never had the chance to apologise for what had made her say those awful words to him that night. That he had known Simon was cheating on her. That, as a friend, he could—and *should*—have warned her. But he hadn't managed to tell her.

Because messengers often got shot, didn't they?

And he couldn't be the one to tell her because of how he'd felt about Nikki. Because he'd potentially had something to gain by breaking up her relationship. But that was so far in the past it didn't matter now. He could apologise. And be sincere about it. After all, it was hardly Nikki's fault that she'd only ever seen him as a friend. The chemistry had been one-sided and that was just…life. Some people got lucky in love and others didn't and it would be very self-destructive to get bitter and twisted about it.

He made his tone deliberately casual as he spoke again. 'I could take the paperwork that needs to be signed, if that's not too much of a breach of protocol?'

Hopefully, that paperwork would contain personal details that he might have trouble accessing otherwise. Like her address?

John looked relieved, as though he was offering to take a problem off his hands. 'Not at all,' he said. 'Sounds like the best way forward to me. She hasn't even called to arrange a new appointment yet, which means it's probably necessary to bend the rules a little. Drop in to my office any time tomorrow and my secretary will have all the paperwork ready for you.'

So…

Pedro Garcia…

The quiet achiever at medical school. The good-looking Spanish guy who'd been at university in the UK long enough to perfect his English and was so focused on getting a medical degree with distinction that nothing else seemed important in his life. Her friend. The person who had set the bar for how hard she needed to work to be proud of her achievements and the person who'd bailed her out on more than one occasion by providing his meticulous notes for any lectures she had missed.

Nikita wasn't at all surprised that he'd ended up being an orthopaedic surgeon who could cope with the demands of a busy big-city hospital, but it had come as something of a shock to realise that he'd been doing *her* job for the last year or so.

Not only that, but he loved living in Bristol and had been delighted to hear that he was in the running to be awarded the position on a permanent basis if Nikita didn't return. As the HoD had said, in the phone call he'd made, he was only letting her know this private information because he understood that she knew him well enough to understand how important it was that he could plan his future with confidence. And how disappointing it had been when Nikita had missed her appointment to deal with the paperwork involved. He'd ended the call with the brisk suggestion that she contact his secretary to make a new time in the next day or two that she would manage to attend.

'I need to make that call, Duncan,' she said with a sigh. 'But we need our exercise too, and we've waited long enough for it to stop raining this morning. Maybe I'd better get the call over with, though—after we get back from the beach?'

Duncan, the huge Clydesdale cross horse she was brushing, having removed his warm cover, seemed far more interested in the hay net hanging in front of him in the stable. A few chickens who were scratching hopefully amongst old hay on the cobbled floor also ignored her, but the dog sitting quietly in the corner, watching Nikita adoringly, thumped his tail. Mind you, Earl the English setter approved of pretty much everything Nikita said so she had to take his opinion with a grain of salt.

The stable was almost too small for a horse as big as Duncan but the cosiness of this property had been why Nikita had fallen in love with it when she'd been on the hunt for a refuge. Elm Tree Cottage was on a small patch of rural land, only just big enough to keep a horse, and the house was just the right size for Nikita and Earl. Tiny enough to feel safe, with low ceilings and walls that were close enough to feel like a hug when she'd needed it the most.

She didn't bother with a saddle today. Duncan was wide and solid enough to be as comfortable as an armchair and they weren't going far. It was only a mile or so around the corner and down the lane to the beach and it wouldn't take long for the chilly sea breeze today to blow away any cobwebs. Even Earl might be happy to give up hunting for treasures like smelly seaweed or a dead crab amongst the smaller stones near the waves on a wintry day like this.

She could stoke up the pot belly stove to warm up when they got home again and she'd make sure Duncan was tucked up in his warm coat with plenty of hay and then she'd make that phone call. She should have done it much sooner, but it had been an awkward enough proposition to make her procrastinate.

It was a relief to forget about summoning the courage to make that call for a while longer too. Nikita wanted to simply be in the moment and enjoy the movement of Duncan plodding steadily down the lane as she watched Earl sniffing the unkempt hedgerow for evidence of rabbits. She couldn't stop the ambush of what was becoming a cringe-making thought, however.

Had Pedro told John about her excruciatingly embarrassing meltdown in the stalled lift?

It seemed likely, because John hadn't asked whether there was any reason for why she had missed their appointment. He hadn't mentioned it, or offered any concern about her current mental health, but that didn't surprise Nikita. John was well into his sixties and had always been old-school when it came to personal issues. A stiff upper lip was required at times in life, as far as he was concerned, and letting it ruin your life or career was no more than a sign of weakness. Clearly, he'd been disappointed in Nikita because he'd thought she was made of sterner stuff and had, in fact, been the first to approve and extend her annual leave so that she could head into war zones to do what she could to help.

Now, he couldn't wait to get rid of her. And give her job to Pedro Garcia, of all people.

Nikita hadn't thought about Pedro for a very long time. He'd been a good friend at medical school, but only in the academic side of her life—attending lectures and study group and, later, sharing clinical electives where they were posted to hospital departments to work in a real medical environment. She'd almost never seen him at student parties or as part of the groups who gathered to go to a movie occasionally or play a game of cricket over summer. He'd never missed a single lecture as far as she knew, which was why she'd been able to count on him to share his notes if she'd slept in after a late night or had been away for a long weekend with Simon.

She knew there were plenty of girls who very much wanted to be noticed by Pedro, but if he dated anyone it never lasted long. To his credit, he seemed to remain friends with everybody, even if his relationships were only casual, but Nikita had only observed from a distance, of course. It was no surprise that she and Simon had hooked up during Orientation Week at university. Their parents had known each other and moved in the same circles for many years and maybe the familiarity had been the attraction. Not that Nikita had minded being chosen by the most popular guy on campus so that, as far as her dating life went at medical school, was that.

Until it wasn't.

It was no wonder that memories of that awful graduation night were resurfacing again.

The way she'd blamed Pedro, so unfairly, for the humiliating disaster of that relationship imploding so publicly. The way she'd shouted at him in front of so many people crowded onto the dance floor of that graduation function.

I hate you, Pedro Garcia. I will never forgive you...

As if it was his fault that she'd found her boyfriend passionately kissing someone else just outside the door? That he'd been two-timing her for long enough to make up his mind who he was going to choose to marry—and it wasn't *her*?

The pain of that had faded relatively quickly. Almost as soon as she'd realised that someone who'd think it was remotely acceptable to behave like that certainly wasn't the man she wanted to be with for the rest of her life.

But Pedro had been left believing that she'd blamed him for her graduation night being such a disaster.

Oh, dear Lord. Nikita realised there was more to feel awful about as she headed back up the hill towards home.

What if Pedro somehow thought she might be blaming him for the lift malfunctioning? Or the fact that she was walking away from a career that had been her life?

If only she'd apologised for saying such dreadful things to him all those years ago, but how could she have, when she'd been so devastated that night and when she and Pedro had gone their separate ways the very next day? She'd been too embarrassed to ever go looking for him, so she'd never known where he'd ended up.

Until now.

Now there was no excuse and she was almost home. The cottage was just around the next bend in this narrow country lane.

Normally, Nikita was very careful of this corner, just in case there was a driver who'd decided to see how far they could get towards the beach or people on bicycles or dog walkers who might give them all a fright but, today, her mind was on something else. A part of her past she'd never thought would become relevant again.

Until something that was probably the last thing Nikita would have expected to come around that corner suddenly appeared.

A tall, solid lone man, rugged up in a black leather jacket, scarf and beanie, which made him look intimidating enough to startle even placid old Duncan, who shied sideways with enough speed that Nikita had no chance to grab a handful of his mane.

The jolt of pain in her ankle was severe enough to suggest something might have broken as she landed with a nasty thump on the cold, hard ground. Nikita found herself looking up at Pedro Garcia for the second time this week and her first reaction was to simply close her eyes again.

Her words were more like a groan. 'Oh, *no...*'

CHAPTER THREE

'*DIOS MÍO*… Are you hurt?' Pedro crouched beside Nikita. 'I'm *so* sorry. Does anything hurt?'

Instinctively, Nikita was rolling away from him, onto her knees. Scrambling to her feet. Dodging his hand that was outstretched to help her up.

'I'm fine.'

Except she wasn't. The fright and Pedro's proximity were creating an emotional response that meant Nikita had no choice but to try and defend herself and anger was another instinctive reaction.

'What the hell are you doing here?' Ignoring a stab of pain in her ankle, Nikita stepped towards Duncan and caught the reins of his bridle, even though he was standing as still as a rock, bless him. 'And how did you even find out where I live?'

Earl was well aware of the anger in her tone. He came to stand beside her, protectively leaning against her leg, but he was looking up at Pedro and the plume of his tail was waving softly. Her dog was ready to defend her if necessary, but clearly didn't find this stranger remotely threatening.

Pedro's grimace added embarrassment to an expression

of abject apology. 'I know… I shouldn't have been given the information. But I can explain.'

'Go ahead.'

There was no way Nikita could climb back on board her enormous horse without a mounting block or a fence. She certainly wasn't about to ask Pedro to give her a boost but she also wasn't about to stand here and let the animals get any colder. She clicked her tongue and began leading Duncan down the lane, trying hard not to limp, despite a stabbing twinge in her ankle every time that foot took her weight. She didn't look over her shoulder to see if Pedro was following her but, when he spoke again, she knew he was within touching distance.

'I told John that we were friends at medical school.'

Nikita nodded. That was true. Until she'd ruined it.

'I also told him that I was coming to visit you and… well, I offered to take the paperwork you'd missed signing the other day.' The short silence suggested that Pedro didn't really want to confess any more, but then he cleared his throat. 'I was kind of hoping your address would be there, as part of your personal information. And it was.'

The audacity of gaining information in such an underhand manner should have made Nikita even more angry but, now that the initial shock of the fall was wearing off, she was aware of something beneath that need to protect herself.

Curiosity?

'Why did you say that?' she asked. 'Why would you want to visit me?'

'Because we *were* friends. And…because I've been thinking about you.'

Nikita avoided the urge to turn and catch his gaze. Or

the confession on the tip of her tongue that she had been thinking about *him* as well—as recently as mere moments before he'd appeared in the lane.

'And I wanted to know if you were okay,' Pedro added. 'After…you know…what happened in the lift…'

It was Nikita's turn to feel embarrassed. In a way, the pain in her ankle was a good thing, because it gave her something else to focus on. But it was also a bad thing, because it seemed to draw Pedro's attention to it as well.

'You're limping,' he said. 'You *are* hurt.'

'It's nothing.' The paddock gate was open and the stable wasn't far away. 'Just a bit of a sprain, I expect.' Nikita led Duncan into the paddock. 'Shut that gate behind you, please,' she told Pedro. 'I'll be letting Duncan loose out here when he's got his cover on again.' She could see past the stable to her little cottage with the huge weeping elm tree in front of it. A big black SUV was parked under the twisted bare branches of the tree. 'I'm guessing that's your car?'

'Yes.'

'Why don't you go and find that paperwork? And a pen, if you've got one. Bring it out to the stable and I'll sign whatever needs signing and then you can be on your way.'

'No.'

'Excuse me?' Nikita turned her head sharply.

'I don't have a pen.' Pedro's gaze was steady. 'And it's too cold out here. Let me help you with your horse. It's the least I can do after causing your accident.'

That was true. And Pedro was a lot taller than she was. Getting Duncan's wool-lined canvas cover on was always a mission. Even getting his halter on after undoing his bridle would have needed Nikita to stand on a small ladder if her old horse wasn't cooperative enough to drop his huge head to her level.

'Fine.' She tied the lead rope loosely around the post. 'See that pile of canvas over there?'

'Yes.'

'It's Duncan's winter coat. There's a single strap and buckle on the front and two longer, thinner straps at the back. Throw it over his back so that the fluffy bit on the front of the cover is over his withers.'

'What is a withers?'

Pedro's English might be very close to perfect but there'd always been moments when his grammar or accent slipped enough to remind her of his European heritage. Along with his olive skin and those wickedly dark eyes, his unique voice had always been a big part of his undeniable charm.

'The lump at the bottom of his neck.' Nikita had a hoof pick in her hands and Duncan obligingly lifted each foot so that she could make sure he didn't have any stones caught in his dinner-plate-sized hooves. From the corner of her eye, she could see Pedro picking up the cover and checking which end was which. His coat and jeans were already covered with a layer of horse hair by the time he approached Duncan. Nikita could sense how nervous he was and, while there was no reason for her to want to make *him* feel better, she was reluctantly impressed that he wasn't letting his nervousness stop him from what needed to be done.

'Duncan's big but he's a gentle giant,' she told Pedro. 'He wouldn't hurt a fly.'

'He bucked you off. You could have been badly hurt.'

Nikita felt the tension of this unexpected visit suddenly evaporate. She actually laughed out loud. 'This horse couldn't buck to save his life. It was a shy. Not even that. He just stepped sideways, that's all, and I wasn't fast enough to grab his mane. If I'd been using a saddle, it wouldn't have been a problem.'

Pedro was tall enough to lift the cover easily over Duncan's back and it only took a moment for Nikita to tug it into place. She unclipped a back strap. 'I'll pass this through, between his legs,' she told Pedro. 'You can clip it to the ring on your side and then pass me the clip for the other one.'

She got another biscuit of hay for Duncan when he was warmly covered and then took off his lead rope. 'He's all good,' she said. 'I'll leave the stable doors open and then he can choose whether or not he wants to be outside.' She turned to unbolt the bottom half of the door but the movement was enough to generate a new and much sharper pain in her ankle. Enough to make it impossible to stand on. Nikita reached to hold onto the door to keep herself from falling as her leg gave way beneath her, but Pedro got there first and she found herself clinging to his arm.

Touching him.

Again…

She was holding her breath now. Waiting for the adrenaline rush and the desperate need to escape—like she had when she'd realised how physically close she'd been to him in that lift—but, weirdly, it didn't come. Because she was holding onto him and not the other way around, perhaps?

No. If that was the case then, when Pedro lifted her in his arms to carry her into her house, the feeling of being overpowered by someone would have triggered complete panic.

The kind Nikita used to feel if someone—especially a man—merely brushed against her in passing. But maybe because Pedro wasn't a stranger by any means—or it could be that Earl wasn't showing any signs of mistrust—it was enough for her not to feel that fear. To feel, instead, that someone was taking care of her?

To feel…*safe*…even?

The notion was so astonishing that Nikita completely forgot about the pain in her ankle. Or the reason Pedro was here, until he put her down on the couch in her living area, put a couple of cushions beneath her injured foot and then straightened—as much as he could, anyway, given that he was taller than the ancient beams on the ceiling.

'Don't move,' he commanded. 'I'll be right back.'

Caramba…

Pedro hadn't really had any idea what to expect when he'd decided to turn up, unannounced, at Nikita's address. He hadn't even been at all sure it was a good idea and he'd been right, hadn't he?

How stupid had he been, startling the biggest horse in the world like that and causing an accident? If Nikita's ankle was actually broken he would have achieved the total opposite of his intention, which he had hoped would reassure him that she was okay. Not only that, holding her in his arms and carrying her inside had stirred up more than just the random memories of this woman he'd been grappling with in the last couple of days.

Pedro had the horrible feeling that he wasn't as over her as he'd believed he was.

With a sigh, he picked up the manila folder containing the resignation paperwork from the passenger seat of his car. The sooner this was over with the better.

But then he hesitated after shutting the front door and blew out his breath in another sigh before opening the back hatch of his vehicle to take out the first aid kit he always carried. He knew that Nikita would tell him she was fine, but he wasn't about to drive off until he was quite sure he wasn't leaving an injured woman alone in such an isolated house.

He'd been too aware of having Nikita in his arms and that sinking sensation in his gut when he'd gone inside the cottage the first time to notice much. This time, he was looking everywhere except directly at Nikita and noticing everything was a great way to avoid thinking about himself.

The house was tiny. Stone-built with a slate roof and a door and one window on the front wall. The interior walls were roughcast over stone and the space he'd walked into was the living room and kitchen. The couch Nikita was on faced the window that looked out onto the front garden and the huge tree through leaded diamond-shaped panes and, to one side, was a bare stone fireplace with a pot belly stove installed inside it and a cane basket full of small logs of wood nearby.

The mantelpiece made Pedro imagine decorated children's stockings hanging from it and it was only then that he noticed a complete absence of any reminder that Christmas was rapidly approaching. There wasn't even a sprig of holly to be seen, but it wasn't surprising that she didn't want any reminders of the season when he could hear the echo of something the HoD had said to him.

'A hospital she was working in got bombed just before Christmas last year. Absolute carnage...'

The kitchen was small but pretty, with an antique Welsh dresser stacked with blue and white crockery and a deep square sink with brass taps above it. Pedro even noticed how shiny those taps were and the way that advertised the person living here cared about their surroundings. A downsized version of an Aga stove was set in a wooden benchtop and there was a pot with curls of steam above it on the hotplate. The most delicious smell of just baked bread was coming from beneath a tea towel draped over a bleached wooden board.

A set of shelves behind the couch was crammed with books and he could recognise some of his own favourite medical textbooks on the lowest, widest shelf, along with a stack of medical journals. A specialist orthopaedic publication was lying on the rustic low table right beside the couch and Pedro knew it was the latest edition because he'd been reading it himself only this morning, over a leisurely breakfast on his day off.

Pedro was frowning as he put his kit on the floor and the manila folder onto the table. Why would someone who wanted to walk away from her career be interested in keeping up with the latest developments and peer-reviewed articles?

'There's a pen on the desk just inside the door over there.'

'Okay.'

Pedro could see enough through the open door to know that it was a bedroom. Which presumably meant that the only other door leading from this space was a bathroom. The floor area of this cottage with its dark, wide wooden planks was probably less than half of his apartment in Bristol. Just big enough for one person. And a dog.

It was not only isolated. Surely it was lonely?

He turned his head to catch Nikita's glance, knowing that the question could well be visible. Somehow, he wasn't surprised when she lifted her chin defensively.

'A pen?' she repeated patiently.

'In a minute. I want to check your ankle first.'

'There's no need. I'm an orthopaedic surgeon, remember?'

'So am I. And I'm not leaving until I'm satisfied I don't need to drive you into Bristol Central for an X-ray and a plaster cast.' Pedro took his jacket and hat off and dropped them out of the way. He also held her gaze. Or maybe she was holding his. And, for a little too long, neither of them looked away.

'Fine.' It was an admission of defeat, underlined by the way Nikita didn't just break the eye contact, she turned her head enough to be looking past him and out of the window.

Pedro swallowed. 'I need to take your shoes and socks off,' he said. 'On both feet.'

He couldn't afford to think about it in any terms other than a clinical need to compare two joints. Totally professional. But Nikita wasn't wearing normal shoes. She had elastic-sided jodhpur boots on.

'I might need to cut the elastic on your boot,' Pedro warned. 'I don't want to exacerbate any injury you might have.'

'Oh, for heaven's sake.' Nikita sat up straighter and leaned forward. 'I'll do it myself. I don't want my boots ruined, thank you.'

The uninjured foot was no problem, but Pedro saw the way she was gritting her teeth and becoming rather pale as she pulled the footwear off her other foot. She didn't make a sound, however. And she didn't pause until she could toss the boot to one side.

'There…see? No obvious bruising. Not even any noticeable swelling.' She slumped back against the arm of the couch and closed her eyes.

'Not yet,' Pedro agreed. 'But neither of those processes are necessarily instant, are they? Can you wiggle your toes?'

She could.

'Does it hurt?'

'Not much.'

She flinched as he touched her toes. 'Normal sensation?'

'Yes.'

He touched the top of her foot lightly, checking the warmth and colour, but also looking for the pedal pulse that would confirm circulation.

Then he moved his hand to her ankle but still kept his touch gentle as he palpated the areas where the tibia and fibula met the ankle bone. He didn't need to ask if that hurt because he felt her flinch again.

'Hmm… No obvious crepitation.'

'Good. No fracture, then.'

'I didn't say that.' Pedro cupped her foot in one hand and put a little pressure on the top with his other hand to test plantar flexion. For some reason, using both his hands suddenly made him far more aware of the feel of Nikita's bare skin and it was an effort to keep his focus.

'Pull your foot up,' he instructed, rather more abruptly than he'd intended.

Then he swapped and put pressure on the bottom of her foot. 'Now push it down.'

Nikita sighed loudly, having complied. 'We could skip the rest,' she muttered.

For a split second, Pedro was tempted to agree. He had a feeling that every moment of this physical examination might come back to haunt him later, but he had to finish what he'd started so he ignored her suggestion. He tested the internal and external rotation of her foot and made another check on her limb baselines.

'You've got some bruising starting to come out now.'

'Only to be expected with a sprain. I'll do RICE,' she said. 'I've got a bandage I can use for compression somewhere and there's bound to be a bag of peas in my freezer.'

'I've got a bandage right here.' Pedro unzipped his first aid kit. 'I still think an X-ray would be a good idea. You know as well as I do that if there's tenderness over the posterior malleoli, the likelihood of a clinically significant fracture is increased.'

'I wouldn't want to waste anyone's time. If it's not a lot better tomorrow, I'll think about having an X-ray.'

'I hope you do.' Pedro started bandaging her foot and ankle. 'Put ice on it for twenty minutes every two to three hours and keep your foot elevated above the level of your heart.'

'Yes, Doctor.' Nikita's breath came out in an exasperated sigh but the corner of her mouth twitched as if she was trying to suppress a smile, but then her face stilled.

'Where are those papers?' she asked quietly as he fastened the end of the bandage. 'Let's get this over with, shall we?'

Exactly what Pedro had wanted to do only a very short time ago but, to his own surprise, he found he'd changed his mind.

'No,' he said again. Even more firmly this time.

Was it supposed to be a joke?

Nikita almost started to smile but, oddly, she could feel a prickle of what could be tears behind her eyes. Delayed shock from the fright of that fall, perhaps?

Or maybe it was the way Pedro was looking at her. Giving her that strange sensation that someone cared about her and was going to keep her safe.

No…not someone.

Pedro Garcia.

He hadn't broken the eye contact since he'd refused her request so calmly. 'I don't think you should sign them,' he said. 'Not yet, anyway.'

Nikita blinked back that prickle. And then she gave a huff of incredulity. 'Don't you think that's my decision to make?'

'Of course. If it's really what you want to do.' Pedro straightened and turned to look out of the window. 'I'm not convinced it is.'

Nikita found herself staring at that broad, solid back. At the way this man stood, as if he was more than happy in his own skin and quite content with his world. Nikita would give anything to feel like that. So, instead of snapping back at him to tell him to mind his own business, she found herself speaking softly.

'Why not?'

It was a long, long moment before Pedro turned back to her. He didn't look directly at her either, but let his gaze sweep around the interior of her cottage. He lifted both his hands as if he was holding everything he could see.

'This…' he said. 'This picture-perfect country life, riding your horse on the beach and baking bread and living in a hobbit house with just your dog for company?' He shook his head as he blew out a breath. 'This isn't the Nikita Wallace I remember. It's nothing like you, Nikki. It almost feels like you're hiding. From yourself as much as anyone else.'

Okay…that threat of crying had just returned with a vengeance. A single tear escaped but Nikita swiped it away.

'Maybe I'm not the same person that you remember,' she said quietly.

'Yes, you are.' Pedro took a step back towards her. 'Deep down. I know you've had stuff happen and that can change how people feel and behave, but I don't believe that what makes a person who they are ever really changes. And I don't believe that the real Nikki wants to hide from the world. Or not do the work that mattered so much to her.'

He was talking nonsense. The real Nikki was who she'd become. Who she was right now. But there was something in his words that was giving her something just as powerful as making her feel like someone cared about her.

Hope…?

'Who is she, then?' she demanded. 'This "real" Nikki?'

Slowly, Pedro moved to the end of the couch where her bandaged foot was resting on the cushions. He perched on the arm of the couch.

'The Nikki I remember,' he said, 'was so full of life that she would light up a room when she went into it. She had hair that could catch the sunlight and look as if it had caught on fire and eyes that sparkled when she laughed. And she laughed a lot. Everybody knew she came from a very wealthy family but she was never snobby. She could get on with anybody, even a Spanish boy who'd grown up in the slums of Barcelona...'

Nikita could actually feel her jaw dropping as she listened to Pedro. Hearing him talk as if he had been... what...*attracted* to her was astonishing. Shocking, even. He'd just been the smartest guy in her study group, which had made him the best to work with. And, okay, he'd seemed as keen as she was to gather and retain every drop of knowledge and skill possible, but he'd never shown any sign of wanting to be more than a friend.

As if he was reading her thoughts, Pedro continued. 'She was the cleverest student in our year. She could have easily beaten me at every single test and exam, but only missed out sometimes because she had more going on in her life than study. Everybody wanted to spend time with her so she had too many parties or concerts or dinners to go to, but she still managed to do so well because she was so passionate about being a doctor. A surgeon. And it wasn't just for the prestige or the money. The Nikki I knew was the most genuine person I'd ever met and she was determined to get out in the world and help the people who needed it the most.'

Pedro stopped. The look he gave Nikita was an apology.

'Sorry,' he said quietly. 'You can probably tell I had a crush on you. I was hopelessly in love with you, even.'

Nikita was still staring at him. No wonder she had felt

as if he cared about her. As if she was safe in his arms. Perhaps her body recognised something she'd been blind to in every other way?

Pedro was shaking his head now. 'It's all ancient history,' he said lightly. 'Don't worry—I got over it too many years ago to count. But I do think you should take some more time to think about this resignation. I just can't imagine you want to turn your back on medicine completely.' His gaze went to the medical journal on the coffee table beside them. 'In fact, I think it's obvious that you don't want to.'

'But if I didn't resign, you'd be out of a job.'

Pedro shrugged. 'I can always find a job. I never stay in one place very long. I should probably go back to Spain for a while and be near enough to visit my mother more often, even though she doesn't recognise me any longer. My youngest sister has nearly finished medical school in New Zealand so I could go there for a year or so. I'd love to go back to the States, where I did my surgical trauma training, and do some postgraduate study. It's a specialty in its own right over there and it's growing.'

He sounded as if he couldn't wait to move on. As if the possibilities for his future were unlimited and exciting. Nikita had forgotten what it was like to feel like that.

Pedro was smiling at her now. 'So there you go. I'll be leaving soon anyway, so you shouldn't let the fact that I've been holding your position influence your decision in any way. But please…hold off a little longer before signing your career away. I'll leave the papers here. And… I'll leave you my phone number. I can pick them up any time.'

He reached for his leather jacket and took a pen from

an inside pocket to scrawl a number on the front of the manila folder.

'You *did* have a pen,' Nikita exclaimed.

'I forgot.'

Nikita knew he was lying by the way he avoided her gaze. He hadn't just come out here to check on her or deliver those papers. He'd intended trying to talk her out of resigning all along, hadn't he?

'I'm employed until the New Year.' Pedro put the pen away and shrugged himself into his jacket. 'That's not too long to wait, is it?'

'I guess not...'

'Now...can I find a bag of peas or some ice for you to put on your ankle before I go?'

'No. I can do that.'

'You should be resting.'

'I'll be careful about how much weight I put on it. It's feeling so much better with the bandage on.' Nikita sat up and then stood up cautiously. 'See? I think you've cured it.'

Pedro smiled but he was turning away already to pick up his kit. Nikita followed him to the door of her cottage.

'Thank you,' she said.

'No need to thank me,' he said. 'It was my fault you hurt yourself in the first place.'

'That wasn't what I was thanking you for. You've given me quite a lot to think about.'

He was giving her that look again. The one that seemed to be melting its way through all the protective, healing barriers Nikita had so carefully constructed over the last year.

Did he really believe that she was, deep down, the person she'd always been? Was that why he could say things that gave her more hope than hundreds of hours of counselling had achieved? Why he could touch her without her feeling the need to flee?

The skin-to-skin contact they'd had as he'd examined her foot and ankle would have been her worst nightmare not long ago. She'd never thought she would ever, ever, be able to allow a man to touch her again.

Or had that been because it was purely professional, in order to make a medical diagnosis?

A personal touch…like a hug, or getting anywhere near an intimate touch, like a kiss, would undoubtedly be an entirely different matter.

That thought was in Nikita's mind at the precise moment that Pedro turned to say goodbye as he reached the door. And maybe her balance wasn't perfect because she was trying to keep the weight off her injured ankle, because she didn't stop right away and Pedro put his arm out to steady her.

Another touch that didn't scare her was enough for something to shift inside Nikita's head. Or her heart? Whatever…she needed to know…

So she used her good foot to stand on tiptoe.

And she kissed Pedro Garcia.

On his lips.

CHAPTER FOUR

IT WAS NO more than a featherlight touch of her lips on his but it packed a punch that sent Pedro jerking backwards.

'What the *hell*…?'

Nikita was staring at him in horror. 'Oh, my God,' she said through fingers she had pressed to her mouth. 'I'm *so* sorry.'

Pedro couldn't find any words that might capture the astonishment of what had just happened so, with a disbelieving shake of his head, he turned and walked towards his car. He wasn't even sure how he was feeling. Surprised? Sure. Angry? Yeah…he could feel that if he let himself. But there was something more than that. Did he feel almost…betrayed?

He'd only gone a few steps but he swung back to face Nikita.

'How could you *do* that?' he demanded. 'When I'd told you how I used to feel about you?'

'I'm sorry,' she repeated. 'I can't believe I did that, but… I can explain.'

'Go on, then.' Pedro's invitation was icy. She looked more than sorry. She looked mortified—as well she should.

'Not out here. It's too cold.' Nikita was wrapping her

arms around herself and there was a plea in her eyes. And her voice. 'It's getting late for lunch and I've made some soup. And some…um…bread?'

The face she pulled made Pedro remember he'd singled out her bread making as something that didn't fit with the person he'd known her to be. As if it was somehow a shameful skill to have acquired? He hadn't meant it to be an insult, he'd just been puzzled about how much she'd changed. The idea of sitting down and having a meal with her after she'd just kissed him was definitely a step too far, but he was curious about her explanation.

He could also remember saying exactly the same words—*I can explain*—when he'd offered to justify how he'd managed to gain access to protected information like her private address. And how much he had wanted to be given that opportunity.

'I don't need lunch,' he said. 'But I'll come inside. You shouldn't be standing around on that ankle.'

Nikita sat on one end of the couch but she didn't elevate her foot. She drew her knees up instead and hugged them and Pedro didn't suggest she did anything else because he knew instinctively that she needed this comfort right now. He sat on the other end of the couch but didn't make direct eye contact. Earl climbed into the space between them and that seemed to cushion the atmosphere enough for Nikita to be ready to talk.

'I don't know how much John's told you about why I took leave from work.'

'He told me that you were working in a hospital that got bombed. "Carnage" was how he described it.'

Nikita nodded. 'That pretty much sums it up. But the devil, as they say, is in the detail. The missile was a direct hit. Half the building collapsed and it was hard to see through the dust and smoke so we had to try and find people that were buried or injured by touch or listening for their cries. We found a girl whose leg was so badly injured it had to be amputated so we carried her into what was left of the theatre and I gave her a femoral block as the fastest kind of anaesthetic we could do. We could hear gunfire outside and I told everyone else to run, but I couldn't leave a child to bleed to death on the table.'

Pedro could almost hear her swallow hard.

'She died anyway.'

'Because you had to get out to save your own life?'

'No.' Her voice was no more than a whisper. 'Because I wasn't allowed to finish the surgery. The…insurgents, guerrillas—whatever you want to call them—came into what was left of our hospital. Into my theatre and…and they captured me.'

Pedro knew how hard she would have fought to protect that child. She would have had to be dragged, kicking and screaming, away from that operating theatre.

'I couldn't help anyone.' Nikita was fighting tears. 'I could see people everywhere. The amazing local nurses and other doctors from MSF. Patients and their families. Terrified people trying to help. Or escape. So many of them so badly injured and dying. I was the only hostage they were interested in, but I didn't know that then. They were so rough that I thought they were taking me outside to…' She sucked in a breath. 'To kill me.'

Pedro swore under his breath. How terrifying would that have been? And what did 'so rough' mean and did he really want to know? He was feeling too angry already and it had nothing to do with anything Nikki had done to stir up ancient hurt feelings.

'To cut a long and very unpleasant story short,' Nikita said quietly, 'they didn't want to kill me. They wanted to use me as a pawn in a game of getting some of their own people released from captivity, but I didn't know that. I just knew I was being held and I had no idea what was coming.'

Pedro nodded, understanding now why the event had been kept top secret. But he felt sick to his stomach imagining what she had gone through. Earl seemed to understand the undercurrent of this awful revelation and lifted his head to lay it on Nikita's arm.

'Did they...' He could feel his face scrunch up as he tried to formulate a question he didn't really want to ask.

He didn't need to, because she was shaking her head.

'They didn't hurt me but I did develop an uncontrollable fear of anyone touching me.'

'I'm not surprised,' Pedro said quietly.

'Even someone being close enough to touch me could set off my fight or flight response. My heart rate would accelerate, my hands got clammy. I even threw up once.'

Pedro nodded slowly. He could totally understand why the automatic physiological response of the sympathetic nervous system would kick in.

Nikita reached out to stroke Earl's head. 'It's a year ago now and I'm a lot better,' she said. 'But I'm not that comfortable being in a crowded building, especially a hospital, and what happened in the lift the other day means the fear of flashbacks I have is justified. I think it was the shuddering movement. Or the noise. We heard the bomb coming and it was like being in an earthquake when it hit.'

Pedro looked up. 'I wish I'd known,' he said softly. 'I wish I could have known why you needed comfort. I might have been able to offer more support...'

'You helped,' Nikita said simply. 'More than you know.' But she looked away from him. 'That's why I have to resign,' she added. 'I don't really have a choice. What if I was in the operating theatre and someone dropped a tray of instruments or just a kidney dish, even, and I had another flashback and ended up crouched in a corner and somebody died?'

Pedro was listening but something she'd said earlier was overriding her last words.

'What did you mean,' he asked, 'about me helping more than I know?'

'Because something was different.' Nikita licked her lips as if they were suddenly dry. 'You were holding me. Touching me. And it didn't make things worse—it helped. And today, when you carried me inside, it...it almost felt safe. Even when you were touching my *skin*—on my ankle and foot, I didn't get that fight or flight reaction at all.' She gave a huff of sound that wasn't quite laughter. 'I thought maybe that was because it was a medical touch and it would be different if it was something personal like a hug...or a kiss...and I was thinking that when you were standing so close to me at the door and...then I stopped thinking and I just wanted to find out, that's all...' She was biting her lip now. 'It didn't even occur to me to remember what you'd told me. I was just thinking of you as the Pedro I'd known back then. Before graduation. A friend. Someone I could trust...'

Oh… Pedro's heart was breaking as he watched a single tear roll down Nikita's cheek. He wasn't far off tears himself. How brave had she been to try that kiss? If only he'd known how big a thing it was. But if he had, they wouldn't be having this conversation now and it was an opportunity that he'd never expected to have—a chance to heal something from the past that had never quite gone away.

'You said you hated me,' he murmured. 'That if I'd been a real friend I would have told you that Simon was cheating on you.'

'I know you tried. And I shut you down because I didn't believe you. I didn't *want* to believe you. It wasn't until I saw them together at the graduation party that I realised I was the cliché. The woman who was the last person to know about the *other* woman. I'm sorry, Pedro. I should never have blamed you like that. My world had just crumbled and I was so devastated, but I guess I wanted to hang onto at least a shred of dignity before I walked out on him and being angry was the easiest way to do that. And when I turned my back on Simon, you were the first person I saw…'

'And maybe I should have tried harder to tell you what was going on behind your back but…you were so sure it couldn't be true and I knew you would hate me if I proved it was correct. And…and I couldn't bear the thought of you hating me.' He let his breath out in a resigned sigh. 'But you ended up doing that anyway.'

Nikita was shaking her head. 'I didn't. Even by the next day I had my head together enough to know I needed to apologise, but… I couldn't find you.'

'I was all packed and ready to leave before I even

went to that party. I took a night train up to Glasgow and I started my first real job as a doctor the next day. I couldn't wait to get started.'

Or to finally be in a position to really help his family, who'd made this dream career possible. It was time his mother stopped working so hard and he'd wanted to make sure there were no financial obstacles for his younger siblings to get tertiary education if that was what they wanted to do.

'Well, it's taken far too long, but I'm apologising now, okay?' Nikita's face was scrunched into shades of regret. 'You *were* a good friend. I would never have done as well as I did in med school if you hadn't had my back. You were always there in study group, pushing me to do that little bit more. And you saved me so many times by giving me your lecture notes. I relied on you more than you know and I knew I could trust you.' There were tears in her eyes now. 'You're still exactly the same person you were, Pedro. It's just me that's changed so much.'

'With good reason.' Pedro found a smile. One that hopefully told Nikita her explanation had done far more than excuse her from an uninvited kiss. Past hurts had been forgiven and it felt good. Something else—something unexpected—was fighting for recognition as well.

A feeling of pride?

He'd helped Nikita in a moment that could easily have been unbearable for her as that lift had jerked and screeched to a halt.

He was the one who'd been able to touch her when she hadn't let anyone that close for a very long time.

And she'd cared about him more than he'd realised in the past. She'd depended on him. Trusted him…

'Did you say something about some soup?' he found himself asking. 'And homemade bread?' He glanced at his watch. 'It is getting very late for lunch, isn't it?'

Nikita seemed to understand that he was offering to forgive and forget anything that had come before this. That he was offering a chance to rekindle their first friendship?

'It's what I call "Everything Soup" when I use up all the vegetables I can find in the garden and the fridge and throw in any leftovers—like the spaghetti bolognese I had the other night.'

'Sounds delicious.'

Nikita smiled at his obvious trepidation. 'It's hot, anyway. I'll get you a bowl.'

'Uh-uh.' Pedro shook his head. 'You stay right there and get that foot up on the cushions again. I'm quite capable of finding some bowls and buttering some bread. I'll find something cold to go on your ankle too.'

The soup was, in fact, surprisingly delicious. So was the bread. The conversation became easier as they pulled out memories from medical school and caught each other up on parts of their lives in the last ten years.

'So...' Nikita sounded curious although her words were a little cautious. 'Do you have a family of your own now?'

Pedro tried to brush off what felt like an admission of personal failure by making a joke. 'Can't afford one,' he said. 'I'm keeping my mother in a very expensive rest home and helping my sister through medical school. I can only afford to rent an apartment the size of a broom cupboard in central Bristol, so there's no room for anyone but me.' He pasted a smile onto his face. 'But that's the way I like it. There are worse things than being able to go wherever I want and do whatever I want. Maybe I'm making a choice by not making a choice.'

'What do you mean?'

'That I'm choosing to be single for ever because I'm not choosing to look for someone to share my life with. And I have no desire to change the status quo.'

'Maybe I'm doing that too,' Nikita said. 'I haven't even given it a thought in the last year, but even before that I always kept things casual.' Her smile was wry. 'I guess Simon left me more "once bitten, twice shy" than I realised.'

Pedro was watching her face carefully but he couldn't detect any sign of lingering heartbreak.

'Where's Simon now, do you know?'

She shook her head this time. 'Been married twice. Divorced twice. I believe he's working on a cruise ship now. Probably even more popular than ever.'

Pedro could have happily kept talking but the afternoon had all but disappeared and it was already getting dark outside.

'I'd better head home,' he said.

'And I need to move,' Nikita said. 'Even if it's just to go to the loo.'

'How's your ankle feeling?'

'It's okay. I'll take some paracetamol and I'm sure it'll be much better tomorrow.'

'Let me know if it isn't, won't you?'

Nikita nodded. She followed him to the door but Pedro paused before he opened it.

'Can I ask you something?'

Nikita grimaced. 'It's okay… I'm not going to try kissing you again if that's what you're worried about.'

'Not exactly. I was wondering if you'd been right and that a personal touch might have triggered something?'

'No…' Her tone was thoughtful. 'I don't think it did.'

He could hear the hesitancy in her voice and he thought he knew why. 'It wasn't really enough of a kiss to find out, was it?'

Nikita didn't say anything but she was watching him carefully and he saw the way her eyes widened. He wasn't going to say anything else but if she could read his mind and chose to accept his offer, he wasn't going to back down either.

'You think I should try again?'

Pedro's words were careful. 'Only if you want to.'

She was silent again but she gave the tiniest nod and her gaze was hanging onto his as if breaking that eye contact would be enough to change her mind.

Pedro felt a weight of responsibility he'd never had before. Nikita was trusting him with something that was so big, it felt like an honour that he'd been chosen. This had to be the best kiss that had ever been given to any woman. Ever.

So he was gentle. He held Nikita's chin with his fingertips and kept that eye contact with her as long as possible so he'd know if she wanted him to stop at any point. Because he would understand completely if she did want to change her mind.

She didn't. And when his lips covered hers and it was the realisation of something he'd thought about countless times, both during the time he'd known her at medical school and in the years since, Pedro didn't want to stop either. He deepened the pressure of the intimate touch and he felt her lips moving beneath his, responding to that pressure in a subtle conversation that was purely physical.

A slow kiss that could have developed into something much more, but Pedro didn't let that happen. He pulled back the instant he felt her lips softening and parting beneath his because he knew it would be a mistake to go any further. For both of them.

But when he lifted his head he smiled at her. 'You're not running away.'

She smiled back. 'I'm not, am I?'

Ay, hombre… He was the one who needed to get away—before it occurred to him to offer Nikita an opportunity to test her trigger points even more thoroughly.

'I'm the one who's running this time,' he said lightly. 'I really do have to go.'

The nightmare was so familiar that, on some level, Nikita was aware it was only a dream. As if part of her brain was watching another part misbehaving.

Unfortunately, that wasn't enough to stop the attack on her senses feeling like reality. She could hear the eardrum-shattering noise of the shell's impact and explosion and the screams of terrified and injured people. She could smell the smoke. Taste the blood from the cut on her lip caused by flying shrapnel. Feel the heat of fire and the fear…

That never got any less horrific, experiencing that kind of fear, even though—when it was happening—she'd been able to push it to one side as she, and others, desperately tried to shift debris, carry people to safety or do whatever else they could to try and save their lives. She could still feel the pulse of an artery beneath her hands as she tried to stem bleeding that would soon be fatal and fingers digging into her like claws as she was dragged away. The last thing she had seen clearly, before her head was shoved into a hood made of rough hessian, was a blood-soaked rope of silver tinsel—a token reminder of the season for foreign medics working in a country that didn't recognise a Christian festival—that had somehow become caught on her foot.

This was the point she usually woke up, her heart racing and her skin slick with perspiration, and Nikita braced for the transition to reality as she fought her way back to consciousness, but then something changed.

For the first time, the sensations of her nightmare morphed into something very different. She knew that the hands she could sense on her body were not a threat. Quite the opposite, and she didn't need to fight them any longer. She could let go. Let those hands and arms pull her into a place of safety. Drift back into sleep, even, instead of having to spend the rest of her night awake.

There was no face attached to those hands in her dream and perhaps it was the feeling of safety that was the only important part of the difference, but Nikita knew perfectly well who had created this difference and if waking up with an aching ankle was the price she had to pay for what felt like more than a small miracle in her road to recovery, it was more than well worth it.

Because that feeling stayed with her during a day where she limped around doing only her most essential chores and spent the rest of the day curled up on the couch in front of her fireplace, reading a book. Reading her medical journals. Deliberately *not* reading the paperwork in that manila folder.

Just knowing that she could feel that sensation of safety, even if it was only for a few seconds, was priceless. It didn't matter how it had happened, because it *had* happened and it had sown a seed that Nikita knew was capable of growing. She had learned all sorts of techniques for controlling her fear and living with the aftermath of trauma, but this feeling was nothing like controlling or avoiding anything. It was more like a comforting hug that she could lean into.

And who was she kidding? It did matter how it had happened because maybe there was something about Pedro Garcia that had made the difference. Something to do with his confession that he'd had a crush on her? Been in love with her once upon a time, even? Nikita found herself trying to retrieve every memory of medical school that had included the big, good-looking Spanish guy, but he was only ever in the background of her memories—eclipsed by the blond, charismatic Simon, who had made it clear very early on that they were perfect for each other. That he was smitten by her.

Ha… Smitten by the inheritance she would one day receive from her wealthy parents, more like. He wouldn't have had to wait too long either. The accident that had tragically claimed the lives of both Nikita's parents had been only a few years ago and, while she had initially moved back into the old family home in one of the most affluent areas on the outskirts of Bristol, the house had been so overwhelmingly big and empty that the prospect of living there again in the wake of the bombing had been terrifying.

Doing something about the house, which was being looked after but not occupied, was the second item on her list of the things that needed to be sorted in the New Year. Thanks to the financial security her parents had bequeathed her, it had been possible not to have to make decisions about her childhood home but still be able to take a lease on this wee cottage and to take time away from her career to find the best treatment available to help her conquer PTSD.

It could well be the foundations that excellent therapy had built that had put Nikita into a space where it was possible for Pedro's touch—and that *kiss*—to move her off whatever plateau had seemed to be as far as she was ever going to get.

Or maybe it was just that there was something totally unique about him that her soul had finally recognised, despite failing to do so all those years ago.

Whatever alchemy was responsible for making it happen, Nikita was beyond grateful. It felt like a gift.

Almost a promise that things were going to get better. That the future might actually be a whole lot brighter than she'd been hoping for.

If only the stupid swelling in her ankle would go down a bit faster. The longer it took, the more Nikita had to consider the possibility that it was, indeed, fractured and might need more than home remedies to heal.

She might hate the idea, but it wasn't beyond the realms of possibility that she would have to go back to Bristol Central—as a patient this time, instead of a doctor.

CHAPTER FIVE

THE DAY SURGERY list for the orthopaedic department was always an extremely busy one because so many operations that used to require open surgery and hospital stays could be done with minimally invasive arthroscopic procedures with one small incision to insert the thin tube with the video camera and other incisions to insert whatever surgical instruments were needed. Light general anaesthetics or sedation and local anaesthetics contributed to patients being able to be discharged the same day.

Pedro always enjoyed the rapid throughput and variety of cases that were put under his care. He'd started the list with a shoulder of a man who needed a decompression for a bursitis which was seriously hampering his work as a builder and he spent an hour or so removing the bursa and enough bone from the irritated area and the rotator cuff tendons.

He'd cleaned out an elbow for someone who'd been diagnosed with septic arthritis in their elbow after that, taking care with the surgical debridement and cleaning of the joint so that the IV antibiotics would have a better chance of being effective.

His senior registrar rolled his eyes when they were scrubbing in for their fifth carpal tunnel release that afternoon—a quick procedure under local anaesthesia, to divide the transverse carpal ligament and decompress the medial nerve.

'It's time we moved down the body a bit further, isn't it? Shoulder, elbow, wrists…what's next? A hip or knee?'

'I do believe we've got a meniscus repair to finish up the list for today.' Pedro was smiling. He hadn't taken note that they had been systematically moving down a list of body parts. 'I don't think we'll get time to fit an ankle in, though. We'll have to get on with the post-op ward round and discharging everybody.'

The thought stayed with him, however, as they set up for treating one of the more common injuries that came through the day surgery clinic. Their patient was a nineteen-year-old rugby player who'd been stretchered off a field mid-game, unable to put any weight on his knee after a high-speed pivot, and an MRI had revealed a tear too large to repair and displaced tissue that needed to be removed. The young man was already under anaesthetic and the theatre staff were still draping his leg and setting up the arthroscopic equipment after Pedro had scrubbed in.

It was more than enough time to think about what he'd flippantly said to his registrar about finding time to fit in some ankle surgery.

To wonder whether Nikita's ankle was a lot better after a couple of days to start healing.

To remember, yet again, the extraordinary end to that visit when he'd ended up doing something he'd never dreamed he would ever get to do.

Kissing Nikita Wallace.

Properly…

Pedro had tried to put it to one side. To tell himself that

it was simply closure for something that had haunted him from the past. To pat himself on the back, in fact, that he'd been able to help someone move past a fear of being touched that was a physical barrier that could have made a significant difference to their quality of life.

That might well be something he could be pleased about, but it was now also in the past. Done and dusted. He needed to walk away and not look back. To not think about it so much it was becoming more significant than it had any right to be.

He needed to get on with his own life, as well as this surgery that was going to make a huge difference to his patient's quality of life.

'Scalpel, thanks,' he requested. He quickly made the first small incision to insert the arthroscope probe with its built-in camera. 'Overhead lights down, please. Let's have a look and see what we can find, shall we?'

It was easy to focus now. Especially when he had a first-year doctor starting a rotation in the orthopaedic department in here to observe this afternoon.

'When I started out learning this surgery,' he told her, 'we used to do at least a seven-centimetre incision and we'd remove the entire meniscus in open surgery.'

'That would have left a bone-on-bone situation for the knee joint, wouldn't it? Sounds painful.'

'We've certainly improved the process. We generally only remove about five to ten percent of it now, which leaves a much better cushion between the femur and tibia.' The bright light of the camera was visible beneath the skin as Pedro manipulated the camera to inspect the entire joint.

'There's the major tear. And that's a sizeable flap of displaced tissue that needs to come out. I'll make another

incision so we can get in with the punch and shaver.'
Pedro glanced up at the clock. 'We should be done in
about fifteen minutes.'

The shaver made a rasping sound as it smoothed out
the ragged edges of torn meniscus and sucked out the
debris. After another sweep of the camera to check that
nothing had been missed, including damage to the an-
terior cruciate ligament, Pedro left it to his registrars to
close up the incisions and bandage the knee.

'I'll start the post-op round,' he told them. 'Come and
join me when you're done. By the time we get back to
this guy, he might be ready to go home.'

And by the time he'd checked on all his surgical cases
for today, done an orthopaedic ward round and caught
up on his paperwork, Pedro would be more than ready
to go home himself.

Except that he changed his mind about that as he was
about to walk out of the main doors of Bristol Central.
Coming towards him, walking rather slowly, with a noticeable limp, was Nikita.

Dammit... Pedro's heart sank as he realised that it was
not going to be as easy as he'd hoped to walk away and
get on with his own life.

Because the very first thing that was filling his mind,
and creating a very physical reaction throughout his entire body, was the memory of that kiss.

Along with an astonishingly strong desire to do it all
over again...

It hadn't been quite as daunting as it had been last time,
walking into the main foyer of Bristol Central, even
though Nikita had had to walk past a group of carol sing-

ers outside the main entrance and the haunting notes of 'Silent Night' had followed her inside, where there were even more Christmas decorations to be seen, including the dreaded tinsel. It was looped overhead from the top of the Christmas tree to various points where the ends could be attached, along the front of the reception desk, dangling from light fittings in the cafeteria and completely covering a wire trolley in front of the pharmacy that was full of gifts like scented soap and hand cream wrapped in pretty red paper and tied up in silver ribbon.

Maybe it was because it was late in the day so the usual buzz of a busy city hospital was dialled down.

More likely, it was because Nikita could see Pedro Garcia walking towards her and she felt a frisson of the feeling of safety he somehow managed to convey without even trying.

Or was it because she could feel the memory of that kiss…?

He wasn't looking happy to see her, mind you. He was frowning quite heavily by the time he got within speaking distance.

'You're limping,' he observed. 'Your ankle's not improving, is it?'

'It's a bit sore,' Nikita admitted. 'I thought it might be sensible to get an X-ray, after all.'

'Don't move,' Pedro ordered. 'I'll be right back.' He turned on his heel and headed towards the reception desk.

Nikita did what she'd been told and stood still—a human obstacle to one side of a flow of people leaving the building. Visitors perhaps, like the woman who was wearing earrings that flashed red and green, holding the hand of a small child who had a Christmas sweater featuring a plum pudding with a sparkling sprig of holly on top. Or they could have been here for an outpatient appointment, like the elderly gentleman who was walking with the aid of a stick that had a tinsel bow tied around it. Some people were clearly staff members, like the pair of nurses in scrubs with lanyards hanging around their necks, who were sniffing the soaps outside the pharmacy and nodding, as if they approved of the price and what an easy gift they would make for someone well down on their list—like a neighbour or their child's schoolteacher?

Pedro had spoken to one of the receptionists and was now coming back towards Nikita, pushing one of the hospital wheelchairs available for anyone with restricted mobility.

'I don't need that,' she protested.

'I'll believe that when I've had a good look at your X-rays.' Pedro's stern tone told her that there was no point in trying to argue with him. 'Hop in. I happen to know exactly where you need to go.'

'I was just going to go through ED,' Nikita told him. 'Like any ordinary person with a sore ankle.'

But Pedro shook his head. 'It's coming up to shift change and you know what ED gets like at this time of the year. You'd be in the waiting room for hours, sitting amongst people coughing and sneezing and spreading their winter bugs and watching the antics of the ones who got drunk at their work Christmas parties and managed to injure themselves.' He gestured at the chair. 'Sit,' he commanded.

Nikita sat. She was, for the moment, still part of a workforce that devoted themselves to caring for others and that made her a part of a community that looked after each other. X-ray technicians in the radiology department were only too happy to squeeze in an extra patient when she had been one of their top orthopaedic surgeons and was in the company of another.

'I'd like the usual anteroposterior and lateral views to rule out a fracture,' Pedro told them. 'And an AP mortise view too, please, so we can get a clear shot of the articular space.'

It was Pedro and the consultant radiologist on duty who examined the films a short time later.

'The good news is that there's no sign of a fracture,' the radiologist told Nikita. 'The bad news is that you've got some decent bruising and swelling there so it's going to be sore for a while. And what you don't want is to do any more damage to it, so you need some decent support to stop you twisting it again.'

'We'll go down to fracture clinic.' Pedro nodded. 'Might be a good idea to get a compression ankle brace fitted properly. Or a moon boot.'

The fracture clinic was right beside the emergency department and it was an area of the hospital that Nikita knew like the back of her hand. There were familiar faces working here and it was quite humbling to find how welcome she was.

'It's so good to see you back,' one of the senior nurses told her. 'We've missed you.'

'I needed a bit of a break,' Nikita confessed.

'Not in your ankle,' someone else quipped. 'But it looks like you did your best to get one.'

They did a superb job of fitting a walking boot with Velcro strapping and a rocker sole and the difference in comfort was astonishing.

Nikita tried walking a few steps. 'It's not hurting at all now. Thank you so much.'

'I wouldn't go hiking for any distance,' the nurse advised. 'Or riding that horse of yours. And if it starts getting sore, then rest. Use the boot for a couple of weeks and it should speed up your recovery considerably.' The nurse smiled at her. 'Think of it as Central's Christmas gift for you.'

Pedro was nodding. And then he smiled at Nikita and she was aware of an odd spear of sensation deep in her belly.

'You may as well have a ride back to the front door,' he said, opening up the wheelchair that had been folded and put to one side of the area. 'I've got to take the wheelchair back to Reception anyway.'

But that odd feeling in her gut had reminded Nikita of that kiss and, embarrassingly, the fact that Pedro had confessed to being in love with her a decade ago. And yes, he had told her he was completely over it and it was ancient history, but knowing that he *had* felt like that and she'd been unaware of it was…weird.

Disappointing, even?

She also knew he would never have offered to kiss her 'properly' if she hadn't kissed him first—and how shocked had he been by that?

Even more disconcertingly, however, she could still actually *feel* what it had been like to have his lips touching hers and that sensation intensified now into something that felt very much like the desire to feel it again.

'I can take the chair back,' she said hurriedly. 'You've done more than enough and it's getting late. I'm sure you're more than ready to go home.'

'I'm walking that way, anyway.' Pedro shrugged. 'We can argue about who gets to push the chair on the way.'

He held the door open for Nikita, but she couldn't go through it because someone was blocking the way. Someone she hadn't seen in a very long time.

Aiden, an emergency department consultant, was looking just as surprised.

'*Nikita*... What on earth are you doing here?' Then he shook his head. 'I heard Pedro was here.' He shifted his gaze. 'We need you, mate. There's a guy on his way in—ETA five minutes. Twenty-five-year-old male who's been caught in machinery and sounds like he's in danger of losing his dominant arm. Open fracture radius and ulnar, elbow dislocation and an arterial bleed that's being controlled with a tourniquet en route, but he's lost a lot of blood already. The trauma team's been activated but we need Orthopaedics on board and someone told me you were here.' His looked back at Nikita. 'And you're here too? With your talents in vascular surgery? Our patient might have just won the lottery in having the best team possible waiting for him.'

Nikita could see that Pedro was already intently focused on the information he was receiving. She could also see that there was no question of him being available to do whatever he could to help with an injury that could be life-changing, if not shattering.

And Aiden was suggesting that *she* became involved?

Because he knew this was exactly the kind of scenario she had become an expert in. He could probably see that Nikita was just as focused as Pedro.

How badly damaged was that artery? Could it be repaired or had too much of it been destroyed and a graft would be needed using a synthetic material or an autologous transplant with one of the patient's own veins? If a blood supply couldn't be re-established quickly, the patient was far more likely to end up with a poor result or having an amputation, and the clock was already ticking.

The critical timeframe for reperfusion for an upper limb might be eight to ten hours, but how long had it been since the injury occurred? How long had it taken to extricate him from the machinery? It could take considerable time to stabilise a patient who was probably in hypovolaemic shock from blood loss and tests such as X-rays or CT scans might be needed. Wounds had to be debrided and cleaned and fractures sorted before vascular injuries could even be assessed, let alone treated.

But consideration of the whole process was filling Nikita's mind and her fear of being unable to perform in an operating theatre was fighting with a desire to be a part of the team working to save this young man's arm.

And that desire was winning the fight.

As if both the men beside her caught her thoughts, they turned towards her. She could see that Aiden simply wanted her input to help shape the priorities for stabilising and treating a serious trauma case, but Pedro's gaze told her that he was aware of what a huge step it would be to even walk back into an emergency department as a medical professional. There was something else in his gaze as well.

Encouragement?

She could hear an echo of his voice in the back of her head.

'*I don't believe that the real Nikki wants to hide from*

*the world. Or not do the work that mattered so much to
her...'*

She could even hear something he hadn't said at the
time.

You can do this, Nikki...

And...maybe she could if he was right there beside her.

If she didn't do it with the kind of support he could
provide, she might never find the courage to find out if
she was still capable of doing it at all. She would end up
walking away from a career that had been everything to
her and might well regret not taking this opportunity for
the rest of her life.

It was Pedro's gaze she was holding as she gave a single decisive nod.

'Let's go,' she said.

Seeing Nikita wearing scrubs was like stepping back in
time to when they had shared a clinical elective in a hospital as part of their medical school training.

Being simply observers as the trauma team began work
to stabilise their patient by securing his airway, breathing and circulation gave Pedro plenty of time to take in
the fact that, outwardly, Nikita hadn't really changed at
all in the last ten years, but he was more concerned with
the awareness that what *had* changed inwardly could impact the care of this patient.

The resuscitation area was crowded as the ambulance
crew did their handover and the trauma team moved
swiftly into well-practised protocols. Portable monitoring of vital signs like blood pressure, blood oxygen saturation levels and heart rate and rhythm were changed to
the department's equipment and oxygen was hooked up

to the overhead supply. Clothing was being cut off and Aiden—the doctor at the head of the bed in charge of the airway—was reassessing his patient's level of consciousness.

'Can you tell me your name?'

'Kyle…' The response was a groan.

'Do you know where you are?'

'…hospital?'

'Yes. You've injured your arm. How's the pain at the moment?'

'It's bad…'

'Score out of ten, with zero being no pain and ten being the worst you can imagine?'

'Nine…'

'Okay, Kyle. We're going to give you some more medication for that.'

Blood was being taken for a type and cross match. Fluids were being hung on IV poles to try and restore blood volume to raise blood pressure. Antibiotics and a tetanus booster were ordered. The dressings covering his arm were carefully removed once more analgesic drugs had been administered and, after no more than a glance to take in a shocking traumatic injury that looked like a partial amputation, Pedro focused on Nikita's face. How was she dealing with an injury that looked as though it could have been the result of a bomb blast, with bone tissue and blood vessels clearly visible in the pulverised muscle?

She was wearing a mask and a hat, but Pedro could sense the way her whole body had stiffened and he could see the intensity of her gaze as she stared at the injury. Could she even hear the crisscross of verbal communication or notice the positioning and movement of equipment and people around her?

'What's the systolic pressure now?' There were more pain-killing drugs being given to Kyle.

'Ninety.'

'Loosen that tourniquet again,' someone directed. 'How's it looking?'

'There's still bleeding, but it's not pulsatile.'

'How much blood loss did the paramedics estimate?'

'Up to two litres.'

'Oxygen saturation's down to ninety-one.' Aiden was looking up at the monitor as an alarm sounded. Was he wondering whether he might need to consider intubation if they couldn't get the blood pressure any higher?

If Nikita was finding the tense atmosphere in this resuscitation area overwhelming she wasn't showing any signs of not being able to handle it. Pedro wasn't worried about her having a meltdown of any kind as he stepped closer to the bed.

'Can I check the limb baselines?'

'Sure…' The nurse who was removing the dressings stepped aside.

'Kyle, can you feel me touching your hand?' He rubbed a pale-looking palm that was clearly not getting enough of a blood supply.

'Kind of… It feels weird—like pins and needles.'

'Can you move your fingers?'

Pedro watched for any twitch in the hand but couldn't see anything.

He pinched one of Kyle's nails between his forefinger and thumb.

'Capillary refill greater than five seconds,' he reported

for the benefit of the scribe who was recording the resuscitation. 'Skin cold to touch.' He felt both sides of the wrist, pausing for several seconds. 'Radial and ulnar pulses both absent.'

He glanced up but he'd known that Nikita was watching him like a hawk and that she'd heard everything he'd said. No pulses meant that there was major damage to the arteries in Kyle's arm. The tissue below the level of injury would die without an oxygen supply.

'Can everyone not wearing a lead apron step back, please?' A technician was moving overhead equipment. 'We're ready to take some X-rays.'

Even without the information the X-rays would provide, it was obvious there were major orthopaedic injuries, not just in Kyle's elbow. The jagged end of his radius was visible through the skin of his forearm and the deformity in the forearm suggested a severe displacement of both the radius and the ulnar bones.

Pedro was closer to Nikita as she stepped further back.

'Mess...' she murmured quietly.

Pedro was tempted to try and defuse the tension around them by agreeing that the arm in front of them *was* a mess, but he knew she was referring to something far more clinical. 'What's your score estimate?'

A MESS score was a Mangled Extremity Severity Score. Anything over a score of seven meant that amputation was more likely to be needed, but in someone Kyle's age and with the loss of a dominant hand potentially catastrophic, they were going to do whatever they could to save it.

'His age is in his favour, with no score for under thirty years old.'

'But the ischaemia score is at least two with no pulses and poor cap refill.'

'At least a two for the mechanism of injury.'

'And he's still hypotensive—that's another two.'

Pedro held Nikita's gaze and he saw the level of determination increasing in her eyes. He waited, holding his breath, as if he knew—or at least hoped—that she was about to take an even bigger step in her recovery.

'We're in with a shot, then,' she said. 'We need to get him to Theatre ASAP.'

CHAPTER SIX

IT WAS THE first time Nikita had been inside an operating theatre since the day of the bombing and her capture. If she'd given herself any time to think about it she might have backed off, being so sure that it would trigger a paralysing flashback.

But she was in control.

Remarkably calm, in fact.

Because Pedro was right beside her and she knew—as she always had known, despite that one instance where she'd made a horrible mistake—that she could trust him. Right now, it felt like there was a human rock in the midst of the potentially dangerous currents she had chosen to step into and she could catch hold of that safe anchor if she needed to at any time.

And maybe that was why she could focus so completely on what was happening in front of her. Even her hands were reassuringly steady as she assisted Pedro in managing the injuries to the elbow joint and the bones of the lower arm. They had already debrided all the obviously dead tissue, along with removing any foreign matter and giving the huge wound a thorough wash with saline. The dislocation and fractures needed to be stabilised before Nikita could explore the wound to see how much vascular damage had occurred.

The elbow was the first priority and she watched Pedro's careful relocation of the joint and then attaching lightweight external fixation.

'We don't want this joint moving while we're working on the rest of his arm,' he said.

Nikita turned to look again at the series of X-ray images on screen of the fractures and wasn't surprised when Pedro made a new incision in Kyle's forearm to access the ulnar bone. What did surprise her was the dexterity and skill Pedro displayed in achieving meticulous realignment of the bones and then manipulating the small plates and screws to hold them close enough to ensure the best result possible as they healed.

And then it was Nikita's turn to step into the lead.

'Do you want the technicians to set up for angiography?'

She shook her head. 'The ischaemia's obvious and… how long has it been since injury now?'

Pedro looked up at the clock. 'Nearly five hours.'

'I don't want to lose any more time. I don't imagine this will be a quick fix for the vascular damage.'

'Are you going to be all right standing on that ankle?'

Nikita nodded. Thanks to the support of the boot and the adrenaline rush of being back in an operating theatre, she had actually forgotten about what had brought her into the hospital in the first place and she wasn't about to let a minor level of discomfort distract her now—especially as she carefully explored the huge open wound and confirmed how long her part in this surgery was likely to take.

'We've got destructive injury in the brachial, ulnar and radial arteries and it's big. More than twenty centimetres. It's not going to be possible to suture them directly.'

'Will you use a synthetic graft?'

Pedro was watching her work with the same intensity she had watched him. Was he just as impressed?

'No. I'm going to remove all the bruised segments and do a reversed, bifurcated saphenous vein graft. It's the best option to maintain arterial continuity.'

Nikita only glanced up to meet Pedro's gaze for a heartbeat but…yeah…she could see he was impressed and that was just the boost her confidence needed to take her focus to the next level.

The level she'd always worked at and, in a situation like this, spurred on by urgency due to a limited time span if she was going to succeed.

Pedro wasn't the only person in Theatre to be impressed when, nearly three hours later, the first pulse could be felt in Kyle's wrist. The pale, lifeless-looking hand was beginning to take on a pink tinge and Nikita let out her breath in a sigh of relief that came from somewhere very deep within her. Not that they were finished here quite yet but, happy there were no leaks in any of the vascular suturing and with no obvious nerve damage that needed immediate attention from the neurosurgeon in Theatre with them, it was time to move on to the last step in this painstaking attempt to save a young man's arm and hand.

'I'll do the prophylactic fasciotomies,' Pedro offered. 'You must need to rest that ankle by now.'

She did, but she didn't want to step away from the table just yet. Someone brought her a stool so she could sit while she watched Pedro make openings in the thin casing around the muscles so that the pressures from swelling in compartment syndrome couldn't undo all the work they had just done and then close the soft tissue injuries and finally close the skin as neatly as the ragged wound would allow.

Kyle would need further surgeries, there was no doubt about that, but there was now a very good chance that he would not only keep his arm and hand but hopefully end up with a good level of function.

Nikita was proud of their efforts, but what she was even more proud of was that she had just done what she'd been so sure she would never be able to do again. She could actually feel herself welling up with an emotional reaction as she walked out of Theatre and the enormity of what she had done finally hit her. She took in a huge breath and lifted her chin, hoping nobody had noticed, only to find that Pedro was right beside her.

He had not only noticed, he was smiling.

'You did it,' he murmured. 'I knew you could...'

Dammit...those tears were threatening to multiply. She knew he was being completely genuine. He had believed in her and that was why he'd refused to let her sign those papers and give up on her career before she was completely sure it was what she wanted to do.

He might have single-handedly changed the entire rest of her life. Not just careerwise, but because he might have made it possible for her to believe in herself again.

No wonder emotion was threatening to get the better of her. It also didn't help that Nikita was aware that her foot was aching badly and she was limping as much as she had been when Pedro had seen her arrive so many hours ago. The urge to lean on Pedro was so strong she could almost feel herself tilting. She pulled in another deep breath as she straightened her back.

'I've got to get home,' she muttered. 'Poor Earl will be wondering where on earth I am. At least I gave him his dinner early before I came in.'

'Did you have *your* dinner early too?'

'No.'

'Neither did I. Although it's probably closer to breakfast time now. I wonder if there's a bacon and egg sandwich in one of those vending machines. I might have a look after I check on Kyle in Recovery.'

He was smiling at Nikita again and she could feel the warmth of it despite, or perhaps because of, her tiredness and emotional fragility. The warmth was enough to make it feel like something was melting inside her, leaving a puddle of…what was it?

A longing to be close to someone?

To actually look forward to having human company instead of the limiting but trusted alternative of having only her animals around her.

Yes.

And no.

Yes, she was yearning for the closeness.

But no, not just to someone.

This man.

Only this man.

She was standing in front of a vending machine in the foyer, not far from the huge Christmas tree with its lights twinkling in the dim light of the early hours. The star on the top of the tree was providing an anchor for long tendrils of red, green and silver tinsel that were radiating out like the spokes of a wheel and attached to points like an information screen near the reception desk and over the entrance to the café.

A weary-looking security guard was patrolling the front door. Nikita looked even more tired. She was staring through the glass window of the machine as if she had no idea what she wanted and that, along with her slightly hunched shoulders, made her look kind of sad.

Lost, even?

He'd never seen her look like that when he'd first known her and it was breaking his heart that she could look like this now.

Pedro found himself swallowing a lump in his throat as he walked up to her.

'I thought you'd be long gone by now,' he said.

'I took a shower and had a coffee. I didn't want to fall asleep while I was driving home.' Her face brightened a little. 'How's Kyle doing?'

'Good. His hand is warm and pink. He woke up while I was there and the first thing he did was look to see if he still had his hand attached. And then he tried to move his fingers, and when he got just the smallest twitch he was so relieved he burst into tears.' Pedro could feel that lump back in his own throat again so he cleared it and changed the subject. 'Are there any bacon and egg sandwiches in there?'

'No. There's an egg and cheese.'

'Not the same.'

'No.' Nikita shook her head in agreement. She looked up at him with a half-smile on her face but then, to his dismay, her gaze slid to something over his shoulder and her expression changed to one of disgust. Horror, even?

He turned his head sharply to see what it was she was looking at. One of the strands of tinsel had detached itself from high on the wall beside the main entrance and was drifting down to coil up like a shimmering snake on the floor.

'I *hate* Christmas.' Nikita's tone was vehement. 'I hate Christmas decorations most of all.'

Pedro put two and two together with the speed of light as he remembered that it had been just before Christmas when Nikita had gone through the terror of the bombing and her capture.

'Take a deep breath,' he said quietly. 'You're okay, Nikki.'

He could see the way she was struggling to swallow so that she could speak. 'It's tinsel,' she whispered. 'Red tinsel. That's the worst.'

Pedro shifted so that she wasn't watching the security guard collect the end of the tinsel and shift it away from where people would be walking to get through the doors. When she lifted her gaze to his, he held it.

'Can I ask why?'

'It's something that's always in my nightmares.' Nikita bit her bottom lip and closed her eyes, as if she was seeing it again. Or perhaps it was easier to tell him something personal while she was hiding how she felt about it. 'It was silver tinsel—or it had been until it got covered with blood. It was caught…around my foot.' She opened her eyes again. 'But yeah… I used to love Christmas decorations and that's just a stupid piece of tinsel and I'm not going to let it do my head in.'

'Bravo,' Pedro murmured.

'Can't say I'm hungry now, though. I think I'll just go home.'

'I'll walk you to your car. Is it in the car park?'

'Yes. On the far side. I could ask the security guy to get someone to go with me.'

'I'm going that way anyway.' His glance must have told her that he would be better for both company and protection, because he knew there was so much more to this than the time of night and being vulnerable to any undesirable people who could be lurking in the shadows. He knew about the shadows that Nikita carried with her wherever she went and whatever time of day it was.

'Thanks, Pedro. I'd appreciate that.'

He was pleased to see that Nikita wasn't limping so much as they walked into the night, even after being on her feet for so long, so that boot was doing its job.

'What do you do with Earl when you're out like this?'

'He has a lovely warm bed in the stable. He's probably curled up and fast asleep now. And Duncan will be in there, keeping him company. They're the best of friends.'

'So he wouldn't mind if you stay out a bit longer?'

Nikita's sideways glance was startled. 'Why would I do that?'

'I thought I could buy you breakfast. To say thank you. You did a much better job than I could have with that vascular repair. Without it, Kyle might not have woken up with his hand still attached.'

Nikita shook her head. 'My car's right here. There wouldn't be anywhere open for breakfast at this time of night, anyway.'

'My apartment is. It's only a few minutes' walk from

here.' Pedro raised an eyebrow. 'Bacon and eggs is one thing I'm good at cooking, so I always have supplies in the fridge. I could even throw in a hash brown, seeing as it's a special occasion.'

'A hash brown? Now you're talking.' But Nikita was shaking her head again. 'Thanks, anyway, Pedro, but I think I need to get home for myself as much as my animals. I…feel a bit wrecked, to be honest.'

Yeah…that tinsel had been the last straw on top of what had already been a difficult time. Pedro's smile faded as his tone became serious. 'What you did in Theatre was very impressive,' he told her. 'You know that, don't you? And I'm not just talking about a vascular reconstruction.'

Something softened in Nikita's eyes. She knew he was talking about the way she'd won the battle she'd had to fight against her fears. That she had broken through what had seemed an impenetrable barrier.

'I couldn't have done it,' she said very quietly, 'if you hadn't been there.'

Pedro held her gaze. 'I'm still here,' he said. 'I could be here long enough for you to try again. To be there, but just in the background—so that you can know you're capable of doing this. And capable of keeping the career I know you love so much.'

Yes…it was there. He could see that flash of hope in her eyes, but then it was snuffed out.

'It's too big,' she whispered. 'I can't even start to think about it.'

Except that Pedro knew, on some level, she *was* thinking about it already. Maybe she had been, ever since she'd turned her back on her career in order to focus on her own health.

'Go home,' he said gently. 'Get some sleep. We'll talk about this when you've had time to think about what an amazing thing you did tonight.' He watched as Nikita unlocked her car and opened the door. He didn't want her to leave just yet. The thought of her going home and having nightmares about blood-covered tinsel was too awful and he desperately wanted to be able to help.

He touched her cheek gently. 'Tinsel can't hurt you,' he said softly. 'You know that. I seem to remember a Christmas thing when we were on an elective together and you got dressed up as a fairy. With tinsel in your hair and a sparkly star on a stick...'

There'd been other medical students involved but it was only Nikita that Pedro could remember so clearly.

'Oh, good grief... I'd completely forgotten that. We went around the wards at St Nicholas Children's Hospital, giving out presents, didn't we? I think I was supposed to be an angel and the tinsel was my halo. And didn't you do the honours dressed as Father Christmas?'

'I did. I had a pillow in my jacket to make me fat enough.'

There was a shimmer to Nikita's eyes that suggested tears. 'It was fun... Those kids were so happy to see us.'

He nodded. Just once. Slowly. 'It *was* fun. Try to remember that,' he said. 'And *this* Christmas is different too.'

'Why?'

'Because it just is. It's a new Christmas. And *you're* different. You just did something you didn't think you could do any longer, didn't you?'

She hesitated but then she nodded.

'So there you go. It's the start of something new. And we'll talk tomorrow, when you've had that rest. I could bring you some dinner when I've finished work,' he said.

'You don't need to do that.'

'I want to do that.' Pedro's tone was firm. 'And you know you need to talk to me.'

'Why?'

'Because I'm not going to let you resign until I'm sure that it's what you really want. I'm going to make sure your resignation isn't accepted if I'm not sure.'

Nikita shook her head again. 'That's John's call as HoD, not yours.'

'I'm making it mine. So, why don't you tell me what your favourite thing to eat is, or I might turn up with bacon and eggs.'

There was a flash of something else in her eyes now. Not hope but something warmer, like humour. Or appreciation, perhaps?

'If there's a hash brown thrown in, I wouldn't say no. An all-day breakfast is right up there with my favourite things to eat.'

Oh…this felt like a win. It felt so good, in fact, that Pedro knew his smile was too wide.

He knew he was holding her gaze for too long as well, but he couldn't help it because he felt as if he needed to hold something to keep his balance, so that he wouldn't fall.

Which was an odd thought.

His feet were solidly on the asphalt of the car parking area and he wasn't even moving, so how on earth could he fall?

And then the thought evaporated anyway, because it was being replaced by a desire to kiss Nikki again.

One of those *proper* kisses…

It looked as if she might be thinking the same thing but…it was late and Nikita had to be exhausted, both physically and emotionally, after the way she'd pushed past those barriers tonight. Kissing her right now would be taking advantage of someone who had told him, only minutes ago, that she needed time to get her head straight.

So he simply smiled softly instead.

'Drive carefully,' he said. 'I'll see you tomorrow evening.'

There was the hint of a smile curling the corners of Nikita's mouth too. 'Don't bring any eggs,' she said. 'My chickens would be highly offended.' Then her smile widened and there was a gleam in her eyes that Pedro could feel even more than he could see. And it was making him feel very good.

Very good indeed.

'But don't forget the hash browns,' she added. 'Or *I* might be highly offended.'

CHAPTER SEVEN

IT SNOWED DURING the day a little.

Just enough to coat the bare branches of the weeping elm tree like a dusting of icing sugar and for it to be cold enough for Nikita to have had her pot belly stove, as well as the little Aga in her kitchen, well stoked all day. It was completely dark well before Pedro arrived but the cottage was warm enough for Nikita to be wearing only jeans with frayed knees and a soft sweatshirt with the sleeves pushed up. Pedro discarded his leather jacket as soon as he'd put the bags he was carrying down on the kitchen bench.

'It's as warm as…' Pedro frowned. 'What's the expression? Toast?'

Nikita nodded. 'Yep. Warm as toast.'

'In Spanish we'd just say it's nice and warm—*bien caliente* Why toast? It never stays warm for long after it's popped.'

'I suppose it dates back to before electric toasters, when people used to put slices of bread on a fork and sit in front of an open fireplace to toast them in the flames. They would have been close enough to get pretty hot.'

Pedro tilted his head in acknowledgement but he was clearly thinking about something else now.

'We have another saying in Spain,' he told her. '*Nuevo año, nuevo yo*, which means "New year, new me".' He picked up one of the paper bags. 'This isn't food,' he told her. 'But I saw it in the window of a shop beside the supermarket and… I thought of a new saying. Why not *Nuevo Navidad, nuevo yo*? New Christmas, new me?'

The bag was heavy. Nikita opened it and took out an oddly shaped parcel wrapped in tissue paper. She took the paper off to find quite a large three-dimensional star made out of clear glass pieces joined by lead lighting. There was a short chain to hang it up with and a small door that opened to allow a tealight candle to go inside.

It was beautiful.

'It's a Christmas star,' Pedro told her. 'Because it's a symbol of something wonderful happening. And it's to remind you that Christmas has been good in the past and it will be good again in the future.' He looked up at the beams that were within easy reach for him and his tone was casual—as if this was no big deal at all. 'Where would you like it? If you have a hook, I could hang it up for you.'

He didn't want her to put it away in a corner and forget about it, did he? Surprisingly, Nikita realised she didn't want to do that either. It wasn't as if he was asking her to string gaudy tinsel from her beams or put a plastic reindeer on the windowsill. A star wasn't just for Christmas. It was something you could wish on as well. Wishing for the possibility of a 'New Christmas, new me' couldn't hurt, could it?

'Have a look in the left-hand drawer of the dresser in the kitchen. It's my "useful" drawer, which actually means it's full of junk. There may be some cup hooks left over from when I put them in to hang mugs under the shelf.'

There was a small brass hook to be found amongst batteries and extra keys and old phone chargers. There was even a screwdriver that Pedro could use to start a tiny hole in a beam that was probably as solid as concrete and some pliers so that he could turn the hook until it was firmly in place. He lit the small candle inside it and then closed and latched the little door. Nikita had chosen the corner nearest the door of her bedroom so it was hanging in a spot that was shadowy enough to make the glow of the candle fill the interior of the star and glow brightly as it flickered.

'I love it,' she told Pedro. 'Thank you so much.'

'I've got some gingerbread men for our dessert too,' he said. 'It's not really a Christmas decoration if you eat it, is it? Now, show me how to use this oven so I can get the hash browns cooking. And where is your frying pan?'

He hadn't just been thinking of ingredients for their meal when he'd been shopping, had he? Pedro had been thinking about *her*. Not just about the issues that had completely changed her life but about how he might be able to help her. Nikita could feel that odd warmth of something melting deep inside her again—a feeling that only this man seemed to be able to create.

And it was *such* a lovely feeling…

'Let me help,' she offered.

'No.' Pedro shook his head. 'You're supposed to be resting that foot. You can tell me where things are while you're sitting on the couch.'

Nikita gave in gracefully. 'As long as you tell me

how Kyle's doing as well. I've been wondering about him all day.'

'I knew you would be. I went to see him just before I left work. He's got a very lumpy arm so it's just as well we cut the fascia to prevent compartment syndrome. His limb baselines are all acceptable and he's got slightly more movement in his fingers but he's still very sore. And sleepy. You should come in and see him yourself in the next day or two.'

Nikita made a non-committal sound but the idea was attractive. She wanted to see the results of her work. Would it be even easier to walk back into the hospital a third time?

Nuevo Navidad, nuevo yo.

The all-day breakfast that Pedro put together was impressive. Epic, even. The hash browns, crunchy on the outside and soft in the middle, were used as a base for perfectly fried eggs. Crispy curls of bacon, aromatic mushrooms and the baked beans Nikita had insisted were a vital component of the meal filled the rest of their plates. Pedro had already stacked gingerbread men into a bowl he'd found and put them on the mantelpiece in the living room.

'For later,' he said.

He'd filled two glasses with a rich red wine as well.

'For now,' he said with a grin.

They ate with quiet enjoyment, sitting on the couch in front of the pot belly stove. Earl lay on the floor beside them, his nose on Nikita's foot, just to make sure she knew he was there. Or maybe he was waiting for a morsel of bacon to fall off her plate.

The sound of Pedro's phone ringing cut through the

companionable quietness just as Nikita was eating the last corner of hash brown, smothered in egg yolk and attached to half a button mushroom.

'Sorry…that's the hospital,' Pedro apologised as he glanced at the screen of his device. 'I'd better take the call.'

'Of course.' Nikita nodded. Even though Pedro stood up and moved away, it was impossible not to listen to his side of the conversation.

'No…really? And he was in Theatre at the time?

'How serious is it? Has he had an angiogram?'

Nikita swallowed her mouthful of food in a hurry at that point. Had something happened to Kyle? Had he been rushed back to Theatre in an emergency? Had one of her vascular repairs failed?

'How many stents?' Pedro gave a silent whistle. 'Just as well he was where he was when it happened, then.' He listened for a long minute, making sounds of agreement. 'Sure thing,' he said, then. 'Let's have a departmental meeting at eight o'clock tomorrow morning and decide how we're going to plug the gaps.'

He ended the call and then took a deep breath before turning back.

'John Barlow's had a heart attack,' he told Nikita. 'He collapsed in Theatre just after he finished a hip replacement this afternoon. They got him to the catheter lab less than an hour later and he's now got four stents in place to deal with two major occlusions.' Pedro shook his head. 'Talk about being in the right place at the right time. He's a very lucky man.'

His voice trailed into silence but he was still holding Nikita's gaze. 'We're going to be seriously short-staffed,' he said. 'We're already covering for people who have taken extended leave for Christmas and there's the usual winter bugs going around.' He paused to take another breath. 'How would you feel about coming to the departmental meeting tomorrow and possibly coming back to work with us? Even just for a few days would be helpful while we get some new rosters sorted.'

Nikita's jaw dropped. She could feel her heart rate increasing and her muscles tensing as her adrenaline levels suddenly shot up but—just as suddenly and far more unexpectedly—it didn't last for more than a moment. One deep breath was all it took to steady her.

Because she was still holding Pedro's gaze. Because she could see in his eyes that he believed she could cope with going back to work.

He believed in *her*.

Vaya...

Pedro couldn't look away from those eyes. He'd always been intrigued by the kaleidoscope of colours, with those flecks of gold and even green against the soft brown background and the way they could change.

He'd seen them glow with determination or satisfaction, sparkle with amusement and flare with anger. More recently, he'd seen the chill of real fear in them and an uncertainty that he'd never seen before.

Right now, in the wake of his suggestion that she came back to work in her job as an orthopaedic surgeon, he could see a battle going on. She wanted to, but something was holding her back.

What was it?

And could he help her through it?

What a gift that would be for the woman he'd once loved to a level of distraction he hadn't been able to afford. And what better time to offer that gift when it was just days away from Christmas—a time when you gave gifts to the family and friends you cared about the most.

'What is it, Nikki?' he asked quietly. 'What are you afraid of?'

'You already know that.' Nikita broke their eye contact. 'Triggers. Being unable to do my job. Putting someone in danger.'

'You didn't put Kyle in danger. You saved his arm.'

'That was different. You were there. I knew you'd be able to step in if something went wrong.'

'What if I promised to be there to do that again? At least until you get your confidence back enough to trust in yourself?'

She still wasn't looking at him. She seemed to be staring at the glass star he'd hung in the corner of the room. For the size of the candle inside, it was certainly providing an impressive glow and lasting a long time.

'What was it that you said you're most afraid of?' he asked. 'Loud noises? Something being dropped? Like this?' He walked towards her, picked up the fork he'd been using to eat his dinner and dropped it back onto the plate.

Nikita's eyes widened at the clatter but she didn't look terrified. 'I could see what you were doing.'

'Shut your eyes, then. I'll go and drop it somewhere else.'

'But I know it's okay.'

'You'll know that in Theatre as well. You'll know it's

just a pair of forceps or a kidney dish and they're no more dangerous than a fork.'

Nikita looked as if she was chewing the inside of her cheek. She still didn't look convinced. Pedro crouched by the end of the sofa.

'Tell me,' he urged. 'Please… What's the thing you're *most* afraid of?'

She stared back at him. 'Someone coming up behind me,' she whispered. 'Touching me. *Grabbing* me…'

That fear was changing the colour of her eyes again. Making them darker. Tears were gathering as well, and Pedro could feel his breath catching in his chest.

'*Oh, cariñito,*' he murmured. He couldn't find words to tell her how well he understood or how sad he was that she'd been left with this fear, and maybe it was the wrong thing to do to touch her in this moment but she didn't seem to mind. It almost felt like she got to her feet so that he could hold her more easily in his arms. Tightly enough, he hoped, for her to feel safe.

And then he had an idea.

'What if we practised it?' he suggested. 'Like dropping the fork? Just slowly. The first time, I could walk up behind you and not even touch you. And then I could tell you I was going to touch you?'

'But I'd know it was you and that I was safe. Like I knew it was the fork.'

Pedro was caught for a heartbeat, knowing that he was capable of making her feel safe, but he also knew that this felt like the right track to be on if he wanted to give her the gift that could change the rest of her life.

'And you'd know that the people who might brush past you would be your colleagues. The doctors and nurses and technicians you've worked with before, and they're no more dangerous than I am.'

'I guess…'

'Shall we try?'

'Okay…'

'You stand over there, then. Under the star.'

Earl took advantage of not being watched to steal a last piece of bacon from Pedro's abandoned plate and then he climbed onto the couch to settle down and watch.

Pedro kept his voice calm as he walked up behind Nikita the first time. 'I'm coming towards you. I'm almost there. Now I'm standing right behind you.'

He walked up without saying anything the next time but still didn't touch her.

And then he touched her but warned her first. 'I'm just going to touch your shoulders, okay? I'm not going to grab you.'

'Don't tell me next time,' Nikita said. 'I think… I think I'm okay with this.'

So Pedro didn't say anything. He walked slowly towards Nikita. He could see the candlelight from the star above her head picked out russet flecks in her dark hair. Did she have her eyes closed? Was she listening to his footsteps on the ancient wooden boards of her floor?

Did she still feel safe?

He touched her gently, with open hands loosely cupping her shoulders. For a split second he thought she had frozen beneath his fingers, but then he felt her move as she turned to look up at him. She didn't need to say anything, he could see that she felt like she'd broken through another barrier. Her smile was wobbly but she wasn't trying to move away from his touch, so Pedro deepened it. He was holding her now. Really holding her.

Looking down at the face—so close he could see the reflection of the candle star in her pupils. He could see the moment those pupils dilated and then it hit him all at once. The sensation of her body beneath his hands. The candlelight. The warmth of the fire. The smell of Nikita's hair and even her skin. The fact that they were alone in the middle of nowhere and that, just behind the door on the other side of the star, was a bedroom. Nikki's bedroom.

That he could make this woman feel safe.

And, most of all, that he could see she wanted him to kiss her as much as he wanted to.

Pedro was aware of that odd falling sensation again, but this time he thought he knew what it could be.

Was he falling in love with her all over again?

Playing with fire?

But, if that was the case, he was old and wise enough to make sure there was a safety net. To not let it get out of control in the first place, even. He knew better than to hope for something that was never going to happen. He'd long ago accepted that any chemistry between them had only been on his side.

And this wasn't really about him, anyway, was it? This was about Nikki. It was a moment in time that might never be repeated but could possibly be an important part of the key to giving Nikita what she needed to believe in herself again.

Okay, it might also be the only opportunity he would ever have to step into a dream that he'd known would haunt him for the rest of his life, and it didn't feel as if he would be taking advantage of her this time because she wanted it as much as he did. And…what if his dream had been beyond anything that was likely to be found in reality? It could be that he could stop looking for something that didn't exist, and that might make it possible to find a person he could share the rest of his life with. To create a family with.

So maybe…this could be a gift for both of them?

There was only one way to find out.

He was going to kiss her.

But he was moving so slowly to lower his head and touch her lips with his own.

Too slowly.

A part of Nikita's brain told her that it was deliberate. Not because he was teasing her, but because he was giving her the chance to change her mind before things got out of control. He knew how she felt about people touching her.

Another part of her was aware of the astonishment of wanting this kiss so much. To want more than simply a passionate kiss. Nikita was desperately wanting someone to touch her in a way she'd never thought she would want—or even be able to tolerate—to be touched again.

No, not someone.

This man.

Only this man.

Because he'd earned her trust long ago. *She'd* been the one to break that friendship, not him.

And because he made her feel so safe.

She could feel the warmth of his lips even before they touched her own and yes…there was a beat of fear there now. A choice to be made. She could pull away, and she knew that Pedro would absolutely accept that decision. Or…she could take what felt like an even bigger risk than picking up a scalpel again. She could find out if she was capable of being this physically close to anyone again. To touch—and be touched—in the most intimate way possible.

And, because of the trust that was already there, Nikita knew that this was very likely to be the only opportunity she would ever get to feel safe enough to find that out.

So she didn't pull away. Instead, she found herself rising onto her tippy-toes as she felt his lips touch hers. She wrapped her arms around Pedro's neck and let herself sink into his kiss. When they finally broke that kiss and she could see the question in his eyes she did no more than snatch a breath.

'Don't stop,' she whispered. 'Please…please don't stop…'

When he scooped her up into his arms and carried her into her bedroom, her head brushed the glass star as they walked beneath it. The light flickered wildly around them but then steadied.

The glow was bright enough to reach the bed that filled this small room, but soft enough to allow other senses to be so much more important than sight. The deep rumbling murmur of Pedro's voice was something she could feel as much as hear, but it was what her other senses were so aware of that Nikita knew she would remember for ever. The smell and taste of this man. And the touch. Most of all the touch—the gentleness of it.

The feeling of safety that brought tears to her eyes.

A touch that was bringing her body back to life. Providing a pleasure she'd forgotten even existed.

A gift, that was what this was...

Something totally unexpected.

Something precious.

CHAPTER EIGHT

'NIKITA... HOW GOOD to see you.' Lewis Sugden's smile, as an old colleague and acting HoD, was as welcoming as his tone. 'I couldn't believe our luck when Pedro rang this morning to tell me you might be available to come back to Central a little earlier than planned.'

'I'm thinking about it,' Nikita agreed cautiously. 'I've come in for the meeting so I know what needs covering and how much time might be expected.' She hesitated for a moment, wondering how much Lewis knew. 'Did Pedro say anything else?'

'Only that he wanted to be available to be in Theatre with you for any initial surgeries. Just until you feel completely back up to speed after a long break.' Lewis's brow creased. 'I'm sorry I haven't been in touch. Even sorrier that you had to go through that dreadful experience of your hospital being bombed.' He shook his head. 'None of us were surprised that you needed some time away. We were getting worried that you might not come back at all.'

'Pedro talked me into it.'

Nikita looked towards the other end of the long table in one of Bristol Central's conference rooms. Pedro, who was standing near a whiteboard talking to other members of the Department of Orthopaedics, turned his head as if he could feel her glance. He gave a tiny nod, acknowledging her arrival. He didn't give the slightest indication that they had spent the night together before driving into the city separately.

'Ah…' Lewis had noticed the direction of her glance. 'I did hear that you happened to be here and could help with that nasty arm fracture that came in the other day. And did someone tell me that you and Pedro were at medical school together?'

Nikita nodded. 'I think that was part of the reason why Pedro suggested I might be able to help with the caseload while John's out of action.'

Not the biggest part, though. Pedro could see this as a way for her to put some of the broken pieces of her life back together and…he cared enough to want to be able to help her do that?

Oh…it had felt as if he cared about more than that last night, hadn't it? As if he'd wanted nothing more than to put another broken piece of her life back together. Almost as if he'd wanted to make love to her as much as she'd wanted him to.

She was probably letting her imagination run away with her. Pedro had made it very clear that he was completely over his old crush. He'd been helping her—as a friend. Like the way he used to help her out by lending her his lecture notes. He'd been helping her regain her confidence in a professional environment and deliberately touching her was only an extension of trying to defuse her triggers. And, okay, it had escalated into sex, but she'd initiated that—the same way she'd made that first kiss happen. Good grief…she had practically begged him to take her to bed.

Nikita knew there was nothing more to it, but the way he'd made love to her last night had felt far more signific-ant than any one-off or casual sexual encounter could possibly feel.

She'd felt as if she might be falling in love with Pedro Garcia. Or was she confusing gratitude and trust for love? Reading too much into a rekindled friendship because a physical boundary had been crossed?

Yes, of course she was. She knew that Pedro had his life mapped out for the near future, with a wealth of amazing opportunities to choose from. In no time at all, he'd be living in Spain or America or totally on the other side of the world in New Zealand. He couldn't wait to get away.

Last night wasn't going to change any of that. But it had felt…

So totally different to anything Nikita had ever felt before as far as sex went. Intimate on a level she hadn't known existed.

Tender enough to make her cry.

Exquisite enough to make her realise how far from feeling completely alive she had been for a very long time.

Even the flash of remembering the sensations Pedro's touch was capable of generating was enough her make her smile, but that didn't matter because Lewis was al-ready smiling himself.

'It would be a godsend to have you back,' Lewis said. 'Even if it's just temporary. Please sit down. I'd better get this meeting underway before everybody needs to be somewhere else.'

The fact that Nikita had come to this meeting at all

gave the impression that she would be prepared to put her name on the roster to help cover the immediate pressures.

The fact that Pedro was sitting at the other end of the table gave her the confidence to not only offer to help but to believe that this was the way back to a career she hadn't realised quite how much she'd been missing, and that was…exciting.

Her body had been brought back to life during the most amazing night she'd ever had last night, but it was her brain that was kicking back into life this morning and the combination felt as if she had taken a substance that was fizzing in her veins. Had she ever felt quite like this before? Like when she had finished her training and was ready to take on the world?

No. Because she hadn't known what it was like to lose hope for her future, and that made how she was feeling… a bit of a miracle.

'Christmas…' she heard Lewis say. She tried to catch what she'd missed by being distracted. Something about getting through the season that brought a sharp increase in the number of orthopaedic injuries from road traffic accidents and falls?

It fitted with her somewhat distracted thoughts this morning, anyway.

Because miracles were more likely to happen at Christmastime too, weren't they?

'I've still got a bit of time before my outpatient clinic starts,' Pedro said to Nikita as the meeting broke up. 'Let's go and collect that pager and a lanyard for you, and would you like to come with me and see how Kyle's doing?'

'Oh, yes, please.' Nikita was folding a piece of paper

she'd been making notes on. 'I must buy a diary or calendar on the way home,' she said, 'so I can make sure I don't forget the roster for the next few days.' She caught his gaze. 'It feels a bit weird that I need to take notice of what day it is again.'

Pedro just smiled. He knew that she was a bit nervous about the commitment to come back to work that she'd made during that meeting, but he could see how far she'd come since he'd seen her in the lift that day, looking so scared.

So lost…

She still looked different to how he'd remembered her from the past, but in a good way. Older and wiser. And maybe that wisdom had been very hard won, but he had a feeling—even if Nikki didn't realise it yet—that it had made her stronger and more compassionate and…admirable?

Sí…

Pedro knew he was right when he saw the expression on her face as she clipped the paging device to her pocket and officially became a working member of Bristol Central. He saw that balance of professionalism and deep compassion again when she was at Kyle's bedside a short time later. She brushed off their patient's gratitude at still having his arm with a modesty that was covering a pride she had every reason to be feeling, and the empathy she showed as her examination revealed how long his journey to a complete recovery might be was completely genuine.

He'd always known how skilled she was, though, hadn't he? And what a special person she was. He would never have been so smitten otherwise. Her qualities were magnified now, however. Even more special because she'd come very close to believing she'd lost them?

'I'm really happy with the colour of your skin and how warm it is,' she told him. 'You've got a good blood supply getting everywhere it's needed. We'll see how much sensation comes back when the swelling's gone down more, but I do think it's likely that you'll need some more surgery to repair nerves. We'll get the best neurosurgeon we've got here to come and see you very soon.'

'Will these lumps on my arm go away? It looks as if I've got tennis balls under my skin.'

'That's because we needed to release pressure from any swelling,' Pedro told him. 'It'll disappear completely soon.'

'And can I go home?'

'We'd like to keep you in for a bit longer. We want to make sure there's no infection happening and that the fixation on your elbow is adequate. You'll be at more risk of doing too much if you're at home.'

Kyle's face fell. 'I really need to be home,' he begged. 'What if I'm careful? Could I get out just for a few hours?'

'For Christmas Day?' Nikita asked. 'Have you got children, Kyle?'

He nodded. 'About sixteen of them,' he said. 'And it's Christmas Eve that's the important day.' His face tightened as if he was fighting back tears. 'This'll be the first year I've missed,' he said. 'And...and what if they can't find someone else?'

But Pedro was still processing the first thing he'd said. 'Did you really say *sixteen* children?' he asked.

Kyle nodded again as he sniffed loudly and used his uninjured hand to rub his nose. 'Not mine, exactly,' he said. 'But they're from the kind of homes I grew up in and they don't have much. I've been helping a group called the Secret Elves that puts on a special Christmas treat for disadvantaged kids every year. They get nominations from schools or social welfare and other organisations and we take them on a magical mystery bus trip on Christmas Eve and finish up having a party and I get to dress up as Santa and give them all a present. I've been doing it for nearly ten years.'

Since he was only about fifteen himself? Pedro was impressed. What had he been doing for others at Christmastime that he could be proud of? The only thing that sprang to mind was a long time ago.

'I dressed up as Santa once,' he told Kyle. 'And Nikki here was a Christmas angel. We went round the children's wards over at St Nick's and gave out presents.'

'*My* girlfriend helped me last year,' Kyle said. 'But she was an elf, not an angel. She said she wouldn't do it again though. I reckon that was one of the reasons I broke up with her.'

Pedro was trying to avoid looking at Nikita after the emphasis Kyle had put on his words that made him realise he thought he and Nikki were an item.

Had this young man somehow sensed what had happened last night? Was there some kind of current in the air because they were standing so close together? If so, it was just as well they'd been sitting at opposite ends of the table in that departmental meeting. How embarrassing would it be for Nikki if everyone knew she'd jumped into bed with her locum?

Pedro still hadn't quite got his head around what had happened last night.

The overwhelming impression he'd been left with was that he'd been right all along. Sex with Nikita Wallace was on a level he'd never experienced before and, now that he knew it really did exist, he was never going to be able to settle for anything less.

Even so, he wasn't going to regret what had happened last night.

Without thinking, his gaze slid sideways as he wondered whether Nikki might be regretting it. He hadn't expected her to be looking straight at him, probably for the same reason, as she wondered about his reaction to Kyle's assumption that they were in some kind of relationship.

What was even more unexpected was that it was so easy to see exactly what she was thinking.

She wasn't regretting anything either.

And was he imagining that he could also see an invitation to do it all over again?

He didn't get the chance to hold her gaze long enough to be sure because Kyle was trying to sit up straighter and had jolted his injured arm.

'*Ow...*' he groaned. 'That really hurts.'

'Push your button,' Nikita advised. 'You can control the amount of pain relief you're getting through your IV line that way.'

But Kyle looked from Nikita to Pedro and then back again, his expression a desperate plea.

'Maybe you could help? They'll never be able to find someone else when it's only a few days away. It's almost impossible to find people that are prepared to give time the day before Christmas anyway. That's why the same people keep doing it, year after year—like Mikey, the bus driver. He even owns the bus—a vintage one like an old school bus that he painted years ago to try and make it look like a giant sleigh with reindeer on the front. And there's Steph, who's old enough to be my grandma, and she's been doing it since it started.'

Pedro could see how much pain Kyle was in, but he was ignoring it because this was far more important to him.

'They're such good kids,' he added with a catch in his voice that wasn't simply due to pain. 'And I know their favourite part of the whole day is getting the presents with their names on the labels. You should see the way they just light up and stand a bit taller. I reckon it's the first time some of them have ever felt special.'

Pedro had a bit of a lump in his own throat. He knew all too well what it was like to grow up poor. For Christmas to be just another burden on a family that was struggling to cope anyway.

And Nikita was looking at him almost as hopefully as Kyle was.

'You were a really good Santa,' she said. 'I remember the smiles on those kids' faces when you arrived in the wards.'

'Christmas Eve?' Pedro shook his head. 'I think I'm working.'

'It wouldn't take that long,' Kyle said. 'An hour or two at the most. And the play zone place where we have the party isn't that far away from here.'

Nikita was nodding. 'I'm sure someone would cover for you for a while if you weren't finished in time to do it. *I* could… This roster I've been given has me on call overnight, but I don't have to be in the hospital until seven p.m. I could come in earlier and let you get away for a couple of hours.'

Pedro shook his head again. 'The only way I'd consider doing it,' he said, 'is if you do it with me. Come and be the angel again. Or an elf.'

It wasn't quite the truth. He already knew he wouldn't be able to say no if there was any way he could make it work. He also knew that asking Nikita to attend a Christmas party—to dress up, even—might be a huge step too far. But he would be there with her and...she trusted him, didn't she? Would she realise that he was trying to offer her a bit of time travel, here? A chance to go back to when Christmas didn't have any unthinkable associations for her? A time when they had the kind of friendship he would really like to have with her again?

Maybe she did. Because she took in a quick breath that was almost a gasp and then she held it for a long moment before letting it out slowly. A little shakily, perhaps, but she had that determined look in her eyes again.

'Okay,' she said. 'You're on. You find some cover and I'll get the details of the organisation from Kyle and give them a call.' She glanced at her watch. 'Aren't you due to start that outpatient clinic about now? *Oh...*'

Nikita visibly jumped at the strident beeping of her pager. 'They must be testing to check that it's functioning,' she said.

'Uh-uh...' Pedro was reaching for his device. 'Mine went off at the same time—that's why it was so loud.' He read the message. 'They need an orthopaedic consult in ED. Pelvic fracture from an RTA. Sorry, Kyle, someone's had a nasty car accident by the sound of it.'

'No worries, man. Thanks for coming. You won't forget about Christmas Eve, will you?'

'I won't,' Pedro promised.

He turned towards the door, but could see in his peripheral vision that Nikita wasn't following him. Because she wasn't officially on the roster just yet? But if she wasn't ready now, she wouldn't be ready tomorrow morning either and...if she wasn't being drawn towards a potentially life-threatening emergency as strongly as he was, perhaps his admiration in her courage and strength was misplaced?

'Coming?' he asked.

A single nod from Nikita and she was moving. Fast. Pedro was ahead of her as they raced towards the emergency department so she couldn't see the satisfaction that was probably written all over his face.

He wasn't wrong about her.

He never had been.

And right now he was feeling very proud of her.

Okay...maybe he was a bit in love with her all over again, but did it really matter when it was only temporary? He knew that Nikki would be back in her job on a permanent basis very soon and that would signal that it was time he moved on to a new job. A new adventure.

Nuevo año, nuevo yo wasn't just a mantra for Nikki. Pedro could feel big changes ahead for himself as well. A new beginning that would see his life going in a completely different direction than Nikki's. They might never see each other again, but at least this time he could be sure they would part on a much more positive note and the memory of their time together would be welcome and not painfully haunting.

* * *

Her name might not be filling a gap on a printed roster just yet but this felt as real as it got as Nikita hurriedly pulled on a set of scrubs and shut her belongings into an empty locker.

She arrived in the resuscitation area before Pedro to find the space crowded with medical staff—members of the trauma team including other surgeons, nursing and technical staff and every available doctor from the department, including Aiden, the same consultant who'd taken care of Kyle the other day.

The patient had been intubated and was on a ventilator with the doctor tasked with the role of looking after the airway monitoring him closely. An X-ray technician was collecting the lead aprons that had been protecting the staff who couldn't step away from the table and a nurse was hanging a second bag of fluid on an IV stand. Another doctor was using a bedside ultrasound machine on the patient's abdomen.

A quick glance at the overhead monitors showed Nikita that the accident victim's heart rate was too fast and his blood pressure was too low.

Aiden noticed Nikita entering the room and tilted his head to invite her to join him, where he was looking at a computer screen. Then he looked past her.

'Have we got the CBC back?'

'Yep. Haemoglobin's down to one three five.' It was the doctor who was doing the ultrasound examination who responded. 'And we've got free fluid in the pelvic cavity. Looks like he's lost a significant amount of blood internally.'

'SPO2?'

'Still in the nineties on high flow oxygen.'

'Let's get an arterial blood gas.' Aiden shifted to let Nikita see the screen well. 'High impact collision,' he told her. 'Motorbike versus truck. C-spine and chest X-rays clear. Open book fracture of his pelvis, here, so it's no surprise he's been bleeding.'

It wasn't. There were many branches of arteries within the pelvic cavity that could be damaged in trauma that was severe enough to break bones. The question was whether the pelvic binder that had been put in place by paramedics on scene had been enough to control blood loss.

Nikita blew out a breath. 'He's got anteroposterior compression fractures—here…and here…' She touched the screen. 'It's a complete fracture of the right iliac wing and…look…there's sacroiliac joint and pubis disruption.'

'There could be a small degree of vertical shear as well.' It was Pedro's voice, just behind Nikita's shoulder, and the sound of it was enough to loosen an unpleasantly tight knot in her stomach. Just the presence of this man was enough to change everything, wasn't it?

'Sorry I took a while,' Pedro murmured. 'I needed to get my registrar going on running the outpatient clinic.'

'We've had plenty going on to stabilise him so we've only just done the X-rays,' Aiden said. 'He's not out of the woods yet, by any means, but the tranexamic acid and blood products have got us back from the brink of irreversible shock.'

'Did you get a chance to assess movement and sensation before you intubated him?' Nikita asked.

'Yes. They were grossly normal. And he had palpable distal pulses.' Aiden looked up at both orthopaedic surgeons. 'ORIF?'

Nikita nodded. Dealing with this many fractures was going to need an open reduction and internal fixation. But not just yet. They needed to be sure the fractures were stabilised as much as possible to prevent any further damage from movement that could exacerbate blood loss. She caught Pedro's glance. 'I'd prefer to do external fixation before he's taken to Theatre for an emergent laparotomy or any other investigations. I'm not happy with the alignment that's there with just the binder.' Her raised eyebrows were asking his opinion.

'Exactly my thoughts,' he said.

Temporary external fixation could save a life in a complex fracture situation like this. It stabilised both bones and soft tissues but still allowed access for both assessment and surgical procedures and did not interfere with either CT or MRI imaging to provide more information on any injuries.

Scrubbing in to perform the surgical task of inserting self-drilling screws into the iliac crests on both sides of the pelvis and then attaching, checking placement and adjusting the carbon fibre rods was only the start of the management of an unexpected and complex case that Nikita was leading.

Pedro went back to his outpatient clinic while a CT scan was performed and a consultation with an interventional radiologist to discuss bleeding control by embolisation was started but then abandoned due to the condition of their patient deteriorating. He came back to scrub in and join Nikita in Theatre and, when she had dealt with the artery that was the likely cause of most of the blood loss, he assisted her in repairing the multiple fractures with both screws and pre-contoured plates.

It was well into the afternoon before the patient was safely transferred to the intensive care unit for the monitoring he would need for some time and it was dark by the time Nikita got home after dropping in to talk to a neighbour to see if she could help look after Earl while she was working for the next few days.

Or possibly longer than a few days?

Because, while Nikita was a little beyond tired as she greeted and cared for the needs of her animals, she was more than ready to do all this again tomorrow.

Maybe even without Pedro hovering in the background like a guardian angel?

Confidence was a building process, it seemed. Pedro had given her what felt like a solid foundation and she had added considerably to that structure today and Nikita felt...good.

No. It went way beyond good.

She felt as if she was finding herself again. Remembering why she had wanted this career so much and how important it was to *who* she was.

And she had Pedro to thank for that.

It wasn't just on a professional level either. Last night had given her a glimpse into the possibility of a life that was far bigger and brighter than anything she had imagined in recent times.

How did you go about thanking someone for doing that?

With a gift?

How big a gift would that need to be, though? So big it might be something that money couldn't even buy?

Earl followed Nikita as she went into the living room to get the pot belly stove going. She screwed up newspaper and added kindling and then reached for the matches which were on the mantelpiece beside that bowl of gingerbread men they'd never got around to tasting last night.

As the flames caught and grew, Nikita added some small logs. She took the gingerbread men out of the bowl and stood them up on the back of the mantelpiece like a row of children holding hands. With their bright, candy-covered chocolate buttons and smiling faces they looked far more like Christmas decorations than edible treats.

And Nikita found herself smiling back at them.

She found another match and lit the little candle inside the glass star, making a mental note to buy more candles on her way home from work tomorrow. Maybe even Christmas candles scented with something like cinnamon or pine.

And then she sat down on her couch and cuddled Earl, wondering why her tiny cottage suddenly felt a bit empty, even though this small space was still just as full of furniture and books and everything else.

Why was she feeling so satisfied with what she'd achieved today and happy that such positive change was happening in her life but a little sad at the same time?

The answer to both was all too obvious and the realisation came with a yearning that astonished Nikita with its ferocity.

Pedro wasn't here.

And she really, really wished he was.

CHAPTER NINE

TIME SEEMED TO speed up over the next few days—as it always did in the mad rush towards Christmas Day.

Outpatient clinics were now suspended for the holiday break until after the start of the New Year, but it didn't seem to make any difference to how busy the orthopaedic department of Bristol Central Infirmary was. Wet, icy weather, crowded streets and roads and everybody being in a hurry to get those important tasks done before they could kick back and enjoy a day of feasting and gift-giving led to a spike in the kinds of injuries that were treated by orthopaedic surgeons. Falls on slippery streets or icy steps meant fractured bones and dislocated joints. Reduced visibility and too much speed in winter conditions increased both the frequency and severity of road traffic accidents.

Nikita seemed to be so busy and so immersed in her work that she almost didn't notice that Pedro was stepping back from being her support in Theatre. He began arriving each time after she'd got started and leaving a little earlier. And then, just a day later, he didn't show up at all. He phoned her to apologise, telling her that there'd been a trauma team activation in the emergency department that he had to respond to. The relief of finding that

Nikita had coped perfectly well without him there with her had Pedro leaning against a wall and closing his eyes as he listened to her voice.

'I can't believe it, but I actually forgot to think about it—because you've been later sometimes? I thought you'd turn up at some point so I just got on with it and my registrar is great. By the time we were in the middle of things and it occurred to me to wonder where you were, I realised that it didn't matter if you weren't right there in Theatre. I knew I could cope.'

She sounded so happy it brought a bit of a lump to his throat. Pedro had achieved what he'd set out to do, to help her find her confidence and get past the barriers that were stopping her living her best life. She knew she was capable of going back to the work she loved and the life she'd had before her world had been so abruptly tipped upside down. He could hear the Nikki he'd known and loved all those years ago reappearing and...this wasn't just a gift for her, was it? It really did feel like it was just as much of a gift for himself, but not quite in the way he'd hoped—that would make it easier to walk away and not look back.

Was that why it felt as if his part in her recovery wasn't quite finished? That the gift he'd wanted to bestow wasn't quite complete? That it was still too fragile, perhaps? On both sides?

Would she understand—and forgive him—if she discovered that there hadn't actually been a trauma team activation and he'd simply chosen not to go into Theatre with her so that she could take that next step and discover she could do it alone?

It had been a risk that had been enough to have Pedro

holding his breath at times, wondering how it was going. *Wanting* to be there with her...

'We should celebrate you flying solo,' he found himself saying. 'How 'bout dinner after work? Somewhere nearby—I've got a mountain of paperwork but I should be sorted this evening.'

'I'd love to, but I can't. I've got my neighbour down the lane, Deidre, looking after Earl while I'm working and she's got a Christmas function to go to tonight so I need to pick him up.'

'Come back into town? No, you don't want to do that.' Pedro remembered the road where it ran close to the coast near Nikita's house. She'd be tired after a long day and that drive needed concentration—especially that bit where there was just a low barrier by the cliff down to the jagged rocks on the beach. He wasn't about to let Nikita risk her safety just so that he could have some private time with her.

'We'll find another time to celebrate,' he told her. 'Lunch in the cafeteria tomorrow, perhaps?'

Nikita laughed. And then she caught her breath. 'Oh... there's something I have to tell you. I saw Lewis in the theatre suite when I arrived and he told me that John Barlow's wife has put her foot down and told him that it's high time he retired and that this heart attack was a warning he shouldn't ignore. Apparently she's booked them on a world cruise. So that means there'll be a permanent consultancy position in the department being advertised very soon.'

Pedro didn't say anything, but his thoughts were racing fast enough to collide with each other. He could apply for that position and possibly stay here at Bristol Central and work with Nikita for the rest of his professional life.

He could watch her go from strength to strength in her recovery and her career. Maybe he would even see her meet and fall in love with someone and know that he'd helped her get to that point because he'd been the one to break the barriers she'd had about being touched.

And there it was.

The reason that his part in Nikita's life felt unfinished. This gift was supposed to have no strings attached whatsoever. To not be dangerous enough to mess with his own life because it was only temporary. Something for old times' sake because he still cared that much about her.

Warning bells had been ringing for days now, however. Getting louder every time he remembered their night together.

Every time he found himself longing to make love to her again.

He'd known he was playing with fire but he'd still believed he could prevent himself becoming seriously burnt.

Again.

He'd known that getting close to Nikki wasn't going to magically change the way she'd always felt about him or make her see the mistake she'd made all those years ago in not realising that they were meant to be together. She hadn't felt like that about him then so why would she now? As she'd said herself, he was still exactly the same person she remembered. He hadn't changed.

She'd let him make love to her because it was part of her journey to get past another barrier that was holding her back in her life, not because of any overwhelming attraction or wanting something more than friendship from him.

Pedro had been only too happy to give her the gift of rediscovering her own confidence but there was a point where he had to protect himself.

And perhaps he'd just reached it?

'So you don't have to lose your job if I come back to work properly.' Nikita sounded…hopeful? 'You *could* stay…'

'Mmm…' The sound was wary. For his own safety he needed to create a little more distance between himself and Nikki so that he could regain control of how he felt. He also needed an insurance policy—an escape route he could take at any time he felt he might be in danger of completely losing that control. 'But I was talking to my sister last night.' He managed to keep his tone light. 'And I said it might be possible for me to come and work in New Zealand for a while. Or for a holiday, at least. She's so excited.' He cleared his throat. 'So am I.'

'Oh…' There was a moment's silence that felt…odd. But then Nikita sounded as if she was smiling. 'That is exciting. When do you think you might go?'

'Soon. Maybe I can be there to start the New Year.'

'*Nuevo año, nuevo yo?*'

It was Pedro's turn to laugh. '*Exactamente.*'

She couldn't shake that weird feeling of being happy but sad at the same time. If anything, it was getting stronger.

Because Nikita knew she was going to come back to work properly.

And she knew that, maybe as soon as the end of next week, Pedro was going to be on the other side of the world.

It was so busy it felt like she might not even get any time alone with Pedro any time soon. No chance to tell him how much he'd changed her life. To thank him for a gift that was so priceless she still had no idea how to acknowledge its significance in a way that could encompass how much it meant to her.

One of the things on Nikita's list for today was to go and visit Kyle, to follow up on the arrangements that were being made for her and Pedro to help out with the children's Christmas party which was only two days away now. Almost bumping into Pedro as she arrived on the orthopaedic ward was a very unexpected bonus. She hadn't seen him all day. Hadn't even spoken to him since the phone call this morning when she'd learned that the clock was ticking very loudly when it came to any time she had left with Pedro.

'I'm just going to see Kyle. Have you found out the details for the party? Like the address?'

'Not yet. I was going to ask him but he had a visitor with him. An older lady. I thought it might be his mother. Or grandmother.'

'I'm sure he won't mind if we interrupt. I've only got a few minutes before I need to head home.'

'Okay... I'll come too.'

Nikita wondered if she'd made a mistake when they got to Kyle's bedside. The older woman was sitting on a chair beside the bed and she looked as if she'd been crying. Kyle was also looking miserable.

'I'm so sorry,' Nikita said. 'Have we come at a bad time?'

Kyle shook his head. 'It's something you should know about,' he said. 'This is Steph. I think I told you about her. She's the one who came up with the idea of the Secret Elves but I knew her a long time before that.'

'I fostered Kyle for a while,' Steph said quietly. 'He's one of my boys.' She blew her nose. 'Sorry. We just had some bad news. It looks as if the party might not go ahead at all.'

'Oh, no...what's happened?'

'The children's play zone place where we always have the party had a flood last night. A pipe burst—probably after it got frozen—and the rooms were under six inches of water by the time anyone arrived this morning. They've had to shut.' Steph blew her nose on the crumpled tissues she was holding. 'I feel terrible for them because they've always been so good to us. They always gave us the use of the playground and kitchen for free because they knew our budget only ever covers the caterers.'

Nikita bit her lip. If it was only a matter of money, she could fix this. There was more to her inheritance than the huge property her parents had left her and maybe it was time she began thinking about other people's problems instead of being trapped by her own.

'What if we could find a donation that would cover the cost of another venue?'

'We'd never find one. I've been on the phone all day but, even if we had limitless funds, there's nothing that's available at this short notice. Not on Christmas Eve.'

'What about the bus trip?' Pedro asked. 'Does that have to be cancelled as well?'

'No.' Steph brightened a little. 'We can still take the kids to Clifton Observatory, which is always our first stop.'

'Isn't the bus trip in the afternoon?' Pedro asked. 'You can't see the stars then, can you?'

'No.' Steph smiled. 'And it's usually overcast and raining. It might even be snowing this year by the sound of things, but it's a special place.'

'You haven't been?' Nikita could remember school picnics and even a friend's wedding that had taken place at the observatory. 'It's a Bristol icon. Started out as a windmill and then got converted into an observatory. It's got an amazing view across the city and the Avon Gorge and the Clifton Suspension Bridge.'

'Best of all, there's a creepy tunnel that leads to the Giant's cave,' Kyle put in. 'That's the most fun bit for the kids, especially if it's bad weather and all dark and a bit slimy.'

'Then we head off to the beach for an ice cream,' Steph said. 'Which is always a surprise because nobody goes to the beach and has ice creams in the winter, do they? There's a café in Clevedon that loves to cater for our group and goes all out with the staff wearing Christmas jumpers and turning ice creams into reindeers with red lolly noses and chocolate stick antlers.'

'And then it's Westonbury Castle along Cliff Road,' Kyle said.

'That's near where I live,' Nikita exclaimed. 'But…it'll be freezing and there's nothing there but the old towers and walls of the ruined castle.'

'I know.' Kyle nodded. 'That first trip I went on when I was just a kid, I couldn't believe we were getting taken to some old ruins, but it turned out to be a treasure hunt and there was a small prize for everybody. Once you found one, you got back on the bus to stay warm.'

Steph sighed. 'Mikey, our bus driver, would blast Christmas carols on the trip home, but then came the big surprise at the end, with the party and lots of games and all the treats to eat and finally Father Christmas coming in with his sack and giving everybody a proper wrapped-up present—just for them. I guess we'll just have to give the presents out on the bus this time.' She looked at Pedro and then Nikita. 'Could you still help with that? We could park somewhere near here.'

'Of course,' Pedro said. He caught Nikita's gaze. 'Is that all right with you?'

But Nikita didn't answer immediately. She turned to Steph. 'What is it that you need in a venue?' she asked. 'Does it have to be a playground type of place?'

Steph shook her head. 'Any space would do. We've got all the games ready, like pin the tail on Rudolph and Snowman Slam—which is a kind of skittles with paper cups and...oh, there's enough to keep them all entertained for an hour or so. Then we serve the party food and Father Christmas arrives to do the presents and it's time for the kids to go home. We can set everything up and clean up afterwards but...' her sigh was even heavier this time '...we need more space than my living room's got for more than twenty people.'

'What about a house in Leigh Woods?' Nikita asked slowly. 'Not that far from the Clifton Observatory, in fact. A house that has an old ballroom that's been divided into different living areas with folding doors that can be opened up to make one really big space. And there's a huge kitchen and a dining table that can seat about sixteen people.'

Everybody was staring at her.

'Who lives there?' Kyle asked.

'Nobody,' Nikita answered. 'I used to. I grew up there. It's too big for me to live in now, but I haven't got around to deciding what to do with it. It's been empty for ages but there's been a caretaker keeping an eye on things.'

'And you'd be happy to let us use it?' Steph was looking at her as if she'd waved a magic wand.

Nikita nodded. 'I'll go and check it out after work tomorrow, but I think all it'll need is for dust sheets to get pulled off. I'm sure there are any number of Christmas decorations in the attic too. My mum used to do parties for various charities and I'm sure she got her inspiration from places like Chatsworth House or Holkham Hall.' She smiled at Steph and Kyle. 'I'd love to do at least a part of something like that again. In her honour. It might even help me make those plans for the future of the house and what better time than a new year to be doing that?'

'I could help with the decorating.' Steph was sounding excited now. 'I'd love to help. I've got a few boxes of things like tinsel and I'll have time tomorrow morning.'

'Let me see what I can find,' Nikita said. 'It won't be the level of decoration that my mother would have achieved, but I should have plenty of time to get it looking festive enough for a party. Give me your phone number and I'll let you know if I need any extra help tomorrow.'

Pedro was looking at her as if she'd grown a pair of wings. Or a halo, perhaps?

And no wonder. Nikita could almost hear that vehement tone of her own voice and what she'd said to him not so long ago.

'I hate Christmas. I hate Christmas decorations most of all.'

But this felt different. A link with not only the best parts of her past but with the promise of both a new future and something that would always make her think of Pedro.

Nueva Navidad, nueva yo.

New Christmas, new me.

'I'll help,' Pedro offered.

'Don't you have a mountain of paperwork to get sorted? I'll probably come back in this evening to go and check out the house.'

'I can get most of it done by then if I get on with it. I'm not having you climbing ladders into attics all by yourself in an empty house.'

Steph was nodding. Kyle was smiling.

'Do what he says,' he said. 'He just wants to look after you.'

That look in Pedro's eyes told Nikita that Kyle wasn't wrong and it came with a rush of memories.

She'd always been able to rely on Pedro looking after her, hadn't she? Lending her his lecture notes, helping her understand complicated study topics, making sure she knew where she was going in a hospital they hadn't been in before.

She'd thought he was simply a good friend, but now she knew he'd loved her.

She must have hurt him so badly, not just by being unaware of how he felt but, far worse, actually telling him that she hated him.

How stupid had she been? It was no wonder he was completely over the way he'd felt about her. She'd destroyed that love in that moment without even knowing it existed. Or how precious it was. Refusing his offer of help now might pale in comparison but he still didn't deserve even a hint of rejection.

'I'll text you the address,' she told him. 'I should be there by seven o'clock.'

The contrast between Nikki's tiny seaside cottage and this mansion within Bristol's city limits couldn't have been greater.

It brought back memories of things Pedro had heard about her at medical school that had made him realise that, even if she hadn't been with Simon, he came from such a different world, she would never have considered him as a partner.

He'd been a scruffy kid, playing football barefoot in the streets of the poorest area in Barcelona. She'd been going to pony club or playing in the woodland that bordered the property. He'd worked in whatever jobs he could get to help put food on his family's table. He'd heard about her being absent from lectures or study group because of some charity event she was attending—like a ball after a polo match that she'd watched Simon participating in.

This house was like nothing Pedro had ever been in. There were lights on the ground floor that revealed huge bay windows on either side of a grand entrance, but it was completely dark on the second floor and the dormer-style windows on a third floor. Was that the attic? Thank goodness he'd insisted on coming to help Nikki tonight, Pedro thought. He knew how courageous she was but she shouldn't have to be doing something like exploring creepy, dark, deserted attics alone.

The ornate wooden door opened as Pedro climbed the wide steps that led to the entrance of the house.

'I saw you arriving,' Nikita said. Earl squeezed past her to greet Pedro but he was staring at an enormous shrouded object propped to one side of the door.

'What on earth is that?'

'A tree. I knew there wouldn't be a fake tree in the attic because my mother hated them. I got on the phone as I left work and ordered the biggest one still available to be delivered. I've set up the stand for it but it was too heavy for me to shift.'

'I can do that.' Pedro picked the tree up easily. 'Show me where it needs to go.'

The hallway was a room on its own, with a sweeping staircase straight ahead. To either side were even bigger spaces and Pedro could see furniture shrouded with white sheets through a door on his right. It felt cold and their footsteps echoed on the mosaic tiles of the floor.

'I've just pulled the sheets off on this side,' Nikita said, leading Pedro through the door on his left. 'And I've opened the folding doors. I've turned the heating up but it's still a bit cold. I've asked the caretaker to come in early tomorrow and get the fires going and the kitchen sorted for the caterers to be able to use. Steph's going to come in the morning before she goes on the bus trip with the kids and we can do any final touches to the decorating then. She's bringing the Father Christmas outfit for you as well.'

Pedro slotted the tree's trunk into the stand and then began unwinding the netting restraining the branches. 'And your angel costume, I hope?'

'Might be an elf.' She looked up at him. 'Do you think it'll be okay?'

'You being an elf instead of an angel?' Pedro grinned. 'I think it will be way more than okay. You will make an adorable elf.'

Nikita laughed. 'No… I meant this…' She waved an arm to take in a room with scattered carpets on a polished wooden floor and an ornate plaster ceiling—vast enough to make a grand piano look like a toy in one corner and countless comfortable couches and armchairs dotted in front of more than one open fireplace.

'It'll be wonderful,' he told her. 'If we move a few chairs to make space for the games it will be absolutely perfect. It's very generous of you to make it possible.'

'This house needs to be brought back to life,' she responded. 'It's years now since my parents died in an accident and it was just too hard to do what I should have done long ago.' Her glance up at him was almost shy. 'Sometimes you need a push to do something. Especially if you've started to believe it's just too hard.'

There was a softness in her gaze that told Pedro she was talking about a lot more than opening up the house she'd grown up in. It felt as if she was trying to thank him for what he'd done for *her*—pushing her past her barriers back into the life she deserved to have.

And, okay, maybe he could take the credit for the fact that she had taken the huge step of going back to her career and he'd had the privilege of taking her past the barrier of accepting physical touch, but she was leaping over this particular obstacle all by herself and it felt as if she was really starting to embrace life again.

Maybe she'd end up living in this amazing house again herself one day. With a husband who adored her for the kind of courage and compassion she had that Pedro was so aware of. Here she was, with every reason to still hate everything to do with Christmas after what she'd been through, but she was about to throw herself into making this space as festive as possible for the sake of children who had their own reasons for not finding this season as fun-filled and happy as it was supposed to be.

There was so much else about her that would make any man want to be with her. Things that were so admirable, like her intelligence and dedication and abilities to do a difficult job under pressure and to do it exceptionally well.

And then there were the things that Pedro was never, ever going to forget, like that adorable smile and the way she could say things without saying a word, with those astonishingly expressive eyes.

Whoever won Nikki's heart would be the luckiest man on earth, wouldn't he? There had to be at least half a dozen bedrooms upstairs. Plenty of room to cater for the creation of a perfect family...

Oh... *Dios mío*. He couldn't hide from it now. He couldn't pretend he was in control of his emotions.

He'd never really stopped loving Nikita Wallace, had he?

Not that he would let her know that. Why would he? He had made it very clear that he was only in her life as a friend. Temporarily. That there were no strings attached because of anything that had happened in the past.

She was taking her first steps back into truly living

again and that was the gift Pedro had hoped he could give her. Why would he spoil that by making her feel guilty that she didn't feel the same way about him as he'd always felt about her? That she never had and never would. Or worse, feel sorry for him because he was still hoping something might change?

This was his problem, not Nikki's. And he could deal with it. He'd had practice, after all, hadn't he?

It was Pedro who broke the eye contact. And then he cleared his throat so that he could speak past that odd tightness.

'We'd better get on with this, hadn't we? We're both working tomorrow and I'm sure Steph will be too busy to have much time for decorating.'

The branches of the fir tree had settled into their natural conical shape. Pedro could just touch the very top of the tree with an outstretched hand.

'That's good,' he said. 'We won't need a ladder to put the star on.'

'We might for the windows. There should be big golden paper bells to hang from red ribbons that hook onto the curtain rails. And long strings of fairy lights that go from the chandeliers to the walls. I seem to remember there are little hooks hidden above the picture rails for that.' Nikita's eyes were shining. 'You're right, we need to get going. Come on—there's a secret staircase to the attic hidden behind a door in the upstairs hallway.'

The word echoed in Pedro's mind as he followed her up the main staircase.

A secret.

Un secreto.

Exactly what his feelings had been for Nikki all those years ago.

And exactly what they needed to remain now.

CHAPTER TEN

THE ATTIC NIKITA led Pedro into had the same floor area as the ballroom they were planning to decorate and it appeared that most of this attic space had been devoted to storing Christmas decorations, neatly packed and boxes labelled with stickers such as 'Light ropes/nets', 'Bells for windows' and 'Silver and white ornaments for tree'.

'I can't see any boxes of tinsel,' Pedro noted. 'That's good.'

'Something else my mother didn't approve of,' Nikita said. 'Like the fake trees. But you know what? I think I'm getting over my aversion to decorations—even tinsel. It might have been you reminding me about my angel halo that did it.'

Or perhaps it had been the beautiful star candle holder. Or the gingerbread men. Or the way Pedro had been there like a human rock when that piece of tinsel had fallen in the foyer and he'd promised that she was okay.

And she had been. Because Pedro had been there beside her.

But he wouldn't be for much longer and it felt as if the tick of that clock measuring how long it was until Pedro disappeared from her life completely had just become even louder. So loud it was impossible to ignore.

'When will you leave, do you think?' she asked as she handed him a box. 'If you want to be in New Zealand for the New Year, you'll have to leave straight after Christmas, won't you? It's a long trip.'

'My contract actually expires at the end of December, but I'm owed quite a bit of leave. If things are under control and you feel ready to take over your position again, there's no reason for me to stay.'

And every reason for him to leave?

'You won't miss this winter weather.' Nikita tried to keep her tone bright. She wanted Pedro to leave knowing how much he'd helped her and how grateful she was. She was not about to make him feel guilty about getting on with his own life. 'It'll be summer there. So different...'

Pedro disappeared to take a box down the secret staircase but came straight back for another.

'Different can be exciting,' he said. 'Even if it's just a new routine that shakes off things from the past you don't need or want in your life any longer.'

'That's true.' Nikita put down a box that was labelled 'Table decorations'. 'What is it they say? Something about not looking in the rear-vision mirror because that's not the direction you're going in?'

Pedro nodded but the next box Nikita found was enough to remind her that nothing was ever that black and white.

'This box is special,' she told Pedro. 'It's the nativity scene that goes in the middle of the dining table on top of the red tablecloth. It's something that's been passed down through the family for generations and I've always loved it—especially the lambs and the donkeys and the little baby Jesus in his crib, all carved out of wood.' She caught a breath. 'Some things from the past are worth keeping. The trick is to know which ones, isn't it?'

Again, Pedro nodded. 'But that's one of the benefits of trying something completely new, I think. You find out what you miss and you can decide if you want to bring it back into your life or not.'

They didn't talk for a while after that as Nikita dragged box after box after box to the top of the secret staircase and Pedro carried them down, but she was wondering what it was that he might miss about his life in Bristol.

Would he miss her?

As much as she knew she was going to miss him?

So much that it was, quite literally, breathtaking.

So much that she knew that she had gone past any warning signs that she might be falling in love with Pedro. Somehow, at some point in the last week, it had already happened.

Nikita headed for the darkest corner of the attic to ensure that Pedro wouldn't notice that she needed to stand very still for a moment. To press her hand onto her chest as if it could soothe the ache that was sharp enough to feel like a piece of her heart was breaking.

She couldn't even tell Pedro how much she would miss him, let alone confess how she really felt about him. She only had to remember how horrified he'd been when she'd kissed him without invitation that first time, after he'd told her how he'd once felt about her. It had been such a thoughtless thing to do it had crossed the line into cruelty, even. She'd not only opened an old wound, she had rubbed salt into it.

Imagine how much worse it would be to confess she

was finally—and far too late—feeling the way he'd once felt about her?

She couldn't—*wouldn't*—do that to him.

He'd made it clear that those feelings of his were ancient history. That they no longer existed. He wasn't in love with her, even if he'd made love to her as if he was. He had plans to move on and take his life in exciting new directions and he was about to make them happen.

And something was becoming clear to Nikita as well. She'd wanted to find a gift for Pedro to thank him for what he'd done in bringing her back into a world she'd thought she'd lost for ever. This was it, even though she couldn't wrap it up. He wouldn't actually know it was being given either. Or how hard it would be to bestow.

But Nikita could give him the freedom to move forward with his own life. To not be dragged back to a point in the past where hurtful things could be remembered or even relived. And she could make sure they parted as friends this time. With something happy to remember, like a children's Christmas party.

Well over an hour later, Pedro carried a ladder down to the ballroom and Nikita came down after him.

'I think we've got more than enough to get started,' she said. 'Otherwise we'll be here all night and you're working from early tomorrow so that's not an option.'

'I'm good for a few hours yet,' he told her. 'I seem to remember a time when we both used to manage to stay up all night and then work the next day.'

'We were a lot younger then. And a lot less wise.' Nikita lifted her eyebrows. 'Have you had something to eat this evening? I've got sandwiches and soup in the kitchen if you're hungry.'

'Is it your "everything" soup?'

'Yes.'

'Did you make the bread for the sandwiches?'

'Mmm…' Nikita's gaze shifted to where Earl was making himself at home on a velvet-covered couch and she'd hunched her shoulders a little as if she was embarrassed.

Was she remembering what he'd said about her ability to make homemade bread being one of the signs of how much she had changed since he'd last seen her? Evidence of how she'd been hiding from the real world.

But they both knew she wasn't hiding now.

'I'd love some soup.' Pedro could feel his smile softening his whole face as Nikita looked up at him. Could she see how proud he was of how far she'd come in such a short time? That he was seeing an even more amazing version of the 'real' Nikki he'd never been able to forget?

'But let's wait until we're really hungry.' Pedro turned to survey the sea of boxes. 'I agree that we need to get started. Why don't I set up the ladder and you can bring me the lights that need to go all over the ceiling? Or shall we start with the tree?'

'Ceiling then tree,' Nikita decreed. 'Even if that's as far as we get, it will make the room look like it should for a Christmas party.'

They wrapped nets with tiny fairy lights attached around the tree and tested the programming to find a sparkle that was pretty but not over the top. Pedro hooked the ends of long ropes to the main lights and then Nikita unrolled the coils so that he could attach the other ends to the hidden hooks. These lights didn't sparkle but lit up the ceiling like a night sky full of stars. They put the ribbons and bells over the windows and opened boxes of shiny silver ornaments for the tree, but Nikita said they needed a break before they started that big job so they went into the kitchen to heat the soup and toast bread.

They sat at a scrubbed wooden table in the kitchen near the double sinks and long working bench. The smell of hot soup and toast didn't quite banish the feeling that this room had been cold and empty and unused for too long but, on the positive side, it felt so comfortable sharing an impromptu midnight meal with Nikki that it seemed like they'd been doing it for their whole lives.

It felt like…what home should feel like?

Pedro knew that a large part of that was because of how he felt in the company of the woman he'd cared so much about a decade ago. Those feelings might have been hastily buried after the awful way they'd parted but they had never died and he hadn't been able to prevent himself uncovering too much of them by trying to help Nikki through the last hurdles of the trauma she'd experienced. But he'd never tell her how he felt because she'd never felt the same way so why on earth would he expect that to have changed?

And perhaps at least a part of that yearning for this feeling of home was because Pedro had been away from his real home for so long that he'd forgotten how important his own country might be to him.

'I might only go to New Zealand for a holiday,' he found himself saying aloud. 'It might be time for me to go back home to Spain after that.'

'Oh?' Nikita was focusing on him intently. 'Are there

parts of the past that you're missing? Your family? The place you grew up?' Her gaze shifted for a moment. 'I'd forgotten how much I loved this house. I could never live here again, but it's kind of special to be here, doing this.'

'I don't think the place I grew up even exists now,' Pedro told her quietly. 'And that's a good thing. It was a tenement block that was no better than a slum.'

Nikita's eyes widened. 'I never knew that,' she said. 'It must have been hard for you to get to medical school—in another country, even.'

'My family made a lot of sacrifices so that could happen. That's part of why I was so boring—all work and no play. I owed them everything.'

'And you've been supporting them ever since you graduated, haven't you?' There was an admiration in her eyes that almost felt like...love?

He was in trouble, wasn't he? Enough to be seeing what he wanted to see rather than what was real?

'They must be very proud of everything you've achieved,' Nikita said.

Pedro's smile felt poignant. 'I think I told you that my mother doesn't know who I am any longer, but she's in a wonderful home and will be very well taken care of for the rest of her life. I go and visit regularly but...'

'But there might be other things from your past that are worth keeping?' Nikita finished for him.

Pedro nodded slowly. 'Maybe I've been looking in all the wrong places for what's missing from my life. Home is a background, isn't it? A setting that is imprinted on your DNA? A place that gives you comfort and familiarity and the strong foundation that can let you be exactly who you want to be? Perhaps I left too soon and there's something more I need to find there?'

He stopped himself before he could say anything else.

Something about hoping he could find a person who could fill the huge gap in his life that leaving Nikki behind was going to create? Again…?

Pedro stood up to end the conversation. He picked up the empty soup bowls and moved to the sink to rinse them. He didn't realise that Nikita was following him until he turned around to go back to the ballroom and found she was right behind him, a tea towel in her hands to dry the bowls with. She was so close he had to put his hands out to catch her shoulders so he didn't bump into her.

He didn't let go even when he knew she was in no danger of being bumped off balance any longer, however.

How could he, when she was smiling at him like that?

So softly, it felt as if it was touching his heart. But how was it that such a gentle touch could create something so close to pain?

And that look in her eyes. As if…

As if…

No. He couldn't allow himself to think that she might have feelings she was about to confess. To allow hope to gain a foothold and only make things so much harder in the very near future.

Maybe it was simply this physical proximity. Being properly alone again for the first time since they'd made love.

Did she want him to kiss her again?

He couldn't make love to her again, no matter how

much he might want to, because it would be too hard to hide how he felt. But a kiss?

That couldn't hurt, could it?

Just a soft one.

Like a farewell? Nikita knew he was leaving very soon. She just didn't know why, and it was much better that she didn't.

So Pedro leaned down and placed a soft kiss on her lips. And, okay…maybe it lingered just a little too long, but it was never going to escalate into anything more passionate. It was poignant, that was what it was…

'I really hope you find what you want,' Nikita whispered when he lifted his head again. 'You deserve the best of everything that life can provide. You're the nicest person I've ever known, Pedro, and I'm so sorry for the horrible things I said to you on graduation night. They were never true. Ever.'

'I knew that,' Pedro lied. And then he said something truthful. 'They're forgotten,' he said. 'I'll only ever have good memories of you now.' He let go of her shoulders before he was tempted to kiss her again. 'Let's go and see what we can do with that tree, shall we? I'll need to head home before too long and get some sleep.'

'You should go home now.' Nikita was smiling at him. 'It's so late. I'll go home myself soon and I'll get Steph to come and help with the rest in the morning.'

Pedro knew he should get some sleep. He had to be on top of his game in Theatre first thing in the morning. 'Are you sure?'

'You've done enough.' Nikita nodded. 'Way more than I can ever thank you for. Go on…go home… I'll be absolutely fine.'

* * *

It began snowing on the morning of Christmas Eve.

Just a little. Enough to be pretty and get people excited about the possibility of a white Christmas, but not enough to settle and make the roads too dangerous, much to the relief of all the Secret Elves who would be involved in creating magic for a small group of children that afternoon. Nikita was keeping a close eye on the weather reports, however. She was planning to go home by lunchtime, take Earl for a walk and then try and catch a couple of hours' sleep, ahead of working a night shift at Bristol Central tonight.

By lunchtime the skies were leaden but there were no snowflakes to be seen sifting down and no forecast of an imminent blizzard. The lawn and the ornamental bay trees clipped into balls on either side of the front door of Nikita's childhood home had a dusting of snow on them and the heavy cloud cover dampened the daylight enough to make the lights appear to sparkle twice as brightly, which was…perfect.

The caretaker of the house was married to the gardener and they'd both arrived much earlier than Nikita to crank up the heating, light fires and make sure the cloakrooms were ready for an influx of visitors. And then they stayed to help finish the decorating and show the caterers around the kitchen when they'd finished unloading their van.

'It's so wonderful to see the house being used again,' they told Nikita. 'And for such a good cause. Your parents would love that this is happening. Can we come back for the party?'

'Of course.' Steph, who'd been on the doorstep by the

time Nikita got there, just in case she could help, beamed at them. 'The more the merrier, as they say.'

The wooden table where Nikita and Pedro had shared the late supper of soup and toast was laden with treats for the party and Nikita tried to keep her focus on it and not turn her head towards the sink, but it didn't help. She was reliving that moment when Pedro had turned and caught her to stop her bumping into him. When he'd kissed her with such heartbreaking tenderness.

When he'd told her that the past was forgotten and, presumably, forgiven.

When he'd looked at her as if he would rather stay with her all night than go home, but he'd gone home in the end, without a backward glance, and that was probably a very good thing because if he'd stayed he might not have got very much sleep and she knew he not only had a back-to-back theatre list today but he was on call for the emergency department's trauma team.

Had that been the last chance they would ever have to share a night together again? Nikita was working tonight. Pedro was on call for Christmas Day and...

It was also a good thing that the caterer's cheerful voice distracted her from the space her thoughts were rushing into—the one that was all about how little time she had before Pedro was gone for good. The one with potholes that she was afraid might trip her up. She might think she could cope without him being nearby, but what was it really going to be like when it became a reality?

'We always do lots of hot food.' The caterer must have noticed how intently Nikita had been staring at the table. 'The kids will be cold and hungry by the time they've finished their treasure hunt. We'll put the oven on at about four o'clock and we can get the sausage rolls and pizza and chips nice and hot for when they roll in.'

'I'll be back in time to help you serve it. I can disappear while they're playing games to get changed into my elf outfit. Oh…' She turned to Steph, who was unpacking platters of gingerbread Christmas trees. 'Have you unpacked the costumes for me and Pedro from your car? I should make sure mine fits.'

Steph waved a hand. 'Don't worry. They're on the big side, but they've got elastic everywhere that counts,' she said. 'They'll fit anybody.'

Bowls of red jelly and whipped cream were going into the fridge and chocolate biscuits with white icing snowflakes on them came out of another box. Nikita's eyebrows rose at the rather lurid green shade of bottles of soft drink Steph began unpacking.

'We call that Grinch juice,' Steph told her. 'The kids love it.'

'I'm sure they do.' Nikita shook her head. 'Okay… I think we've done everything we can for now. I'm going to head home for a bit.'

She was smiling as she walked through the ballroom. The fairy lights and chandeliers were looking just as much like a starry sky as they had last night. The Christmas tree was sparkling, with its lights flashing and reflecting off all the silver balls and the tinsel that Steph had ended up bringing just in case. Nikita had been the one to climb the ladder and attach the glittery silver star on the top of the tree this morning. It was beautiful, but she didn't love it nearly as much as the glass star hanging in her cottage, right outside her bedroom door.

A gift that she was going to treasure for ever. One that

would remind her of Pedro and maybe even make it feel like there was a part of him that would stay with her for ever. A private space in her head—and her heart—that she could tap into when she needed to remember that life was capable of providing joy. Or that she was capable of coping, even when it didn't.

Nikita lit the candle in the star when she got back from walking Earl. She curled up on her bed, wrapped in her duvet, watching it flicker, but she didn't manage to fall asleep. That was partly because she didn't really want to. She wanted to stay cuddled up like this, remembering the time she hadn't been alone in this bed.

It was also partly because Steph was on the bus trip with a crowd of excited children and she was sending messages and photos through to Nikita's phone.

The view over the gorge from the cave at the end of the tunnel had been magical with the air sprinkled with tiny snowflakes. There was a video of the children singing a very enthusiastic rendition of 'Rudolph the Red-Nosed Reindeer' in the bus and then a close-up of a reindeer ice cream with its own red nose.

Nikita gave up trying to sleep at that point. She checked on Duncan and shut the chickens back into their coop, concerned that the snowflakes were getting bigger and falling more thickly now.

'I'm going to head back into the city,' she told Earl. 'Let's get you some dinner and I'll leave you inside where you'll be safe and warm. If I get stuck by the snow, Deidre will come and rescue you in the morning, okay?'

Snowflakes caught by the headlights of her car as Nikita began to drive back into Bristol gave the impression of rushing towards her, even though they were falling straight down. Big feathery flakes that were threatening to interfere with visibility and settle into a dangerously slippery layer on the road.

Had the bus left the café in Clevedon yet? They wouldn't still go to the ruins of Westonbury Castle with the weather closing in like this, would they?

Nikita was on the coast road herself now and she found herself watching for headlights coming in the opposite direction, because the visibility was already too limited to drive without them on. A car went past and then a motorbike and then the road was empty until she was approaching the point that she liked the least on this route—where there was nothing more than a low metal barrier on the side of the road as protection from a sharp drop to the rocks on the beach below—when another set of headlights came into view. The vehicle was no more than a smudge of colour behind the lights through the veil of snowflakes, but she could see it was red. And larger than a car.

She knew it was the bus and found herself slowing down. Should she flash her lights and try and warn them that they should turn around as soon as they could and head back into the city? Or were they already trying to find a space big enough to turn without creating a traffic hazard?

Nikita slowed, suddenly worried about how slippery this road was and what could happen if she slid into the path of the larger vehicle. She stopped completely when she felt the hairs on the back of her neck start to prickle so she had nothing to distract her from what she was seeing in front of her.

She watched in horror as the bus bounced as it got too

close to the side of the road and ran over some uneven ground or rocks, perhaps, that were now hidden by a layer of snow. Correcting the direction of the large vehicle put it into a slide that gained speed and the back of bus came into view as it rotated. Nikita's heart missed a beat as she thought she was about to witness it rolling towards where she had stopped, but it stayed upright.

Sliding uncontrollably towards a metal barrier that had no hope of even slowing its path. She saw the sparks of metal on metal and heard the sound of the barrier being torn apart.

She watched the bus disappear over the edge of the cliff.

She was out of her car by the time the sounds of the bus hitting the rocks below the road got swallowed by the snow and darkness.

And then Nikita could hear the worst sound of all.

Utter silence…

CHAPTER ELEVEN

No...

No, no, no...

Nikita had no memory of getting out of her car but here she was, standing in the glow of her own headlights, right beside the torn metal of the safety barrier, looking down several metres to where the bus lay on its side, wedged amongst the rocks. If she shaded her eyes from the glare of the headlights, she could see the broken windows on the side facing upwards. She could also see the painting on the side of the bus—wooden runners and door handles that made it look as if those windows were part of a giant sleigh. Reins with bunches of bells looped between the windows until they got to the front of the bus. The reindeer were too small to be pulling such a huge sleigh, but they had happy smiles on their faces and...and tinsel trailing from their antlers.

And the moment Nikita noticed that, she also heard the first scream from a terrified child trapped inside the bus.

Oh, dear Lord...

The only way to get to them would be to climb up on the rocks and try and break enough glass to be able to climb inside. There had to be injured people, both children and adults, in there. There would be blood. Screams of pain, or worse, total silence from the ones who hadn't survived the impact.

The flashback was so intense, Nikita could hear the escalating whine of an approaching missile that was about to make the world around her explode into horror. She found herself crouching—the way she had when the lift had shuddered to a halt that day—but there was no corner to shelter in here. Nobody to put their arms around her and tell her that she was safe. That she wasn't going to fall. That he was holding her and she would always be safe…

Okay…maybe she'd made that last bit up but…but it felt like it was the truth. And maybe that was why, when she pulled her phone out, knowing that she had to call for help *right now*…it was Pedro's number her fingers fumbled to push, not the emergency number which had somehow jammed somewhere in a brain and body that was doing its best to freeze into total immobility.

By some miracle, Pedro wasn't in Theatre and unable to hear his phone.

'Nikki? How's it going? It's not time for me to come and play Santa yet, is it?'

He must have been confused by the silence but Nikita couldn't make any words emerge. And maybe he felt it. The same kind of panic he'd seen her experience once before. Because his voice somehow managed to focus intently but become softer at the same time.

'What's happening, Nikki? You can talk to me, you know that.'

She struggled to pull in a breath. To find the right words. Any words…

'I'm here,' Pedro said. 'Tell me, *cara*…' The plea in his

voice was almost desperate. Could he hear the screams coming from the bus now?

'The…bus,' Nikita managed, her voice hoarse. 'It's gone over the cliff.'

There was a heartbeat of silence on the other end of the line but Pedro's voice was still gentle. 'Tell me where you are. Is someone there with you?'

'No…' But that wasn't quite true, was it? 'Just you…'

'Are you on the road?'

'Yes. Beside…where that barrier is. *Was*… The metal one…?'

'I know it.' Pedro's voice was grim. 'Hang on just a second, Nikki. Don't go away, okay? Don't hang up…'

'I won't.' How could she when the sound of Pedro's voice was the only rock she had to cling to?

When she was fighting to keep her nose above the rushing water of the flashback and she knew she would drown if she lost her grip on the Pedro rock? She could hear him. Was he in the emergency department at the moment? He was giving rapid instructions for someone to contact the police, fire and ambulance and activate a major incident response. To get any and all available resources on the way to the location of an accident that was likely to involve multiple patients. And then, within what felt like only seconds, she could hear the sound of movement—muffled but rapid thumping, as if Pedro was running.

'I'm heading for the car park.' He sounded out of breath. 'I'm on my way, Nikki, but you need to start without me, okay?'

'I… I don't think I can…'

'You can, *cara*. You know you can... Tell me what you can see...'

She wouldn't be able to see anything if she stayed crouched on the roadside like this. Nikita closed her eyes, gripped her phone like a talisman and pushed her body harder than she ever had before. Finding herself on her feet and actually walking towards the gap in the barrier was more than she had expected she could do. She looked down at the bus.

'I can see the bus,' she told him. 'It's on its side. On the rocks. The door is underneath but the windows are broken on top. I can hear them...' She caught her breath in a sob. 'The children... I can hear them calling for help.'

'I can hear them too. That's a good thing, sweetheart. If they can call, they're not unconscious. They have patent airways. Is the bus in the water at all?'

'No...but it's not far from the waves and I don't know if the tide is coming in.'

'Is it possible to climb down to it? Without putting yourself in danger?'

'I...'

Nikita bit her lip and looked at the gap between herself and the bus. It was steep but the slope was made up of rocks so it would be easy enough to climb if it wasn't so dark or the rocks slippery with snow trying to settle on wet surfaces.

Could she do it?

More importantly, could she do what would need to be done when she got that far?

Relying on help to arrive wasn't good enough. She could hear the engine of Pedro's car starting up, but it would take him at least thirty minutes to get here. Probably longer, given that the road was getting bad enough for no other traffic to be appearing.

And there were people who desperately needed help. Children…

She had to do something. She only had to take it one step at a time and…and she had Pedro so close it felt like his lips were against her ear.

'Yes,' she told him. 'I can get down.' But she turned away from the edge of the cliff. 'I need to get my first aid kit out of the car.'

It was in the back, a small pack with not much more than dressings and bandages, an airway device or two and some basic gear like scissors and tweezers and an old stethoscope. Nothing of any real use for major trauma, but at least it was something that might make Nikita feel a little less helpless.

Even better, she had Pedro talking to her and that made her feel as if she could do something to help until better-equipped and more confident rescuers arrived.

'Use the torch on your phone.' She could hear the sound of a car door slamming in the background after she told Pedro she was back at the top of the cliff and about to climb down. 'It won't cut me off. I've got you on speaker phone now so I can talk to you all the time. There's help on its way. Tell me everything you see…'

Pedro was torn.

He had to focus on his driving and not allow himself to get distracted and possibly be involved in an accident himself, but that meant fighting against what he really wanted to focus on—Nikki's voice and what she was telling him.

He could hear the fear. The gasp of breath and alarmed cry when she almost slipped and fell climbing over slippery rocks. He needed to be there so badly. To put his hand out to steady Nikki. To keep her safe. But all he could do was keep talking.

'Hang onto that rock. Find a secure foothold before you let go...'

'Don't climb onto the side of the bus if it doesn't feel secure. You might have to wait for the fire service to arrive. They're on their way...'

Pedro knew she wasn't going to sit back and wait. Not when he could hear the crying and screaming so clearly now from inside the bus.

'Make sure there's nobody too close to the window while you break the rest of the glass.'

He heard the glass breaking. He heard the grunts of effort as Nikki climbed into the bus through the window. He heard her hesitate for a heartbeat and take in a deep, deep breath but nobody else would have known about any struggle she was having. Her voice was strong as she called out loudly enough to be heard over the sounds of chaos within the vehicle.

'Can everybody hear me? Wave your hand if you can.'

Clever, Pedro thought. In a normal situation you would ask everybody who could move to come towards you and that would immediately show you where you needed to go to the more seriously injured victims who couldn't move or might not be conscious. It wasn't possible to do that in a bus that nobody could get out of unaided and it might be difficult to move around bent seating and a less than level position of the floor. By waving their arms,

Nikki would know that they were conscious, able to follow commands and that they could move.

A police car flashed its lights at him as he slowed for a red traffic light and then pulled up beside him.

'You're speeding, mate.'

'I'm a doctor. I'm trying to get to a major incident. Bus crash on the coast road past Clevedon.'

'We just heard that activation. Follow us…' They put the beacons and siren on and took off through the red light with Pedro right behind them. He could see more flashing beacons in his rear-view mirror, coming in the same direction. Nikki would have all the help she needed very soon.

But in the meantime she needed him.

'Oh, my God, Pedro.' Her voice was a shaky whisper. 'There's a girl here. Unconscious. I've opened her airway but she's got a compound fracture of her femur and she's bleeding badly. It's a pulsatile blood loss.'

She didn't have to tell him that she was facing her worst nightmare. A flashback that had come to life. A girl whose life was in danger and would need to be taken to an operating theatre ASAP to stop the haemorrhage definitively and reduce the fracture. Pedro sent up a silent plea that the injury wasn't so severe it might sound an alarm that amputation might be a possibility because that could be shocking enough to tip the balance of whether or not Nikita had the strength to face this challenge. It was, after all, only a short time ago that she had been ready to give up the idea of working with any seriously injured people ever again.

'Have you got a tourniquet in your kit?' Pedro kept his voice as calm as he could. As if he was standing by her side in an operating theatre and could provide support for what was a perfectly manageable complication of surgery. As if he had complete faith in her ability to manage this situation.

'Yes…' But Nikki was talking to someone else now. 'Could you hold this for me, please, darling? Thank you… I just need to get something out of my bag to put around her leg. What's your name?'

There was a child's voice that was too muffled to hear properly. Pedro could tell the phone had been put down beside the first aid kit because he could hear a zip being opened and packaging ripped apart.

'Oh…is this your sister, Mohammed?' Nikki's voice was more distant now, as well. 'What's her name? Adeela… That's a pretty name. I know this looks awful but this is going to help. I'm going to turn this little stick and…look…it's making the bleeding stop. I'm going to cover it up with a dressing to help it stay clean, but can you stay with Adeela and make sure the dressing doesn't fall off? You could hold her hand too, because that will help her not to be so scared if she wakes up. I need to check on everybody else but I'll be back as soon as I can and there will be more people arriving to help very, very soon.'

Pedro could hear her reassuring terrified children as she moved towards the front of the bus, telling them they were going to be okay. That she knew how scary this was, but there were more people who were on their way to come and help look after them and, in the meantime, they could help look after each other while she took care of anyone who was badly hurt. He could hear a growing confidence in her voice too.

'You're doing this, *cara*,' he said. 'Keep going.'

His own voice felt a little shaky. Pedro had never been more proud of Nikita.

He'd never loved her more…

Then she found someone he knew Nikki recognised and he caught his breath as he listened to the catch in her voice.

'Steph…are you okay? No, don't move. You've got a nasty bump on your head and you might have hurt your neck. Here…hold this dressing in place and put some pressure on it to help stop the bleeding. Try and keep as still as you can until we can get a collar on you.'

'I'm fine… I need to get up and help but…it's my arm… I think it's broken…'

'Stay there. Use your other hand to press on this dressing.'

'But…that's Adeela on the floor back there, isn't it?'

'Yes.'

'Is she badly hurt?'

'I've got the bleeding under control. I'll get back to her in a second. I've just got to check on the driver. What's his name?'

'Mikey…' Steph sounded as if she was crying. 'It wasn't his fault… The forecast said it wasn't going to start snowing for hours, but it started so suddenly. He was trying to find somewhere to turn around… And Adeela only came because her little brother was too scared to come by himself. Mohammed's only nine. Adeela's sixteen…their mother died last year…the father's long gone and she's been trying to raise her baby brother all by herself…'

Pedro could feel an ache deep in his chest. These children already had more than enough to cope with in their lives. This was supposed to be a special Christmas treat for them and it was all going so horribly wrong.

Except for one thing. The silver lining in a very dark cloud was that Nikita Wallace was coping with this emergency. Alone. He could hear the strength in her voice.

'Steph…listen to me… There's more help coming. It'll be here any minute. Please don't try and move just yet. I've got to check on Mikey…'

'Yes…of course you do…'

Pedro knew she was moving again. He heard Nikki swear under her breath at the same time that there was a cracking sound, as if the phone had hit a metal bar. Then he heard muffled static that went on long enough for Pedro to wish he wasn't driving and that he could be on a video call and see what was happening as Nikita was obviously trying to make her way towards Mikey.

'The front of the bus has had the most damage,' she told Pedro seconds later. 'It looks like Mikey's pinned by the steering wheel. I'm just going to put the phone down and try to move it with both hands.'

'He may have chest injuries. Check his breathing first.'

'Mikey? Can you hear me?'

Pedro couldn't hear any response and Nikki's voice was barely audible. 'Does it hurt to breathe?'

He listened to sounds further away from where she was. Children still crying. A siren in the distance. And then a startled exclamation from Nikki.

'Nikki…' he called loudly to try and catch her attention. 'What's going on? What's wrong?'

She must have reached for the phone because her voice was clear again.

'We just got splashed, that's all. The windscreen's broken and some spray from a wave came through. We're closer to the waves than I realised.'

Pedro's adrenaline level went up another notch. If the tide was coming in and Nikki was inside that bus, she was in danger as well, but he couldn't go any faster to get to her. If anything, the pace was slowing as they left the city behind and the snow was falling on dark roads ahead of them, but he could see flashing blue and red lights ahead of him and the larger wheels of an emergency vehicle had left tracks in the snow on the road that he could follow. And surely they couldn't be too far away now?

The sudden silence on the other end of the line had only lasted a couple of heartbeats but it had even more of an effect than the splash of icy water that had just caught the side of Nikita's head.

'Are you still there, Pedro?'

He had to be. It was knowing that he was there that was giving her the strength to push through the fear of being trapped in the metal shell of the bus. Alone in her responsibility of providing urgent medical care to people who might die without it. Fighting the pull that was trying to drag her back to the most terrifying moments of her life. Pedro's voice seemed to be able to cast a spell to keep that fear at bay. To let her believe that she could do this.

And she could—she was already doing it and she knew that, but hearing his voice again gave her a wash of relief so strong she had to blink back the threat of tears.

'I'm still here, *cara*. I'm getting closer every minute. Talk to me.'

'Mikey's conscious and talking but his breathing is

rapid and shallow and I'm not sure his chest movements are equal. He's in enough pain to have fractured ribs.'

'Can you listen to his chest?'

'Yes… I've got a stethoscope in my kit. I'll have to put the phone down for a minute. Oh…'

'What now?'

'Someone's here. At the back. Climbing in. I think it's a fireman.'

'And I can see a fire truck that's stopped on the road ahead of me and a police car. I think I'm here, Nikki… And there's an ambulance right behind me…'

A sob escaped Nikita. Real support had arrived, starting with the personnel to help everybody who could move to escape the bus. A glance showed her that there was more than one fire officer at the open window she'd used to climb into the bus and children were already being helped to climb out.

The skills and equipment that might be needed to treat the more seriously injured, like Steph and Mikey and especially Adeela, was also arriving with Pedro on scene and an ambulance crew just behind him.

Nikita could step back if she wanted to, confident in the knowledge that she'd managed the initial triage and could point responders to those who needed help urgently. She too could climb back out of that window and escape the nightmare of being inside this crumpled bus with the cries of fear and pain still in the air around her and the personal fight in the back of her own head to not let this situation drag her into the past.

But she didn't want to step back.

And she didn't need to.

The phone connection with Pedro had been cut—possibly because he didn't want her distracted by the noise of the people around him now, his attention on collecting the gear he wanted brought in and then his need to concentrate on climbing safely down to the bus.

And it was then that Nikita realised—like she had in Theatre that day when he hadn't arrived—that his physical presence would be a huge bonus but she didn't need to depend on it like she had that first time. She didn't need the reassurance of his voice on the end of a phone line either. She didn't even need to be in the same part of the world as the man who'd given her back her confidence because he was always going to be with her— like he was in this moment of silence as she hooked the earpieces of her stethoscope into place and put the disc against Mikey's chest.

He'd be there as a quiet voice at the back of her mind. Or a squeeze on her heart that would remind her to believe in herself because *he* always had…

Nikita could hear Mikey's breathing and knew he wasn't about to collapse with a tension pneumothorax. He did need some oxygen and pain relief and then the experts to free him from the wreckage so they could get him into the back of an ambulance and start monitoring him properly as they took him to hospital.

'Hang in there, Mikey,' Nikita told him. 'We're going to get you out of here very soon. There are people outside now to help.' Including paramedics, from what she could see through the broken windscreen. Had they not been given the all-clear to climb inside yet? 'I just need to check on someone a bit further back,' she told Mikey. The person she now knew was the most seriously injured because she'd been able to check everyone.

'Is it Steph?'

'I'll check on her too. She's had a bump on her head and may have broken her arm, but it's Adeela I'm more worried about.'

'Please…' Mikey said, his voice breaking. 'Go… Take care of them both…'

Someone else was climbing into the bus as Nikita clambered back to where Adeela was lying in the aisle. Someone who had turned to take a kit being passed through the window. It would contain the IV access gear and fluids that would be needed to combat shock from blood loss. Pain relief and splints to make it possible to move Adeela with that nasty fracture in her femur where the bone had come right through her skin, doing untold damage to her muscles and blood vessels.

And then the person was coming towards Nikita.

'*Pedro…*'

Nothing else mattered in this moment except that she had the best assistance she could hope for and all the equipment and backup either of them could need. There was certainly no thought of stepping back from this confronting scene.

Quite the opposite. Nikita knew exactly what needed to be done here.

She also knew, on some level, that this was possibly the final barrier she needed to overcome in order to put the pieces of her own life back together and, thanks to Pedro, she was almost there. If she had to, she would fight for the chance to finish what she'd started.

But she didn't have to.

'Tell me what you need me to do,' Pedro said as he opened the kit on one of the bus seats and crouched on the other side of this seriously injured teenager in the limited space they had available to work.

Adeela's brother was being led away by a paramedic but he was struggling.

'*No*...let me stay...'

'It's okay, Mohammed,' Pedro told him. 'We're going to take the very best care of your sister, I promise. Doctor Nikki knows exactly what to do.'

The accident scene was swarming with emergency service personnel now. There was the sound of sirens outside as more vehicles and people arrived. Pneumatic cutting gear being used to free Mikey from the wreckage was much nearer and louder but it was still possible to hear radio messages and instructions being relayed from the scene commanders. The children with minor injuries like lacerations and bruises were already being transported to St Nicholas Children's Hospital for further assessment and treatment. Steph was being attended to by paramedics.

Nikita was barely aware of the background noise and chaos around them. She was totally focused on the patient that she and Pedro were trying to stabilise in order to transport her as quickly as possible to where she could get the treatment that could save her leg, if not her life.

This was all that mattered right now.

And it mattered so much it felt as if a huge part of Nikita's life might also be hanging in the balance.

CHAPTER TWELVE

THEY WERE SIDE by side at the sinks, scrubbing in to enter Theatre together. Pedro and Nikita had done this before, but this time it felt very different. He hadn't had to encourage her to believe that this was possible.

They were standing here as equals. She was just as confident and competent as he was.

The gift had been completed.

It was many hours now since Pedro had arrived at the scene of the accident and worked with Nikita to try and save the teenager who'd been the most critically injured person in the bus crash.

He'd held a torch for her as she'd put in a line that could deliver the fluids needed to combat blood loss and the drugs to take away Adeela's pain. He'd watched, in awe, as Nikita found the tourniquet hadn't stopped the arterial bleeding completely and she'd searched for the damaged major blood vessel amongst mangled tissue and clamped it. They'd splinted the leg as quickly as possible and then a whole team of rescuers had helped to put her into a scoop stretcher and carefully manoeuvre her out of the bus, but the clock was ticking, counting down and diminishing the window of time they had to save the leg, and Pedro was as invested in a successful outcome as Nikita was.

But he wanted it for Nikki as much as for Adeela.

He wanted what seemed to represent the ghost of what had changed her life so dramatically to be left in the past. Overwritten by facing a similar challenge—and winning.

Nikita had travelled in the ambulance with Adeela and they'd been followed by Pedro in his big SUV. They'd both stayed with her in the emergency department as the team had worked to stabilise her. X-rays had been taken. A CT scan had been done.

Had Nikita picked up on his thought?

'I'm so glad we did that CT,' she said. 'We could have missed that Hoffa fracture extending through the medial condyle.'

Pedro lifted his hands to start rinsing off the soap suds. 'We'll need to fix that before moving up to the repair of the femoral shaft.' He turned to take the sterile towel from the scrub nurse assisting them. 'We could be in for a long night.'

Which was fine by him. Because Pedro had the feeling that this might be the last surgery he ever did with Nikki.

He couldn't be this close to her for much longer without the risk of that secret of how he felt about Nikki being exposed and, if that happened, it might be impossible to ever get it back where it belonged, hidden deep in his heart.

Public holidays might make it more difficult to do, but it was time to use the escape route that was available. If he cashed in on the leave he'd accrued, it might even be possible to slip away tomorrow.

Which meant he would need to say goodbye to Nikki before he left tonight.

Sí... The longer this surgery took, the better...

It was a long, complex surgery with a big team that covered several specialties but Nikita was involved every step of the way and having Pedro in Theatre with her was...perfect, that was what it was.

It took time to position Adeela's leg to allow for reduction and there were multiple fragments of bone to deal with, along with a soft tissue injury that needed thorough debridement and cleaning. X-rays were taken at varying points throughout the procedures to painstakingly repair the fractures with plates, rods and screws.

There was no real reason for Pedro to stay in Theatre once Nikita was focused on the repair of the femoral artery but it felt like everybody here was now part of Adeela's story.

A story that had captured nationwide interest because it involved a bunch of kids, a vintage bus and volunteers who had only wanted to give them a special Christmas treat.

They had news coming in at frequent intervals, via theatre technicians and staff working out of the sterile area who had access to phones and social media.

'You guys are famous,' an X-ray technician informed Nikita and Pedro. 'You're on every news bulletin, with footage of you getting Adeela out of the bus and into the ambulance.'

'They've got cameras at St Nick's too. There's a whole observation ward being set aside for the kids once they're through the ED.'

Most of the bus crash victims had been taken to St Nicholas Children's Hospital and, fortunately, most had only minor injuries. Reports were coming through at intervals about them all.

'Violet, ten years old, has had a head lac fixed with skin glue and an X-ray to check a finger wasn't broken.'

'Sonny—twelve years old—has had stitches in his lip. He banged it on the rail of the seat in front of him. He's got a black eye too.'

'Molly's fine—just a few bruises, but she doesn't want to go home without her friend Sara, who's getting a Colles fracture plastered.'

'Mohammed's not injured but he won't talk to anyone. He must be worried sick about his big sister...'

The siblings had been separated, with Adeela being brought to Bristol Central along with the injured adults, Steph and Mikey. This decision had been made partly to spread the patient load, partly because she was old enough to be treated as a young adult and not a paediatric case, but mostly because she was already under the care of two of Bristol Central's orthopaedic surgeons and it seemed that Pedro would have been just as reluctant to hand over the case as Nikita.

Getting this right mattered on so many levels. For a young girl who'd taken on the responsibility of her younger brother when they'd lost their only parent. For the frightened little boy who was waiting. For Nikita, because this was like the universe was offering her a chance to try again at what she'd desperately wanted to do but failed to achieve in the catastrophic aftermath of that bomb blast.

And it mattered for Pedro too. Because he'd believed

in her and she wanted him to know that his faith hadn't been misplaced. She could not only go back to doing her job but she could do it very, very well.

She wanted him to be proud of her.

Christmas Eve had long since become Christmas Day by the time Adeela had woken up properly in Recovery and was ready to be transferred to the intensive care unit for close monitoring for a day or two. Her first words were to ask about her brother.

'He's fine,' Nikita reassured her. 'But he's missing you. He'll be so happy to know that the surgery went so well.'

'I need to see him…' Adeela had tears rolling down her cheeks. 'He'll be so afraid—like he was the night our mother died.'

'He's being very well looked after,' Pedro told her. 'I've heard that they're keeping all the kids in the hospital until tomorrow morning. A lot of the parents can't get in because of all the snow. There'll be arrangements made for somebody to look after Mohammed—and you—until you're well again.'

'I wish I could see him.'

Nikita and Pedro shared a glance. They both knew that being anxious and upset wasn't going to help Adeela's recovery at all.

'Let me see what I can do.' Nikita took out her phone. She knew that Steph had gone over to St Nick's as soon as her head wound had been dealt with and her broken arm put into a cast and a sling. She sent a text that was answered immediately. A minute later and a video call was happening between Adeela and Mohammed. Just a short one because Adeela needed to sleep and begin a long healing process and it was in a language Nikita didn't understand, but the fact that Mohammed was talking felt like a gift.

And she could speak to Steph after Adeela's eyes drifted shut and a nurse moved in to check her vital signs again. She and Pedro went out into the corridor and kept the video call going.

'They're all okay,' Steph told her. 'But most of them cried themselves to sleep. They're so sad about how the day ended.'

Mikey was also there at St Nick's. He was sore, with his cracked ribs and a lot of bruises, but he wasn't going home any time soon.

'We'll stay until all the kids get collected tomorrow,' Steph told her. 'And I'm talking to Social Services about taking Mohammed home with me. Maybe they'll let me look after Adeela as well, when she comes out of hospital.'

'You're an angel, Steph,' Pedro told her. 'I wish I could do something to help.'

'Maybe you could…'

'Just name it,' he said, smiling.

'You've got a car that can cope with the snow, yes?'

'I have.'

'Could you go to Nikita's house and collect the presents for the children? Maybe some of the food too? We could give them a Christmas breakfast with sausage rolls and Grinch juice and their presents to take home. It's not much but…it would be something…'

'I think that's a great idea,' Nikita said. She grinned at Pedro. 'You could pick up the Father Christmas outfit at the same time and be the one to give out the presents.'

'Are you offering to be my elf?'

He was smiling at her but his eyes held a different message. Something that looked…almost sad?

As if that clock had suddenly sped up and this was part of how they were going to say goodbye to each other?

If so, it seemed like this was perfect as well. A happy note to end on, with Christmas wishes and presents to make children happier. A memory that would be a happy one for everyone. Even Adeela, if she was awake again and feeling well enough to join in by a video call. And how happy would she be if she knew what Steph was planning and might have approval for by then?

Nikita could feel a squeeze on her heart that was so tight it hurt but she didn't let that dim her smile.

'You're on,' she told Pedro. 'As soon as I'm off call in the morning, we'll go and rustle up a bit of Christmas magic.'

Steph and Mikey were waiting for them at the front entrance of Bristol's St Nicholas Children's Hospital as Christmas Day was dawning. They had wheelchairs ready to pile the bags of food and the sack of gifts into.

Steph was smiling despite the bandage on her head and a very impressive black eye. 'Merry Christmas,' she said.

Pedro smiled back. '*Feliz Navidad*,' he said.

Mikey had an arm across his chest, supporting painful ribs, and he looked too worried to smile. 'How's Adeela?' he asked.

'She's doing very well this morning,' Nikita told him. 'She's not going to lose her leg and she's stable enough to be moved to a ward later today. She really wants us to video call her when the children are with Father Christmas.'

'We're all set.' Steph nodded. 'We've got kitchen staff

ready to heat up the sausage rolls and get the Grinch juice and have everything hidden in a meal trolley. They'll arrive just after you give out all their presents. We've arranged a private space for you both to get changed that's just down the corridor from the observation ward the kids are in. Come with me...'

The reception area of St Nick's seemed oddly crowded for this time of the morning on a public holiday. Like Bristol Central, there was a huge Christmas tree in the foyer, with sparkling lights and a huge pile of brightly wrapped gifts beneath it. People were coming in behind them too, with parcels in their arms.

'Do you know if we just put them under the tree?' a woman asked Steph. 'It's a gift for one of the children from the bus crash.' She beamed at them. 'I just wanted to start my Christmas Day this year by being a Secret Elf.'

Another person was staring at Pedro and Nikita. 'You're the doctors,' he said. 'I saw you on the news. You saved that girl who was so badly hurt. How's she doing?'

'She's going to be fine,' Steph told him. 'We're going to make sure of that. Excuse us, please—we've all got a very important appointment to get to.'

'Of course.' The man winked. 'Secret Elf stuff, yeah?'

'You're not going to believe it,' Steph said as she ushered them through the reception area. 'The Secret Elves have gone viral. People have been bringing gifts and treats into the hospital ever since the story hit the news. Even more amazingly, there are donations pouring in.'

She had tears in her eyes. 'The accident was a terrible thing to happen but...what's happening now is...oh, my goodness, I don't even know what it is...'

'Maybe it's magic,' Nikita suggested. 'Christmas magic?'

Steph sniffed hard. 'Maybe it is. We haven't told the children anything yet because we need Father Christmas here. And his elf. And the presents that have got their names on them. They do know there's a surprise coming, though, so we need to hurry…'

Steph opened a door. 'Here you go, Father Christmas.'

Mikey parked the wheelchair, with the sack of gifts that he'd insisted on pushing himself, beside the door.

'And you can go in here.' Steph opened the next door for Nikita. 'The rooms are tiny so you'll both need some space. Text me when you're ready so we can get set for the surprise. The observation ward is just down this corridor on the left after the fracture clinic. You can't miss it. The nurses all have reindeer antlers on their heads and there's a little Christmas tree by the door.'

Nikita was holding the bag with the elf costume in it.

She stuck her head out of her door as Steph and Mikey disappeared down the corridor, presumably taking the food to the kitchens.

'See you soon, Santa,' she said softly.

Her eyes were shining as she looked up and smiled at Pedro and he could actually feel his heart breaking because he wanted to kiss her *so* much.

Because he loved her so, *so* much… Which was precisely why he couldn't kiss her, because he'd never be able to keep his secret, and the last thing he wanted was to spoil the magic of what they were about to do for these children.

So he found a smile instead. '*Sí…mi elfo de Navidad,*' he murmured.

'What's Father Christmas in Spanish?' Nikita was disappearing behind her door.

'*Papá Noel.*'

* * *

Steph had been quite right when she'd told Nikita that the elf suit would fit anyone. At least the elastic on the bottom of the baggy green pants held up the loose red and white striped socks. She had bells on the points of the red collar adorning the green top and the hat was large enough to keep falling down over her eyes but Nikita didn't care. This wasn't about her.

This was about the children.

And Christmas.

And Pedro.

Apparently with a bit of magic being sprinkled over the whole occasion, with the possibility that the Secret Elves would be financially secure from now on, and that was making it already joyous.

Something else she would be able to look back on and remember about this time of having Pedro Garcia back in her life that she'd been gifted so unexpectedly.

Nikita laughed out loud when she came out of her room at the same time Pedro came out of his, dressed in the red and white suit, with a fluffy white beard and the curls of a wig peeping out from beneath the long hat with the white trim and pompom. The finishing touch of the round gold-rimmed spectacles was fabulous.

'*Feliz Navidad*,' he said, making his voice louder and deeper than usual. 'Merry Christmas. Ho-ho-ho…'

'Something's not quite right.' Nikita tilted her head on one side. 'I mean, you look gorgeous, but not quite what the kids might be expecting *Papá Noel* to look like.'

'It doesn't fit very well, does it? This suit…' Pedro pulled on the front of a jacket that was hanging in very loose folds.

'Oh… I know exactly what we need.'

Pedro followed her back into the consulting room she'd been in and watched as she took both the pillows from the bed. 'We'll just borrow these,' she said. 'And put them inside the front of your jacket.'

Pedro obligingly undid the black belt and then the buttons of the jacket. Nikita hadn't expected him to not be wearing anything underneath and she was careful not to look up and meet his gaze as she helped position the pillow and button the jacket up around it.

Because she didn't want Pedro to notice that she was struggling with a level of desire that was powerful enough to be painful.

She wanted this man *so* much…

She loved him even more…

And yes, maybe he had kissed her as though she was the most desirable woman on earth and he'd made love to her as if he adored her but…he hadn't initiated any of that physical intimacy himself, had he?

She needed to gather a bit of pride now and keep her feelings hidden. For both their sakes. Because this was her gift for him. A fond farewell and…freedom.

'That's much better,' she announced brightly, patting his now well-cushioned stomach. 'Let's get going, shall we?'

But Pedro didn't move.

Startled, Nikita looked up and when her gaze met his, she couldn't look away. She felt as if she were falling. Off a cliff. Into a space she'd never known existed.

Somewhere…

…magical…?

The words came out of her mouth before Nikita could even think of biting them back.

'I love you, Pedro,' she whispered.

He looked completely stunned. He opened his mouth and then closed it again as if he had no idea what to say.

So Nikita kept talking and once she started the words kept tumbling out.

'I know I shouldn't tell you, and I wasn't going to, and I was trying and trying to think of a way to say thank you for everything you've done to help me and my present was going to be to *not* to tell you that I love you, so that you can just go and get on with all the exciting things you've got planned in your life and not have to remember any of the past, with me being so horrible to you. But… but…it feels like I've already given you the only thing that could let you know how precious you are to me…' Nikita took in a huge gulp of air. 'And it's not letting you go. It's…it's…my heart. My love…' She could feel tears escaping. 'They're going to be yours for ever, Pedro, and I know it's the last thing you want…'

Pedro's voice sounded raw. 'How do you know that?'

'Because…you told me. That you'd had a crush on me but that was for ever ago and you were so angry when I kissed you and…and I can't blame you for that.'

'And you told me that you trusted me. That I had helped you, and that made me feel like I was ten feet tall. That I could keep helping you because I still cared about you. What I *didn't* know was…'

Nikita jumped in to fill the gap when he hesitated to catch a breath. '…was that I was going to fall in love with you? I didn't know that either. How could I? We'd only ever been friends…'

'And I was still the same person—you told me that too. That I hadn't changed at all.'

'But *I'd* changed. So much. I can see life in a very different way now, and I can't believe I hadn't seen what was right there in front of me all those years ago. My... my person...'

She wanted to say more. That she knew now that Pedro was her soulmate. Her rock...

But she'd said too much already.

'You don't have to say anything,' she assured Pedro. 'I understand that you want to go to New Zealand to see your sister and that you need to go back to your home—Spain—so you can find whatever it is you're looking for. The thing that's missing from your life. I would never ask—'

Nikita stopped talking as Pedro put his finger gently against her lips.

'I don't need to go to Spain,' he said quietly.

Her lips moved against that finger. 'But it's your home...'

'Do you remember what else I said? That home is about comfort? And familiarity? That it's the foundation to be exactly who you want to be?'

Nikita nodded.

'Home doesn't have to be a place, Nikki. It can be a person. What's that English expression about home?'

'That it's where the heart is?'

'*Si*...that's it. And my heart's always been with you. That's what I was trying to tell you. I knew I wanted to help you and I thought I could do it as a friend—that you would never want anything more than that from me. But what I didn't know was that I'd never stopped being in love with you.' He cleared his throat but it didn't stop his next words sounding as if they were coated with an emotion that was coming straight from his own heart. 'I never will.'

How ridiculous was it to have a Father Christmas declaring his undying love for her?

Pedro was barely recognisable in that costume but, behind those silly spectacles, were a pair of dark, dark eyes that were looking at her with an intensity that was making something melt deep inside Nikita's soul. She could see so much love in those eyes.

As much as he was seeing in hers?

Yes…

That was why he was pulling her into his arms like this. Why he was kissing her as if he'd just been given the best Christmas gift ever. As if there really was magic in the air today and anything…*everything* was possible…

Nikita knew exactly how that felt…

EPILOGUE

Two years later...

THE FATHER CHRISTMAS suit still needed two pillows to fill out the jacket.

And Pedro Garcia looked just as gorgeous as he had the first time he'd worn this costume. Nikita's smile was distinctly misty as she stood back far enough to admire her husband.

'This is my favourite part of Christmas,' she announced.

'Mine too.' Pedro was smiling down at her. 'I do believe this is where *Papá Noel* gets to kiss his *elfo de Navidad.'*

'Mmm... If he can get close enough.' Nikita put her hand on her hugely pregnant belly. 'It's a good thing that this elf costume has so much elastic in the trousers.'

Pedro put his hand beside hers on her belly.

'It might have helped if you hadn't decided to get pregnant with twins,' he murmured.

Nikita was still smiling. 'We had a lot of time to make up for.'

'We did...'

As if they knew who was touching them, their unborn twins wriggled beneath their hands. Pedro had no trouble getting close enough to their mother to place a lingering, tender kiss on her lips.

And then just one more…

Nikita sighed happily after that. 'We'd better go downstairs,' she said. 'Or Steph will know what we've been doing when we should have just been getting changed.'

She smiled as her gaze met Pedro's again and it was another of those shared memories that was part of building a life together. Decorating the 'home' that was the love that bound them together. Because they were both remembering that first kiss on Christmas Day in that consulting room at St Nick's. When Steph had come to find them and had come into the room after a brief tap on the door to find them kissing each other so passionately, but she hadn't seemed at all shocked. If anything, she'd looked rather pleased about it.

'*I thought it was Mummy that Santa Claus was supposed to be caught kissing*,' she'd said, trying to hide a smile. '*Not his Christmas elf*.'

Nikita held out her hand and Pedro took hold of it. She had a feeling that Steph would still be delighted if she knew what was going on in this upstairs bedroom and that she and Pedro were more in love with each other with every passing day.

Steph, along with Mikey, had come all the way to Spain when Pedro and Nikita celebrated their wedding in Barcelona. They'd helped them move into the big house in Leigh Woods because Elm Tree Cottage would never be big enough for the family they couldn't wait to start. It was far more practical for them both to be near the hospital where they were still working together, until Nikita took her maternity leave and, as a bonus, there'd been more than enough room for Duncan and the chickens in the old pony paddock between the house and the forest. And, along with Kyle, Adeela and Mohammed, those two original Secret Elves had insisted on looking after Earl and keeping an eye on Duncan and the chickens when Nikita and Pedro took a slightly belated but extended honeymoon in New Zealand.

Steph and Mikey's lives were busier than ever now that the Secret Elves had grown to become a registered charity with a huge number of supporters and generous donors and they'd been able to start helping so many more children.

There were fifty of those special kids downstairs in the ballroom right now, beneath the sparkling fairy lights that ran from the chandeliers all over the beautiful ceilings like a starry sky. The fires were lit and the enormous room with its spectacular Christmas tree that seemed to be getting bigger every year was as warm as toast. The kitchens were bursting at the seams with a Christmas Eve feast that the caterers were putting the finishing touches to and she and Pedro had decorated the dining table themselves last night—with the family heirloom wooden nativity scene taking centre stage.

The Secret Elves had employees as well as volunteers now and Adeela, who worked for the charity around her first-year university studies, was waiting at the bottom of the staircase as Pedro and Nikita went down, hand in hand. Earl was helping her guard the huge red sack that was filled with the gifts that had been carefully selected, wrapped and named for each of the children chosen to go on the magical mystery bus trip this year.

A big bus now, to cater for all the extra children that

could be given a Christmas treat they might not otherwise have received. Mikey's old red sleigh bus had been lifted from the rocks at the bottom of that cliff and repaired, but it was towed to its final resting place in the car park of the new headquarters for the Secret Elves—who weren't so secret any longer.

'I hear you came top of your class again this year, Adeela.'

Pedro was using his 'Father Christmas' voice. Nikita could feel its deep rumble right into her bones and it made her smile. She was also smiling because she knew there was a parcel for Adeela in the bag—an anatomy textbook with amazing diagrams and pictures.

'Well done.' Nikita gave her a hug. 'You'll be heading off to medical school before we know it.'

'Oh, I hope so, Nikki.' Adeela's face lit up. 'That's what I dream about—being a surgeon, just like you and Pedro. Maybe a specialist for children so I can work at St Nick's.'

The door to the ballroom opened and Steph poked her head out. 'Are you coming in?' she asked. 'There's just a few rather excited children waiting in here.'

Mohammed appeared beside her. He was holding a large bell and had the biggest smile on his face that Nikita had ever seen. 'Is it time?' he begged. 'Can I ring the bell?'

Pedro picked up the bag of gifts and put it over his shoulder. 'I'm ready,' he announced.

Steph turned back into the room. 'Guess who's here?' she called.

They could hear a cheer coming from the children and all the helpers.

Mohammed began ringing the bell as he went back to the gathering. 'He's arrived,' he shouted. 'I saw his sleigh and now he's here…'

Pedro paused for a moment longer. Just long enough to kiss Nikita again. One of those slow, tender kisses she would never want him to stop giving her. 'Are you ready, *mi cariñito*?' he asked. '*Mi elfo?*'

'I'm so ready,' she replied with a smile.

And she was. She was ready for this magical evening and a new Christmas Day tomorrow and a new year to begin next week. She was ready for their babies to arrive and change their lives for ever and she was more than ready to embrace the joy of her own future and every Christmas to come that she would share with this man she loved *so* much…

Yes…she was ready.

Let the magic begin…

* * * * *

BABY SHOCK
FOR THE
MILLIONAIRE DOC

MARION LENNOX

MILLS & BOON

PROLOGUE

SHE HAD TO give this baby away.

At two in the morning, sleep deprived to the point of illness, this final decision was tearing her apart.

It was the only one available.

Baby Lily, six weeks old, had been released from hospital a week ago, but no matter what Misty tried, she wouldn't settle. Misty was the sole doctor for Kirra Island, but in the last few days there'd been no time for medicine. No time for the islanders.

There'd been no time for anything.

Misty had abandoned almost everything to be with her tiny niece. She'd crooned and rocked and slept in snatches of no more than an hour. Her grandmother had rocked her back and forth in her wheelchair until she swore she was wearing wheel ruts in the kitchen's linoleum. Both women had put everything they knew into caring for this tiny bundle, and all the time, Misty's nephew, seven-year-old Forrest, was hunched under his bedclothes, knowing—no matter what he was told—that somehow this was All His Fault.

Forrest was turning into an Eeyore, Misty thought dismally. Just the way she'd always been.

Tigger and Eeyore. That's what their mother had nicknamed her two daughters, after the happy go lucky tiger and the doleful donkey in A.A. Milne's beloved *Winnie the Pooh*. Misty's older sister, Jancie, had been Tigger, out for a good time, no matter what. Misty had been Eeyore and now Forrest was turning into an Eeyore, too. A little boy who never expected anything good to happen.

Twelve months ago, Misty had finally gained custody of Jancie's son and she'd sworn she'd give him a childhood where he could be happy.

Well, Jancie had done her best to see that wouldn't happen. Her sister's anger at losing custody of her neglected little boy had been off the scale. In what must have been an act of pure defiance, she'd fallen pregnant again almost as soon as she'd been released from her latest stint in prison. Thus here was Misty, forced again to handle the consequences. Forced to take care of this tiny newborn.

But Misty's capacity to care had reached its limit. She was the sole doctor for Kirra Island's six hundred permanent residents. Her grandmother, wheelchair bound after years of struggling to control her diabetes, did her best to help, but there were times where Misty had to help her. And Forrest…how was she to give him any sort of happy childhood?

To keep this little one, Misty's only choice would be to give up her career to care for them all. Sadly that couldn't be an option. There was no other doctor willing to work on Kirra Island and besides, she was broke—Jancie's legal and medical fees had seen to that. She'd be raising them all in poverty.

As she struggled with these choices, in her head she could hear her sister's mocking voice and, before hers, their mother's.

For some reason she'd been remembering a childhood morning. Seven-year-old Misty had been awake, dressed in her second-hand uniform, desperate to go to school. For Misty, school had always been a sanctuary, but as often happened, her mother refused to take her.

'Oh, for heaven's sake, Misty, stop whining. What does

it matter if you miss school? You're not my conscience. I'm taking my headache back to bed.'

For as long as she could remember, that's what she'd felt like, her mother's conscience. Misty had been Eeyore, spoiling her mother's fun—and as Jancie got deeper and deeper into trouble, her sister's, too.

In her arms Lily gave a protesting mew and Misty looked down at her sister's baby with exhausted eyes. She was close to the edge. There had to be lightness somewhere.

But maybe it was here.

On her desk sat her sister's computer. It had taken a couple of local computer geeks some time to break into it, but now she had access, complete with internet history.

She was looking at history from almost a year ago, and there it was. There *he* was.

Doctor Angus Firth
Thirty-two
Runner up in the Gold Coast Surf Championships

She was looking at colour photographs of a lean, ripped surfer, sweeping in on cresting waves. His body had been glistening from surf and sun—and probably sun oil? His sun-bleached, wavy blond hair was a bit too long, but not long enough to hide gorgeous blue eyes.

Doctor Angus Firth, surfer from Melbourne, was riding waves with skill and looks good enough to catch the eye of professional media photographers. He was concentrating, but he'd obviously been relaxed enough to see the photographer and he'd given him a wicked, teasing grin. Like, I can do this and enjoy myself, too?

Attached to the photograph was a newspaper report extolling his skill, discussing how sheer bad luck had robbed him of the championship.

But Jancie's internet searching hadn't stopped with surfing. Misty had found social media searches, searches of academic records, career background. The files were a compilation of fact after fact.

And dating from the following weeks there'd been searches of accommodation bookings. 'She's hacked into all sorts of places,' the computer experts had told Misty. 'Wow, even there!'

There had been a booking at a luxury hotel near the Gold Coast Surf Championships. Easier to find had been another booking by Jancie, at the same time, for the same hotel. There'd then been timetables of the championship event and then a spreadsheet of appearances, of restaurant bookings, of so much.

And then there'd been ovulation charts, neatly documented. For such an irresponsible woman, Jancie had sometimes been extraordinarily clever.

So tonight, while Lily fitfully slept and complained, Misty had scrolled on, reading and rereading all the information Jancie had collected on Angus Firth.

So what was there? No responsibilities as far as she could see. A family background of wealth and privilege. A medical career, but seemingly not one he took seriously.

Was he like Jancie, another Tigger?

And it seemed Jancie had plotted to meet him. Ten months ago, her planned campaign was all mapped out in her sister's internet history. It seemed Dr Firth had serious family money and Misty could almost see Jancie's plan to hit him for support payments in the future.

But the future was now. If all this evidence proved he was indeed Lily's father... If Lily indeed had a living parent...

Maybe that support could happen straight away?

'Enough,' she told Lily, as the tiny creature in her arms decided that she'd had enough, too, and opened her mouth and wailed. 'I'm sorry, sweetheart, but it's time for this

Eeyore to share, and if this man is indeed your dad... Forrest needs a chance to be a carefree kid and maybe even I could use a sliver of a chance at being Tigger.'

Then she looked again at the photograph of the blond, carefree, surfer-cum-doctor. 'So, Dr Angus Firth,' she said out loud, 'have I got a surprise for you.

CHAPTER ONE

FIVE O'CLOCK AND Mrs Marjorie Field's nit problem was not only boring, it also extended well over her normal consultation allocation.

The society matriarch had housed her three grandchildren and their nanny while their parents were interstate, but had been appalled to discover they were nit-infected.

Everyone concerned had been treated. The parents had returned. Marjorie had handed back her grandchildren, along with lectures on irresponsible sons and daughters-in-law who dared not check their children before handing them over—and you would have thought the drama was over.

But Marjorie wasn't one to let a grievance go, nor could she be totally satisfied that her beautifully bouffant hair was completely nit free. She needed Angus to check for himself and she needed something for the anxiety—'Oh, the palpitations when I saw them, Doctor!' Her booked short consultation thus became long.

He hoped it didn't matter. Summer in Melbourne meant there'd still be a couple of hours' beach time. On Thursday evenings he usually joined mates paddling kayaks round the bay. Tonight's wind meant it'd be choppy enough to be interesting.

But they were meeting at six thirty and he had a final patient booked.

The receptionists knew the rules—Angus worked four

days a week, nine to six, and that was that. His city clinic employed sixteen doctors, with after-hours patients outsourced to locums. Thus he accepted no bookings after five.

'What gives?' he'd demanded of the guys on the desk when he'd seen this last appointment. 'Misty Calvert? Do we have a history?'

'No, mate, she's new to the clinic, but I felt sorry for her.' Don on the desk was new, a soft touch. He'd toughen up, Angus thought. He'd learn the rules. Doctors here valued their time off above all else. Emergencies, long consultations, social issues—they could all be handled at another clinic.

By doctors who cared?

He did care, he conceded. Just not if it interfered with his surfing.

'Why did you feel sorry for her?' he'd asked, in a voice that made Don wince. 'Why not just put her into a locum appointment?'

'She wanted to see you. She has kids with her, a little boy and a baby. She came in just after lunch and asked to be seen urgently, but only by you. To be honest, she looked exhausted and so did the kid. Tired, sad, beat. She said…she said her baby needed to see a doctor and there was something she needed to tell you. Something about her sister… a Jancie?'

Jancie? It clicked with Misty's last name, bringing back a flood of memories, most of them excellent.

Jancie Calvert. He'd met Jancie almost a year back, at the surfing championships on the Gold Coast. He'd been gutted that he hadn't won—he'd been so close. But Jancie was gorgeous and funny and intent on making him forget his disappointment. They'd had a great time, but she was a no-strings person, just like him. They'd said goodbye with no regrets and that was that.

But now? Had something happened to Jancie? Was that why this woman was sad? Had she thought there was something more to their relationship than there was? Was she coming to tell him bad news?

He found himself bracing as he walked through to the waiting room to meet her.

But this woman looked nothing like Jancie. Jancie had been gorgeous, blonde—bottle-blonde, probably, but who'd been caring? She'd been perfectly manicured, beautifully attired—and pretty damned sexy.

He remembered the first time he'd seen her, in the bar at his hotel. He'd been there with surfing mates, and some time during the night one of his friends had introduced them. 'Hey, Firth, meet one of your greatest fans. Jancie's been telling us all about why you were robbed!'

She knew it all, everything about him, right down to details of every last wave he'd ridden during the contests. She'd lifted his shattered ego and made the night fun. She'd even made him decide to stay a few nights longer.

And this was her sister? This tired, milk-stained woman, cradling a baby, with a little boy huddling beside her as if he was afraid of the very room?

Her hair, mouse brown, curly—very curly—was bunched into an unruly knot. Dark-shadowed eyes looked out from a face devoid of make-up. She was wearing faded jeans, a stained white shirt and grubby sneakers.

She was probably around the same size as Jancie, not tall, not short. Slim build, if he could guess behind the stained shirt—though if the baby in her arms was any indication, she'd still be post-partum. In that case she was too thin.

She was about as far from the glamourous Jancie as it was possible to get.

But as he entered the waiting room, the little boy cringed and huddled tighter, and the woman looked up at him with exhausted eyes. Despite his confusion, the doctor part of him kicked in. He had rules about limiting his medical practice, but every so often something got under his skin. The fear on the little boy's face, the look of exhaustion on the woman... Okay, maybe his kayaking mates might have to go without him.

The woman rose, lifting the baby with her and tugging the little boy up to stand beside her. As his last patients for the day, this little group had the waiting room to themselves and both woman and boy looked...afraid? What was going on?

'Good evening,' Angus said gravely and gave her his practised, doctorly smile. 'Ms Misty Calvert? How can I help you?'

There was a moment's pause while she seemed to brace. Then she took a deep breath, her chin came up and she met his gaze head on. 'I'm Dr Calvert,' she said bluntly. 'But I don't think you can help me at all. It's Lily here who needs help.' She motioned down to the baby in her arms. 'I'm here to tell you that my sister's dead. Jancie. She died during childbirth, but Lily survived. So... I'm sorry to spring this on you, but unless...unless I'm mistaken, we're here to give you your daughter.'

There were some moments in life that felt like a seismic shift...when the earth almost seemed to disappear.

It had been like that for Angus when he'd learned his parents and kid brother had been fatally injured in a car accident. He'd been nineteen. He still remembered the sensation when the police had come to find him at his university college, when he'd stared at them blankly, not able to believe the unbelievable, feeling as though the ground was no longer under his feet.

And this was the same. His brain simply stopped working. There was some sort of fuzz going on. He couldn't figure where to go from here.

'You might need to sit down,' the woman—Misty—said.

He didn't. If he moved, that might make this real.

'That's not my baby.' Maybe it was a dumb thing to say, but they were the only words he could find. They were the only words that could possibly be true.

'You'll need DNA to confirm it,' the woman said, briskly now. 'But I can't find any alternative. You slept with my sister almost a year ago, right? Jancie Calvert? You spent two weeks with her on the Gold Coast? Jancie kept meticulous records and it seems it was planned. After her death I found spreadsheets, ovulation charts, all the preparations to make as certain as possible that she'd get pregnant and that she'd get pregnant by you. She kept records of your time together. She documented everything.'

'I don't…' The air seemed to have been sucked out of his lungs. 'I don't believe you.'

'That's understandable,' she said, not without sympathy. 'But I think it's true.' She motioned to a folder on the chair near where she'd been sitting. 'It's all there if you'd like to see. You're not on the birth certificate because…'

'Because she didn't know who the father was?' He was grasping at anything, but his capacity to think was way beyond reach.

'Because she died.' The answer was flat. 'As I said, she died in childbirth. My sister had…friends who weren't exactly reliable. At almost nine months pregnant she got into a car with some others who were drug affected. She…she might have been drug affected, too. Lily was born that night, by caesarean section, just before she died.' She glanced down at the bundle in her arms. 'The authorities had trouble tracing connections, so I only found out ten days ago. Because they couldn't find any relatives, the nurses tentatively called her Lily, but I guess you can change that if you want. If you're her father, that's your right.'

'I'm not her father.' His voice sounded strange, not his own.

'As I said, all the evidence she left says that you are.' Misty's voice suddenly gentled. 'I'm sorry. I know it's a lot to take in, but the truth seems to be that Jancie targeted you. She wanted a baby, she saw your photograph, she researched you and decided you'd make a good father. Or not actually a good father—a suitable sperm donor, without the trouble and expense of finding one commercially.' She hesitated and her voice gentled even further. 'So now I guess you need to look at her.' And she tugged back a corner of the shawl so he could see the baby's face.

He didn't step forward—he couldn't make his feet move—but she stepped forward instead.

Shocked as he was, or maybe instinctively avoiding looking at the baby, he still saw the compulsive movement of the little boy by her side. He'd been clutching the hem of her shirt, as if she might be about to run, and now he clutched it even harder.

There was a sliver of thought—the doctor in him—that wondered what was going on here? But then he saw the baby's face and everything else faded to nothing.

He'd seen photographs of himself as a baby, of course he had, and he could see a resemblance. But there was more than that.

Angus had been eight years old when his little brother was born. He remembered his mum, fresh home from hospital, setting him up on the lounge room sofa and carefully placing Baby Archie into his arms.

His kid brother.

'He's ours,' his mum had said, smiling through happy tears. 'He's ours to love and care for, for ever.'

He hadn't exactly cared for Archie, he thought, but he'd surely loved him. He'd ached for him to be old enough to be interesting. He'd kicked the footy back and forth to him—probably kicked way too hard for a toddler. He'd pushed him to put his head under water in the pool while his mum and dad had protested, 'He's too young to learn to swim, Angus, he's just a baby.' He'd pulled the training wheels off his bike and taught him to go it alone. When Archie was seven he'd taken him for his first surf.

Blue eyes, wispy blond hair, a tiny, cherubic face… The resemblance… Archie…

The memory of those awful last few days flooded back.

No! This was a nightmare.

'She has nothing to do with me,' he said, but his voice sounded…like it wasn't his?

'I think she has.' The woman was studying his face. 'I was almost certain before I came, but now I'm here…the resemblance is striking. But do a DNA test if you want. I've taken on the parent role for ten days because there was no one else, but I can't take it on permanently. She's spent five weeks in hospital, but now…' She hesitated again, but then forged on.

'There were…drug issues with Jancie and Lily's needed care. By the time the authorities located me they'd declared her well, but it's left her unsettled. But you're a doctor, you'll understand. If you want to keep her, you'll find her medical notes in the pram, plus a care guide. The basket has everything you should need for the next few days. I'm sorry this has taken you by surprise, but there doesn't seem an alternative.'

'What…what are you saying?' His voice…was that his voice?

'It's simple. I've brought you your daughter and it seems you're the only parent this little one has.'

'I'm not...'

'Look again,' she said, gently now. 'I think you know that you are.'

'But I can't... You're her...you're her...aunt?' The panic he felt was almost overwhelming. 'You have to care for her.'

'But I believe you're her father.' A certain amount of steeliness entered her voice. 'I was contacted ten days ago to be confronted by Jancie's death and Lily's existence. I took Lily in because there seemed no one else, but I can't continue to care for her. If you're her father...'

'You can't prove...'

'I don't need to prove it. It's not my role to prove or disprove anything. The authorities have assumed I'll take care of her, but I have Forrest to think of.'

She smiled wearily down at the little boy at her side. 'Jancie gave me Forrest to look after, too. She was his mum, but I've had his care for the last twelve months. We're doing our best, aren't we, Forrest? I also have a disabled grandmother and a community of patients dependent on me. I can't do more. So if you can't keep Lily...' She paused, took another deep breath, then continued, her chin tilting up again. Defiant?

'I'm sorry, but if you can't accept responsibility, then I need to hand her over to Social Services for adoption and I need to do it now. I've talked to the authorities—to her case worker. It seems there are lots of potential parents just aching to have a little girl as perfect as your daughter, and the sooner that happens the better. I'm prepared—I'd even like—to stay in touch, let Forrest be her half-brother. I am her aunt, after all, but I can't take care of her any longer.'

She paused, but then forged on, almost as if her speech had been rehearsed.

'Doctor Firth, I believe—and I think you do, too—that she's your daughter and if that's true, then what happens next needs to be your decision. I can't look after her any longer. If you're not prepared or able to take responsibility, then I need to hand her over to people who can. I'll let Social Services know what I've discovered—I dare say they'll contact you before any adoption takes place—but for now it's over to you.'

And before he knew what she intended, she lifted Lily into his arms.

Misty had planned—hoped—she could say her piece and walk away. But thinking and doing were two different things. Her head felt as though it was exploding. Her heart was wrenching and as she backed away, Forrest tugged at her shirt, forcing her to look down.

'Is he going to look after her?'

'I hope he is,' she said. 'He's her daddy. Looking after Lily is his job.'

'But what if he doesn't know how to stop her crying?'

'He'll learn,' she managed. Then she thought, *I* don't know how to stop her crying. He can hardly do any worse than me.

And she had to do this.

She'd looked at it from every angle. Her research had told her this man held down a respectable job, that there were no blemishes to his name, no criminal convictions, nothing to say that he wasn't as qualified to be a parent as... well, as qualified as she was. He was also wealthy—very wealthy. Old money, the blurb she'd read on him said. His family dated from the squattocracy.

Jancie had obviously known this and tricked him into being a parent. Who knew what had gone on in that fancy hotel room they'd shared, but the look on his face as she'd produced Lily had her guessing that he'd thought pregnancy was impossible.

Such a scenario wasn't unthinkable. Lies could be told. Condoms could be interfered with. Morals had never been allowed to interfere with what Jancie wanted and she'd obviously wanted this man.

There was a part of her that even felt sorry for him.

Sympathy or not, though, he was Lily's father. As far as her research had taught her, his responsibilities were limited to a strictly defined four-day-a-week medical practice, Monday to Thursday and nothing else. This was a man who'd have time—if he was prepared to give it—to be a parent.

And her? The thought of continuing to care for this needy little girl was too much, but Forrest was looking up at her with anxious eyes. Despite what she'd said, she knew she couldn't just walk away.

'Why didn't you ring me?' Angus was saying, in a voice that sounded almost strangled.

'Would that have helped?' She sighed. 'I thought of it, but you needed to see her. So much easier to refuse over the phone, don't you think, than when you're looking down at a little girl who looks like you?'

And that brought silence.

'Forrest and I are staying at the Oakview Motel,' she said at last. She wasn't planning on leaving him completely high and dry. 'We arrived last night to figure out where you were and set up this appointment. We live on Kirra Island, just out from Brisbane, and I need to be home by Monday. I'm the island's only doctor, so that's non-negotiable, but we can stay on for a couple of days, to make sure there aren't any...'

'Monday?' He sounded panicked. 'That's three days. You'll keep her until then?'

'No.' She made her voice implacable—there was no way she could relent. 'I can't. I haven't slept for ten days. I know this is a bolt from the blue, but it was for me, too, and my choice now is either handing her to you or taking her straight back to Social Services. Forrest… Forrest has nightmares and his mum's death has made them worse.'

'Forrest is Jancie's son?' He was holding a bundle of baby—blessedly asleep now. He was looking down at Forrest as if he was struggling to find reality.

'Yes,' she told him. 'But I've had custody for the last few months, and before that, while Jancie was in jail…'

'Jail!'

'There's a folder there that'll tell you all about her,' she said. 'It's divided into two parts, the stuff you might want Lily to know as she grows up and the parts you might want to censor. Also, there's the documentation Jancie made of your time together—I believe she may have had a future paternity suit in mind. Look, if there's anything else you can contact us at the motel.'

'But I can't look after a baby.'

She flinched then, remembering the automatic assumption of the welfare authorities that she'd do exactly that. She was back in the hospital nursery, looking down at her niece, whose very existence had blindsided her. She remembered staring down at the tiny baby, feeling overwhelming grief for a big sister who, despite all the pain she'd caused, she'd once adored. But she was also thinking of the overwhelming panic as they'd handed Lily over.

The assumption was that if she was already looking after one of Jancie's children, then of course she'd care for another. But how could she? Emotion surged and when she talked again her voice was little more than a whisper. 'What makes you think I can?'

'You're a…'

'Woman. Yep, I get it, but I don't have lactating breasts.' Deep breath. Get this over with, she told herself. Just do it. 'There's nothing I can do that you can't—and as far as I can see you have way, way more time to care for her than I do.'

She softened a little. 'Look, if there's any real need you can phone me, but Forrest and I are heading back to the motel. I'm desperate for sleep.'

She motioned to the pram she'd brought in with her. 'Everything's there, everything she'll need for the next week or so. Her medical notes are on top. I'm sorry, but unless there's any major reason why you can't look after her, unless you want me to take her straight to the authorities, there's nothing more I can do.'

Nothing.

He stood with an armful of baby and he couldn't think of a single thing to say. And now there were other emotions superimposing themselves over his shock.

The baby was warm in his arms. She curved against his chest almost as if she was meant to be there and weirdly his body was responding.

Lily. It was a strangely old-fashioned name for such a tiny being. She was awake now. Her blue eyes were gazing up at him, still slightly unfocused, but definitely...definitely looking at him?

His daughter.

He could refute this absolutely. Right now, without DNA profiling, there was surely nothing to prove she was his. This woman was her aunt. He could simply set her down into the pram and walk away.

But there was something in this woman's voice that told him she was making no idle threat. She'd take her straight to Social Services.

'Please, at least for tonight...' he managed to say. That sounded pathetic, but maybe any man who'd just had the floor pulled from under him would feel the same.

'I'm sorry, but I can't.' Her voice was implacable. 'I told you, I'm past exhaustion and I'm already...' She hesitated, but then forged on. 'I'm already getting attached and I can't afford to be any more so.'

'I'll pay.'

'What?'

'I meant… I'll pay for her care, at least until DNA tests come back.' That'd give him time to take things in.

But the look she gave him made him feel as though he was something that had crawled out of cheese. Ouch.

And it hit him then, the enormity of what she'd been saddled with. Maybe even more than the responsibility she was thrusting on him?

'I don't need your money.' Her voice was almost savage. 'I need sleep and, to tell you the truth, I can't see past that. Sorry. I've done what I came for.' She stooped and gave the little boy a hug. 'Forrest, we need to go now. Doctor Firth is going to look after Lily and he'll do it really well.'

'What if he doesn't cuddle her?' He sounded worried.

'He will cuddle her,' she said, definitively. 'Won't you, Dr Firth?'

Would he? His brain was refusing to function. But as she took Forrest's hand and turned to leave, panic gave way to desperate thought.

'Please,' he said. 'Stop. Give me a moment.'

She stopped. She didn't turn, but there was something about the set of her shoulders that told him that she was finding this almost as hard as he was. The way she'd looked at Lily as she'd turned…

Her words were replaying.

'I'm already getting attached and I can't afford to be any more so.'

In that statement lay a chink of light.

'You can't hand her over to Social Services tonight,' he said.

'No, but I don't need to. That's your call.'

'I can't hand her over at this hour.'

'Is he giving Lily away?' Forrest's voice was thin and distressed and he thought, why had she brought him? This was so unfair, to all of them.

And for some reason she seemed to read his thoughts.

'Forrest needed to come with me,' she said. 'There was no choice. I'm his security blanket, aren't I, Forrest? He stays with me for ever.' She stooped and faced the little boy straight on.

'I'll never leave you, Forrest. I've told you that and it's true. But Lily has a daddy and he'll do the very best he can for her. If that means he needs to find another mummy and daddy who'll care for her, then he will, but we need to leave them alone now to make their decision.' She rose. 'Your receptionist has my contact details,' she said. 'I'm sorry, I know this has thrown your world into turmoil, but mine's been thrown the same way, once too often. Your turn.'

'But tonight…'

'No.'

He was thinking, frantically. 'Look, my house…'

'You're not going to tell me your house isn't fit to hold your daughter?'

'I…of course not. But I live not far from here and the house is big.' His head was clearing, just a little—was that panic kicking in and giving him straws to clutch? He looked at Misty's wooden face and decided talking to Forrest might be best. 'I have a swing in the garden and there's a park right across the street,' he told the little boy. 'It's by the river and there's a great playground.'

Then he took a deep breath, thinking this might just work.

'I know the Oakview Motel where you're staying,' he said. 'It's rundown and it's very noisy.' That much was true—it was close to his clinic, on a busy street, dilapidated and obviously meant for cheap stays. 'Can I ask if you…'

he was still talking to Forrest, sensing this might be a weak link in Misty's resolve '…if you and your aunt would stay with me for a couple of days? Or at least for tonight? Just to help me learn…how to cuddle Lily?'

'She's easy to cuddle,' Forrest ventured, eyeing him distrustfully. 'Unless she's crying, but she cries a lot. I think she's missing Mummy.'

He closed his eyes for a moment, pushing back a vision of the lovely, laughing Jancie. A woman as different from this one as it was possible to be.

Mummy. The vision didn't fit, but the woman facing him now fit the bill exactly.

There must be some way he could make this work—but he needed time.

'I have five big bedrooms,' he told Misty, facing her again. 'I often have friends staying, but right now, apart from me, the place is empty. There are beds already made up. My housekeeper keeps the fridge stocked with food. The garden's great. You could sleep…'

'I can't and won't care for your daughter overnight.' It was flat, inflectionless, totally non-negotiable. 'I'll fall over if I don't get some sleep. My decision's been made. I just… can't.'

'I'll look after Lily tonight,' he said. Anything to keep this woman here, while he figured his way forward. 'The master bedroom's at one end of the house, the other bedrooms are divided by the living areas. You won't even have to hear her, and tomorrow we'll make a decision.'

'You'll make a decision,' she said bluntly. 'I already have.'

'Then I hope you'll help me see my way forward,' he told her. 'Please, this has been an appalling shock.'

'You get used to shocks, after a while.'

That made him pause. For a moment his own shock receded, enough to acknowledge her absolute weariness, obvious in her voice and on her face. She really did look as though she was about to fall over.

The medical side of him was suddenly surfacing, assessing. He saw few such women in this affluent Melbourne suburb, but during his training in the big city hospitals, he'd occasionally seen them. Women who'd been given burdens too great for them to bear.

'My housekeeper sets up the spare rooms so they can be used at a moment's notice,' he said, gently now. 'It's only a five-minute drive away. Down by the river.'

And at that her head jerked up. 'You have a five-bedroom house, by the river—with a housekeeper? In this suburb?' Her voice was incredulous.

'My parents left it to me.' He gave a rueful smile. 'Yeah, it's far too big for one, but I've never got round to selling it.'

'Jancie's research said you were well off, but…'

'Jancie's research?'

'She seemed to have targeted you as the perfect father. Maybe she was even right.' She was staring at him as if she was seeing another life form, but Forrest was tugging her hand.

'Misty, I don't like our motel,' he whispered. 'There were men yelling last night and it was scary. Doctor Firth says there's a garden with a swing.'

She closed her eyes and took a deep breath. Then another. When she opened them, she seemed to have come to a decision.

'You say beds are already made up?'

'They are. And I know my housekeeper's left a lasagne in the fridge.' He'd been expecting to kayak tonight. His home, large, central and welcoming, was often used as a base for his mates when they returned from kayaking and it was too late to find a pub meal. He'd asked Pat and she'd promised there'd be lasagne.

'I like lasagne,' Forrest ventured, and he saw Misty crack.

'Fine,' she said, sounding goaded, then she softened. 'Sorry. That sounds ungracious. What we've done to you sounds appalling and I'm aware of it. It's just that Jancie's done the same thing to me and I'm left with no choice. So thank you for your offer, Dr Firth. Forrest and I would like to stay with you tonight. That way Forrest can see what we both hope will be Lily's new home.'

That wasn't exactly what Angus had planned when he'd offered accommodation, but he'd take what he could get. Keep her here, he thought, and tomorrow…well, who knew what tomorrow could bring? Some way of getting him out of this mess?

CHAPTER TWO

DOCTOR ANGUS FIRTH'S house was stunning- an idyllic fantasy of what a true home should be? It was big, old and weathered into the landscape, a house that looked as if it had been there for a hundred years. French windows opened to wide verandas and then to the huge garden. Its age and beauty seemed almost a welcome in itself.

It was set on sloping bushland leading down to Melbourne's iconic Yarra River. Misty climbed out of his car—an SUV with a bright red kayak on the roof rack—and was met by a chorus of evening birdsong. The smell of eucalyptus, the sight of the flowering gums, the massive crimson bougainvillea trailing along the cast-iron lacework of the veranda…it almost took her breath away.

You could almost imagine you were in the country in this place, she thought—the sounds of the city had simply disappeared.

Automatically she turned to lift Lily from the baby capsule she'd hired at the airport—and then she paused. This was no longer her role. Starting now?

She looked across to Angus and she didn't move. Nor did she say a word. Their eyes locked.

'You mean this, don't you?' he said at last.

'I don't have a choice.'

'Fine. We'll sort it in the morning.'

'You can sort it in the morning,' she said, then she relaxed. 'But I'll help.'

'That's big of you.'

'It's the least I can do.'

There was a moment's silence, then something in his face changed. 'It seems you're between a rock and a hard place,' he said at last.

'You'd better believe it.'

'We'll sort this mess somehow.'

But that made her eyes flash. 'It's not a mess. It's a little girl called Lily. A little girl who's your daughter.'

That made him wince, but Forrest was tugging Misty's hand, demanding attention. 'I see the swing. Misty, Misty, will you come and push me?'

'Sure,' Misty told him and then turned back to Angus. 'Lily's just woken and she's due for a feed. There's everything you need in this bag. Is it okay if Forrest and I explore the garden?' She softened a little. 'Please... Forrest desperately needs one-on-one time and there's been so little...'

And he got it. The strain in her eyes. The exhaustion. The need. Something lurched inside and strangely it wasn't just pity. She was a woman with her back to the wall and she was fighting with everything she had. Not just for herself, though, he thought with a flash of insight. For the little boy at her side. Maybe even for Lily?

She could have just handed Lily over to the authorities, he thought. Why hadn't she?

Courage?

Where had that word come from? Wherever it had, when he spoke again he did so gently.

'I can cope,' he told her. 'I'll put the lasagne in the oven and figure out a bottle. Dinner in half an hour? Forrest, there's a cubby house round the back of the house and strawberries in the vegetable patch. See you soon.'

He took a deep breath and reached in and lifted this little girl, who might or might not be his daughter, from her car seat. Surely he could block the resemblance. Misty had cared for this little one. Surely he could, too?

Or maybe he couldn't.

Lily did more than wake when he lifted her from the car, she opened her small mouth and screamed. He took her inside and then fought panic as he tried to take stock.

He had a baby.

His baby?

When he'd first looked at her she'd been sleeping, and in repose the likeness to his baby brother had been remarkable. The piercing pain, the tug of immediate connection, had left him floundering. He hadn't been able to refute fatherhood straight off.

Now though, with her entire being arched into howls, there was no resemblance at all, but weirdly the connection seemed to be growing. He looked down at her and he thought, what a mother she'd been gifted, a woman who'd conned him, who'd lied, who'd been in jail…for what? A woman whose drug use and lifestyle must have meant this little one was lucky to even be alive.

But at least she'd been blessed with an aunt who cared. Misty. Despite his shock, his bewilderment, his total confusion, he did sense the care.

What was her story?

And Forrest? He glanced out the window and saw Forrest was already on the swing. Misty was pushing him, but only a little. Very small swings for a little boy who seemed fearful of the world.

But as he swung, Misty had her face turned upwards towards the sinking sun. The last rays would be warm on her face and she seemed to be soaking them in almost greedily. He had the impression that she was a woman for whom such moments of peace, without responsibilities cramming in from all sides, were rare indeed.

Responsibilities. This little girl.

'All right, sweetheart, let's get you changed and fed,' he told her, feeling strangely confident. Which he was. Sort of.

Not only had he been Forrest's age when his little brother was born, old enough to help with the caring, he'd also done a stint as a neonatal intern. He knew the routine—you changed before you fed. Babies often dozed after a full feed and who wanted to wake and change them then?

Which meant he had to spread her change mat on the kitchen table, then wrangle a flailing baby—easier said than done—and figure out how to clean her. Sheesh, he should have prepared…

Then he had to wait an interminable thirty seconds while the pre-prepared bottle—thank you, Misty—heated in the microwave. While he managed to pour himself a much-needed beer. While she kept on screaming.

He needed another hand—or six—but somehow he succeeded in carrying Lily, bottle and beer out to the veranda.

'Done,' he told his…daughter? 'Who's a clever…?'

And then he hesitated. A clever what?

A clever daddy?

Some things were too hard to take in. Just do what comes next, he told himself, and manoeuvred the teat into the little girl's mouth.

And then, mercifully, blessedly, there was silence.

She stood in the gorgeous garden with the sun's sinking rays on her face, pushing Forrest gently back and forth and she thought: *it's done*.

She'd listened to Lily's wails of indignation that her demands hadn't been instantly met. She'd been torn—what was she doing, leaving her niece to the mercy of someone she didn't know? But then she'd heard the screen door slam above the wails, she'd glanced up and seen Angus settle himself with his bundle of noise—and then, blessedly, she'd heard silence.

He was feeding his daughter. *His* daughter. There'd obviously be DNA testing to be done, but the look she'd seen in his eyes…he knew she was his. And now he was sitting on his veranda feeding his little girl and she thought she just might have engineered an outcome that wouldn't rack her with guilt for the rest of her life.

The thought of going down the adoption route had been doing her head in. Yes, there'd be great parents out there, but this little girl was her niece, she was Forrest's half-sister, she was…family.

To Misty's mother and sister, the concept of family had meant nothing. Or actually, it had. It meant they'd known they could depend on Misty, no matter how outrageous their demands had been. She recalled a midnight phone call from a police station the night before her final exams as a med student. 'Misty, come and bail me out, will you? And bring my red dress and black stilettoes because there's a party I'm missing…' It had been her mother, but it could equally have been her sister.

The pair of them had been out for a good time, no matter what. The responsibility had been all Misty's.

But now some of that responsibility might have shifted. She glanced again through the trees and saw man and baby, settled together. He looked almost like an expert, cradling Lily in the crook of his arm, bottle perfectly tilted, a beer in the other hand.

She could see why Jancie had chosen him, she thought. He was almost absurdly good looking, long and lean, superbly muscled and tanned from surf and sun. Jancie would have described him as hot, she thought, but right now his looks weren't what she was focused on. He looked settled, as though all was right with his world.

And she thought, to be like this… To have a home, unencumbered by debt. To work only four days a week because you wanted to have fun the rest of the time… If she had that, how much difference could she make to Forrest's life?

But strangely it wasn't envy she was feeling but…what? Hunger?

She thought of the two weeks Jancie had spent with this man. Two weeks of abandonment to pleasure, with no thought except fun and sexual desire.

That wasn't what she was hungry for, she thought, surely? She couldn't even imagine what such a time would be like. But she could still see Angus. She could still sense the innate gentleness that had come through, despite his shock. She could sense the underlying warmth in his eyes, and she thought, someone to care…someone to sit on her veranda…

Well, that wasn't going to happen. Number one, the floorboards of her veranda were rotten—she'd rebuilt the stumps leading to the front door, but that was as far as she'd been able to manage.

What if she could stay here?

Where was her mind taking her? To a seduction scene? She wasn't like Jancie. She almost managed a smile at that, thinking of Jancie's gorgeous image, though produced at what cost? Even when they were small, any available funds left from her mother's extravagance had been channelled Jancie's way. Her mother had been fond—or as fond as she was capable—of the pretty Jancie. Misty had been an accident, unwanted from the start.

So what was she thinking? Seduction? Was there any way she could con this guy into taking not only Lily, but also herself and Forrest? What about Alice, her grandmother? And who was looking after the islanders while she was away? Martin was a competent nurse, but in an emergency...

Okay, forget the hunger, forget the stupid feelings the sight of this guy cradling his baby was creating. Just be grateful that, for now, things seemed to be working. She needed to tie up the threads and go home.

'I like it here.' Forrest's small voice cut across her thoughts. He'd been swinging almost dreamily, as though this was time out for him, too.

Once this drama with Lily was over, she'd be able to spend time...

As long as Alice didn't get worse.

As long as there were no dramas among the community of Kirra Island. The increasing number of tourists were creating a nightmare of a workload and it showed no signs of stopping.

As long as...

Oh, for heaven's sake, she told herself, stop being Eeyore. Just soak up this moment and then sleep. From now on she needed to steel herself to step away. She'd checked Angus's work commitments via his online booking system before she'd come. He worked Monday to Thursday only, therefore tomorrow there'd be no need to reschedule appointments, no excuse for him not to take over Lily's care.

So please, tomorrow this nightmare would be over?

To say he had a bad night was an understatement.

As part of his training Angus had spent six months working with babies who were premature or ill, and he'd prided himself on his handling skills. 'A baby wrangler,' one of the nurses had labelled him when he'd managed to get a desperately ill premmie to settle. And when he'd seen tiny George Drakos carried home in his parents' arms four weeks later, he'd felt a surge of pride. He'd felt he was good with babies ever since.

But he wasn't good with Lily. He fed her, but she didn't seem to appreciate it. She whimpered as he and Misty and Forrest ate their lasagne. She whimpered as Misty resolutely took Forrest's hand and headed for the bedrooms he'd shown her to. 'Goodnight and good luck,' she said and an hour later, with Lily still complaining, he was starting to realise what she meant.

He changed her and fed her again. He walked the floor with her. He took her outside to show her the garden in the moonlight. She wasn't impressed. He read the medical notes Misty had left for him and thought about clinical care of babies born to drug-affected mothers. With Lily in his arms he headed to his own books and read up on the symptoms, but they didn't seem to fit. Nothing seemed overtly wrong—Lily seemed just plain pissed off with being in a world that…didn't seem to want her?

His heart lurched a bit at that thought, but by then Lily's wails had turned to screams, the noise was doing his head in and he had to walk a bit more.

All the time he was half expecting—certainly hoping— for Misty to appear and offer to help. She and Forrest were sleeping at the far end of the house. There was a dining room and living room dividing them from the kitchen where he paced, but surely she could hear? He knew she needed sleep, but at three in the morning, when feeding, crooning still failed, when nothing worked, it was hard not to feel anger.

What sort of woman could just hand a baby over and walk away?

But she hadn't walked away. He could head to her bedroom right now and tell her to take her back.

His pride kicked in then, but the attachment…the tug he felt when he'd first seen…his daughter?…was growing very thin indeed.

Blessedly, as dawn rose over the bend in the river, finally she sank into an exhausted sleep. He laid her in her pram and thought about bed himself.

But he knew he wouldn't sleep. So many thoughts, so much…responsibility?

He didn't do responsibility. He'd let that go ten years back, the night his family's car had slid on black ice and crashed.

The night the police had knocked on his university residence door. 'We're so sorry, sir, but we regret to tell you…'

He flinched at the memory of that moment and what had come after, of the enormity of the caring and the loss and the eventual resolution that he could never again expose himself to that sort of pain. He couldn't exist with that possibility.

And now this. A daughter?

No. Muzzy from lack of sleep, his head was doing its best to find a way out of this mess. If Lily *was* indeed his daughter, there'd have to be a way to do it without…losing himself? The concept of loving as he'd loved his family made him feel physically ill.

But some time in the night he'd read Jancie's documentation and realities were kicking in. If he really was Lily's father—and he probably was—then what? Adoption? That was messing with his head. At least in the short term, until he could figure things out, maybe he could hire a nanny? He could set up the house so nanny and baby were basically at one end, with himself at the other. He could pay whatever it took.

But he couldn't pay anyone right now.

It was six in the morning.

Six. Friday.

Swimming squad.

Every Friday, for as long as he remembered, he'd swum, with a group that varied from two to twenty. They swam in the ocean, almost a kilometre in either direction between two jetties, winter, summer, no matter what.

One of his mates—and he had lots of mates—had dragged him along in the weeks after his family had died, and fighting the surging tide and the cold water had somehow numbed the grief, the shock, the total, awful emptiness.

It was one of the reasons he never worked on Fridays. Like the kayak group on Thursdays, the swimming squad had become another pillar of his mental health. As were his mates, an assorted group of friends who seemed to have the same attitude to commitment that he did.

So now, with Lily finally sleeping, he had the urge to be with those friends. Maybe giving them a quick heads up about the baby before he hit the water, seeing their reactions—which he imagined would be just the same as his— might help. And then he'd be in the water again, blocking out the world.

Once he thought it, the need was overpowering. His whole overtired, shocked body seemed to be screaming for that release.

Could he?

Misty and Forrest had gone to bed at eight the night before and he'd heard not a sound since. He acknowledged that Misty had been exhausted, but she'd now slept for ten hours. He'd—nobly?—kept the dividing doors closed to block out the noise, but she hadn't come out to check.

Lily would surely sleep for at least a couple of hours. If he rolled the pram to the other end of the house, opened Misty's door and left the pram beside it, then he could head off for his longed-for swim. Lily shouldn't wake before he returned, but even if she did, he'd leave a note in the pram.

Surely that was fair. He'd given Misty a good night's sleep.

Don't overthink it, he told himself. Misty's been responsible for over a week. Surely one more morning won't hurt.

Just do it.

'Misty, Lily's crying and the man's not looking after her.'

She emerged from such a deep sleep that she felt almost as if she'd been drugged.

Forrest had slept with her, in the great king-sized bed. With Forrest cradled beside her, with a responsible adult— a doctor!—taking care of Lily, with no islanders about to plead for emergency medical aid, she'd slept like she hadn't remembered sleeping since she'd learned that Jancie had died.

She could sleep still. She clung to the last vestiges of slumber, but Forrest was up, standing beside her, his voice anxious.

Well, what was new? Forrest was always anxious.

'Misty, she's crying and she's all by herself.'

That brought her awake, fast. She sat up as though she'd been hit with a cattle prod.

How many times had she woken like this? To medical need from the islanders, or worse, from family drama. 'Doctor Calvert, we have your nephew here. Your sister's not capable of caring for him and he seems to be alone.'

Or… 'Doctor Calvert, we've just arrested your sister and there seems to be a child…'

And that last appalling time… 'Doctor Calvert, are you Jancie Calvert's sister? I'm sorry to have to tell you this, but we believe your sister died five weeks ago and there's a baby…'

She'd gone to sleep the night before almost as soon as her head had hit the pillow, but she'd heard Lily as she'd drifted off, the plaintive whimpers of a baby who couldn't figure what she needed, but knew there was something wrong in her world.

But Angus had closed the doors between the guest bedroom and the living areas. She'd hardly been able to hear the whimpers and she'd done enough research on this guy to know that she wasn't any more capable of solving Lily's problems than he was. Forrest had needed reassurance—these last weeks had almost shattered his fragile security. Priorities, she'd decided. She'd carefully, deliberately, closed her heart to the whimpers, hugged Forrest close and let them both sleep.

Now, though, Lily's cries were closer. Much closer. She looked across to the door which she'd shut the night before. It was slightly open and the wails seemed as though they were right on the other side.

'I peeped out and he's not there,' Forrest whispered. 'The man.'

And Misty closed her eyes for a millisecond as responsibility swept back over her like a grey, fog-soaked rug. Last night she'd gone to sleep thinking maybe, just maybe, there could be a happy ending for baby Lily.

Who was she kidding?

But maybe Angus was just in the shower, she thought. She'd had to do that herself, let her cry while she did the urgent stuff.

But couldn't a shower have waited?

By this time she was out of bed, padding over the thickly carpeted floor and tugging open the door. The door led to a passage, which led to the vast, gorgeous sitting room she'd been almost too tired to see properly the night before. But

Lily wasn't in the sitting room. Her pram was tucked right beside their door.

'Was this door open?' she asked Forrest and he nodded, looking scared. Was there something in his aunt's voice that was scaring him?

The feeling sweeping over her was scaring *her*. She'd reached the pram. Lily was a ball of misery, red-faced and screaming, her entire being wailing for help Misty had started thinking she didn't know how to give.

Instinctively she scooped her up and laid her against her shoulder.

'Hey. Hey, it's okay, little one. There.'

She cradled and rocked until the screams turned to whimpers and she was able to look into the pram. A note.

Six a.m. and all's well. I swim with a squad for two hours every Friday morning. I'll skip coffee with the guys, which means I should be home around nine. She's just had a full bottle and is soundly asleep, so hoping you might not hear from her until I get back.'

'Misty?' Forrest's hand was clutching her nightgown, his small face screwed tight with anxiety. 'Misty, you look angry.'

'Not angry,' she said and closed her eyes, laying her cheek on Lily's downy head. 'Just…reassessing.'

'What does that mean?'

'It means I thought Dr Firth might be…might be someone who could love Lily,' she whispered. 'But, Forrest, I think we might have to think of something else.'

'I'd like to stay here longer,' Forrest said plaintively.

'I'm sorry, Forrest, but that's not possible.'

'But we can't just leave Lily.'

'We're not leaving Lily,' Misty told him, trying to keep the desolate acceptance she was feeling from her voice. 'We're taking her with us.'

* * *

The swim was great. With his head down, powering through the waves, feeling the surge of the sea, the chill of the ocean currents, this had been his time out ever since his family had died. The first half-hour or so he let his mind go blank. Slowly, though, as his body found its rhythm, thoughts of the future seeped in. And finally the future seemed doable.

When he'd first started swimming all those years ago, that future had simply seemed like the possibility of surviving, the prospect of being able to take one step after another without grief leaving him crushed and flailing. Then it had been the idea of getting back into his studies. Of somehow opening his books again.

And gradually his world had opened wider. The last Friday he'd swum he'd been looking forward to a weekend with Lisle.

He'd been seeing Lisle for a few weeks now—nothing serious, but she was fun. The last thing he needed—ever—was more emotional commitment, but Lisle understood. Any girl he dated had to.

As did the patients he treated. He gave good service, but with the first hint of emotional dependence his books were suddenly closed. There were other doctors in his clinic they could move to—for heaven's sake, some of his colleagues even seemed to like the emotional stuff.

So this morning, while it took a while for the shock to ease, the ability to look forward finally emerged. To plan his future, but to also plan his boundaries.

It seemed he had a daughter.

Nothing was proven yet. This seemed like a giant con, yet he knew instinctively that there was nothing of the con woman about Misty.

Had he been conned by Jancie?

Obviously yes.

He needed space to sort it out, but Misty was giving him no time. He should feel anger, but if he believed her—and it seemed he did—she'd been given no time either. They were as shocked as each other.

As he swam, the idea of accepting responsibility seemed like the only option. If he was the father...well, fair enough.

His swimming mind was busy making plans. If Lily really was his, how would his life have to change? That created a groundswell of panic that almost had him faltering. But the swim was helping clear his head and he had an hour or so to sort something out of this mess.

A good nanny would be essential. Funding wouldn't be a problem. With a nanny attached, she could even spend time with her aunt. School holidays? That sort of thing.

It all made sense and by the time he climbed from the water he was pretty much resigned.

He just had to go home and tell Misty how things would be.

CHAPTER THREE

WHEN HE GOT home there were suitcases on the veranda. And a pram.

Had she decided to leave? Straight away?

That produced a moment's panic, then he took a couple of deep breaths and switched himself back into swim mode, forcing himself to think this through.

The pram was with the baggage. That meant…she was taking Lily with her?

Confused, he edged past the baggage and headed for the kitchen.

What met him was a scene of domesticity. Misty was sitting at the kitchen table, cradling Lily. This was a cleaner, fresher version of Misty. Her curls were neatly brushed. She was wearing clean jeans and a shirt, her face looked scrubbed and somehow…she looked a little younger? That'd be from a decent sleep, he thought, congratulating himself on giving her that. The baby in her arms was absorbed in a bottle—damn, she'd woken earlier than expected, but at least Misty had had the night off.

Forrest was intent on dipping toast soldiers into a boiled egg. He glanced up as Angus appeared and then quickly down again, as though scared someone might have caught him looking.

Misty didn't look up from the baby.

'You're leaving?' Possibly it wasn't the wisest start to a conversation, but it was front and centre in his mind.

'Good morning to you, too,' Misty said. She glanced up briefly, then went back to focusing on keeping the bottle steady, keeping Lily's feed undisturbed. 'Did you have a good swim?'

'A great swim,' he told her. 'I'm glad you found breakfast.'

'We found everything we needed,' she said. 'Except you.' And then, as Forrest finished his last toast soldier, she turned to him. 'Forrest, could you go clean your teeth and then maybe have one last swing in Dr Firth's garden? We only have half an hour before the taxi arrives.'

'You've booked a taxi?' he asked, cautiously, as Forrest cast him a fearful look and then bolted past him for the door—as if Angus himself was something to be feared.

'I have. I've made a mistake,' she told him. 'So I need to fix it as fast as possible. We have a flight at midday.'

'We?'

'The three of us.'

He wasn't sure where this was going. He stood against the wall, feeling its solidity behind him. He needed it. Last night his world had changed and it seemed it was about to change again.

'You're taking Lily home?'

'No,' she said shortly. 'I told you, I can't do that. I've looked at it every which way. I don't have the resources to care for her and I can't afford to fall for her…any deeper than I already have. But I've been in contact with Social Services from the moment they found me. They placed her in my custody. There seemed no choice. But there is a choice now and they know what I'm doing. So…' She took a deep breath and seemed to brace.

'The idea was that if you didn't want, or couldn't accept,

custody then I'd hand her to them,' she told him. 'It was always part of the plan when I brought her to you. She'll go into foster care—and you needn't look like that, you're a doctor, you know foster carers are awesome. Lily will only be given to carers who have the time and resources to give her what she needs, affection and security. From there she'll go on the list for adoption. There are so many potential parents out there aching for a baby—she'll find the loving home she deserves.'

'I thought,' he said slowly, 'that I agreed I might take her.'

'And then you proved you couldn't.'

'I'm sorry, what?'

'You walked out on her. You had the responsibility for one night and you ended up propping her outside my room and leaving.'

'That's hardly fair. I knew you'd wake.'

'You knew no such thing,' Misty snapped. Lily had finished her bottle and was now drifting towards sleep, cradled against Misty's breast, as if she belonged. Misty glanced down and her face changed. And Angus thought…was that grief he saw? Regardless, her voice softened.

'You know nothing about me,' she whispered, still looking at her niece. 'Nothing. My sister was on drugs. She was totally irresponsible, so how do you know I'm not the same?'

'I assumed…'

'You assumed what? That I hadn't taken sleeping pills or worse? That I'd wake and jump straight back into caring mode?'

'She's survived this far, so you can't be all that bad.' He said it lightly, even attempting a smile. He didn't get one in return.

'You didn't know that.'

'You have Forrest.' He was starting to sound defensive and that annoyed him. 'You obviously care.'

'Does Forrest look like a child who's been cared for his whole life?'

'You explained…'

'And you believed,' she said flatly. 'Because you wanted to go swimming. You're a medical professional. Even without the personal ties here, to walk out on the job without handover…how responsible is that?'

'Misty…'

'Enough,' she said wearily. 'This was a dumb plan from the start. I was too tired to think straight. Yes, I needed to let you know about Lily, but it was dumb to think you'd take one look at her and turn into a loving dad.' She closed her eyes for a moment and he could still see pain. 'But you see, I had a romantic, stupid hope that you'd fall so hard that fostering, adoption, would be out of the question.'

'I do want her.' But did he? He heard his own uncertainty and could have kicked himself.

'Then you'll need to fight for her.' She rose, lifting Lily with her. 'You know, once upon a time, when I was a little girl, maybe about six or seven, our next-door neighbour's cat had kittens and I wanted one. I wanted one so badly. But Mrs Baginski told me I could only have one if I paid five dollars. She said I could take the kitten home and ask Mum. So I ran all the way home and pleaded with Mum, but of course there was no five dollars.'

'Ouch.'

'Ouch is right,' she said. 'So I had to take the kitten back and I cried so hard, and Mrs Baginski seemed really sad, too, but she said if my mum wouldn't pay five dollars, then she wouldn't think the kitten was worth anything and she wouldn't care for it. And you know what? She was right.'

'But…' To say he was confused was an understatement. 'What's that got to do with me?'

'Everything. I was about to hand you your daughter for free. I should have known better.'

'You mean…you're comparing Lily to a kitten?' His voice was incredulous.

'I know what I mean,' she said. 'And I think you do, too.'

'If she's my daughter… I have rights.'

'Then fight for them,' she said, suddenly harsh. 'I became Lily's carer because there was no one else and she's definitely my niece, but with parentage unproven, you have no rights at all. You know now that she may or may not be your daughter. Now it's up to you.'

'I've told you. I'll take her.'

'That's big of you, I don't think,' she snapped. 'How will you take care of her?'

'I'll sort it. I'll get a nanny.'

'She doesn't need a nanny. She needs love.'

'I'll take care…'

'I said love,' she said, even more harshly. 'And I was an idiot to think that could happen on sight. So now she's coming back to Brisbane with me and I'll hand her over to foster care. The steps for adoption will begin. If you want any say, then you'll need to fight.'

'Fight…'

'For one, you'll need to prove to the authorities, not just to me, that you're her dad. You'll need to put in a court application for DNA testing, then you'll need to prove to Social Services that you're responsible. Then prove, *really prove,* that you want custody, that she'll get a good life with you. And believe me, after the start she's had, Social Services are going to be tough to convince. But that's my equivalent of the five-dollar test, Dr Firth, and after your actions this morning, it's set in stone. Now if you'll excuse me, I need to give Forrest one last push on the swing.'

'You can't just go.'

'Watch me,' she said, weariness coming back into her voice. 'You have no grounds to ask me to stay. I made a mistake by coming.'

'You didn't make a mistake. I needed to know…of her existence.'

'Well, now you do. It's up to you what you do next.'

He glanced again at Lily, at her little face drifting into replete sleep, and his gut seemed to lurch. Then he looked up at Misty's face and what he saw there…

Desolation? Pain? This was killing her, he thought suddenly. Handing over a baby…

'You already love her,' he said, with a note of discovery, and she flinched.

'I can't afford to.' Her voice dropped to almost a whisper. 'I just…can't. My grandmother… Forrest…they need me so much and if I don't work there's no money for anything. This trip has already cost me far more than I can afford, so please, Dr Firth, stand aside and let us go."

He had no choice. He helped put her gear into the taxi. Then he stood on the veranda as she tucked Lily into her baby seat, as she fixed Forrest into his seat belt and then she climbed in after him. Forrest gave a very tentative wave, but Misty stared straight ahead.

He stood, feeling like…a king-sized rat?

Maybe he should be relieved, he thought, as the taxi disappeared. He didn't want responsibility. The last thing he wanted was family.

Misty had family in spades.

She was ridding herself of it, though, or at least part of it. She was about to pass Lily on to unknown bureaucrats, so nameless people could take care of his daughter.

His daughter?

The whole situation could still be wrong, he told himself.

Maybe this was the way to go, put the child in care until it was proven either way.

The child.

His daughter.

No. Don't think of her like that, wait until it's proven. Relax.

But the confusion he was feeling about Lily was also overshadowed by his impressions of the woman who'd just left. Of the pain he'd seen on her face.

She already loved this baby.

And suddenly he was hit by a sweep of emotions so strong it made him feel dizzy. Was she feeling what he'd felt? The pain of loss... The sheer effort of ensuring he never got so close again...

Misty loved. He knew it. She loved Forrest and she also loved this unknown grandmother. There were probably more people she loved, who knew? And now she was giving away a baby...because she loved?

The story of the kitten was suddenly front and centre. He could see a six-year-old Misty carrying a tiny kitten home to her mother and could imagine what reaction she'd have received. He found himself flinching on her behalf, then remembering the pain he'd seen in her eyes as she'd left.

She'd wanted this to be a happy outcome, he thought. Maybe she'd hoped that one look at Lily would have seen him melt, that the love she obviously already had would be instantly felt by him.

That was a fool's hope. He didn't do love.

The memory of those last few days by his little brother's bedside were suddenly crowding in again, as they'd crowded in over and over ever since...

Hell.

He raked his fingers through his salt-stiff hair and tried to sort facts from the myriad of unwanted emotions.

One thing stood out—it had to. If Lily was indeed his daughter, then despite his emotions, despite unwanted memories, he had to act. There was something hard wired inside him that absolutely rejected the idea of handing her over to foster care. It wasn't love, he told himself—how could it be? It was duty.

The duty that had seen him walk away this morning? Leave her outside Misty's door?

That had been reasonable, he told himself, but maybe he shouldn't have… Shouldn't have…

Hell, he was so confused. But as he stood there watching the empty driveway, but still seeing the conflict on Misty's face, he knew he had to do something.

She'd said their plane left at midday. It was now only a little after nine and from here it was less than half an hour's drive to the airport. That meant she'd have two hours to wait for the plane, but she'd clearly thought it was preferable to spend time there rather than here.

Two hours.

Come on, Firth, he told himself. *You don't want family. You don't want this. You were conned into fatherhood, so why should you care?*

It wasn't Misty who conned you. He was arguing with himself. *And it's not her baby. Why should she care?*

She does and you know damned well that it's going to kill her to hand Lily over to the authorities.

He stood silent, the minutes ticking by as he fought conflicting emotions. But there was a bottom line. No matter how much he'd been tricked into fatherhood, if Lily was indeed his daughter then the responsibility was his. Misty had told him what his five-dollar test was. He'd need to go through bureaucratic hoops to win her back. Maybe he could do that, but meanwhile Misty would be handing over…a baby she already loved?

Was that his imagination? Fantasy?

He knew it wasn't.

He hardly knew Misty, but still he flinched inwardly at the thought of her handing her—his?—baby to strangers.

She didn't deserve that sort of pain.

So circumvent it, he told himself harshly. Take responsibility.

Was he nuts? How much more sensible would it be to head for his bedroom and get the sleep he hadn't had the night before?

He couldn't do it. Something he didn't understand was demanding he act and it was demanding he act *now*.

CHAPTER FOUR

AIRPORTS WERE NOT designed for kids and they had two hours to wait. But Forrest didn't complain. He sat, silent and stoic. He'd been silent and stoic ever since Misty had gained custody.

This was what Jancie had taught him, to shut up and not bother her. In the year since Misty had cared for him, there'd been glimpses of the child he might be. She'd seen it this morning as he'd swung in Angus's wonderful garden, his face alive with effort and wonder. Then she'd seen his face shut down again as she'd bundled him into the taxi.

She had picture books in her luggage—she'd given him a couple and he was pretending to read, but that was a learned response, too.

Oh, Forrest…

And, oh, Lily.

She was struggling not to cry. This had been a mad trip, a desperate hope that somehow she could hand responsibility over without searing guilt. So much for that.

Then Forrest glanced up from his book and stared back at the security gate they'd passed through half an hour ago. 'He's here,' he said, almost in a whisper.

'Who…?'

She turned and there he was—Dr Angus Firth. He was wearing jeans and a loose, linen shirt, his sun-bleached hair combed but still unruly, a faded leather holdall swinging from his shoulder.

He looked like a surfer heading off to find some waves. As though he should have a surfboard under his arm.

He stood, searching the crowed airport terminal—and then he found them. And there was the smile she'd seen in the media reports, maybe the same smile that had made Jancie decide this would be a good father for her child. It was a smile that seemed almost wicked, a mix of concentration and fun. A smile that said, 'I can do this, but I can enjoy myself, too.'

It was a smile that took her breath away.

Oh, for heaven's sake, this was hardly the time to turn hormonal, she told herself fiercely. Why was he here? He obviously wasn't here to claim his baby. His carry-all said he was a traveller.

Then, to her surprise, Forrest raised his arm and gave him a wave. It wasn't what you could call a big wave, but Angus saw and waved back, and started weaving through the general airport muddle to reach them.

Because they were early, Misty had been able to snag a couple of seats right by the windows. She'd hoped Forrest would look at planes. He hadn't, but it had given them a slight oasis away from the bustle. Angus headed straight for them and her illusion of oasis was gone.

What now?

'I'm glad I caught you,' he said, by way of greeting. His smile caught her and held—for long enough to do something to her insides that she had no hope of dealing with—and then he stooped and addressed Forrest.

'I've decided to come with you,' he said, almost as if he was suggesting he might go with them on a walk to the corner store. 'If that's okay with your aunty.'

'You mean...my Misty?'

'With your Misty,' he agreed.

'She is my aunty,' Forrest explained, 'but she's my Misty. She says that's what she is. Gran's my gran, and Gran's Misty's gran, too, but Misty's my Misty.'

'That's great,' he said and smiled at Misty. 'So, Forrest's Misty, is it okay if I come with you?'

'W-Why?' She could scarcely get the words out.

'I've decided that I can't let you go alone,' he told her. 'If Lily does need to be adopted, if she is my daughter, then I can't let you wear that decision yourself.'

Whoa. What was there in that statement that made her world seem to still?

I can't let you go alone...

The last ten days had been an exhausting, tragic roller coaster. She'd never felt so alone in her life as when she'd made the decision that she couldn't keep Lily, but now...

Had this man guessed the thought of handing Jancie's baby—Forrest's sister—over for adoption was killing her? She knew she had to do it, for all of their sakes, but to actually walk away... She knew she must, but she also knew that she'd bear the weight of this decision for the rest of her life.

It was a burden she was bracing herself to carry, but now Angus Firth was offering to share.

Since the call had come to tell her of Jancie's death, she'd held herself rigidly under control, but right now emotions were threatening to overwhelm her. She was too tired, too confused, too...whatever.

Crying had been mocked and/or slapped out of Misty Calvert a long time ago. But the combination of this guy's presence, his smile, the way he'd stooped and faced Forrest, the way Forrest had glanced at her and made what seemed to her to be a momentous decision... The way he'd said *my Misty*.

The way Angus had said, 'I can't let you go alone.'

She couldn't help it, her eyes started to well.

And Angus noticed. Without a word he sat on the seat beside her and produced a large, blue-on-blue man's hand-kerchief. He handed it across and deftly removed Lily from her arms.

The motion was so swift, so decisive, that she blinked the tears back and stared at him in astonishment. As her gaze met his, his smile returned, directed straight at her. And tangentially, stupidly, she found herself thinking: *If this guy was my doctor, I'd be finding all the excuses in the world to go and see him.* If this was his bedside manner, then his clinic should be overbooked for months.

But he didn't do overbooked clinics, she reminded herself. He was a part-time doctor with rigid boundaries. Smiles, empathy, care would only be available four days a week, nine to five.

Like his care for Lily. He'd care for her only when he couldn't find someone else to do the caring.

So why was he really coming?

She took a deep breath and handed the handkerchief back.

'What's wrong with my handkerchief?' he demanded.

'I don't need it,' she said, grabbing tissues from her ca-pacious carry bag. 'But even if I did, I wouldn't blow my nose on that. Is that …a *monogram*?'

And at that his grin widened. He held it up and there, in the corner, was a discreet embroidered AF.

She stared at it in disbelief, everything else suddenly pushed into the background.

'You get your handkerchiefs embroidered?' she stam-mered.

'Not guilty.' He looked a bit self-conscious, but then he shrugged. 'My mum sewed. She…well, she had a fall from a horse when she was a kid and hurt her back—she damaged T11 and T12. She was in a wheelchair and had a fair bit of pain. The doctors said if she'd done a better job of breaking she'd have been in less pain, but what mobility she had she really valued. When things were really hurting she used to sew. Our...*my* house is thus full of embroidered table cloths, tapestries... You might have noticed the patchwork quilt on your bed last night?'

She'd been too tired to even notice. 'I'm... I'm sorry,' she stammered, but she looked again at the handkerchiefs. 'So she embroidered handkerchiefs for her son?

'Sons,' he said, a trifle stiffly. And then the smile returned again. 'It's okay, she wasn't nuts. She knew the chance of either of us using monogrammed handkerchiefs...well, a snowball's chance in a bushfire is a decent analogy. But my father was called Andrew and he loved her enough to use them with pride. When they died, I discovered a cache that took up half a shelf in the linen cupboard and, sod it, I've been using them ever since.'

When they died...

There was enough in that to have her look at him sharply, to catch her breath. *They?* Did they die together? But he was looking down at Lily, moving on. 'Hey, she's gone to sleep.'

'Of course she has,' Misty said, somehow collecting herself. 'She'll be storing energy so she can wail at full strength on the plane and have everyone hate me.'

'They can hate me,' he told her. 'I'm coming, too.'

She took a deep breath. 'You're... I think you'd better explain.'

He nodded, serious again. 'Okay. I hope it's okay with you, but I've reorganised the tickets so we can sit together. You'll need to reconfirm at the gate—I gather there'll be no problem swapping back if you wish...'

'You're really coming with us?'

Reorganising tickets seemed small fry in the scheme of things. In *his* scheme of things.

'I figured…' He took a deep breath and met her gaze full on. His smile had gone now, replaced by…what? She didn't understand. She saw confusion, resolution, but also…fear? As a family doctor she was used to reading expressions and the look she saw on his face now…

She was reminded suddenly of a farmer she'd treated a while back, a guy with a wife, three small children, a struggling dairy farm. He'd come because he'd found a lump in his groin. He'd actually found it weeks before, but it had taken all that time to gather the courage to make an appointment.

The lump had turned out to be a benign cyst, but when he'd first walked into her clinic his expression had been exactly the same as the one Angus was wearing.

'Angus, you don't have to do this,' she told him. This wasn't a potentially cancerous growth he was facing—it was something that might be even bigger.

Fatherhood?

'I know,' he said, faltering a little, which cemented her impression of fear. 'And maybe…maybe things won't work out. But I need time to come to terms with what you've told me and I don't think I can have that while Lily goes into foster care. Not while I…while *we* won't have control over what's happening in her life.'

'So what are you proposing?'

'That you keep control for a while.' He grimaced. 'No, don't look like that. I accept that you can't care for her. But I realised almost as soon as you walked out that what you care about most is Lily's well-being. So I agree, leaving her with me was a risk you couldn't take. Also, I have no rights to take care of her. There's no proof that she's my daughter. No, I'm not attempting to deny it, but legalities are there for a reason. I need to prove fatherhood, for both Lily's and my sakes. But while I do, I don't think I want to go down the foster care route. I want…to get to know my daughter.'

'And once you do?'

He paused at that. He sat silent for a moment and then raked his sun-bleached hair with his long fingers. All at once he seemed young, Misty thought. Vulnerable.

This man was nearly thirty years old, a doctor, very much an adult, but all at once she had the impression that underneath he was a scared kid, struggling to find a way to cope with a situation that was almost overwhelming.

For a moment she felt sympathy. He'd been conned by Jancie, and Lily had arrived seemingly out of nowhere. It must have been a bombshell, shattering his lovely, carefree existence, yet here he was, struggling to find the right thing to do.

But he was an adult, she told herself, and there was no room in her crowded world for sympathy. Nor could she be distracted by the way he was looking, which was big, sexy and gorgeous. The fact that he was now holding a baby only managed to accentuate his sexiness. The women around them were glancing sideways and some weren't even bothering to do it subtly. She could see why Jancie had chosen him, she thought. Eye candy didn't come close to describing him.

Don't! she told herself frantically. Don't you dare think about how he looks. This is *not* the time to get distracted.

When was there ever time to get distracted?

'So what are you suggesting?' she managed to say, and if her words came out sounding a bit strangled, she couldn't help herself. But the words themselves seemed to make both of them move on. He quit the hair raking and met her gaze.

'Is your house big enough to accommodate me?' he asked. 'For maybe a month or so? For however long it takes bureaucracy—and you—to trust me?'

And that took her breath away all over again. She stared at him open mouthed and he reached up and tilted her chin, closing her lips.

'There's no need to look so shocked,' he said. 'I checked out Kirra Island on the internet in the taxi on the way here. There's holiday accommodation. It's almost the end of holiday season, so I have the alternative to rent somewhere nearby. I've found a good place that's available, close to the town and medical clinic, but if you have room, I'm thinking maybe you'd feel better if Lily stayed near you.'

'I don't… I can't…'

'You can't take care of her any longer,' he said, gently now. 'I get that. So what I'm saying is that I'll take care of her. I'll take responsibility.'

'But your job…'

'You already know I'm a part-time doctor. Our clinic is huge—sixteen doctors. My absence will scarcely be noticed.'

What sort of world was it when a doctor's absence didn't make a difference? That was astounding all by itself, but there were bigger issues crowding her mind right now.

'So you want…you want to stay with us?'

'Is there room?'

'I guess,' she said, trying to get her confused mind to function. 'Our clinic was started forty years ago. There was mining on the island and the population was over two thousand. The mining company built a five-bedroom doctors' residence. We never had that many doctors and now Kirra's lucky to have me.'

'You're the sole doctor?'

She was still struggling, thinking of the big, ramshackle house—but somehow in the fog she was thinking…okay, she did have room. 'Yes,' she said. 'Martin helps out. He's a nurse practitioner, but he's semi-retired. He has four Labradors and a wolfhound. Our house is big, but his dog pack is bigger. He lives down by the beach.'

'So there's room for me?'

What was he asking? That she accept another month of being responsible for Lily? Another month of falling deeper and deeper in love with her sister's baby?

As if he guessed her thoughts, he shook his head. 'Misty, I'm not asking you to form any deeper a bond with Lily than you already have. She'll be my total charge, I swear it. If you're not happy, then all you need to do is what you're intending to do now: hand her over to Social Services. I assume you have that right. I messed things up badly last night...this morning...but now I'm asking, can you give me this chance?

'I can't...'

'Do any more than you've already done?' His gaze was surprisingly gentle now, his smile suggesting empathy. 'I realise that. I'll stay out of your way as much as I can, but you can check up on us both at any time.' He hesitated. 'And, Misty, if you're the island's sole doctor and if I'm to stay for a month... If there are gaps in minding Lily, I might even be of use to you.'

'Gaps in minding a newborn? Good luck with that.'

'There might be,' he persisted. 'I remember my Mum with my little brother. She had a sling she used to carry him in while she worked. He seemed happy as a pig in mud while he was in that sling. I thought...maybe I could get my own sling? Do the odd consultation. Take the pressure off you for a bit.'

'You'd work with a baby in a sling?' She stared at him, incredulous. The vision of this man acting as a doctor, with a baby attached...

'If mums can do it, I don't see why I can't,' he told her. 'I can't see myself dealing with drunks or life-threatening injuries—and to be honest, that's not my style of medicine—but a nicely snoozing baby while I do a diabetic check or run a life insurance medical...'

'That's the style of medicine you like?'

'And no other,' he said, with a firmness that made her blink.

'We don't get much call for life insurance medicals on Kirra.'

'Then I'll do what I can. Misty, I have the plane ticket. Let me come.'

And it was said almost humbly.

Oh, for heaven's sake, what was happening here? She was so confused.

This would be more of the same, she decided—it had to be. Her entire life had been punctuated with shocks, trauma and disasters. She should be over the surge of adrenalin, the innate response of fight or flight.

Flight was her urge now. She had an almost primeval urge to run. From this man. From the way she was feeling.

Instead, here she was, in her fall-back position. Bleak acceptance.

'Fine,' she said. The word was surely churlish, but he gave her a long, assessing look, then nodded.

'I deserve nothing less,' he said. 'Misty, it seems you've been landed with something that's totally not your call. I've also been hit with a tsunami of a shock, but it was of my own making. I swear I won't add to yours. I'll look after myself and I will look after Lily. What's more, if decisions need to be made after DNA testing, then you won't be making those decisions alone. Alone sucks, Misty, and if we team up then we might just manage something good for this little girl. I'm thinking she's a victim of Jancie's machinations as well.'

We team up...

Three little words. Why did they make her feel as if they had some sort of power all on their own?

We team up...

'So can I come?'

'I...yes,' she said before she had time to think any further and he smiled, and that smile...

That smile might mean she was making a very bad decision, but it seemed the decision had been made.

'Right. Moving on,' he said. 'Do you need coffee?'

And that hit a nerve. 'I'd kill for coffee,' she admitted. Abandoning their oasis, carrying Lily and towing Forrest across to the airport cafe to buy coffee, had been too much to contemplate.

'Me, too,' he said cheerfully. 'Right, team. Misty, seeing as Lily's asleep, could I ask if you would kindly hold my daughter while I buy you coffee?'

And there it was—another statement that caused a seismic shift in her head. *My daughter?*

'I...of course.'

'And, Forrest...' he looked down at the little boy who'd stayed silent during this whole conversation '...you're not really reading those books, are you?'

'No.' It was a monosyllabic response, which was practically all she ever got from Forrest.

'And we have over an hour before we board. Let's go find you a snack and you can help me choose some glossy magazines. We need them.'

'We need them?' she asked. 'For you? I don't...'

'Need glossies yourself? That's your choice, but Forrest and I definitely need them.'

What the...? 'He probably won't be interested,' she told him, figuring she needed to tell it like it was. Forrest didn't even seem interested in the jets taking off. If they didn't interest him, magazines would hardly cut it.

But here was that smile again, a grin that was almost magnetic. 'You know, magazines have more than one use,' Angus told her, carefully sliding Lily back into her arms. 'I'm looking at the big planes out of the window, but thinking what's needed are little planes. Come on, Forrest, let's go find us some building material.'

Angus Firth was a qualified doctor. According to media reports, he was an extremely skilled surfer.

He could also build and fly paper planes better than anyone she'd ever seen.

Five minutes after they left, man and boy were back, with a large, double-strength coffee for her—she hadn't realised how much she'd needed it—snacks for the boys and a pile of expensive-looking, glossy magazines. *Yachting Holidays for the Rich and Famous*, *Glorious Gardens of the World* and *Sea Life of the Great Barrier Reef*. They were also carrying two pairs of children's scissors. While Misty tackled her coffee, the two of them knelt beside her and started construction.

It seemed the magazines hadn't been chosen for their content, but for the colour and glossiness of their paper. Yachts, gardens and sea creatures were being ruthlessly chopped into rectangles for plane construction.

And what construction! Angus made the first plane, a simple form that even Misty recognised from school days, but when it launched it flew half the length of the terminal.

'This is the Dart,' Angus told Forrest. 'It's probably the simplest design, but some still say it's the best.'

Then he helped Forrest make one. Its launch was spectacular. It flew almost all the way to the security gates and Forrest was hooked.

As were others. As their production increased, kids gravitated planewards, grabbing the planes at the end of their flight, bringing them back and then staying to watch. They were invited to help. Angus cut more rectangles and in minutes paper darts were flying everywhere.

Then Angus took things up a notch.

'This is the Sea Glider,' he told Forrest. 'She's a drifting glider that can make really respectable distances.'

Then... 'How about a Concorde? If you make the nose really sharp, you can burst a balloon with one of these beauties.'

Half an hour later the terminal was a flight path and Forrest's face was alive with excitement. And pride, Misty thought. Angus was acting as if Forrest was his kid and Forrest was even showing other kids how to make the Dart. Had Forrest ever had this before? A grown-up helping him and other kids obviously jealous of what he had?

And the construction line was growing. The F-15 Eagle '—great for twists—' was followed by The Spyder '—limited distance but, boy, can this baby turn!'

Adults were hooked as well, and when the announcement was made that their flight was delayed there wasn't a whisper of dismay. Kids, parents, businessmen and women—so many were dredging up forgotten skills and learning more.

Misty even made one herself. Her plane swooped in a long loop and hit a security guard. He launched it back at her and Forrest whooped with excitement. And so did Angus. She met his gaze, he grinned and that smile...

It was her paper plane's success that made her feel like this, she told herself.

Wasn't it?

When finally their flight was called, the whole terminal seemed disappointed, but Misty's pleasure stayed with her as they boarded. This man had transformed a dreary two hours into fun. More. He'd given Forrest joy and she could have kissed him for it.

Um…not.

But, oh, the relief of someone else caring for Forrest.

Someone else helping her.

As their flight was called, he gathered his gear and brought Forrest across to her. 'Do you need the bathroom before we board? I'll take over Lily.'

'She's still asleep,' she warned. 'Gearing up for flight mode.'

'I'm in charge of flight mode,' he told her. 'People can glare at me when she screams. Not your problem, Misty.'

And the twist in her heart when he said that…

'Be careful,' she told herself as she took Forrest's hand and headed across to the terminal facilities. 'this guy could seriously get under your skin.'

As if.

Or okay, maybe he could, she conceded. There'd been guys before, men who'd shown interest and she'd been interested in turn. Always, though, there'd been obstacles. Putting herself through med school had meant holding down two jobs as well as studying. There hadn't been room for romance. Then, almost as soon as she'd graduated, there'd been the need to provide an intermittent home for Forrest and the need to care for her grandmother. And the island's needs. What man would ever look sideways at a woman with those sorts of ties?

It hadn't stopped her looking sideways at men, though, but she'd looked in the way a child watched other kids going to parties. There was never the money for party clothes, or anyone to take her.

All her life she'd been on the outside, looking in.

So get a grip, she told herself. *You might have a few weeks coping with this guy until custody is decided, but you're an adult and charming guys are not your scene. You don't have time, now or ever.*

CHAPTER FIVE

THE FLIGHT TO Brisbane took two hours, and the ferry to Kirra another two. For all that time, plus during the messy transfer in the middle, Angus kept his promise. He cared for Lily.

To her astonishment, Misty discovered that not only had Angus organised sitting near them on the flight, he'd also upgraded them to business class. Misty and Forrest had two huge seats together. Angus and Lily were over the aisle and a row in front. They were thus apart and, not only that, he didn't refer to her once during the flight.

But she could watch him. The seat next to Angus was occupied by a middle-aged woman who looked dressed for business. Fifteen minutes into the flight, from Misty's point of view, it looked as though they were already the best of friends. When the meal was served, she was even more astonished to see the stranger taking a turn holding Lily. When Lily wailed, the woman seemed amused rather than annoyed. She and Angus looked as though they were swapping baby advice.

For Misty, who'd wrangled Forrest and Lily in cramped cattle class on the way up, and had even been abused for disturbing the peace of the guy squashed into the third seat... yeah, she was bemused, but there was also a sliver of resentment. Charm and money can get you anywhere, she thought bitterly.

But not very bitterly, because she and Forrest had this glorious time to themselves. They gazed out the window and made up stories about cloud formations. They giggled over a silly cartoon on the airline's entertainment system and discussed the menu choices like grown-ups. Forrest then tried to teach Misty how to make a Spyder from the squares Angus had cut and packed—then giggled over the impropriety of launching them. Maybe even aiming them straight at Angus?

It was the same on the ferry. Angus sat apart and was almost instantly being admired and assisted by seemingly every woman who came into his orbit. He had that *noble male doing his best* façade down to a T, but Misty didn't care—she was counting dolphins with Forrest. And when Forrest snuggled against her and went to sleep, when she felt his usually tense body relax, she could even grin as she saw two middle-aged ladies tutting over Angus's baby-changing techniques—and finally take over. Who knew what pathetic tale he was spinning? Helpless, deserted dad? It didn't matter. She and Forrest had time out.

But then they pulled up at Kirra Island's ferry port and, the moment she stepped into the terminal, her time out was over.

Cath O'Donoghue was in the queue, waiting to board for the return trip to Brisbane. Cath was her gran's cousin, and also her best friend, a woman whom Misty had known and loved from childhood.

A trip to the mainland was a big deal for most islanders. To go to Brisbane, she'd have expected Cath to be wearing her Sunday best, but instead she was wearing her gardening skirt and cardigan. There were crimson stains smeared across her shoulder and the wisping curls escaping from the unruly knot of her silver-white hair didn't completely disguise what looked like dried blood on her forehead.

And she was carrying a dog.

Misty knew this dog well—he spent a lot of his time under her kitchen table. Doozy was a muddle of dachshund, terrier—and maybe poodle? Now he was clutched to Cath's chest and she could see bloodstains on his hind quarters.

As Misty and Forrest walked through the glass terminal doors, Cath saw her and her face sagged into what looked like relief.

'Oh, Misty, you're home,' she said and burst into tears. 'Oh, my dear. Your grandmother said…she wasn't sure… oh, Misty, I need you to…' Her voice cracked on a sob, but somehow she forced herself to continue. 'Misty, I need you to…to put Doozy down.'

Misty stopped dead, staring at the elderly lady in shock.

She remembered the first time she'd met Cath's dog, five years before. Cath's husband had been a fisherman who spent most of his time in the island pub and was known for punching first, asking questions later. There'd been no question of a dog while Trevor was alive, but two months after his death Cath had quietly taken the ferry to Brisbane and come back with a half-grown, straggly pup.

He was indeed straggly, an odd shape for an odd little dog, but in Cath's eyes he was beautiful. 'He's a real doozy,' she'd beamed as Misty had given him his first injections.

Because as well as being island doctor, Misty was also the island's sometime vet.

Doozy spent a lot of his time sprawled on the floor, waiting for inevitable crumbs as Gran and Cath nattered. But there was no nattering now. White-faced, tear-streaked, Cath was staring at her with desperation.

'He's in pain, Misty.' Her words came out in a rush. 'Last night…we went for a walk on the beach path and suddenly out of nowhere there was a cat over the road. And Doozy… Doozy… Anyway, Les Irvine was driving his old truck and he didn't mean to hit him, he wasn't even driving fast. He drove us home and you know Les...he's good with animals. He said he thinks his back leg's broken. Only he thinks it might be higher up, in the pelvis. So we rang the Brisbane vet and they said how much it'd cost to fix. The minimum. But they said if Les is right and it's in the pelvis it'll be more. Misty, even the minimum's half a year's pension. And then Les said... Les said he'd shoot him, but I couldn't bear it and you were away.'

She paused, as if what came next was too dreadful to contemplate, but somehow she forced herself to go on.

'Anyway, I cradled him all night. I kept him warm. I did everything I could think of, but he can't stand up and I know he's hurting. And your gran said she didn't know when you were coming back so...so I decided I'd take him to the mainland and get the vet to...get the vet to...' Another sob and then she seemed to brace.

'But you're here now and I know you have the animal euthanasia stuff. If you could just... Could you please just do it?'

The terminal was emptying. The arriving passengers were all off the ferry, streaming out towards the car park. The departing passengers were boarding. Many glanced at Cath and her dog as they passed, but they looked away fast. Grief was obvious.

During the journey Angus had had time to do an internet search of Kirra Island. It was a popular tourist location, but also had a permanent population of fishermen and retirees. Many of those leaving and arriving would be tourists, he thought, but there'd be a fair smattering of locals. This lady and her dog would be recognised.

No one, though, was stepping forward with comfort or offers of help and he could figure out why. Misty would be recognised as the island doctor. She'd therefore be understood to be in charge.

In charge of a devastated woman and her dying dog?

This wasn't fair. To ask such a thing in such a setting, with Forrest hearing every word…

'Can I help?' The words were out before he knew he was about to speak. Misty was looking at the dog slumped in the woman's arms, but she acknowledged his presence.

'Cath, this is Dr Firth. He's here…he's here to help me cope with Lily. Angus, this is my gran's cousin, Cath. My friend.' Then she reached out and gently stroked behind the little dog's ear. 'Hey, Doozy. Oh, sweetheart, what have you done to yourself? Cath, can you pop him down on the floor? Forrest, you can see that Doozy's badly hurt. I need to examine him.'

What, here, in the middle of the ferry terminal, surrounded by strangers and luggage? How unprofessional was this? But Cath was setting the dog down on the tiles and Misty was kneeling to see.

The little dog was obviously badly hurt. He was bloodstained and, as Cath lowered him, his backside sank but his front legs remained straight. He was sitting, almost as if, whatever was coming, he wanted to face it, but there was no doubt there was something very wrong with his hindquarters.

Misty was running gentle hands over him, speaking softly, checking his eyes, his mouth, lifting his front pads, running fingers lightly down his spine.

'I can see scrapes to his pads where they were driven into the road,' she told Cath. 'But otherwise his front legs look fine. And his left side, too. He reacts to the slightest touch on the right, but not so much on the left.'

'That's what Les said,' Cath said tearfully. 'He thinks there's a break high up on the right. Probably pelvis.'

'Les is good,' Misty murmured. She glanced up at Angus. 'Les Irvine's one of our local farmers, great with animals.'

But not good enough to be of solid help here, Angus thought. Except for his offer to shoot.

'Cath, this morning…has he had a wee?' Misty was asking.

'He managed it.' Cath gulped. 'I knew he'd need to and I carried him outside and he did. I had to hold his back up, though.'

'Well, that's a good sign,' Misty told her. 'If he's able to wee, there's less likelihood of internal injury or spinal damage. The vets on the mainland might be able to set his leg.'

'But Les is sure it's higher,' Cath said. 'And the vet says if it's his back or pelvis… The costs… I don't want to take him all the way over there just to have to tell them I can't afford it, and I can't bear him to suffer any more. Even if it's just a broken leg… I can't even afford that. That's why… Misty, if I take him home, could you come there and…and do what you have to do?' Her voice was pleading. 'He needs to be in his own basket, where he knows he's…'

And she couldn't go on.

Misty sighed and rose and, to Angus's further astonishment, she enveloped Cath in a gentle hug. Then she stepped back and handed over a wad of tissues—from the same wad Angus had been accessing during the journey. Monogrammed handkerchiefs didn't cut it in these sorts of situations. Or when travelling with babies.

'I've booked Mack Henderson's taxi to take us home,' Misty was telling Cath. 'There's only one taxi on the island and we don't mind waiting, do we, Angus? Cath, I'll get Mack to drop you and Doozy at the hospital and I'll ring Martin and tell him to expect you. Can you wait for me there? We can't all fit in the taxi, so Mack will need to make two trips. I can't make any promises, but I'd like to take an X-ray and see what's going on inside before we make a final call. If it's a simple broken leg, maybe I can set it.'

What? Angus thought incredulously. Was she offering to set it herself? And...an X-ray?

'You'll do an X-ray? At the hospital?' he demanded, incredulous. Also, he was thinking...this island...did it really run a hospital?

'It's not really a hospital,' she said, answering his unspoken question as she lifted Doozy back into Cath's arms. 'We have two beds we can use if bad weather means we can't get a patient off the island—or maybe if someone just needs rehydrating after gastro and it's not serious enough to send them to Brisbane. The ferry doesn't run after hours and the air ambulance is expensive. The government funds our clinic because of it.'

He was still incredulous. 'Do they fund it for dogs?'

There was a moment's silence and then Misty's chin tilted. Her eyes met his and there was a sudden flash of anger.

'I use what I have to use. You want to report us?'

'I... No! Of course I don't. I was just...surprised.'

And she managed a twisted smile. 'Don't worry, we disinfect afterwards,' she told him, 'though I'm betting Doozy has less germs than the ten-year-old kid I X-rayed last week. Mike Hannon fell off his dad's pigsty wall and hit his shoulder on the trough. The trough was full at the time.'

'Um...' He was searching for suitable words. 'Urk?'

'Exactly,' she told him. 'Right, Cath, there's Mack at the entrance. I'll tell him to take you and then come back for us. I'll be with you as soon as I can settle this lot.' She made a vague gesture that included Forrest and Lily, included their baggage—and included him. That made him feel... as though he was part of the baggage?

But he didn't come here to be useless. This whole scenario smacked of emotion. Angus Firth avoided emotion like the plague, but Misty already seemed to be thinking of him as something that'd just crawled out of cheese and he didn't like it.

So…just offer.

'If it's just a broken leg, I might be able to operate,' he said and he couldn't figure out which woman looked more astonished.

'You?' Misty said, her tone revealing that his analogy of *'crawled out of cheese'* was spot on.

'I might have the skills,' he told her. And then he decided, okay, why not jump all in. 'I did two years of vet science before finishing med school.'

'Vet science?' Misty's incredulity was unmistakable. 'What the…how?'

He hesitated, trying to find words to describe a period in his life that he hated to remember.

There seemed little choice but to say it.

'I did the first two years of med school,' he said, diffidently. 'Then…then something happened to make me think I didn't want to be a doctor. I changed to vet science for two years, but then changed back.'

What he didn't say was that his parents' and brother's death had made him aimless. Nothing seemed to have any point.

He'd thought of dropping out of university—he'd thought he couldn't handle the emotion of medicine. But he'd loved… what he'd done. Finally, at the persuasion of a couple of concerned lecturers, he'd changed to veterinary medicine.

But two years on, seeing life as a vet, seeing the raw emotion of people like…well, people like Cath, he'd decided being a part-time doctor might be a better way to go. He'd changed back and didn't regret it. His career now meant short consultations, not getting involved and passing anything complicated or emotional on to others.

Veterinarians were constantly faced with scenarios just like this. Devastated owners, hard choices, grief. He hated it. He hated what was before him now, but the words were out and Cath was already staring at him with hope.

'You're a vet?' she said, tremulously.

'I'm not a vet.'

'But if you've done two years, you'll know a lot more about vet science than I do,' Misty said, and he didn't like the thoughtful look that had come into her eyes. As though she might already be mentally organising him a list of animal patients for Monday.

'This one time only,' he said hastily and she nodded, though she still looked thoughtful.

'Vet knowledge, eh?' she said, almost to herself. 'And the man says he's here for a month. Well, well.' Then she caught herself and smiled, but the smile wasn't aimed at him, it was aimed straight at Cath. 'Cath, let's not get your hopes up, but maybe this situation isn't as bad as it seems. Doctor Firth says he's here to be useful. For Doozy's sake, let's hope useful starts now.'

Mack and his taxi took Cath to the clinic while they waited at the terminal—apparently one island, one taxi. He was back in fifteen minutes and Misty and her entourage—Angus still had the feeling he was baggage—were driven to her home.

Five minutes from the ferry terminal they turned into the formal entrance of a modern-looking building, signed as Kirra Island Medical Clinic. The taxi didn't stop though. Instead, Mack slowed and drove around the back.

Here, fenced off from the clinic grounds, was a house that looked as though it had seen better days and those better days were a while ago. It was big, with wide verandas and French windows which were mostly open. It could be lovely, Angus thought, but it wasn't. The paintwork was peeling. The corrugated iron roof looked rusty. Bougainvillea seemed as though it had taken a hold, sprawling in great crimson trails along the veranda and over the roof. The overall impression was that any day now the house would simply disappear under a crimson carpet.

'What a waste,' Angus said, before he could stop himself, and Misty cast him a look of dislike.

'That's hardly polite. Government funding goes to the clinic and I don't have time to paint. Besides, we like it shabby, don't we, Forrest?'

Her smile suddenly peeped out and it gave him a shock. Up until now her smile had seemed tight and forced, but now there…a twinkle?

Was it because she was home? Or maybe because he'd offered to share responsibility for her friend's dog? Regardless, the smile caught him. Fascinated him.

What she'd done over the past few years had been epic, he thought. She'd taken on Forrest and then she'd taken on Lily. Somewhere there was a grandma she cared for as well. Not only that, she seemed to be caring for the medical needs of the whole island. Then, in the last couple of days, she'd packed up and taken both Forrest and Lily to Melbourne. She'd have had no idea of the reception she'd receive, but she'd travelled while caring for a newborn, plus an emotionally damaged seven-year-old.

It was a wonder the twinkle was peeping out now, he decided, but it definitely was. And he liked it. He found himself smiling back.

And he thought suddenly, was that why he'd been drawn to Jancie? Had it been this smile?

No. Jancie's smile had been brilliant, her laughter infectious, her whole package a seduction in itself. Misty's smile had nothing of the seductress about it.

It was just a smile.

Wasn't it?

'Moving on,' she said now, still smiling. 'I could demand you apologise for criticising our house, but we don't have time. Come and meet Gran.'

'Gran' was in the kitchen. She was small and plump, with short silver curls and eyes the same blue as Misty's. When she turned to greet them, her smile was almost a perfect match to her granddaughter's.

She was sitting at the kitchen table in a wheelchair.

'So you're home,' she said, spinning her chair to face them, beaming and holding out her arms to Forrest. 'How lovely. I wasn't expecting you this soon. Forrest, love, come and give Gran a hug.'

'N-nuh,' Forrest said, backing up a little, but he managed the vestige of a smile. 'Gran, we brought Lily back. And…and Dr Firth.' And then he edged towards the door and disappeared.

'Well, so you're Dr Firth,' Gran said, eyeing him from head to foot with a long, assessing gaze. 'So you're the man who impregnated my granddaughter.'

'Gran,' Misty said weakly.

'Hmph,' she said. 'Well, I guess the fact that you're here means you're not a total waste of space, but you'll have to prove it. Misty's told me about you—or rather she showed me all about you on the internet. Sorry I can't get up to greet you.'

She motioned to her legs, emerging from a soft print dress. Or rather…leg. There was an empty space where her left leg should be.

'Diabetes,' she said bluntly, following his instinctive gaze and answering his unvoiced question. 'Terribly treated in the olden days—the olden days being before Misty came back to the island.'

'Angus, this is Alice Calvert, my grandmother, Forrest's great-grandmother,' Misty told him. 'Gran, I'm so sorry, but I need to—'

'To go,' Alice finished for her, still eyeing Angus. 'Martin rang me five minutes ago to give me a heads-up. He said you've both offered to help with Doozy. That's great. Cath rang last night, wanting you, but I didn't know when you'd be back. Thank heaven that you're here now. Give me Lily. I'll take care of the kids while you two scoot. Misty, does Forrest…?'

'He knows what's happening, but I'll tell him again,' Misty said. 'He'll be happy to be back in his room.'

'He spends far too much time in that room,' Alice said darkly, but then she shrugged. 'I'll talk to him when you go. I'll ask him all about his trip and you know he'll emerge if I need him. He's a good kid. In the meantime, off you go and see if you can save Doozy. If you can do that, you, Angus, might even go up in my estimation.' And then she glowered. 'You can hardly go down.'

Angus tried to smile. It didn't come off, though. This scene, this kitchen…

A woman in a wheelchair. A little boy. A baby.

Memories were flooding back. His mum, in her wheelchair, stirring a bowl of something at the kitchen table, his baby brother in a sling arrangement across her chest. He'd been around the same age Forrest was now, sitting beside her. They'd been making a chocolate cake, he thought. She'd let him lick…

'Angus? Are you okay?' Misty sounded worried and he caught himself.

'I…yes. I'm fine.' Would he never rid himself of these memories? he thought savagely. He loathed them, the almost supernatural flashbacks, taking him to a time when…when he'd loved. 'We need to see about this dog.'

'About Doozy,' she agreed, still watching him, still looking puzzled. But she knew…they both knew they had to move on. 'Yes, we do.'

It wasn't just a broken leg. Misty stared at the film and felt ill. Doozy's vertebrae seemed undamaged—for what it was worth that was good news—but the hip joint was fractured, and badly.

This was way beyond her ken. She could have splinted a broken leg, but the bone she was looking at was shattered. How to repair it? Impossible. On the table beneath them Doozy lay, anaesthetised. She looked down at him and felt ill.

'It seems your Mr Irvine was right.' Angus was standing beside her, also staring at the film. Cath was being given a cup of tea by Martin. They'd have to go out and break it to her, Misty thought drearily, trying not to think ahead, to the process of euthanising a dog she'd grown to love.

But Angus's tone wasn't despairing. 'The best result here would be a prosthesis,' he said, considering. 'An artificial hip.' Astonishingly, he sounded thoughtful. 'It'd mean replacing the entire hip joint. I've seen it done with dogs. Like in humans, the femoral head could be removed, the cup resurfaced and the head replaced by an implant. Implants have porous coating so bone can grow into it. The leg itself looks fixable.'

But then he frowned, obviously still considering.

'That'd require a veterinary orthopaedic team, though, and the implants themselves are off-the-scale expensive. Human implants are subsidised and, while not quite standard, they're close enough to be affordable. Doozy's not close to any standard I've ever seen. The cost of the prosthesis alone would run into the thousands and fitting it...'

'Impossible,' she whispered. 'Even if we could find the money...'

'So option two?' He said it hesitantly and she braced.

'Hey, I'm not talking of euthanasia,' he said, almost roughly. 'If you trust me...'

'What...? What...?'

'Misty, there are alternatives to a hip replacement.' He was speaking gently, as if he guessed how close to emotional breakdown she was. And she *was* close to breakdown.

These last few days had seemed endless, starting with learning of her sister's death, bringing Lily home and fighting to settle her, trawling Jancie's records, taking the gamble of the trip to Melbourne. Right now she was struggling not to feel numb. Doctors were supposed to have boundaries, but Doozy was her gran's best friend's dog. She loved Cath herself, she'd known Doozy since he was a pup and there was so much going on in her head right now.

And maybe Angus sensed it. He gave her a long look, then continued, still gently.

'Misty, during my training I did a practical placement for a country vet. We had a farmer's collie with just such an injury. It was half a day's journey to the nearest specialist clinic and the farmer couldn't afford a prosthesis anyway. But the dog was past working and the farmer just wanted his mate to be with him as...well, as a mate. The vet I was working with, old school, totally practical, explained that he could do what's called a femoral head ostectomy.'

She stared. 'A what?'

'It involves removing the hip joint and allowing a false joint to develop from scar tissue,' he explained. 'In a human such a procedure can't work—our legs could never bear weight without a working hip joint—but dogs have four legs and Doozy's not overweight. What would be left if we remove it would be a non-painful, fibrous joint. He'd limp for a while, but it should be painfree and he'd learn to use it. I remember some sort of doggy physiotherapy regime the farmer was given to work through, but he jumped at the chance to save his dog. I was interested enough to follow up and it worked out fine.'

And Misty was caught. It'd have to be cheaper, she conceded, but...

'We couldn't. The Brisbane clinic will refer him to specialists anyway. There's no way they'll do that themselves, and the cost will still be—'

'Astronomical. But we can do it here.'

'We?'

'We,' he said, still gentle. 'There are still many places where implants aren't an option and I can get a brush-up on line. If you're up to giving an anaesthetic...'

She stared at him, almost open-mouthed. One minute she was thinking of this guy as...well, almost a waste of space. A guy who'd impregnated her sister and walked away. A man refusing to take full responsibility for his daughter. But now here he was, offering to attempt a surgical procedure way beyond her skills.

Why? He didn't have to. He was here because of his daughter. Was this some sort of attempt to mitigate guilt?

He was stooping now, so his face was almost level with that of the disreputable little mutt on the table.

'No promises, mate,' he whispered as he ran his fingers gently behind a soft, furry ear. 'I'll talk to your mistress and explain that we can only try. We won't let you feel any pain. If we get in there and discover it's impossible...well, we'll have done our best and we'll just let you go softly into the last big sleep. Is that okay with you, fella?'

'Are you up to it?' she asked bluntly, and he straightened and nodded.

'You'd have to trust me, but if I didn't think I could do it, I wouldn't offer.'

'And would you...would you charge?' It had to be asked.

'Of course I wouldn't,' he said, as if it was a ridiculous question. And then he softened. 'Misty, you know there are no guarantees. We'd have to spell that out to Cath, but we could try.'

And for the second time that day Misty found herself blinking back tears. And then...thinking forward. This sounded as though this guy cared! And if he cared about a dog, then maybe...

Cut it out, she told herself fiercely. One step at a time. One problem at a time.

She managed to sniff and then she nodded. Moving on.

Right now she needed to go with Angus and talk to Cath about her dog. And then she needed to brush up on—or, in fact, learn—everything she needed to know about dog anaesthesia.

CHAPTER SIX

THEY USED THE normal procedure room, set up as a theatre.

Government authorities might well have kittens if they could see the use the equipment they'd funded was being put to, but there wasn't an islander who'd object, Misty thought. Disinfecting afterwards would take longer, but Martin hadn't blinked when he'd been told what they intended, just phoned Val, another retired nurse, to come in and help.

'Got a tricky surgical drama over here. We're going to need a full team,' he told her. 'Could you come over and man the fort while we pretend we know what we're doing?'

'Cath's dog?' they heard Val ask. Martin had the phone on speaker while he rang and Angus and Misty, both seated at the desk at reception brushing up on their knowledge, could hear every word.

'Yeah,' Martin told her.

'Thought so,' Val said in satisfaction. 'Mack said Misty was thinking of saving him. And that new guy...the baby's dad... Mack says he's another doctor...he's planning on helping?'

This island... Misty glanced across at Angus and saw a wry smile. The grapevine here worked almost instantaneously.

'I'll be there in ten minutes,' Val was saying. 'Wish 'em all luck from me and give Cath a hug, too.'

'Doc reckons they'll need me in theatre as well,' Martin told her. 'That's the new doc. He also reckons Cath needs a bit of care—she's suffering from shock and he's worried about her blood pressure. So you'll be on Cath duty, as well as caring for any small stuff. Someone's got to care for everyone else while Doozy's under.'

But at those words Misty, still watching Angus, saw his smile slip. And she thought of those words. 'Someone's got to care…' They'd hit her, too, but she couldn't care any more than she already did.

But there must be a part of Angus that was caring, otherwise he'd never have made this offer. He'd also looked tangentially at Cath and insisted she be physically checked before they started. That had made her feel bad—she should have thought of it herself, but her emotions were getting in the way of medicine.

If he could find it in his heart to care for Doozy, maybe he *could* care for Lily?

But then Val was there, taking Cath away for a cup of tea and a lie down—and Angus's ordered surreptitious observation—and Martin had their makeshift theatre organised. They were operating and there was no room for unrelated thoughts at all.

He could do this, Angus told himself, as he watched Misty intubate.

Angus was blessed with an extraordinary memory, almost photogenic. Once seen, never forgotten. He had seen this procedure, so he knew what lay ahead.

But he'd been an onlooker all those years ago, and the feel of this wound under his fingers, the knowledge that there was no back up, the sensation that it was all down to him… This was a weight of responsibility that he'd avoided for years.

So why was he doing this? This whole situation was almost overwhelming. One slip of a girl, with two needy children and one dependent grandmother... One injured dog with a distraught owner... He felt as though he was being hauled in deeper and deeper.

It couldn't matter. What had to matter right now was this excision, this wound, this leg, this beloved dog...

No! He couldn't—mustn't—think of this as a beloved dog. That meant emotion and he didn't do emotion. He couldn't.

He just had to do this.

Keeping an already traumatised dog anaesthetised, when even anaesthetising humans was out of her supposed skill range—though as the only doctor on the island she had needed to do it—should have taken every ounce of Misty's attention. She'd intubated and was now watching every breath.

But Martin was acting as theatre nurse and that gave her space. Martin was dredging up skills he might well have forgotten, but he was rising to the occasion magnificently. A skilled surgeon in a city operating suite could hardly have wished for better nursing staff and that left Misty with glimpses of time when she could see what Angus was doing.

And see his skill.

He hadn't hesitated. From the moment of the first incision, he moved as if he'd trained for years for just such a procedure. He could well have been a fully trained veterinary surgeon.

Her eyes fleetingly met Martin's as they worked and she saw his eyebrows lift in an astonishment that matched hers. What have we here? Martin's expression said and she also saw speculation. Like how can we keep him?

Yeah, as though that was likely to happen, she thought

drily, but as she saw his skilled fingers manoeuvre forceps to remove every sliver of shattered bone, as she watched him wash and wash, check and recheck, then position the saw for excision of the femoral head, she could only wonder.

What sort of doctor was this? A part-time doctor whose main love was surfing? On the surface maybe, but underneath…there was no doubt that part of his leisure time must surely be spent honing skills. Watching these sorts of procedures on teaching channels? Doing online tutorials?

She did it herself when she had time—every doctor tried to—and as the sole doctor in an isolated setting she had reason. But as a part-time doctor in a city practice, where specialist medics and large city hospitals were only moments away, surely there was no need?

There was only one answer to why he'd have been learning and relearning. And that was because underneath the determination to not get involved, to keep himself emotionally distant from his patients, he did love medicine.

And in the slivers of her mind available while monitoring Doozy's vital signs she was slowly starting to consider—if he's capable of loving medicine, could he possibly end up loving Lily?

Maybe he could.

Because tenderness was there. She'd seen it in his interaction with Forrest, in the crazy paper plane session where he'd hauled a little boy out of his perpetual anxiety. She'd seen it in the way he'd responded to Cath, and she was seeing it now, in the way his brows furrowed as he bent over the task at hand.

This was a scruffy, 'bitsa' dog, surely of little account in the scheme of things, but Angus was pouring every skerrick of skill and focus into getting a perfect result. This was breathtaking surgery. Even the young vets in the city clinics would surely need to undertake specialist training to do this, yet here he was...

She glanced again at Martin and found Martin was glancing at her. And the speculation she saw...

After years working together, even partly concealed by their theatre masks, she could read her colleague's expression like a book.

Keep him here, Martin's expression said, and the look he gave her said more.

And there was the way she was feeling.

Well, you can cut that out, she told herself fiercely, as she went back to checking the monitors. But the surgical procedure was long and, as they worked, as she saw what was happening under his hands—the promise of life for a little bitsa dog—there was a tiny part of her that was thinking of Jancie, a hotel suite and this man...

With envy?

Oh, for heaven's sake, Jancie's leavings? Not in a million years. If she could, she'd have stamped her foot in anger at herself.

What was left over from Jancie was one needy little boy and one desperately needy baby.

And absolutely nothing else.

'You two skedaddle.'

With the wound closed and dressed, with Doozy still heavily sedated but breathing for himself and showing every sign of making a good recovery, Martin's orders were firm. 'You've got two kids at home. My dogs are fed and walked. They'll be fine for the night. I'll kip here and keep you updated.' Val had offered to take Cath home and stay with her overnight, so there was only Doozy who still needed watching. He'd need to be on a drip, sedated and on intravenous antibiotics for a couple of days. The wound had been filthy.

'That's great,' Misty said and Angus thought—post-surgery care? Who'd pay Martin? There was certainly no government rebate for dogs.

He would if needed, he thought, but who'd pay normally? Angus hadn't thought past the surgery. In truth, it had stretched him to the limit, or maybe even past his limit. He was feeling a bit punch drunk. But that was surely the culmination of what had happened over the past twenty-four hours, he thought. Was it only that long since Misty had made his world implode?'

But maybe that wasn't fair, he conceded. It hadn't been Misty who'd imploded his world. It had been his own actions almost a year ago.

But despite his self-reproach and confusion as to how he would cope in the future, right now he didn't feel regret. His hand was resting on Doozy's dishevelled coat and he felt good. This dog might live happily into old age.

He'd watched and learned so much medicine, so many procedures, but he hardly used them. He could never explain, even to himself, why he bothered. Intense medical skills called for involvement and he didn't do involvement. But now...

'Fantastic,' Misty said softly, pulling off her mask. 'Oh, Angus, I can't thank you enough.'

And what was there in that to make his feelings swell to a point where...where he had to back off. Because he didn't do this. Whatever *this* was.

But *she* was thanking *him*? How much did this woman have on her shoulders?

But Misty was heading for the door. Martin shook his head as he offered to help clean, and there was nothing for it but to follow.

'So next...' She took a deep breath and he could see her mentally making lists as she walked around the clinic and back towards the house. 'Val tells me Isabelle Graham's rung—she's bringing in her toddler with an ear infection. Jack Ireland's gout's also bad. It seems the island knows I'm back, so there'll be a queue before dinner. Thus prioritising. I'll walk you home now, fix you a bedroom and make sure Gran's okay. She should be all right looking after Forrest, but can you take over Lily?'

'I can do the ear and gout.'

'I'm sure you can,' she told him and he could hear stress building again. When was this woman not under stress? 'But your responsibility is Lily. I can't… I can't get any more attached—I just can't. So let's go.'

She quickened her stride. For a moment Angus stared after her, trying to assimilate just what she had on her shoulders. And why. This wasn't making sense.

'Misty,' he called, but as she didn't pause, he strode after her. He caught up before she reached the top of the steps leading up to the house. 'Misty?'

'I need to hurry.'

'Give me a moment.'

She paused, but she seemed to brace. Was she thinking that this meant something else was expected of her?

'Misty, you can't cope with this alone.' He spoke fast, but he was trying to think this situation through as he spoke.

What she was coping with was impossible. On top of her responsibilities, she now had patients queued to see her, plus the care of an injured dog. The jumbling burden was doing his head in.

'You have Martin,' he said. 'And Val. How much do they help?'

'Did I not say? Martin's semi-retired.' She was looking up at the house as if she wanted to be there. 'When his wife died, he came here to surf, but he gives me five mornings a week, more in an emergency. But he's a dog lover—he'll count Doozy as an emergency. Then there's Val, who really is retired. She's a passionate birder, and it's nesting season for the migrating wading birds. A couple of endangered species nest on East Beach and during this season Val stands guard, warning off anyone who might disturb them. It has to be life or death before she leaves them. I respect that, but she and Cath are friends. Coming in today was a no-brainer.'

He blinked. Nesting birds… Was that another priority for this woman?

'How many people are on this island?' he asked.

'Around six hundred,' she said, with another impatient look at the house. 'A lot more in the tourist season—there's a big camping site at the north end. Look, Angus, I need to go.'

'And you look after everyone?'

'Yes.'

'Why?' he demanded, incredulous. 'Why not just get a job with a city practice, or at least get more staff?'

She sighed, closed her eyes for a brief moment, then faced him full on.

The house they were heading to was built behind the clinic, on the cliffs overlooking the island's sheltered western beach. Straggly salt bush and wind-bent trees dotted the land between clinic and sea. Beneath the cliffs, waves rolled in and out, a wash of white and turquoise colour. Gulls were wheeling close to shore. Some bigger fish must be chasing tiddlers, he thought, as the water was rippling with movement.

The setting was lovely. The waves looked too small for for surfing—he had high hopes for the eastern side of the island—but right now he wasn't thinking about surfing. Nor was he thinking about this magnificent setting.

Why was this woman so alone in this place?

A trained doctor could make a good income in a city

practice, he thought. On the mainland she could surely earn more than enough to support herself, her nephew and her grandmother, too. She could also have time off to care for them, even time off for herself.

Angus earned most of his income from vaccinations and run-of-the-mill minor ailments. That meant high earning, short consultations. But in this situation, few of the ailments Misty faced would be minor and, given the island's isolation, some would be catastrophic. There was little sign of wealth here—she'd be scraping to make a living.

'*Why not just get a job with a city practice?*'

The question hung.

Finally she answered. 'This is my home,' she said at last and crossed her arms over her breasts. Defensive? Almost belligerent.

'But it's surely nuts.' It was so far away from the medicine he practised he felt as though he'd landed on another planet. 'Right now, you're what—returning to the house to check Forrest and your gran are okay, then returning to do a clinical list before dinner? Of whoever turns up. In between you'll be checking on a recovering dog. You'll also be hoping no other dramas occur. I can help today, but usually, surely you need assistance? Anyone can see Alice is hardly able to help. And Forrest himself… I'm no child psychiatrist, but surely he needs time. Attention. Care.'

'He needs a mother,' Misty snapped. 'And Gran needs… well, maybe a daughter, but sadly I'm all they both have. Which is why I can't take Lily.'

'Surely if you moved to the city…'

'I still couldn't take care of Lily.'

'I'm not asking you to,' he said, struggling to think things through. 'But even if you take Lily out of the equation…'

'If?'

He got it then, the surge of anger—maybe mixed with

panic? 'Hey.' He held up his hands, as if in surrender. 'Not *if*. Yes, that was the wrong word. It should have been *when*. Lily will end up either with me or with adopted parents, I get that. But that leaves you with this mess.'

'It's not a mess and where that leaves me is none of your business.' She stopped, took a deep breath, steadied. 'Okay. Short answer. Angus, I stay because I must. Gran saved my life, *our* lives, over and over again when I was a kid. I owe her a thousandfold and I *will* pay my debts.'

He frowned. They were still standing on the steps, with the sun and the sea behind them, but for some reason the setting seemed private. Even intimate?

Like a psychiatrist's consulting room.

But then he shoved the analogy away. This was no professional consultation. What was happening seemed intense, but very, very personal.

'You want to tell me how she saved your life?' What was he doing? he thought. Did he want to dig deep?

He never got involved, yet here he was, living in this woman's home, accepting—for now—fatherhood of his daughter…and he was asking a woman he didn't know for her life story?

Maybe she guessed his confusion. The look she gave him was strained, but also quizzical, as if she suspected he didn't really want to know. But finally she shrugged and spread her hands and answered.

'Okay. You asked. My mum, Gran's daughter, was born on the island, but she…well, I gather she was wild from the start. She hooked up with some deadheads in her teens and left the island with them. From then on it was all downhill. Alcohol, drugs, one appalling relationship after another, one mess after another. She died five years ago.'

'I'm sorry.'

'Don't be.' She shook her head. 'Her death, well—I know

Gran felt grief, but I couldn't. She was a dreadful mother. The worst thing was that she wouldn't give us up, wouldn't give us to Gran or even let us have the security of a foster home.'

'Which is why, with Lily…'

'Yeah, there's a wormhole I don't intend to go down,' she told him. 'But the bottom line was that we were stuck with Mum and Gran could hardly help us. But she sent parcels.'

'Parcels?'

'Every month.' And for a moment he heard pleasure in her voice. 'The most wonderful parcels. There were clothes that actually fit us, great clothes, some she made herself, some she bought new, but with the labels cut off so Mum couldn't sell them on. And there'd be food, huge bags of raisins and nuts, juice boxes, pasta with Gran's instructions, handwritten, made simple so even we could cook it. Mum used to rip the boxes open and swear. None of the stuff in there interested her. Sometimes she'd even hurl the contents at us, but Jancie and I…' She stopped and then made herself go on. 'Well, you have no idea how much we depended on those parcels.'

'I'm sorry.'

'Yeah,' she said drily. 'But there's more. There were a few times when Social Services stepped in. They'd ring Gran and she'd travel to wherever we were and bring us here. Back to her island. And until Mum got us back we'd get three meals a day, and snacks, and soft, clean beds, and we'd go to school.' Her face clouded a little.

'Though Jancie…not so much. She was eight years older than me. I remember the first time she refused to come to the island and how shocked I was. As she got older she even seemed to like Mum's lifestyle. But when we were here… Gran would take us fishing and we'd collect shells and she'd read to us. And the islanders would help her care and we'd be safe and fed until Mum finally came and took us away again. As she got older Jancie resented it—she said she hated the island—but I felt safe here. It felt like my home and it still does. So I guess…you're right, what I want for Lily is a home.'

Then she took a deep breath and seemed to regroup. 'So I guess that's where I am now,' she said. 'This is home and Gran needs me as much as I once needed her. She's a fourth-generation islander, she's related to half the island. How could I ask her to leave? And as for us moving to the city, how do you think she'd cope, in some rented apartment with me working full time? How do you think Forrest would cope? I can't tell you the state he was in when I finally managed to bring him here, but he's getting better. Your lifestyle is your decision, but this is where we stay.'

'But you have to have help. You must be able to have fun.'

'Fun?' She came close to snorting. 'So I can go surfing? Or kayaking at dawn while the kids are asleep? Or dating or clubbing or whatever? As though that's important. That makes you sound just like Jancie.'

That brought silence. It stretched on and on between them. He was like Jancie?

'I don't think I am,' he said at last.

'Really? Is having a good time more important than caring for the people you love?'

Whoa, that was a kick in the guts. *The people he loved…* The number of those was exactly zero and he intended it to stay that way.

But she stood there expecting an answer and he was so goaded that finally he gave her one. He gave her the truth.

'Okay,' he conceded. 'I don't get involved, but there's a reason. My parents and my little brother were killed in a car crash when I was nineteen. That's when I tried to give up being a doctor, because I didn't want emotional ties—only

I soon figured veterinary medicine was as bad or worse. So my clinical medicine now is just that, clinical. I don't do emotional attachment. But that doesn't make me like Jancie. It just makes me…distant.'

And he saw her flinch. She stared up at him, anger fading, leaving her white-faced. Shocked.

There was a reason he didn't tell people. He hated pity almost as much as he feared emotional attachment.

Why had he told her?

'I'm sorry,' she whispered. 'I didn't know. Of course there's a reason.'

'Tragedy does…tragedy changes people.'

'It does,' she conceded, pulling herself together with visible effort. 'If you let it. You know, I never knew my dad, and Mum and my sister are both dead. My family. But losing them, or never having them…it just makes me want to cling tighter. Form a family with whomever I have.'

'Except not with Lily.'

What was he thinking? He hadn't meant it, but intended or not, it came out as an accusation.

There was a moment's silence, where the colour drained from her face, where she stood and stared at him as if he'd just said something obscene. As maybe he had. Then, as a reflex that seemed to come from nowhere, her hand swung up and she slapped him. Hard.

CHAPTER SEVEN

IT TOOK HIM a moment to realise what had happened. It was a moment when he instinctively stepped back, when his hand went to his face—and when Misty's eyes filled with what could only be horror. Her hand went to her own face, as if she was feeling it. As if she herself had been struck.

And then she just...crumpled. She sank to her knees on the stone steps, sagging as if her legs could no longer hold her. But her eyes didn't leave his and her horror was growing.

'No! I couldn't. Angus, I didn't mean... I'm sorry, I'm so, so sorry. I've never hit anyone. How could I...?' But then her voice broke, and in place of words came a tearing, heart-ripping sob. A sob that felt like a gut punch all on its own.

Before he knew it he was stooping, crouched before her, taking her hands in his, tugging them from her ravaged face, lifting her chin so he could face her. Tears were coursing down her cheeks and sobs were sending shudders right through her.

'Misty...'

Her words were scarcely coherent. 'I'm sorry. Lily... I know... I shouldn't... She's my responsibility, my family. How can I give her away? I have no right...'

To say he was appalled was an understatement. What sort of mess had he and Jancie landed on this woman? How could he possibly have implied she should do anything other than what she was doing? 'Misty, you do have the right.'

'I don't. I don't. But I can't…' She crumpled again and he couldn't bear it. Hardly knowing what he was doing, he gathered her to him, cradling her in his arms. He'd sunk back against the stone steps. Her face was buried in his chest and his arms were holding her.

For however long it took.

She cried as if she couldn't stop and all he could do was hold her and wait for it to pass.

And curse himself for his stupidity.

What had she said? *'Losing them, or never having them… it makes me want to cling tighter.'*

And his response? *'Except not with Lily.'*

His words to her had been crass, cruel, goading. There was no way she should be responsible for his and Jancie's daughter. Did he want her to feel guilty? That was surely how he'd sounded.

What an oaf. She'd taken on so much—what right did he have to demand more?

And as he sat there, as he hugged her, as she lay limp against him, exhausted by emotion he guessed must have been building from the moment she'd learned of Jancie's death, for the first time he finally accepted that what had happened *was* shared responsibility. But that shared responsibility wasn't hers. It should have been shared with Jancie—and now it was his.

With that he also had to accept that this was his fault. The stress, the heartache Misty was feeling…

But all he could do right now was let her sob and hope that somehow this cry would release a little of the mountain of tension that must have built up to the point where his thoughtless words had led to a slap. And it was only a slap. He deserved so much more.

Finally it eased. She hiccupped and hiccupped again, and he reached for his father's handkerchief once more. At least this time it might be useful.

It certainly was. She must have sensed his movement because she sniffed and tugged back, accepting the cloth with something like relief. She blew her nose, mopped her face, then stared ruefully down at the very damp cloth.

'Oh, no. Your beautiful handkerchief. And I hit you. I can't believe I—'

'I deserved it.'

'No one deserves that. Ever.' She sniffed again and he thought…he thought…

She's beautiful.

What the…where did that come from?

Beautiful?

He'd thought Jancie was beautiful. Well, she had been. Svelte, glamorous, sexy as hell, perfectly manicured, dressed to kill.

As opposed to her sister. Misty was dressed in faded jeans, a blouse that was frayed at the collar and sneakers that were scuffed and worn. Her knot of soft brown curls had come untied and was half up, half twisting to her shoulders. Her face was blotched with weeping and her eyes were still wet.

She was as far from her sister as it was possible to get and yet…and yet…

The urge to take her in his arms again was almost irresistible.

'Misty…' His voice sounded strangled, but she didn't seem to notice. She was staring instead at his handkerchief.

'I'm… I'm guessing you don't want this back now.'

'I guess I don't.'

'I'll launder it beautifully—you wait and see.' She was obviously fighting for lightness, fighting for calm. 'Angus,

I never should have done that. You could have me up for assault and I'd deserve it. I think… I think I must be pretty close to the edge.'

'I'm sure you are.'

'Well.' She rose and swiped her cheeks with the back of her hands, obviously still fighting for control. 'I'll get there,' she said. 'I had one decent night's sleep last night.'

'I should have let you sleep for longer.' He hesitated. 'Come to think of it, I should have made you stay in Melbourne. Misty, you can't just plough back into work as if nothing's happened.'

'There's hardly a choice.'

'I think there might be.' He hesitated. 'Okay, here's an idea. If I'm to take care of Lily long term, then you're still going to need some help. They say it takes a village to raise a child. I'm starting to realise that might be true. Where's your village, Misty?'

'Gran. The islanders…'

'Yep, they're a start, but they see you as their doctor—at least I suspect the islanders do—and your gran…she needs a village herself. I'm looking at you and thinking you desperately need time off, to come to terms with your sister's death. Also to help Forrest, who seems traumatised. And Alice must need it as well—Jancie was her granddaughter, too. It's been a hell of a week for you all, hasn't it?'

'I can cope.'

In answer he put his hand on his still slap-marked face. 'You did say you don't normally hit people,' he said mildly. 'I know there were solid reasons, but still…you're a doctor, you must have been provoked any number of times. Haven't you?'

'I might have been,' she admitted.

He could have gone on, outlined the plan he was only just starting to formulate, but the way she said that made him pause. Quite desperately, and for reasons he was struggling to understand, he wanted this woman to have time out and this might be a way to do it. 'Give me an example,' he prompted.

'What, of provocation?'

'Yes. Not as bad as mine, I hope. This island, though.... Tell me the worst. A time where you really wanted to slap, but couldn't.'

There was a long pause.

The school of fish down in the bay had obviously attracted a flock of terns. The mass of silver and white birds was wheeling overhead, rising high and then dive-bombing to get their feed for the day.

'Maureen Frobisher's ear,' Misty said cautiously, and Angus nodded. Something—a dolphin maybe—was stirring the fish, driving them into the shallows. Normally Angus would be fascinated, but right now Misty had all his attention.

Why? What was happening here? He didn't get involved.

Liar. He was involved, like it or not.

'Maureen Frobisher's ear,' he prodded, watching Misty's eyes light a little. Like him, she seemed to be searching for lightness. Sifting through memories to try and find something...fun?

And maybe she'd found it.

'Okay,' she said slowly. 'The time I really, really wanted to slap and I couldn't? Well, here goes.' Her face relaxed a little—just a little, but enough.

'Well,' she said. 'A couple of tourists, Tom and Maureen Frobisher, were camping on the far side of the island. Twenty minutes' drive. This happened a few weeks ago, mid tourist season. I'd had a foul day: teenagers in a car crash, multiple casualties with evacuation to Brisbane. Plus I had my normal clinic and Gran was unwell. Then at eight at night

Tom rang and said Maureen had an earache. I was tired and hungry, but, dammit, you know ears can't wait.'

They didn't wait at his clinic, Angus thought, but not because he was conscientious. If they didn't fit convenient appointments, they were sent on to the local hospital. But here? No, they couldn't wait.

'So I said to come straight over to the clinic. I had to miss reading Forrest a story and put my already dried-out dinner back in the oven. Both Forrest and Gran were upset, but over to the clinic I went, like a good little doctor. And then I had to wait for twenty minutes because they took their own sweet time getting there. But finally Tom arrived—with no Maureen.'

'Um…' he said, confused, and she managed a wry smile.

'Um is right,' she told him. 'I think I said, "Where's your wife?"', and all Tom said was: "You didn't tell me I had to bring her with me." He was indignant and of course it was my fault entirely for not spelling it out, but, oh, the desire to slap…'

He was imagining it. Misty, arriving at a darkened clinic, exhausted already, prepared to tend to a woman's earache—but there was no woman. 'I guess…' he managed to say, his voice a little unsteady, 'he was expecting you to hand over some sort of one-size-fits-all Ear Fixer?'

'I guess he was,' she said and then glowered. 'Don't you dare laugh. I was clearly too tired to see the funny side. It meant I had to get in the car and drive across the island to their campsite, only to find out she'd been swimming and her ear was full of water and it took all of two minutes to fix. And of course they had no documentation on them and the next day they were gone, so I couldn't even bill them for the cost of the petrol.'

'And yet you didn't slap?' he said, wonderingly, and she gave a wry smile.

'Nope. I saved my slap for you. Angus, I really am sorry.'

'We're both sorry,' he said. But he was suddenly more than sorry. This strange sensation was growing within. Maybe there was sympathy, he thought, but this was more. A lot more.

Misty was coping with so much.

Angus had lost his family when he was nineteen. He'd been gutted, but how much had Misty lost? The same, but in much more dire circumstances.

He'd been left with funds to cope with life. He had a great home. He had friends. His friendship group was pretty much transient—he never let them close and he chose friends who felt pretty much the same—but there were always friends and colleagues to fall back on. Friends to go surfing with, or kayaking or swimming. Colleagues to swap shifts with if the surf was great.

Misty seemed to have had no support at all.

She had courage though, he thought. Courage in spades. And skill and honour and commitment.

She made him feel ashamed.

She made him feel as though he needed to do more than just care for his daughter.

But caring for Lily, he conceded, might well take more time than he could imagine. And thinking that, the germ of an idea that had seeded itself before the slap seemed to swell and grow.

'Misty, I have surfing friends,' he said, but she was glancing towards the house. She'd be needed there, he thought. She was needed everywhere. 'You realise the east coast of this island is a surfer's paradise?'

'Your point is? Angus, I need…'

'You're so needed,' he told her. 'I can't even begin to imagine how much you're needed. But it's been less than two weeks since you found out about your sister's death,

Forrest's mother's death, Alice's granddaughter's death and, as far as I can see, the only time you've taken for yourself is the two nights you spent in Melbourne. So here's a plan. You all take a break.'

She stopped looking at the house. Instead, she turned and stared at him, as if he'd said something ludicrous.

'What, just head off on a holiday?'

'Yes,' he told her. 'In a perfect world I'd like to put you and Forrest—and maybe Alice, too, if she wants it—on a plane to Hawaii. But I know it wouldn't work. I don't know too much about child psychiatry, but even I can guess that Forrest needs to feel secure, and you and your gran have had enough shocks already. But I think I told you, when I looked up flights to come here, I also looked up places to stay. To be honest…well, if I had to come here I intended to be comfortable and I wasn't too sure of my welcome with you. So I put a tentative hold on a holiday house just along from here. Sapphire Seas. Do you know it?'

Did she know it? Obviously yes, because her jaw dropped. 'You're kidding,' she managed, turning and staring along the cliffs to where they could see a vast rectangle of gleaming glass and granite on the headland. 'That's it there. Do you know who owns it?'

'No.'

She named an actor whose very name spelled money. American. 'He came three years in a row for four weeks,' she told him. 'That was when his current girlfriend was Australian and he hasn't been back since they split. It's supposed to be on the market, but his price is ludicrous. Meanwhile it's being rented out for a sum that'd make your eyes water.'

'It did make my eyes water,' Angus conceded. 'But I can afford it.'

That left her stunned as well. 'How can you afford it?' I mean…with your house, I assume you're wealthy, but this…'

'My parents come from old money,' he told her. 'Actually, not just my parents, but my grandparents and great-grandparents before them. My parents also had massive life insurance policies and I've had a very good investment advisor, so fret not about money. Think about my idea. I'm proposing that you and Forrest and Alice go and stay in it for a month.'

'Us!'

'I know, I'm a better fit for such a place,' he told her and tried a smile. He was hoping he could make her smile back, but it didn't happen. 'Misty, your house is right behind the clinic and everyone knows where you are. I'm betting that's where every local goes when they're in trouble and I'm starting to figure out how much they depend on you. But my plan is to put the word out. Doctor Calvert desperately needs a break and Dr Firth and his team are taking over. Misty, do you have a work phone or do you use your personal phone for everything?'

'I have a separate work phone,' she said, cautiously. 'I can divert it to Martin if I'm caught up.'

'Excellent. We can use that or divert it to mine.' Then, because now he'd said it out loud, it did seem a neat scheme, he let himself grin. He also decided to cup her chin in his hand and force her eyes to meet his gaze. Which felt quite good. Or actually…really good. 'What do you reckon, sweetheart? Good plan?'

But that brought them both up with a jolt. The touch of his hand on her chin. The words. *The word.* 'Did you…did you just call me sweetheart?' she stammered.

'Whoops.' Had he? What was he thinking? 'Slip of the tongue,' he told her hastily. 'I meant—what do you reckon, mate?'

She eyed him cautiously—as though he might be about

to grow two heads—but for some reason his hand was still under her chin and she didn't pull away.

'Okay. So…mate,' she said, 'you're proposing…what, that you and Lily stay in our house, get to know each other and get Lily settled? Lily, who doesn't know what settled is? You're also proposing to take on the medical needs of the whole island while you do it?'

He had to concede it sounded like lunacy, but his plan was extending. It might need finessing, but if the guys were available…

'I told you, I have surfing friends,' he said. 'And many of my surfing friends are also doctors.'

'Um…so?'

'So many of them are available for short-term work.' He hesitated. 'Misty, you know I'm not all that committed to my career.'

'Except for studying,' she said, frowning. She did tug away now, so she could back up and watch him. 'That surgery… Doozy…it was brilliant.'

'Of course,' he said, mock modest. 'Not being totally committed to medicine doesn't mean I've let my skills slip. Many of my friends do the same. We read. We do online tutorials late at night when there's no surf…'

'And no Jancie to keep you amused?' she responded in a flash.

That caught him. His mind flashed back to the time he'd spent with Jancie. He surely hadn't spent his nights studying then—but look where that had landed him.

'As you say,' he said, trying not to sound grim. Focus on the plan, he told himself. 'Anyway, I'm not the only medical student who's decided not to devote all their life to medicine. When I went back to med school I ended up with a like-minded friendship group. Surfing, rock-climbing, kayaking—they're our passions. Medicine's what we do to pay for it.'

'I can't imagine…'

And he knew she couldn't. 'There's not been a lot of time for rock climbing in your life?' he asked gently. 'It's a whole amazing world out there, Misty, if only you look.'

'But do you…do you enjoy it?'

'Of course.'

But did he? There was the rub. His friendship group had morphed during the years, men and women he'd thought totally committed to their fun pursuits slowly dropping out, maybe deciding they wanted to spend more time at work, moving on to specialise, maybe marrying, maybe figuring a once-a-month surf was enough…

The group he surfed and kayaked with now were mostly younger. There were a couple of stayers though, a few even older than himself.

There'd be enough.

'My plan is to call my surfing buddies,' he told Misty now. 'I'll need at least two to make my plan work, but I might tempt more. The east side of the island's stunning for surfing. We can hire beach buggies and the guys can bring their boards. The plan is that I'll be back here with Lily, but I'll also be Doctor in Charge. I'll field calls and organise who's on call or running the clinic.

'We'll work on government rates—if we break the day into shifts, the guys can work for their living, and you say your house is big? So… The island's medical needs will be met. Lily and I will be getting acquainted and you'll be getting a break. Sapphire Seas has a heated pool. There's a beach below the house. You can read. You can spend time with Forrest. What's not to love?'

'But…' She practically gaped. Every one of the prospects he was suggesting made her feel dizzy. She grasped what seemed the closest. Multiple doctors. Here. 'Are these doctors any good?'

'We're all competent,' he told her. 'And you won't be leaving, Misty. You can keep an eye on us from afar, or from close up if you have a set of binoculars. If it doesn't work out, you can move back in again and kick us out. So tell me…what do you have to lose?'

There was a stunned silence. She could hardly take in what was being proposed. How on earth could she answer? 'This seems a joke,' she stammered at last. 'Would they really come?'

'I'd have to ask,' he told her. 'But most are employed casually, as locums, or in the same type of clinic I work in. I'm betting they'll come. The weather in Melbourne's starting to close in. It'll be the surf that lures them.'

'Not for you?' she asked, confused. 'Wouldn't they do it for their friendship with you?'

'We're close, but not so close.'

That made her pause again. She looked at him for a long moment, considering probing further, but then decided to stick to practicalities.

'So…' she said slowly. 'They'd live in our house?'

'I don't see that it'd work any other way. If there's trouble, the islanders will come there looking for you.'

'They'll still want me.'

'But you're on bereavement leave,' he told her, his voice gentling again. 'That's what we'll call it, and if you move out of the doctor's house, if we provide an alternative, the islanders should respect it. Four weeks of nothing, Misty. What do you say?'

What did she say?

What could she say?

Four weeks of…bereavement leave?

She wasn't gutted by Jancie's death—how could she be?

Jancie had been eight years older than her, almost closer to her mother's age than hers. She'd left home when Misty was nine and the next time Misty had had much to do with her was when she'd had that first call from a social worker, asking if she could take care of Forrest. So now... Yes, Jancie's death had shocked her. She had felt grief, but that grief had mostly been for Forrest.

Ever since he'd heard of his mother's death, the little boy had been so subdued that Misty had been thinking that as soon as Lily's needs were met she should organise a trip to a mainland counsellor. Jancie had been an appalling parent, but she'd still been... Mum.

In the last twelve months, living with Misty and Alice, Forrest had started to settle, had started to come out of his shell, had even started to call for Misty when he had a nightmare rather than Jancie. But the news of his mother's death had made him retreat and the subsequent turmoil while she'd tried to care for Lily had made things worse.

What he desperately needed—even more than professional counselling, Misty thought—was time. He needed cuddles and stability. He needed Misty with him for as long as necessary, a Misty who wasn't preoccupied with medicine and a newborn.

And now Angus was offering just that.

'Yes,' she said and the word startled even her. Surely she hadn't meant to say it? Surely she should have thought about it, found out more about Angus's friends, talked to Alice. But her *yes* was already out there. Four weeks of no responsibilities except Forrest and Gran... She'd never had such a thing, never had such a time.

'That was fast.' He was smiling and it was as if the smile was directed straight at her. And maybe it was. Or surely it was. He looked delighted, but there was more than delight behind the smile. He was searching her face, as if he could see right behind it.

'It seems irresponsible,' she said, and his smile deepened.

'Irresponsibility has a lot going for it,' he told her. 'Just ask me. Irresponsibility is my middle name.'

'And yet you will try to love Lily?'

Love… The word hung between them and Angus's smile faded.

'Honestly, Misty, I don't know whether I can.'

What a thing to say. She felt a flash of anger, but then she looked at his face and saw…fear?

Suddenly she thought, this man is in as big a mess as I am. Maybe bigger. I have my gran and Forrest. I have my island, my community. He has, what, friends who'll come here because of the promise of surf?

She'd handed Lily over to him in the hope that he could love her. Could he?

Surely he'd loved once. His parents, his brother, they'd all be somewhere in his heart, and somewhere in there as well was all they'd ever taught him about loving. So what she saw on his face—was that the terror of letting something else—some*one* else—add to that pain?

She was suddenly thinking of kids she'd treated, coming in after falls from bikes, after tumbles from cliffs, cuts, fractures, all the many accidents that happened to island kids. But every child she'd treated—*every one of them*—had a mum or a dad or a grandparent, someone, to hold them, to hug them, to help get them through.

And then Misty was thinking of nineteen-year-old Angus, surely not much older than the kids she treated, surely not old enough to be a man. Maybe he'd been at university when he heard of his family's death, surrounded by kids who were too young to be empathic.

The surfing, the disassociation, the fear of attachment...
She got it.

And as acceptance dawned on just how big the shock of
being landed with a daughter must have been for him, she
looked up and read his expression, and something deeper
seemed to be happening. Their gazes locked and in his
eyes she no longer saw a carefree surfer/doctor fighting to
maintain emotional detachment, but something...some-
one...much deeper.

She couldn't help herself. Before she knew what she was
doing, she raised her hand and cupped his cheek in her
palm. 'You're doing great, Angus,' she whispered. 'You're
doing just great.'

He stared at her as if he wasn't sure what he was seeing.
'It's not me...'

'It is you,' she told him. 'Angus, when your parents
died...did anyone hug you?'

He stared at her blankly. 'I had friends. They took me
surfing, kept me busy, kept the demons at bay.'

'But hugs? Someone to help you face those demons?'

'Misty...'

'I know, I sound like a psychiatrist rather than a family
doctor,' she told him. 'Maybe what *you* need is four weeks'
parental leave, four weeks to get to know your daughter.'

But at that, his look of panic deepened. She smiled, but
didn't take her hand away. For some reason the link seemed
important. 'I know, you need distance, or at least perceived
distance,' she told him. 'You can't get a nanny here, so having friends around you might be the next best thing. But
they can't cocoon you against Lily. In four weeks...if you
let it, might that be long enough to fall in love?'

'Fall...?'

'With your daughter,' she said and still the link of hand

to face remained. 'Angus, your idea is a good one. It might just work for all of us. Thank you.'

And then—because the fear was still there and he was no longer seeming to her like a surfing playboy doctor, but instead she was seeing that bereft, grief-stricken boy—there was suddenly no space for reason. Before she could help herself, she leaned forward, tilted upwards on her toes... and kissed him.

Angus Firth had been kissed by women before. Many women. Kissing was something he enjoyed. He also thought that he was pretty good at it.

This, though, wasn't a kiss like he'd ever experienced.

Misty's kiss landed on his mouth. She possibly hadn't intended that. He must have moved his head. Maybe she'd aimed for a brush against his cheek, the sort of kiss a friend might offer in greeting or farewell. Or in thanks for a gift?

That's what it was meant to be, surely. He'd just organised a break for her, time out from an impossible situation, so a brief, formal kiss was acceptable.

Except this kiss was nothing like that.

Because, with a formal kiss, his hands should have stayed by his sides. The kiss should have been a brush of contact, and then both sides would withdraw. But almost instinctively—it must have been instinct—his hands caught her waist and then the brush of her lips on his mouth became something else entirely.

But this wasn't a seductive prelude to sexual attraction. It was...it was...

Okay, he didn't know what it was. All he knew was that suddenly he was holding her, tugging her body against him and kissing her in return. In response, almost unbelievably, her hands slid around his neck and the kiss deepened.

And the sensation…

He felt as though he'd come home.

The concept was so bizarre that it almost overwhelmed him. He felt light-headed. Spacey. As though this was an out-of-body experience.

Home? What was he thinking?

Home was a house back in Melbourne, or a duffel bag of gear at a surfer's hotel, or even the sanctuary of his sparse consulting rooms at work. It certainly wasn't in the arms of this weary, overwhelmed woman.

And she *was* weary and she *was* overwhelmed, so he had no right, no business, *no reason*, to be kissing her. To be holding her with tenderness. To be feeling tenderness in return.

There was no reason at all to be kissing her like this.

There was no reason at all to feel as though here was home.

What was she doing? Was she out of her mind?

She was kissing the man who'd slept with her sister, who'd fathered her niece, who had nothing at all to do with her, except that she needed him to take some of the responsibility from her shoulders.

But she *was* kissing him, right here, in broad daylight, where anyone passing by could see, where people could think…

But who cared what people thought, because who could think of anything when being kissed like this?

But she wasn't *being* kissed. She'd started this. She'd kissed him.

But she hadn't meant…she hadn't meant…

But there her thoughts ended. She couldn't think, because her body was demanding one thing only: that she kiss and she be kissed. That she let herself melt against this man and be held as if she belonged there. That nothing mattered except right now.

CHAPTER EIGHT

THE KISS ENDED in confusion. Of course it did.

The front door opened and Alice rolled out to the veranda. 'Misty?' she called and then her voice went up an octave or six. 'Misty! What on earth…?'

And they stepped apart as if they'd been hit by lightning. What…what had just happened?

'Misty… Misty was upset,' Angus said, as he stepped back. 'I was…it was just a hug.'

'That didn't look like a hug,' Alice retorted. 'Misty, are out of your mind?'

'I think I must be,' Misty stammered. She carefully didn't look at Angus. 'But I was… I was just thanking him. Gran, Angus has done the most amazing thing.'

'He certainly has,' muttered Alice, giving Angus a death stare to end all death stares. 'I've been trying to stop his "amazing thing" from crying for the last two hours. She's only just stopped and now there's dinner to prepare. I need help.'

'Of course,' Misty said penitently. 'I'll just…'

'Pack,' Angus said.

'As though that's going to happen tonight.' She was feeling weird, maybe even angry? In truth she didn't know how to feel. 'You get your friends here first and then we'll discuss it.'

'They'll come,' he said. 'Maybe tomorrow, definitely by Monday.'

'You really think you can get qualified doctors to drop everything and come?'

'Have you seen the surf report?' He grinned. 'It's a no brainer.'

'What are you talking about?' Alice demanded from the veranda. 'And were you really kissing?' She sounded bewildered, as well she might be. 'Misty, love, are you nuts?'

'Maybe I am,' Misty admitted. 'Because yes, we were kissing.' She took a step back and glared at the offending kisser. Or kissee? She really had no idea.

'I have no idea what just happened,' she said, managing to sound severe. 'But we're not nuts, at least I don't think *I* am. Gran, Angus is promising to conjure up a team of doctors to give me...to give *us* a break. It seems his team can take shifts being doctors and surfers, taking care of the clinic as well as having a sort of holiday.' She took a deep breath, thinking...did this even sound plausible? She cast a cautious glance at Angus and decided looking at him was a bad idea. Somehow she forced herself to go on.

'Angus... Angus thinks his team can live here as well. They'll take over the island's medical needs while you and me and Forrest go and live in the most luxurious house on the island. For a month!'

Alice's jaw dropped. Forrest had edged out to stand beside her wheelchair and she reached out and took the little boy's hand. 'You're joking,' she said, staring at Angus now rather than Misty.

'I'm not joking.'

There was a long silence. 'Of all the promises,' Alice said at last, 'that's crazy. We can't even get a locum.'

'That's because you thought small,' Angus told her, looking smug. 'One locum would be worked to death, just like

Misty's been. Three or more locums, though… A spot of medicine, a spot of surfing, turn and turn about… What's not to love?'

'They won't take medicine seriously,' Misty retorted.

'They'll take medicine seriously enough,' Angus told her. 'But they'll get the balance right.'

'You mean surfing comes first?'

'Misty, we'll always be there in an emergency.' His eyes were on her face as he said it, thoughtful. 'But I imagine our definition of emergency might be different to yours. Brisbane's there, evacuation's there, and we'll use it.'

'But evacuation… That's for…'

'Emergencies. Yes, that's what I said.'

She was staring at him with incredulity, remembering the skill he'd used to save the little dog, remembering the gentleness of his voice as he'd talked to Cath. This didn't fit. 'Would you and your team have sent Doozy to Brisbane?'

He hesitated and then said, 'We might have,' he conceded. 'It was only your reaction…'

'Because I was emotionally involved? Doozy would have died if you'd refused to act.' Her voice sharpened in anger. 'Would you really have done that?'

'Misty.' Her grandmother's voice cut across with unaccustomed sharpness. The elderly lady was staring from Angus to Misty, her face a picture of conflicting emotions. 'Love, is he really… Doctor Firth, are you really offering Misty a holiday?'

'Yes,' he said. Angus was watching Misty's face as well, seemingly bemused by the expressions he was seeing. He didn't seem discombobulated at all, she thought angrily. This was all the same thing. He's used to walking away from emotion. Sorting out others to take on his responsibilities. He walked away from Jancie after a two-week fling.

Then she thought, *He'll be used to kissing and he'll be used to being kissed. It hasn't even thrown him off kilter, whereas me...*

Her thoughts were cut off. Alice had swivelled her chair so she was facing her granddaughter straight on. 'Misty, are you arguing?' she demanded, incredulously.

'Maybe I am,' she said. 'Gran, if he's going to send everything to Brisbane...'

'He's not saying that. Not everything. He's saying there'll be doctors here to do the urgent stuff and for weeks you'll have no responsibility at all. So what if more things than most get sent to the city? It might just save your sanity.'

'Oh, come on...'

'Come on yourself,' Alice said, in the same angry voice. 'Look at you. You're way past exhaustion, way past your limit. You were running on empty even before Jancie died. I've even been thinking we might have to admit defeat and leave...'

'The island? That'd break your heart.'

'Better than breaking *you*,' she retorted. 'But a holiday... four weeks...' She spun her chair again, so she was facing Angus. 'The most luxurious house on the island?'

'Sapphire Seas,' Angus told her. 'I've already booked it.'

Alice gasped. 'You're joking.'

'I'm not.'

'Wow!' She took a deep breath. 'And I rang Martin while you two were canoodling and he says Doozy's going to be okay. Misty, this is sounding like happy ever after.'

'Happy for four weeks,' Misty managed to say and Alice glared.

'Don't you dare quibble,' she said, then she grinned, the happiest smile Misty had seen since they'd heard of Jancie's death. 'Doctor Firth, I'm accepting for all of us. Yes, and yes, and yes. Misty, you were very right to kiss him. Come on up to the veranda, young man. I intend to kiss you myself.'

CHAPTER NINE

TWO WEEKS ON—and he was almost officially a father.

Today Angus had taken Lily across to Brisbane and received the results of the DNA tests. Positive. He'd been questioned for what seemed like hours and filled in enough forms to make a braver man than he was quail. All that was needed now was a couple of government checks to come through, and for Misty to sign forms saying she had no objection to him assuming custody.

Then Lily was his.

He could handle this, he told himself as he took Lily back to the island. But despite the outward control he'd shown in front of officialdom, there was a whole lot of internal panic going on.

But surely there was no need for panic. He'd had two weeks to accept this and think of the future. Surely there was no reason that life in Melbourne couldn't go on almost exactly as it had here.

For these two weeks had worked. There'd been few medical dramas on the island. Yes, there'd been a mass of clinical work—how Misty usually managed it was beyond him—but with four of his doctor mates taking shifts, the workload was more than manageable. What's more, though Lily still had intermittent bouts where nothing seemed to placate her, finally she seemed to be settling.

That must be because she was seldom alone, he decided.

His colleagues had taken on Lily's care with the same dedication they applied to surfing and to medicine. Collectively they'd decided they should use Lily to practise their baby-wrangling skills for future clinical care. Having a baby in the house thus wasn't a problem. The surf was great, their rostered medical shifts were minimal and Lily was perfect for practising their kid skills on.

It also helped that he was paying them more than the government rebates, he thought, though Misty didn't have to know that. He guessed she'd assumed they were doing this for friendship's sake and he wasn't about to disabuse her. His friends thought they were being paid out of clinic funds and he wasn't about to tell them otherwise either.

And this situation had them bemused. He didn't do close friendships, but they were interested, intelligent and fun to be with, and they weren't working very hard for what they were being paid. They were also a trifle stunned by the fact that one of their own had been catapulted into fatherhood.

And now it seemed his fatherhood was about to be official. It should make the path ahead simpler, but as he arrived back at the island, back to the house behind the clinic, the panic returned.

The house was empty. Misty and Alice and Forrest had been settled at Sapphire Seas for two weeks. One of his team would be at the clinic. The others would be surfing.

And there was the glitch in this whole arrangement—he ached to surf. He couldn't. The deal with Misty was that he'd stay with Lily all the time. That had seemed okay when he'd been negotiating this arrangement, but now... He was holding his daughter in his arms and as of this afternoon he was totally, absolutely responsible for her.

And the meaning of the responsibility he'd just assumed was suddenly doing his head in.

Oh, he wanted to surf. He glanced across towards Sapphire Seas. Misty would be there, he thought. Just this once, maybe he could ask…

Was he kidding? The memory of Misty's scorn on that first morning was still raw.

And interspersed with panic, the memory of Misty herself was with him.

Not just her scorn. Her smile?

Did he want to go over and ask her to take a turn with Lily? Or did he want to go over there to see her?

Over and over during these last two weeks he'd found himself looking across to the over-the-top holiday home on the headland and thought he wouldn't mind being over there.

He'd been in contact, of course. He'd taken charge of the island's medical needs and there were logistical things he needed to ask. Thoroughly approving of the arrangements for Misty's holiday, Martin had been more than helpful, but there were things Martin didn't know. He rang nightly to give her an update and seek her advice when needed.

The first time he'd needed her help was for the sort of case he'd normally refer to specialists, the sort of problem he'd do anything to avoid.

'A lad called Nicholas Mickleham?' he'd asked Misty, after one of his team—Jodie—had done a home visit. 'Seventeen years old. Cerebral metastases? Your notes say he's refused more chemo, but he's drowsy and confused and his parents are understandably emotional. They're questioning his decision. Shouldn't we send him to hospital in Brisbane, refer him back to his oncologist?'

And Misty's knowledge of the islanders gave him the answer he needed.

'Angus, Nick's been battling this for a couple of years and he's had enough. He's facing this with a maturity way beyond his years and after his last trip to hospital he swore he'd never leave the island again. I'll ring his parents. Tony and Chris know I'm on a break—so does Nick and they all support it—but if Jodie can't sort it or if Nick wants to talk to me, then I'll go.'

'We can sort it,' he growled. 'But if you want, we will tell him the offer's there. Meanwhile, let's talk about the medications Jodie needs to keep him comfortable.'

And then another case two days later. 'Misty, Dan's seen Nora Wilkins with tummy cramps, but her mum says her cramps clear up at the weekend. Dan's offered to send her to the gastrologist in Brisbane, but her parents reckon she's making the whole thing up, she just doesn't want to go to school. Dan's worried about legal repercussions if we ignore it. Any hints?'

And back came the answer, 'Oh, no, poor Nora.' There'd been a moment's silence while she'd obviously considered what she knew of the twelve-year-old. And then...

'Angus, Nora may well be being given a hard time at school. Nora's dad employed her best friend's older brother as crew on his fishing boat, but word is that Jason kept turning up drunk and he was sacked. Jason holds a grudge like you wouldn't believe. What's the bet he's pressuring his sister to give Nora grief? Donna would be too scared to stand up to him.'

'That's so unfair.'

'Life is,' Misty said briefly. 'I'll give the school counsellor a ring—Pete's great. He'll deal. He knows Jason, too, so things can be sorted from the top down.'

'I don't like you having to ring.'

'Angus, these are my people. I might be on holiday, but I can handle the odd phone call.'

These are my people? What sort of statement was that? It meant a lifetime of overwork and emotional grief, he thought, realising again how much she'd needed this break.

But now there were only two weeks to go. Two weeks before he became the sole carer of Lily.

A nanny had to be the answer. A trained professional would be better than he was at caring—besides, he was missing medicine. Watching his colleagues share the load around their surfing, he'd been starting to feel envious. That was the life he wanted. Part-time doctor suited him perfectly.

As it would surely suit Misty. In two weeks Misty would resume her role as the sole doctor for Kirra Island, a job that was far too big for her.

She could leave, but her words kept echoing.

'These are my people...'

How could she feel like that? Didn't she understand the way to sanity was to keep yourself apart?

Then he looked down at the sleeping Lily, and at the sight of her tiny face the panic welled again. He was scared, he conceded. He felt...alone?

But he liked being alone—he'd designed his life that way. Yes, he needed friends, but his friends were like him. They knew his boundaries. If they were here now, the panic would ease.

If Misty was here now the panic would ease.

Misty.

He glanced over towards Sapphire Seas and saw two figures on the beach. Misty and Forrest. Taking time out to be together?

Surely it wouldn't hurt to walk over. Misty would want to know today's results. He could take Lily in the carry pouch Misty had found for her. She was more settled when he was carrying her, and talking to Misty...it might well make this panic subside.

And as well as that, a small voice was prodding. If Misty was sympathetic, if she was missing Lily but she knew he intended to take over permanently, she might even offer to mind Lily while he surfed. Maybe? That wasn't in the deal, but if she offered…

Why not?

'Let's go tell your aunt and your great-gran that you have a dad,' he told Lily. 'And if, just occasionally, your Aunty Misty wants to share, surely that has to be fine with everyone?'

Misty and Forrest were messing around in the shallows. Just that, messing. There was no pressure to do anything.

Alice was watching from the terrace and Cath was with her. Doozy was dozing beside them, healing nicely, supremely content to be snoozing in a spot where he could occasionally open one eye and look out almost to the mainland. Sharptailed sandpipers were foraging on the sand as the tide came in. Normally Doozy would be seeing the seabirds off, but Doozy was in convalescent mode.

Maybe that's what she was, Misty thought.

For two weeks she'd done nothing.

Okay, she had done some things.

She'd slept, long and gloriously, untroubled by the telephone, by call-outs—or by nightmares.

The master bedroom had a bed that seemed big enough for a small army. The first night here she'd suggested to a nervous Forrest that he might like to share. For the first three days he'd thus slept for longer than she had, his hand tucked in hers.

During the day they'd played—actually played!—in the horizon pool that overlooked the sea—it seemed a waste to have such a pool just for them, but who was arguing? Or they'd wandered down to the beach to play in the shallows.

Forrest was too nervous to do more than wade, but he'd collected shells and made sandcastles and buried his toes in the sand—every now and then glancing at Misty as if he was expecting her to say, *Sorry, Forrest, I need to do...*

But she didn't need to do anything but snooze herself, or read to Forrest, or play and swim and reassure him that she was there for him.

On the fourth night, a beach-sated Forrest had suggested that he might like to sleep in the little room opposite hers because it had a bed that was shaped like a car.

'If you like,' she'd said, diffidently. 'Come back if you get lonely.' They'd left the doors between them open, but he'd decided that's where he'd stay and Misty had the further luxury of her amazing bed all to herself.

Alice, too, was gloriously happy. Cath spent most of the day here, the two women sitting by the pool with a recovering Doozy, happily gossiping about the new order of things on the island.

There was a lot to gossip about. Four qualified doctors—Jodie, Molly, Dan and Ray—all young, all devoted surfers, each of enormous interest to the islanders. There were reports of patients thinking up more than one complaint so they could try out all four.

And late every afternoon Angus rang to update Misty on patients the team had seen that day, to assure Misty that things were going well and that Lily was finally settling.

Currently she and Forrest were building a sand castle. They were also burrowing out a moat, with a channel to the sea they hoped would fill with the incoming tide. The magnificent edifice had taken over an hour to build and how indulgent was that?

When she'd been landed with Lily she'd thought, *This is a disaster.* Right now it was so far from disaster that it almost took her breath away.

Thanks to Angus.

More and more, the emotions in her head when she

thought of Angus had her confused. She'd forced him into fatherhood and his reaction had made her angry. She still wasn't sure that he was accepting responsibility, but he was giving her this.

Plus, his spur-of-the-moment medical team was giving the islanders the most immediate care they'd seen since for ever. Misty was usually booked out for weeks, cramming urgent cases into the edges of her already long days. Now there were fresh young doctors, seemingly ready to drop their surfboards and pay attention.

'Wouldn't it be great if we could keep them?' Alice had said wistfully the night before, but of course they were transient. When the autumn surf turned to cold winter swells they'd be gone and Angus—and Lily—would be gone, too.

Why did that make her heart lurch? And why did her heart race every time the phone rang and it was Angus checking in?

If he was to stay…

Yeah, as if that was likely. She'd handed him a baby and that was enough. She could hardly hand him half a medical practice, a remote island and a lifestyle that wouldn't include his friends.

Why was she even thinking that? Was it that stupid kiss?

If it was, she had to get over it. The stupid niggle that the kiss had caused, the tiny embryo of a fanciful dream… well, it was just that.

Angus had given her the gift of time out, time to recover, time to spend with Forrest. That alone was a gift without price, so why was she wasting any of it dreaming of the impossible?

It took him fifteen minutes to reach Sapphire Seas, walking along the beach path with Lily in a carry pouch on his chest. For most of the walk he could see the two figures on the beach, but even when he rounded the last rockface they seemed oblivious to him.

Misty was wearing a plain black swimsuit, built for practicality rather than style. She looked good in it, though, he decided. No, she looked great. Her curls were damp and tangled from the sea. Her skin was bronzed from the sun.

He'd thought Jancie was the gorgeous sister, but as he walked down the beach towards her, he thought, *Define gorgeous.*

And then came the thought, *I don't want to ask her to take care of Lily while I surf. What I really want is to surf with her.*

Could she surf? If she'd spent much of her childhood on the island she probably could.

How could he organise it?

Um…why did he want to? This situation was complex enough as it was, but as he walked down the beach towards her, the idea stayed.

She and Forrest had dug a moat around their castle and both were whooping with excitement as small waves swept in to fill it. But their castle was in peril. Forrest was desperately trying to shore up his side of the moat, before shouting a warning to Misty. Too late. Misty's side caved in—and then a bigger wave than normal swept up and half the castle crumpled into sand.

Forrest squealed in dismay, but Misty rose from where she'd been kneeling and lifted Forrest and spun him in the shallows. The skinny little kid was whirled in her arms and then hugged tight.

'That's Ocean three, Us none,' Misty said, setting him down and chuckling. 'The odds are against us, Forrest. My suggestion is that we build our next castle higher up the beach and fill our moat with our buckets. What do you say?'

'Yes!' he said. 'We don't have to go inside yet, do we? I'll go get buckets.'

'There's no hurry,' she told him as he raced off and Angus heard the note of satisfaction and thought…he'd done that. He'd given her this month…

Smug R Us? He couldn't quite manage a full-scale chest expansion though, not with a sleeping baby on his chest.

That brought him up with a jolt. It was the arrival of his baby that had put her under such pressure.

His baby? Argh.

He could cope, he told himself. Surely he could cope.

And then Misty saw him. 'Hey,' she said, with a smile that lit her eyes and made him glad all over again that he'd been able to give her this break. And then her eyes narrowed. 'How long have you been here? Have you been spying?'

'I *was* thinking of calling up the cavalry and storming the battlements,' he said, grinning as he surveyed the soggy heap of sand that once was a castle. 'There doesn't seem to be much left to loot and pillage, though.'

'There's a lump of seaweed under this mess,' she offered. 'We used it for bulk. If you really want to pillage…'

'Thank you, but I'm not sure of the black market price for seaweed. My on-selling opportunities seem a bit slim.'

That brought a chuckle and when the chuckle faded, her smile remained.

Oh, it was a great smile.

'So? How did it go on the mainland?' she asked.

So now he had to say it. Out loud. He took a moment to steady and finally the words came out.

'DNA conclusive. One hundred per cent sure, so officially, as of today, I have a daughter. Or almost. They need to run background checks to make sure I'm not an axe murderer or the like. There are a couple of documents you'll need to sign, but after that the thing's done.'

'Oh, Angus…' She stood silent for a moment. Her eyes welled and she blinked back tears. She was smiling, though. Happy tears? Relief for him, or for her, or for Lily? he wondered. Or all three? 'That's…that's wonderful,' she said. 'At least…' She hesitated. 'I think it's wonderful. Is it?'

'Yeah,' he said. And with the sun on his face, with the approval of the social workers still in his mind, with Misty beaming mistily at him, and with Lily warmly cocooned against his chest, maybe it was.

Certainly it was, he told himself. He had to believe it. 'It's working out fine,' he told her. 'And Lily's settling grandly. I told you, it takes a village and that's what my friends and I have. With five of us in the house, baby-wrangling's a piece of cake.'

With five of us in the house, baby-wrangling's a piece of cake…

Why did that statement make something lurch in her insides? Why did that spoil her sense of jubilation?

Why should she even care? Just shut up, she told herself. Your problem's sorted. Lily has a dad.

But this was *her* niece. This was Alice's granddaughter. How could she shut up?

'Really?' she said slowly. 'So baby-wrangling… How does that make you form attachment?'

'Do I need more attachment?' He was craning his neck so he could see his sleeping daughter. 'We're doing okay. Once my friends aren't around I can hire people in Melbourne—a nanny—whatever she needs.'

'So you'll be one carer of many?' Still, she felt uneasy. 'Angus, you're her dad.'

No matter how perfect this set up seemed for him, she still sensed trouble.

But maybe she needed to butt out, she told herself. Angus was now officially Lily's father, which meant Misty would have no ongoing responsibility.

Why the unease?

Maybe she would have felt more comfortable with this situation if they hadn't kissed, she thought. That had been a huge mistake. It had woken something in her that she didn't have time or room for. Watching him now, casually dressed, baby asleep on his chest, looking at ease, a man with his problems sorted… It made her feel…

As though she had no business feeling. It was two weeks since they'd exchanged a meaningless kiss. Surely she should be over it by now.

But was that the reason for her unease? Was she seeing him as a playboy, a Peter Pan who refused to grow up? Would she be more comfortable with him taking on Lily's care if he didn't seem…

So dangerous?

He wasn't dangerous for Lily, she told herself. Dangerous was surely a dumb description.

'I need to be getting back,' Angus said, seemingly unaware of the tension in her voice. 'The guys are setting up a firepit, which means we can have surfer fare, get the guitars out, enjoy ourselves. Jodie—you met Jodie?—sorted some sun damage on Ron Giddie's arm last week and today he presented her with half a dozen snapper.' He hesitated, then said, 'Would you like to join us?'

Her? Join him? Was he kidding? What would it be like to live in a world where she could accept an invitation like this?

'Thank you, but no,' she told him. 'You know I can't leave Forrest.'

'He could come with you. Come to think of it, you could bring Alice as well. We have plenty of fish.'

Oh, the siren song—but she couldn't. Because there was that word again, flashing warning signals in the back of her head.

Dangerous…

Or should that be…impossible?

'We've been on the beach most of the day,' she said. 'Forrest will crash by seven and Gran won't be long after.'

'Could he stay with her while you come?'

She shook her head, resolute. Someone had to be sensible.

'This time is all about getting our relationship sorted. Mine and Forrest's,' she said firmly. 'I need to keep that front and centre.' How hard was that to say? But she'd said it and now she struggled to find something else to talk about.

A grievance?

'You do know that I've coped with Ron Giddie's damaged skin for years and he's never given me so much as a sardine,' she said darkly.

'Something to do with our Dr Jodie looking like a sun-bronzed *Vogue* model?' Angus suggested. But then added hastily, 'Not that you don't look great.'

'Yeah, right.' She was now also having to fight back the image of the gorgeous Jodie. She'd met them and they all looked gorgeous. Young, carefree, joyous.

Except, she reminded herself, that's how Angus came across. But she knew his background now. Who was to say that every one of the team didn't have a backstory? Maybe there was no need for her to feel jealous.

No reason at all?

Oh, for heaven's sake, she was struggling with feelings that were altogether inappropriate. Finally she decided that what she was justified in feeling was annoyed. Lily's arrival didn't seem to have impacted on Angus's life at all. He was the same playboy surfer, surrounded by his mates, sharing his responsibilities.

He did have his responsibility in his arms right now, though, she had to concede, and she had to accept there were more ways than one to parent. So was it jealousy making her feel judgemental?

But he was watching her and the expression on his face had subtly changed.

'When did you last have a night off?' he asked suddenly. 'Without the threat of being called out?'

'I've had the last two weeks off.'

'But before that? When did you last have a night without worrying about Forrest or your gran or your patients?'

That was an easy question. 'I can't remember,' she told him. 'That's why I'm so grateful.'

'But I don't want you to be grateful.' He sighed. 'Okay, it's time for Lily and me to go home, but tomorrow night… What if I organise someone to care for Forrest and keep Alice company? If they were settled…maybe you and I could have a date.'

'A *date*?' Was he out of his mind?

And he must have seen her instinctive recoil, because he went on fast. 'Whoops, maybe that's the wrong word,' he told her. 'We need to talk about future relations with the kids—Lily and Forrest are half-siblings after all. We need to discuss continuing contact. If it'll make you feel better, we can call it a meeting. I'm sure we could fill a whole meal with planning. Maybe, though,' he said, watching her face, 'we could also have fun?'

'*Fun…*'

'Life doesn't have to be serious all the time.'

What followed was a pause. A long pause.

'Misty, we do need to talk,' he said, hurriedly now. 'The social workers say it'll be best for us to keep in touch—

for you and Alice to have some input into Lily's life. We need to figure out a relationship. So here's a plan. Tomorrow evening I'll ask a couple of my team if they can spend a few hours here. I don't see it being a problem—they like kids and they're competent. Alice will be here to give Forrest a sense of security. They can have a barbecue, invite Cath, cook a sausage or six. Alice and Forrest will like my friends and Ray can make better aeroplanes than I can! When they're settled and happy, we can slip away. Maybe even take a picnic?'

'A picnic…'

'The café at the wharf does great take-away picnics,' he told her, speaking a bit too fast again. 'Jodie and Ray took one with them at the weekend and they said it was great.'

'You'd buy a picnic?' This was doing her head in.

'If you don't like that idea, we can do something else,' he told her. 'I can even make something—though my cooking skills are limited. I don't think Vegemite sandwiches are very romantic.'

'Romantic? What the…?'

'I meant delicious,' he said hastily. 'This is not a come on, Misty. I don't intend to make anyone else pregnant.'

'Oh, for heaven's sake! As if!'

'Exactly, so why not come? It looks as though we'll be sort of co-parenting for a long time. We need to figure out some form of relationship.'

'But not romantic,' she said, sounding breathless. 'That kiss…'

'Was an aberration between two stressed people,' he said firmly. 'I know it's left us a bit off kilter, but we need to forget it.'

But then they were interrupted.

Forrest had obviously been waylaid by Alice, but he was now heading back down the beach, waving two buckets.

'Got 'em,' he called. 'Doctor Firth, will you help build an-other moat? And stay for dinner? Gran says she and Aunty Cath are making hamburgers and they say there's enough for you.'

'That sounds great,' he said, looking at Misty appraisingly. 'But my friends will already be cooking my dinner. Forrest, I've asked your aunt to have dinner with me to-morrow, while my friends come over here to eat with you. Ray will teach you to make bigger and better aeroplanes and Jodie's really great at digging. This moat could get hu-mungous. If you're happy, your Aunty Misty and I will go and eat on our own.'

'Why do you want to do that?' Forrest asked, mystified.

'We both like Vegemite sandwiches.'

'Really?' Forrest asked, grimacing, and then decided there was a more important question. 'So what would we eat?'

'What do you like?'

'Sausages.'

'Perfect. Sausages it is.'

'Would you rather eat Vegemite sandwiches than sau-sages?' Forrest sounded incredulous.

'No, but if that's what Misty wants, that's what she'll get. What about it, Misty. Yes or no?'

'What about Lily?' she asked, feeling winded.

'Lily will come with us,' he said, imbuing his words with a tinge of virtue. 'How can you doubt it?' He glanced down at his chest. 'She doesn't eat much, though. I think our Vegemite sandwiches are safe. Come on, Misty, say yes.'

There was a loaded silence while Angus and Forrest both looked at her expectantly. And suddenly her traitorous heart said, why not?

'Okay, yes,' she said, goaded. 'But only if it's fine with you, Forrest.'

'Can your friends bring ice-cream, too?' Forrest demanded and Misty thought of the Forrest of two weeks ago. That Forrest would never have been brave enough to ask such a question.

But... 'Yes, they can,' Angus said and the thing was sorted.

And Misty thought, *What have I done? I have a date with Angus Firth. And his baby.*

CHAPTER TEN

RAY AND JODIE were every bit as competent as Angus had promised. They arrived at Sapphire Seas the next afternoon and went straight into caretaker mode.

'We've competed for the title of Best Paper Planes Maker for years,' Jodie told Forrest. 'And Angus says you're practically a champion yourself. We can mark our best flight length and see if we can set a record. Then we'll cook sausages and have a swim and tell stories on the beach until Misty and Angus get back. They said they'll be back in three hours. Will that give us enough time to do what we want? What do you think?'

Thus Forrest's contentment was assured, as was Alice's—she was watching with a certain level of bemusement—and Misty and Angus were free to go. Angus drove. Lily was settled in her baby capsule, appearing as contented as Forrest. Misty sat in the passenger seat, feeling stunned. Even a bit railroaded?

There were surfboards on the roof rack. Did Angus intend surfing? That made her wonder, what sort of world did he live in where he could just head out for a surf whenever he wanted?

For a moment she imagined a world where she could spend a whole evening on the beach, surfing, with no time limit…even surfing with Angus?

As if. Maybe it was just as well Lily was with them, she thought. The idea of surfing at sunset with Angus…

Well, she couldn't. Even tonight there were restrictions. Someone had to stay on the beach with Lily, and there went any stupid ideas of anything…well, anything stupid.

And then they pulled into a clearing at the side of the road and she almost gasped.

The beach here wasn't known as the best surfing beach on the island, but it was one of the most beautiful. Angus must have done his homework because it was pretty much only known to locals. It wasn't signposted and you couldn't see it from the road. A sandy track, narrow and innocuous, wound its way through the palms to a perfect tear-shaped cove. There were no other cars here and there was a reason.

She climbed cautiously out of the car and gazed around in disbelief. She'd been here during the day, but never in the evening. 'So,' she said slowly. 'Seduction Cove?'

'Cath told me about it. It isn't what it's really called,' he said, but then added dubiously, 'is it?'

'No, but it should be,' she said darkly. 'The unwritten rule is that if there's another car here you leave. It's off the track so tourists don't know about it, and there are plenty of other beaches.'

'None of that's happening tonight,' he said hastily.

'You got that right.' What had Cath been thinking? 'So two surfboards,' she said, cautiously. 'One for you and one for Lily?'

'One for each of us,' he told her, smiling. 'I figure we can take turns, one of us with Lily admiring the other's surfing skills, and then vice versa.'

'You won't be admiring my surfing skills,' she said. 'I haven't surfed for…'

'For years,' he concluded for her. 'Cath told me how much you love surfing, but she also said she hasn't seen you surf since before Forrest came to stay with you. Jodie's lent us her board. I assume yours is under the house, but I figured you might refuse if I asked you where it was.'

Of course she would have refused. What was Cath doing, chatting about her behind her back? 'Angus...'

'Relax,' he told her. 'These four weeks are for you to have a complete break. I'd have liked to have sent you off the island...'

'I couldn't...

'I know you couldn't,' he told her. 'But tonight, and maybe a few times over the next two weeks, you could take time off from being doctor, parent, carer. Maybe you could just... be you.'

'I don't think I know who "just me" is any more.' She sighed. 'Sorry, that sounds dumb. I do know. I'm Misty, the woman who gets up in the morning and does what she needs to do. And what I'd like to do now is eat. Where are these Vegemite sandwiches you promised?'

There weren't just Vegemite sandwiches. Angus had done his homework. His phone call to Cath had produced a gleeful 'Leave it to me!' and Cath and a couple of her friends had more than delivered. Angus carted what seemed an extraordinarily heavy basket down to the beach while Misty carried Lily. Angus headed back for the surfboards while Misty spread out the rug Cath had supplied. When he returned, Misty was squatting on her heels, staring at the basket's contents in amazement.

'A full crayfish, plated ready for eating? Salads? These look like Donna Irvine's home-made bread rolls? Strawberries? Vanilla slices? And wine...and crystal wine glasses! Angus, you *did* know it was Seduction Bay. I should go home now.'

'I swear I didn't,' he said, checking the spread with appreciation. 'Did they not include even one Vegemite sandwich?'

'Oh, look.' There was a tiny, single-serve packet. 'Yes, they did. Hooray, that's my dinner.' She looked again at the lobster and at the bottle of wine in its chilled carrier, and shook her head. 'Someone has to be sensible.'

'Well, it's not going to be me,' Angus told her. 'But you can forget any thoughts of seduction, Misty. We don't have time. We…or at least I, if you stick to your Vegemite sandwich plan…intend to wrap myself round this lot and then surf. Then I'll tell Lily bedtime stories while you surf. Maybe if you get tired I can have a quick surf afterwards. Is that okay with you, Lily?'

Lily, still settled in her capsule, seemed bemused by the whole situation. She was wide eyed, seemingly taking in the gentle surf, the soft white clouds wisping across the sun's last rays, the seabirds swooping overhead.

Angus was kneeling in front of her, and suddenly, amazingly, her tiny face creased into a smile in return.

She was eight weeks old and there'd been no smile until now—not a one. It wasn't surprising considering the start she'd had, but Misty had been starting to be concerned about milestones.

Here it was, though, a huge smile, and it was directed straight at Angus.

She saw Angus's eyes widen in astonishment and then he smiled in return, and she saw Lily's smile broaden into almost a chuckle.

She felt her eyes well with stupid tears. Tears of happiness that finally Lily was smiling?

Tears of relief that here was the bond she'd hoped so desperately for and now seemed to be possible?

Tears of…regret? Tears that she couldn't keep loving this little girl who'd needed her so much?

Angus glanced at her and maybe he sensed the emotions because he turned Lily's capsule. 'A smile! You want to share with your Aunty Misty, sweetheart?'

But Lily didn't. Her gaze tracked back to Angus and held, and Misty sniffed and thought that this was good. No, this was great.

Why was her stupid heart telling her otherwise?

The meal was gorgeous. Of course she abandoned her dumb resolution to only eat sandwiches—though she did eat a corner just so she could assure Forrest that that's what she'd had. Angus did, too. 'Because we're in this together,' he told her and why did that make her feel even more strange than she was already feeling?

But oh, the crayfish and the custard-filled slices—the island baker's specialty—and the strawberries... She even succumbed to temptation and had a glass of wine, and that left her sleepy and sated and wondering why couldn't she feel like this for ever.

Then Lily's patience came to an end and she opened her mouth and squawked.

'I'll feed her,' Angus said. 'You go surf.'

'I didn't bring my swim gear.'

And the man had the temerity to smirk. 'You might as well know I'm an ex-boy scout,' he told her. 'I was raised with "Be Prepared" as my motto. Alice and Cath sneaked your stuff into a bag—give me two minutes and I'll fetch it from the car.'

'They sneaked...?'

'They agreed you'd be too chicken to bring it yourself,' he told her. 'So it's collusion. I even thought of getting Forrest on side.'

Which meant there was nothing for Misty to do but surf, while Angus sat on the beach and fed her...no, *his* baby.

* * *

She was surfing!

Misty had been on the island often enough as a kid to have surfing in her bones. The island kids had accepted her as one of their own. A younger and healthier Alice had brought her to the beach when she was small, and, as she got older, one of the locals would drop by and pick her up whenever the surf was up.

But she hadn't surfed for ever. Since she'd got custody of Forrest there'd never been time. But even before that, well, while she was a med student, while she was working as an intern and then when she was here as the island's sole doctor...there was always something more imperative.

But tonight there was nothing but warm seas and glorious, curving swells, not too challenging for a surfer whose skills were rusty. Forrest and Alice were being cared for. Other doctors were on call, absolving her of all responsibility, and on the beach Angus was feeding his baby. *His.*

She was hardly game to look at him as she caught wave after wave. The surfing, the magnificent feeling of catching and riding the easy swells, should have commanded all her attention, but Angus was watching her and that did something to her insides, something she could hardly understand.

The DNA was proven. He was taking responsibility. Her overwhelming problem was solved, but it wasn't that that was causing this strange feeling. It was the sight of him, a man feeding a baby while she had fun.

The sight of Angus Firth watching her?

She could see why Jancie had targeted him. Skilled, gorgeous, rich...

Vulnerable? Wounded? Scared?

Why did those words spring to mind? They certainly hadn't been on Jancie's desire list.

They shouldn't be in hers either, she thought. She didn't

need to go deep into Angus Firth's mind. For now, all that mattered was that he was Lily's father. And there was another wave to catch.

And that was all.

Half an hour saw Misty done. 'Do you know how long it's been since I've caught a wave?' she demanded of Angus. 'My knees are jelly!'

Lily had drifted to sleep. 'Go surf yourself,' Misty ordered and Angus didn't need to be told twice. Resisting perfect waves was like fighting himself.

Misty settled by the fire he'd made with the driftwood collected from the high tide mark. The night was still and warm, but she wrapped herself in her oversized towel and then used it as a modesty wrap while she dressed.

He was aware of a stab of disappointment as she did. He'd liked seeing her in a bathing suit instead of sensible work clothes, he decided. He'd also enjoyed seeing her surf.

No. He'd *loved* seeing her surf, he conceded. Cath had told him she was good, but until he'd seen her catch her waves with a skill that told him her love of surfing was bone deep, he hadn't realised…what she'd given up.

What sort of life was he leaving her to?

'Surf for as long as you want,' she told him as she settled by the fire. 'I'm warm and happy and I can't believe I'm here, on the beach with nothing to do. If you want to surf until our Forrest-set curfew, it's okay with me.'

So he surfed, but as he surfed he watched the beach. He watched her. She looked content, the firelight showing her face as almost dreamy. How rare was this moment of peace?

And he thought…how could he help her?

How wonderful was it that they took turns caring for Lily while they surfed? How excellent an idea was it to share?

And then he thought…

A thought so perfect it almost blew his mind.

Angus strode out of the shallows and Misty watched him come. The fading evening light accentuated the outline of his body, the man and his surfboard a beautiful silhouette against the waves.

Oh, that body…

'Well, that's Jancie talking,' she told herself, but she managed a smile as he dumped his board, spread his towel and sat down beside her. His body glistened in the firelight and oh, wow…

No! Get yourself together, she told herself. Life's complicated enough already.

And then he said, 'Misty, I've been thinking. I was wondering about the possibility of you moving to Melbourne, sharing my house.'

And her world seemed to still.

'Sorry?' she managed to say at last, staring at him in bewilderment.

'I know,' he said, hurriedly now. 'You won't leave Alice. My house is big enough for all of us, but how could we persuade her to leave the island? But then I thought about how you feel about family. How Alice feels about family. So here's a plan. It's tentative at best, the plan needs finesse, but I want you to think about it.'

'Think about…what?'

'How about we become…almost a family?'

She'd thought her life was complicated. Life was suddenly so much more complicated it was all she could do to breathe.

'What…what?'

Who knew how she got the word out? She was lucky to have even got it out at all.

But he didn't seem perturbed. Nor did he seem conscious that what he'd just said was preposterous.

'I do my best thinking while surfing,' he continued, seemingly unaware of her breathing problems. 'And this thought is a ripper. Misty, you need to be able to surf.'

'I *can* surf,' she said, thinking some sort of hallucinogenic drug might have been in the vanilla slices.

'And do other things,' he continued. 'Have coffee with friends. Go shopping. Go kayaking. I bet you'd like kayaking.'

'I have kayaked.' She was still cautious. Should she back away? Call for a straitjacket? Or had she misheard that first statement?

'I'm not nuts,' he said, pouring himself coffee from the thermos in the picnic basket. 'Thanks for leaving enough for me, by the way. I'm not sure I'd have been that noble.'

'You said…' She took a deep breath. 'You said…family?'

'I did.' He sat, drinking his coffee with appreciation, as if he was considering a totally reasonable proposition. 'You know I'm taking on Lily? You know my house in Melbourne is huge? It's a great place to raise kids, I know it is.'

He hesitated then, staring out to sea for a long moment, but then he regrouped and continued.

'My brother and I loved it—we had the best childhood and I'm betting Forrest and Lily would feel the same. The house would be great for them. And, Misty, my clinic's always looking for new doctors. You'd fit in there magnificently. That'd give you free time to spend with the kids. But also, by raising the two kids together, we could employ excellent childcare and household help. Your gran would get the best medical care, too, and I'm betting she'd enjoy having time to have fun with the kids, but with no responsibility. And for us… Misty, we'd still be free to do what we want—what *you* want, Misty. A life where you have time for *you*.'

She stared at him, dazed, boggled by the whole concept. 'And…and you?' She could still barely get the words out.

'I'll be the dad.' He said it proudly, as though it was the natural conclusion of a neatly laid out plan. 'Maybe even to both kids. I can teach them to surf—you can, too,' he added generously. 'You're a great surfer, Misty. With practice you'd be amazing.'

'No, we're talking about you.' This was sounding more and more ludicrous. 'So you'll teach them to surf? What else?'

'Whatever else they need. It might even be fun.'

'So…fun,' she said, slowly now. 'But you said family?'

'A unit. A practical way to make this work for all of us.'

'Is that what family means to you?' She was having trouble getting her head around this. Anybody would.

'I guess for you it means more,' he admitted. 'But for me it can't. Emotional connection got knocked out of me a long time ago. But, Misty, you already love Lily—I know you do. This way you wouldn't need to give her up.'

'So what are you thinking?' she said. 'This'd be house sharing, with me doing the loving for all of us?'

'I will care.'

'But that's not love.' She hesitated. She should leave now, head back to the car, demand to be taken home. But his proposition wasn't offensive. He even thought it was sensible.

And maybe it might be, she conceded. Except for the way she felt.

About him.

'So I'd love Forrest and Lily and Gran,' she said slowly. 'But…family. What about you and me?'

'We'd be housemates,' he said and then looked at her and gave a crooked smile. 'Okay, this thing that's between us…this thing I feel… We could even… I don't know…be housemates with benefits?'

'You're kidding.'

'Okay, without benefits,' he said hastily. 'But we could try the plan out, see how it evolves. I've been thinking it through while I've been surfing. Social Services would love it—they've said there'll be check-ups because of Lily's background, but this arrangement would totally reassure them. And Forrest and Lily would have a stable home. We all would. And without the massive commitment to this island…'

'You're proposing I leave? Where does that leave the islanders?'

'Nature abhors a vacuum. Some other doctor will come along.'

'After the mining company left, no one came for almost twenty years.'

'My friends came.'

'For a few weeks,' she retorted. This was like some appalling joke, and anger was starting to build. 'I don't know how you got them here, but I suspect payment comes into it. Angus, just how rich are you?'

'Very,' he confessed. 'Which is…'

'Another reason for me to live with you? To stop worrying about my bills?'

'It wouldn't hurt.'

'It would hurt,' she said obtusely. 'I don't want to be rich and I'll be damned if I'm going to be paid to be the loving one.'

'You wouldn't be paid. Just…supported?'

For heaven's sake, he was serious. He was like an engineer, she thought, a man who'd outlined a proposal and was waiting for the unskilled to see the sense in it.

'Angus, this island's my family,' she said.

That brought a frown. 'That doesn't make sense.'

'I guess it doesn't.' Heading for the car was starting to seem the only option. She rose and he rose, too. But now he was a bit too close and that messed with her mind. The whole situation was messing with her mind.

'I care about this island, Angus,' she stated.

'And I care about you.'

'Like you care about your surfer mates? Or…you talked about *"this thing between us"*. Is it physical? The way you cared about Jancie?'

That brought silence. He raked his hair and stared at her for a long moment, seemingly trying to get his thoughts in order. 'I've never wanted to live with anyone but you,' he said at last. 'I never even thought about it with Jancie.'

'Of course not. It wouldn't be sensible. I don't see how you can possibly think this is.'

'It is,' he told her. 'Someone else can look after the islanders.'

'Who?'

'Is that your concern? Haven't you given them enough?'

'I've doled out their ration, do you mean?' Anger was helping now. 'Paid my account? They were good to me so, yep, here's six years' medical care. Enough, you're on your own now.'

'There's no need to be angry.'

'I'm not.' She closed her eyes. 'Sorry. Yes, I am. This is a weird, impossible proposition that's come out of nowhere.'

'I think it would work.' He sounded a bit unsure, but stubborn.

'How would it work when you just admitted you don't want to live with anyone?'

'This is different. The way I feel about you…'

And that stopped her in her tracks. Anger gave way to a sweep of confusion so great she almost felt dizzy and, when she looked at Angus, she saw her confusion mirrored back at her.

The way I feel about you...

He was afraid, she thought, and the realisation hit her like a shock. He was in unchartered territory. He did care. He'd open his house to her, open his life—but on his terms? And those terms must surely be impossible.

They were still too close. For some reason neither of them had taken a step back.

At least she was fully clothed, she thought numbly, for which she was grateful. She'd actually be very grateful if Angus was fully clothed.

Or would she?

'So this...thing...' she ventured, anger giving way to confusion. 'You and me.'

'You feel it, too?'

'You need to tell me what it is.'

'I can't,' he said helplessly. 'But it's there, between us. Misty, I just have to look at you...'

'Like you looked at Jancie?' But that didn't come out right. It was meant to be accusatory. Instead it came out...a little bit sad? As though the idea of anyone like Angus looking at a woman weighed down with so much was unthinkable.

Then, just for a moment, she saw a kaleidoscope image of how life could be in the future Angus was proposing. Living in his gorgeous house. Sharing the responsibility of the two children. Having Gran safe.

Having time for herself.

'I never looked at Jancie like I'm looking at you,' he said, and the kaleidoscope image seemed to whirl and firm into a thought that was suddenly possible.

Then, stupidly, crazily, she let herself look up at him with different eyes. Her gaze met his and for that one impossible moment she let herself believe.

He reached out and his hands cupped her face. He was tilting her chin.

'I'd never have kissed her like this,' he murmured—and kissed her.

They'd kissed before, but he'd accounted for that kiss. It had been almost accidental, a result of shock, of weariness, of confusion and of stress.

The memory had stayed with him, though. The feel of her, the taste of her, the sensation of her body against his. And now...

Why wasn't this like kissing Jancie, or kissing any of the other women who'd fleetingly touched his life? Why was kissing this woman touching something deep within? Setting off a yearning for what might well be unobtainable? Making his life seem somehow both empty and full of promise?

And why wasn't she pulling away?

She was right. His plans were dumb, formed on the spur of the moment, surely not rooted in sense. Or maybe they did make sense on a practical level, but in reality, if this woman was ever in his bed... If she was part of his life...

Would she feel like this?

But right now she did feel like this. This was real. And that was the end of sensible thought, because feeling like this was crazy, but somehow *this* was as if they were two halves, split by fate and magically reunited.

The sensation was mind-blowing. Life-changing? This woman was...

Misty. Nothing more, nothing less. She was a woman who made him feel as he'd never felt before.

And in that moment the defences he'd built so carefully since his family's death crumbled to nothing.

Oh, the taste of her. The feel of her damp curls against his skin. The sensation of her hands on the small of his back as she held herself against him.

For she was kissing him back! The sensation was indescribable and who'd want to describe it anyway? Not when he could feel it. Not when he could *be* it.

Misty.

And in the corner of his brain available for almost coherent thought he decided his plan was not only sensible, it was desirable. To come home to her every night... To have her be part of his home...

He hadn't thought he could ever want a woman in his life, but now it seemed imperative. All he needed was her agreement.

Just as soon as this kiss ended—which couldn't happen any time soon.

It had to end and it had to end now! What was she doing, kissing this man, letting herself surrender to the feel of him, letting herself believe she was desired, that her life could change, that somehow this man could become someone she...loved?

Love? The word was almost terrifying, but once her mind had let it in, it refused to be evicted.

And why not? She was standing in what was surely one of the most beautiful places in the world, she was in the arms of surely one of the most beautiful men, and he'd just proposed that they become a family. That they share their lives.

And he was kissing her and she was kissing him back. No, it was more than just a kiss. She was surrendering all sense, and for this moment she was letting herself believe in some crazy, wonderful vision of the future.

If only she could halt time. If only she could stay in this man's arms for ever—if this kiss could last for eternity. She felt as if she was melting into him. Oh, this kiss…

But eternity was a long time and as the kiss extended, Lily had decided enough was enough. Lying awake in her capsule, obviously noting that neither adult was paying her due attention, she opened her mouth and wailed.

And with that, reality crashed down like an ice wall.

What was she doing, standing in Seduction Cove, kissing a guy who was wearing nothing but boxer shorts? The same man who'd made her sister pregnant. The man who'd just asked her to live with him because…because…

She knew the because. With that wall of ice came the absolute acceptance of what his proposal had been all about. He'd even said it. Yes, he was conceding Lily was his daughter, but he didn't want the emotional responsibility. He'd support her and her family and in payment she'd take over his emotional load.

And she'd leave her island.

But the way she felt…

What? *What?*

Was it love?

There was that word again, slamming back. Was she admitting to herself that she was falling in love with a man who didn't know how to love back?

Could he learn to? Would he even want to try?

What was she thinking? Would she risk breaking her heart by going one step further down a path he wanted nothing to do with?

Somehow she'd broken the kiss. She forced herself to step back, holding up her hands as if to ward him off.

'No,' she stammered, and it was all she could do to get the words out. 'No more. L… Lily.'

'Is hungry.' He sounded as shaken as she was. 'I…it's okay. I have another bottle.'

'Take her home and feed her,' she said, desolation descending like a fog. Was this how Cinderella had felt at midnight? 'She'll settle a little in the car and then you can feed her and put her straight to sleep.'

'Misty…'

'I need to go home, too,' she said. 'Angus, this is stupid.'

'It doesn't feel stupid to me. And you… Misty, you're feeling this, too.'

'It doesn't matter if I am. You said yourself you don't do emotional connections. What else is there if we're to become a family? The idea makes no sort of sense.'

'But you…'

'Yes, I'm feeling emotional connection.' Anger was surging again, fury at the stupidity of what was happening. She took a couple more steps back and let it rip. 'You stand there looking like a Greek god and you smile at me and you save Cath's dog and you smile at Lily and you make my heart… you make my heart… Angus, what I feel…'

'But isn't that a good thing?' He was watching her warily.

'Not if you can't love in return.'

And there was the biggie. Even Lily seemed to sense its enormity, because she stopped wailing and gazed up at them—almost as if she understood that things were being decided here that would affect her future for ever.

'Misty, I don't know that I can,' he said. 'I want you— my body tells me that—but love? Hell, I need to hold myself back.'

'At least you're honest. But me… I *do* love, Angus. I love Gran and Forrest. I love this island. I love my community. I've even come close to loving Lily, but I can't… I can't do more. It seems Lily might have to take a chance on you, but there's no way I can, not when you're too fearful to even try.'

'I don't understand. You want me to tell you I love you? Lie until maybe it happens?'

'Don't be ridiculous,' she said, anger fading, leaving that cold desolation in its wake. 'You're not stupid, Angus Firth, but your proposition certainly is. Lily's your daughter, so she's inextricably tied to you. I'm not. It's time we moved on.'

'Misty…'

'No more. Please, let's go home.'

CHAPTER ELEVEN

COULD HE CHANGE? And why would he want to?

For the next ten days the questions sat in his mind like lead.

The drive home from the beach had been done in silence, with Misty staring straight ahead and Angus trying to figure out what had just happened. He was also wondering if his idea had been as stupid as Misty obviously thought it was.

It had seemed obvious, to bring the kids up together, to share the responsibility and take the pressure off them both. Forming a sort of family had seemed a logical solution, but she'd rejected the proposal outright.

Maybe it was a good thing, he decided, as the days wore on. The way he'd felt as they'd kissed had left him exposed and, as the kiss deepened, so had the feeling that he was on the edge of a chasm. He wasn't sure what that chasm contained.

Or maybe he did. He knew, better than most, what emotional connection cost. The kiss had made him think that the searing pain he'd vowed never to feel again was closing in. The fear. It was just as well she'd refused, because how could she possibly want that?

Clearly she didn't. She was being sensible for both of them.

The next ten days had seen them revert to formality.

Apart from their calls when he updated her with medical information there was no contact.

They'd need contact in the future, though, he thought. She was Lily's aunt and Alice was Lily's great-grandmother. Lily's real family.

But he was Lily's father...*he* was Lily's real family.

The concept felt wrong. He'd lost his family and where they should be was a void.

How could Lily fit into nothing?

But it'd work, he told himself. Children were adaptable and she'd learn to accept the limitations of what he could give.

But over and over his thoughts kept slipping back to Misty. Her commitment to the island was irrational. Her commitment to her gran and to Forrest...maybe that made more sense, but then she hadn't learned to keep her distance as he had. And if she couldn't do that, then her rejection of his idea was sensible as well.

So his proposal had been dumb, but there were still questions that refused to be answered. Questions about the way she made him feel. Questions that made him ask himself, honestly, was there part of him that did want commitment?

Did he want her to fall in love with him?

He couldn't. It'd be unfair, a one-way street where he was protected but she wasn't.

But there was a voice in the back of his head that kept whispering—or sometimes even shouting—that maybe he didn't want to be protected?

So, ten days later he was sitting on the veranda, watching the sun set over the silhouette of the distant mainland—and thinking about Misty. Lily had been settling, but now she woke and decided to complain again. He sighed. She'd had a couple of sessions lately where she'd screamed non-stop for an hour or so before she settled. The team, collectively, had diagnosed colic.

'It's common around this age,' Jodie, one of his team, had told him that afternoon as she'd handed Lily back to him—it was amazing how Lily was handed around like a pet, but almost instantly handed back to him when she started to scream. 'You're lucky it didn't start earlier. By four months they're generally over the worst—you know that.'

Of course he did. How often had he said those same words in his clinic? Superficially. He did his best and then waved the problem goodbye.

But now he conceded that he hadn't been sympathetic enough. Colic was horrid. He rocked her and cradled her and tried not to let his heart wrench when her face contorted in pain.

And he tried not to think about how Misty would do it better.

Because Misty loved?

Don't go there.

Saturday night. She lay in her too-big bed and tried not to think about Angus.

The man had proposed a future where her pressing problems would be solved. Her workload would be easy, her life would be easy...

Her life would be empty.

She lay in the dark and let herself imagine what living with Angus could be like. She remembered the note he'd left back in Melbourne as he'd headed off to swim with his mates. Would they have rosters for who cared for the children? Shared meals?

A shared bed?

She'd go crazy.

Because he'd be asking her to leave this island, she told

herself, but she knew it was more than that. For deep within she accepted that it was because she was in danger of falling in love and she was sensible enough, grounded enough, to know that living with someone who was afraid to love back would break her heart.

So get over it and go to sleep, she told herself, but there was no way sleep would come.

'Because maybe I'm not in danger of falling in love with Angus Firth,' she said at last, speaking out loud into the darkness. 'Foolish or not, I think I already have.'

The phone rang at four in the morning.

With Misty being the sole doctor, locals knew to only ring in cases of dire need—the islanders had accepted that was the only way she could survive. Angus had set up a roster for night calls, but there'd only been two since he'd arrived, one for a toddler with earache and one for an elderly lady with gastro. His team had handled both.

After an unsettled night Lily was now thankfully asleep, but Angus wasn't. He heard the phone ring and Jodie get up to answer. He'd been walking the floor with Lily until well after midnight—but for a reason he couldn't explain to himself he felt guilty for not getting up now.

But Jodie was on call and she could deal with it. If he got up for every call, he'd make himself as exhausted as Misty had been.

As Misty would be again.

And there she was again. Misty. He stared into the night and tried to sort his jumbled thoughts. They refused to be sorted.

He needed to surf again, he decided. Even a long swim might help. Maybe in the morning he could ask one of the team to care for Lily while he…

No. That wasn't in the contract. Misty was expecting him to be sole carer and he would be.

Misty. Damn, why couldn't he escape the judgement he'd seen in her eyes.

Why couldn't he stop thinking of her?

And then there was a knock on his bedroom door.

What? Did Jodie need backup? He slipped out to meet her—no way was he risking waking Lily.

'Problem?' he asked. The young doctor was looking worried.

'I'm sorry to wake you, but… Angus, I think I need to call Misty.'

'We don't call Misty,' he said curtly. That wasn't in the deal. 'We can handle it. What's happening?'

'It's Nicholas Mickleham,' she said, sounding increasingly distressed. 'You remember? Seventeen years old, primary melanoma with cerebral metastases. You talked to Misty about it a couple of weeks back. Nick's made the decision not to go back to Brisbane—he wants no further treatment and his parents and oncologist concur. I did another house call yesterday. He was weaker but there was no sign the end was near.

'But now Tony—his dad—has rung. He's had what sounds like major convulsions and lost consciousness. Tony says his breathing's faltering as well. Obviously they're deeply distressed. They still don't want evacuation to Brisbane, but they've asked me to call Misty. In the circumstances…are you okay with that?'

Was he okay with Misty being called out at this time of night? Three weeks ago he would have said no, but he knew a lot more about Misty by now. What had she said?

This island's my family.

It wasn't sensible, not to him, but with an insight that

he hadn't had three weeks ago, he knew that Misty would want to be called.

'If she'll go, I'll go with her,' Jodie offered.

But he knew instinctively that Misty would go and he also knew she'd be emotionally involved. Then he looked at Jodie and he saw distress. Jodie was one of his mob—medicine without strings. Attending such a situation wasn't what she'd signed up for when he'd asked her to come, but to ask Misty to go alone...

He couldn't. Damn, what was happening to his solitary mindset? He was all at sea here, but with a sinking heart he accepted that it was he who had to go. Whether Misty went or not.

'Would you stay with Lily while I go?' he asked and saw relief.

'Would you?'

He sighed, but inwardly. He was the doctor in charge here. 'I'll ring Misty and see if she wants to come,' he told her. 'But even if she does—and I suspect she will—she'll be personally involved. I can be clinician, as needed.'

At least he could take the practicalities from Misty's shoulders, he thought. Being the doctor in such a situation when it was for someone she loved... It must be impossible.

How did he know she loved?

This was one of her islanders. Of course she loved.

Dammit, she was doing his head in. But he had to go.

'I'll wheel Lily's basket into your room,' he told Jodie, but she shook her head.

'If it's all the same to you, I'll kip on your bed. I heard you up with her earlier. If she's finally settled, there's no way we should risk waking her up.'

Like there's no way I want to go to a deathbed, he thought.

Where was surfing when he needed it?

* * *

She answered on the third ring and her response was instant.

'Of course I'll go. I'll need to wake Gran and let her know what's happening, but I can be there in ten minutes.'

Just like that.

Did she even realise what she'd be facing? A dying kid. A family consumed with grief, gutted as he'd been. Parents who hadn't yet learned to build barricades so this sort of pain could never enter.

And with that came a sweep of emotion so intense it was physically painful. The memory of his brother's death... The thought of enduring that loss... The thought of Misty, even witnessing such grief...

But she hadn't even asked for support.

No matter. She had it. 'I'm also attending,' he told her. 'I'll pick you up on the way.'

'You don't need to.'

'I think I do,' he said and it came out sounding reluctant, but then he forced his voice to change. Authoritative. Confident. In charge. Everything he wasn't feeling. 'Don't tell me you wouldn't like backup?'

'I doubt I need...'

'Misty, would you like me to come?'

That produced a moment's silence, as if she was torn. 'I... Is Lily okay?' she asked at last. 'You said the colic's not settling.'

'She's sound asleep, with Jodie sleeping beside her.'

There was another silence, then Misty sighed. 'You and your team, hey? Lucky you. Oh, Angus, you know I can't get used to having help. But tonight, yes, please, I would like you to come.'

Angus picked her up and they drove the short distance to the Micklehams in silence. There seemed little to say. Angus seemed grim, Misty thought, almost as if he was gritting his teeth for what lay ahead.

As she was, too. Nick was a great kid and the thought of him dying, the thought of the waste, was doing her head in. And she'd known his parents for ever. Before her marriage, a teenaged Chris had sometimes minded the much younger Misty.

Misty had even been a flower girl at their wedding.

She was so involved. Maybe it would be easier to be like Angus, she told herself. But then she arrived and Chris met her at the door, crumpling into her arms and sobbing, and Misty thought, it might *sound* easier to be like Angus, but how could she ever manage it?

And then Angus put a hand on her shoulder, a light touch, as Chris released her and led the way into Nick's room.

'I'm right behind you,' he said softly, and she thought… Strangely she thought, *Who's behind* you?

Angus had introduced himself, then followed quietly as Chris led them to the bedroom. Then, as Tony also folded into grief and Misty hugged him, he had time and space to assess what was happening.

As expected, Nick was certainly deeply unconscious, his breathing already faltering. His path to death seemed to be happening fast. A catastrophic bleed from the tumour seemed the only possible cause, and the time for heroic medicine was long past.

This was a scenario Angus had spent his career avoiding.

In his Melbourne life, if ever there was the risk of this kind of emotion, this kind of grief, Angus would pass responsibility on fast. He'd refer to specialists, to a palliative care team, to anyone but himself. In this situation there were so many memories, all of them appalling.

But there were no 'specialists' here. No palliative care team. There were two parents, Misty and one dying boy.

And Angus.

With Misty supporting a distraught Chris and Tony, Angus had no choice but to take charge. And of course he knew what to do—hadn't he had that drilled into him the hard way? He examined Nick, concurring with what his parents had assumed. There was no response, no sign of anything but brain death. He did what he could to ease the laboured breathing. He checked and rechecked responses and he accepted the inevitable.

'If it's okay with you, I'll administer morphine and midazolam,' he told Tony and Chris. 'I doubt he needs either, but I want to make a hundred per cent sure that he's not in pain, that he doesn't have another convulsion, that he slips gently into death. Are you both okay with that? Misty, do you concur?'

Misty agreed—they all did—but as she helped him administer the drugs and move Nick into a more natural position, remaking the bed, she gave him an odd look—almost as if she hadn't expected him to know what to do? As he moistened the boy's lips and stood back to let Chris and Tony do the same, her look became even more intense. As though there were questions she wanted answered?

But thankfully now wasn't the time for questions he had no intention of answering. There was little to do but wait.

'I'll stay until the end,' Misty told him. 'Angus, you don't need to stay.'

He should go. More than anything else in the world, he didn't want to be there.

But he glanced at her face and, despite how he was feeling, he knew his place was here.

'Unless Jodie needs me, if it's okay with you all,' he said, 'then I'll stay.'

* * *

Nick died an hour later. Peacefully, quietly, while his parents held his hands, while Misty wept silently, while Angus learned…a new way of coping with death?

Was he coping?

What sort of doctor was he if he couldn't cope with this without disintegrating?

He felt drained. It seemed that all the emotions of the last three weeks had coalesced into this moment.

He'd thought he could never do this again, but at least now he could leave. Word was out. With family members flooding in from all over the island, with officialdom covered, he and Misty were free to go. There was nothing more they could do. As they headed out to his car there was the faintest sliver of light on the horizon.

The day felt unreal.

Stop the clocks…

Who'd said that about death? It was surely someone who'd experienced the enormity of loss, the impossibility of the world continuing to spin when someone you loved was gone.

'Thank you for being here,' Misty said. 'Thank you for what you've done. Thank you for sharing.'

'It was my privilege,' he told her, but he was struggling to speak at all. 'Do you…do you want to come back to the house and have breakfast?'

She shook her head. 'I need to go home and have my cry before Forrest wakes up.'

'I'm so sorry.'

'I'm sorry, too. Nick was such…' Her voice broke. 'He was such a good kid. To lose him…'

She couldn't go on and he didn't push. He started the car—and then he realised she was watching him as he drove.

'Angus?'

'Mmm.'

'I shouldn't ask, but your face…as you administered the drugs…as you moistened his lips… Angus, it's none of my business, but…were your family killed instantly?'

He froze for a moment, but then he forced himself to speak. There was no reason not to tell her.

'My mother and father, yes, but my little brother wasn't,' he said, flatly now, consciously dampening down emotion. 'He was…twelve. He was unconscious for two days before he died.'

'Oh, Angus…'

'It was a long time ago. It doesn't matter,'

'Of course it does. Oh, my dear…'

'Please. I'd rather not talk about it.'

And that was that. He drove her back to Sapphire Seas. Then he drove back to the doctors' house. To his daughter.

To responsibility.

To a life that seemed to be cracking at the edges.

'How is she?' Jodie must have been listening for him. She emerged from his bedroom almost the moment he walked through the front door.

'You mean, how are the Micklehams?'

She grimaced, but then gave a wry smile. 'Okay, I meant how are the Micklehams, though I suspect I know. But I'm also asking about Misty?'

'Jodie…'

She shrugged. 'You don't want me to ask? I guess that's our group mantra, isn't it? But you and Misty…'

He stared at her. Jodie had been part of his group for a couple of years now. He didn't know much about her background—yep, his group's philosophy was Don't Ask, Don't Tell—but he suspected that, like him, there were things in her past that had made her the loner she was.

So why was she breaking the rules now?

'The Micklehams are as grief stricken as you'd expect,' he said brusquely. 'But the extended family are gathering. And Misty...' But then he stopped. How to answer?

She was going home to cry? Alone?

And Jodie was still intruding. Not content with that first question, she was heading straight in. 'You're falling for her,' she said and for some reason he heard a faint tremor in her voice. 'Or you've fallen for her. Scary, isn't it?'

'I'm not...'

'I think you are,' she said gently. 'And why not? She's lovely. Why not go for it?'

'I think I have,' he said. Normally he'd never discuss such a personal topic but somehow, right now... His world was already off balance, so why not tilt it further? 'I've asked her to move to Melbourne and share my house.'

Her eyes widened. 'Well, well. But let me guess. She refused?'

'Of course she refused. Though it was a sensible proposition.'

'I'm sure it was,' Jodie said and, to his further astonishment, she took a couple of steps forward and gave him a hug. A real hug, warm and all enveloping. 'This island, though, it gets to you. Tonight, talking to Tony on the phone, remembering Nick assuring me he didn't want to go back to Brisbane, seeing his sheer courage... For some reason I've been remembering a poem from school. A line, something like... *"Anyone's death diminishes me for I'm involved with mankind."* That's Misty with this island, isn't it?'

'Yes,' he said curtly and couldn't go on.

He was standing in the hall. A bunch of surfboards were stacked against the wall and he found himself staring at them with a wave of longing so powerful he had to close his eyes. That's what his life had been before. Before Lily.

Before Misty.

When he opened his eyes, Jodie was watching him with sympathy—and understanding?

'Lily's still sleeping,' she said. 'You know we can cope if she wakes. Why not go find some waves?'

And that was a siren song. To surf…to put these dumb emotions right of his head and enter a space where there was only waves and sand and the sheer power of the sea. A place where he felt insignificant and his problems seemed insignificant as well.

Like walking away from Misty?

That thought did his head in. It was as though there were chasms on all sides and he could hardly move.

And finally, because emotions were building to the point where his head felt it might explode, he cracked.

'Has she woken at all?

'Not a peep.'

She'd cry when she did wake, he thought, as she'd cried most of the afternoon and evening before. He thought of the mums he'd seen in his clinic back in Melbourne, the parents he'd assured blithely, 'They're usually over colic by four months.'

He hadn't been nearly sympathetic enough. Lily's cries… they twisted something deep inside him.

Was it possible he was starting to love his daughter?

Like he'd loved his little brother?

There was another emotion.

But, staring at the surfboards, he felt a sliver of pressure lifting. When Lily was colicky he could do little to help, but in the mornings she'd seemed better. And Jodie was right here.

'Would you…?' He hesitated, but the longing was too great. It was as though those surfboards were calling him.

'Could you stay in charge for a bit longer?' he heard himself say.

And Jodie's face softened. 'Of course. I know why you need it. Surf as long as you want. But, Angus...'

'Yes?'

'I just hugged you,' she said. 'And you responded as though you needed it. We don't do it, do we, in our group? But I've given you a hug and you took it. So maybe you need to pass it on? Take a hug, give a hug—and maybe Misty's waiting?'

She didn't sleep. How could she? She lay and stared at the ceiling and tried to get her emotions in order. When the day began, she was almost grateful.

But the morning seemed to drag. Alice and Forrest decided to bake. She wasn't needed—how rare was that, but she wasn't appreciating it.

She swam in the magnificent pool, but no matter how hard she swam she couldn't lose her thoughts. Angus as a kid. Angus having to cope with the unbearable.

And then Jodie rang and the moment she answered she knew something was wrong. Really wrong. Her anxiety was unmistakable.

'Problem?' she asked, trying to supress her apprehension.

'Misty, I'm sorry to ring but we think Lily has intussusception.'

And that took her breath away.

Intussusception...

She knew it—of course she did. The term referred to a type of bowel obstruction, usually occurring in babies or toddlers, where a portion of their intestine somehow folded inside another. What followed was blockage, swelling and intense pain. In its early stages it was often mistaken for colic, but once things completely blocked it meant agony.

If it wasn't treated fast it could cause irreparable damage to the bowel, leading to lifelong problems. Intestinal tissue could die. There could be internal bleeding. Peritonitis.

Death.

It was a frightening diagnosis at the best of times.

It was the type of emergency that isolated doctors dreaded.

'How…how long?' Misty managed to ask. The words were hard to get out—she felt as though all the air had been punched from her lungs. Lily…the little girl she'd cared for. Her sister's baby.

'It's just turned acute in the last couple of hours,' Jodie told her. 'She woke half an hour after Angus left. For the last few days we thought she had colic, but now there's no mistaking it. She's in obvious pain, she's vomiting and, when I changed her, the staining's unmistakable. Molly and Dan have gone to try to find Angus…'

'Where's Angus?' Her shocked mind was struggling to take this in.

'He went surfing just after he got back from the Micklehams', but he didn't say where and I didn't think to ask. He thought, as we all did, that Lily had settled. Misty, Martin's not answering his phone. Does he walk his dogs at this hour? We have no one to ask about the procedure for evacuation to Brisbane, but that's surely what she needs. Proper evaluation, with a paediatric surgeon on standby.'

'Yes.' Thank heaven for Jodie, Misty thought. Thank heaven there was someone who could think straight.

'So give me details,' Jodie said, calm and sure. 'I'll make the calls.'

'I will…'

'Your voice is shaking,' Jodie said, gentling. 'Tell me who to contact and I'll do it. Then you concentrate on getting yourself over here. If we can't find Angus in time, will you go with her?'

And there was only one answer to that. 'I'm going with her anyway.'

Somehow she relayed the information Jodie needed. Then she went to find Alice. Alice was supervising Forrest spooning honey into muffin batter. When she saw Misty's face she let Forrest's overloaded honey spoon drop into the mix without a word.

'What?'

Misty told her. 'I have to go.'

'I should think so.' Baking forgotten, Alice looked as distressed as Misty felt. 'Forrest, let's finish up here and go pack a bag for your aunty. If Lily's ill, she'll need her.'

'Of course,' Forrest said, wide eyed. Sometimes he really did sound older than his years. 'Like when Misty held my hand when I vomited?'

'Exactly,' Alice said. 'And when the doctors had to take off my foot, Misty stayed with me the whole time. That's what families are for, young Forrest. Right, go give Misty a hug because that's what she needs most and then let's get ourselves organised.'

CHAPTER TWELVE

IT WAS ALMOST midday when Angus finally pulled his board from the water. He'd surfed until sheer physical fatigue forced him to stop. He usually found peace in the surf, but it wasn't there.

His carefully built defences against emotional pain seemed to have been shattered.

Why? How had this happened?

He was trying to shove emotion out of the picture, trying to focus on practicalities. He *could* cope with a future with Lily, he told himself. And being terrified of the sort of scene that had played out last night was dumb.

He needed to persuade Misty to stay in touch, he decided, to have her during school holidays, that sort of thing. And if Lily was upset, if she needed comfort he couldn't give her, then surely Misty would be only a phone call away.

And that was the sticking point. That was what was gnawing away in his gut.

Why did it seem so much better for Misty to be in Melbourne rather than here?

It'd be better for Forrest, he told himself, and it'd be better for Alice. Surely she could see that. It was a practical solution for them all.

Why did it hurt so much that she refused?

But, logical or not, it did hurt and he couldn't stop it hurting.

Finally he gave up. A man could only surf for so long, the wind was building and he probably shouldn't be surfing in such an isolated place anyway. He had a responsibility to Lily that he not get washed out to sea.

And that thought raised more questions. What would happen to Lily if he died? He'd have to change his will, he decided. He could leave everything to Misty, in a trust for Lily. Misty might even come to Melbourne and take care of the kids.

Was she refusing to come to Melbourne because of him? Was her rejection of his proposal all about him?

So many questions. No answers. Finally he caught one last wave, dried himself, loaded the board back on the car and headed for home.

He'd chosen a tiny beach at the south of the island. He'd found it a few days back when he'd taken Lily for a drive. He'd wanted to surf alone and this cove had seemed even more isolated than the one where he and Misty had…had…

Don't go there.

But his head was still there as he drove. He was still thinking of Misty, of that kiss, of that moment- until he topped the headland before the little town and saw a helicopter taking off from beside the clinic.

What the…what had happened while he'd been away?

He swore and pulled over, flipping open his phone. Twelve missed calls, all from Jodie. They must have come through while he surfed.

There must be real trouble.

And he thought… Lily?

That was dumb, he decided, as he pulled back on to the road and put his foot on the accelerator. It'd be someone else. Some accident.

But twelve calls? That felt like panic. Why would Jodie panic? It must be Lily.

Or Alice?

Or Misty?

What if something had happened to Misty?

His gut clenched and for a moment he thought he might be ill.

'You're catastrophising,' he told himself sharply, but his gut refused to unclench. Then he reached the house and Jodie was running down the driveway to meet him. Yelling.

'Where the hell have you been?' This was so unlike Jodie. She was just one of his mates, cool, professional, unemotional.

She didn't sound unemotional now.

'You know I've been surfing,' he said as he reached her. 'Jodie...'

'Stuff surfing. We think Lily has intussusception. She's in real trouble. We called for Medic evacuation. The chopper's on its way to Brisbane now and we have a neonatal team on standby. Misty's gone with her.'

And his world seemed to stop.

Lily.

He'd thought he couldn't care. The fact that he did, and he did so much, almost blindsided him.

For the last three weeks he'd been cradling his little girl against his body almost all the time she'd been awake. He'd fed her, washed her, talked to her, rocked her, seen her first smile...

When he looked at her he saw his brother.

When he looked at her he saw himself.

Intussusception! It was an awful thing. Agony. The thought of his baby... *His daughter*...

And in that moment he knew. Dear God, he loved her. The knowledge was so blinding that he felt as though he'd been physically struck. He couldn't escape the ties he'd spent so long avoiding. He already had them.

'Misty's with her?' he managed.

'Someone had to go.'

'I should have…'

'Yeah,' she said, but then her voice softened. 'But you weren't here and Misty was and, by the look on her face as she arrived, I think Lily's in the best of hands. I'm thinking Misty loves Lily as much as you do.'

He stared blindly at her, hardly hearing. The words didn't make sense. 'I need to get there.'

'I was trying to contact you before the chopper left, but now… There's nothing you can do that Misty can't do.'

'I still need to go.'

'I don't think you can for a few hours,' she said bluntly. 'It's the weekend so there's few ferries. The last one left at twelve and the next one's not until this evening. Misty'll ring if there's news.

'But I have to go,' he said and there was desperation in his voice.

'Well, well.' Jodie managed a rueful grimace. 'So there goes another member of our All Care And No Responsibility Squad.' Her smile faded and she shook her head. 'No matter. There's no way you can get over there until tonight, unless you highjack a fishing boat. Even those'll take a while—they're built for fishing, not for speed. Misty will ring once there's anything to report. If it's me she rings I'll let you know at once.'

Of course Misty would ring Jodie, he thought. Jodie was the referring doctor.

But he? He was Lily's father.

Except he'd surfed while his little girl fought for her life.

It was just as well Misty cared, he thought bleakly.

Why should she ring him? He didn't deserve anything.

* * *

Four p.m. There'd been a terrifying helicopter flight with Lily's condition deteriorating before her eyes. But the paramedics had been awesome, as had the radiologists who'd been on standby the moment they reached the hospital. The diagnosis had been confirmed. Lily had now been in theatre for over two hours and Misty was going out of her mind.

But she wasn't going out of her mind alone. An hour after she'd been ushered into the family waiting area, the door opened and Alice had wheeled herself in, Forrest by her side.

'We knew there wouldn't be room for us on the chopper, but the midday ferry was due to leave just as we found out what was happening,' Alice had told her. 'So I rang and asked them to wait and they did. I've promised to make the crew a big batch of lamingtons in return.'

'And Gran said I could stay with Aunty Cath,' Forrest had added, again sounding much older than his years. 'But Lily's my sister and I thought I ought to come.'

'So how are things?' Alice had asked and they'd both fallen silent as she'd told them.

Then Misty had hugged them both and cried a little, then they'd all settled for the excruciating wait.

Alice was now dozing in her chair. Forrest had played with the toys the nurse had brought him and then decided to nap himself, stretching out on three seats, snuggled in blankets. Even in sleep, though, he held Misty's hand.

The contact helped, Misty thought, as the hours dragged on. Their presence helped.

But it didn't help enough. If only she'd been with her... If she'd held Lily tight... If she'd been a mum to her...

'This is not your fault,' Alice had said to her earlier. 'Angus is her dad. I don't know what he was thinking, going out of contact. It's him that should be with her now.'

'She's ours,' Misty said. 'She always was and you know it.'

'Yes, but she's his, too,' Alice had retorted. 'So why isn't he here?'

And suddenly he was.

The door swung open—not the door that led to the theatre suites, the door she'd been watching for hours, but the door to the corridor that led to the outside world.

His hair stiff with salt. He was wearing jeans and an ancient T-shirt, and on his sand-encrusted feet were disreputable leather sandals.

He looked…haggard.

'Misty,' he said as he saw her, and at that, all her resolve, all her common sense flew right out the window. Forrest's hand was disengaged and she was up and he was gathering her into his arms and hugging her as if he'd never let go.

She cried.

Oh, for heaven's sake, how many times had she cried on this man? She was a doctor, a clinician, a professional.

She didn't feel like a professional. She felt like…a mum?

Somehow she pulled back and what she saw left her stunned.

There were tears running down Angus's cheeks.

They stared at each other for a long moment—and then somehow Misty pulled herself together—sort of—and reached for the tissue box the nurse had strategically left within reach.

'I can't offer you a monogramed hankie,' she said, somehow mustering a shaky smile as she handled him tissues and used a wad herself.

He didn't manage a smile in return.

'Misty, I'm so sorry. I can't…' He shook his head as though shaking off a nightmare. 'How…?'

'I don't know anything other than intussusception has been confirmed and she's been in theatre for two hours.'

'Two hours!'

'They must be repairing...'

But her voice faltered and she couldn't go on. Sometimes intussusception could be remedied by manoeuvring the intestine back into position, but if there'd been a rupture...

'Hell,' he groaned. 'Oh, God, Misty...'

'I know.'

'Thank heaven you...'

'No. It was Jodie and her friends, but you'd have diagnosed it if you were there.'

'I should have been.'

'I've been thinking about that.' She took a deep breath. 'When Jodie first rang I was angry that they couldn't find you. I thought you mustn't care. But I've had a few hours to think now and I was wrong. Lily's almost three months old and you're living with friends who are also doctors. Jodie said she was deeply asleep when you left and, for heaven's sake, even the most besotted parents need to have some time out. And for you... I'm starting to realise that last night must have been dreadful.'

He shook his head, but she put a hand on his arm and soldiered on.

'Please, no guilt, Angus. Pretend you had to go to the dentist for a root canal if that'll make you feel better. It would have been exactly the same—there are times when you need to leave.' And then she frowned. 'But...how exactly did you get here?'

'It seems you can't ring charter companies on Sunday afternoons,' he told her. 'But one of my surfing mates is an airline pilot based here. He's friends with some chopper pilots and one of them knew someone well enough to ask.'

'Wow...'

'So Alice and Forrest?' He signalled to the pair who hadn't stirred.

'They highjacked a ferry, using lamingtons as bait,' she told him. 'Like me, they had to be here. And that brings me to what I need to say.' She took a deep breath. This was momentous, but it was the only decision available. 'So, Angus, no blame about tonight, absolutely none, but Alice and Forrest and I... What we need to say... Angus, we've talked about it and if you agree...if you feel you really can't love her, then we need to keep her. We need to keep Lily.'

Silence—and then she went on in a rush.

'Angus, Lily is Forrest's sister and he knows that. She's Alice's great-grandchild and she's my niece. That doesn't outweigh the fact that she's your daughter, but it seems you have demons you can't help, demons you might not be able to get past. Now I know about your brother...your family... I get it. But, Angus, the good thing about families is that we can be a team. There'll be no judgement. You'll still be her dad, but we'd like to keep her. She feels...like ours.'

He stared at her, expressionless. 'That's not what you said three weeks ago.'

'It wasn't,' she said. 'We... *I* was tired and distressed and shocked. I was coming to terms with Jancie's death and, to be honest, there was also a fair bit of anger in the mix. But we've had time now and, thanks to you, we've had space to see things clearly. And today...' Her voice cracked a little. 'Tonight we've come close to losing her. We still may, but please God, if we don't, when she comes home we're hoping she can come home to us. With you in the background if you like, but the responsibility will be ours.'

'You can't manage.'

She tilted her chin at that. 'Watch us,' she said and then she paused and regrouped. Said what had to be said.

'There'll be sacrifices,' she said. 'The island won't get the medical care it deserves, but I suspect when we lay it on the line we may get help. I need to learn to share a bit more, let the islanders bring Forrest and Lily up, not just me. Much as I'd love to be hands on…'

'I can be hands on.'

'But you don't want to be,' she said, gently now. 'We know you'll do your best, we know that, but loving's not just doing your best. Loving's throwing your heart in the ring, never mind that it might get battered. Alice did that for me—she loved me and before that she loved my mother. Did I tell you that Alice wasn't my mum's birth mother?— Alice adopted her as a troubled teen. But she loved her, no matter what, and she's loved Jancie and me, and now she loves Forrest. And today…' She gave a rueful smile. 'Do you know how hard it is to make lamingtons when you're sitting in a wheelchair? No matter, she's promised them regardless, because she had to get over here.

'So there you are, Angus. You're off the hook. You might choose to have access—maybe you can come up to the island every now and then to surf. You might teach Lily to surf. And also…' She hesitated, but then forged on. 'Alice says I have to ask. If you're able to help financially, just for Lily's costs, we would welcome that with relief.'

But then she faltered. The emotion of the last few hours, the tension, this man's presence…she'd been trying so hard to sound sensible, to talk practicalities, but she couldn't go on. The reality of what was happening behind those beige doors was all too real.

'I don't know why I'm talking of this now,' she said, and swiped the tears away again. 'It all depends…it has to depend…'

'On whether she makes it?' He could hardly say it.

She nodded, then sat down hard on the seat beside Forrest.

'Sorry. For everything that I said. It was unfair to throw

that at you. All I need to say is that we love her and we want her.'

'I want her.'

She shook her head. 'That's just today talking. You know you don't...'

But then the beige doors swung open.

Alice and Forrest woke up and the surgeon was clearing his throat before saying, very gently, 'It's done and we think she'll make it.'

And nothing, not one thing, mattered more than that.

Lily not only lived, she decided to thrive.

She needed to stay in hospital for a few days. Her intestines would be temporarily slowed, so she needed intravenous fluids, plus pain relief, but everything was looking good. She was sometimes even smiling up at them from her little hospital cot.

So she recovered, while Angus tried to figure out where to go from here. His world seemed as though it had been picked up and shaken; nothing seemed the right way up.

All he knew was that he needed to stay with Lily.

And with Misty.

Alice and Forrest returned to the island. 'Now our Lily's decided to live, I have lamingtons to bake,' Alice declared. 'But there's a problem. Cath's offered to help, but rolling them in the icing is a job for at least two. What about it, Forrest?'

Forrest wavered, but the hospital accommodation was boring, Misty was preoccupied, and finally he decided the lamington option was a good one.

Misty stayed on at the hospital, on a trundle bed beside Lily.

Angus got himself a hotel room.

'You don't need to stay,' Misty told him.

There were all sorts of things he should say to that, but he chose the easiest. 'What am I to do if I go back to the island? Surf?'

He waited for Misty to make some comment. Instead she simply nodded.

Was she glad he was staying? He didn't have a clue. She was spending all her time with Lily, talking to her, holding her tiny hand, helping the nurses do what needed to be done.

And Angus sat and watched and tried to come to terms with this new order. With the way his world seemed to have changed.

For now his world was still. The cubicle containing Lily's cot seemed like a cocoon, cut off from the outside world, making every other thing seem irrelevant. He wasn't needed—he knew it—but leaving seemed unthinkable.

So he stayed and sometimes it almost felt as though he was keeping guard. Keeping watch over his family?

That concept occurred to him on the second day, when a nurse bustled in and offered him lunch. 'There's food available for the parents,' she told him, 'and Misty's included. We'll put you on the list as well.'

There was the assumption, that he and Misty were a unit. Mum and Dad. Family. It should have him backing away. Instead it was starting to sound…right.

Family?

There were so many questions in his head it was making him dizzy, but all he could do was sit and watch and wait for things to settle.

He just wasn't sure where that would be, but more and more he knew who he wanted to be with when that happened.

With Misty.

He watched her as she cared for his daughter. He watched her as she made Lily smile. He watched her as she kept her watch over the little girl in the cot, as she touched Lily's hand and let her tiny baby fingers curl around hers.

And as he watched, as he saw tenderness and unmistakable love, he felt ashamed. The courage she'd shown, to care for Forrest, to care for her gran and the islanders, and now, to care for Lily... She was...

No. There were no words to convey the surge of emotion washing through him.

Lily had to stay with her, he thought. But him?

'Come and cuddle,' she told him more than once, but he didn't. He needed to sort himself out. He couldn't make false promises, to allow Lily to think of him as her dad. He couldn't afford to show emotion, to let Misty see what he was feeling...

If he did that he was lost.

But was he lost already? What was he losing by walking away?

Then, on the day the paediatric surgeon announced he was delighted with Lily's progress and he thought he might discharge her the next day, the emotions in his head coalesced into knowledge. And fear.

Misty was about to take her home, but him?

Where was home? Where the heart was? He'd heard that somewhere, read it on a corny card or something.

A nurse came in to take Lily's obs. She'd been awake for a while. Misty had been cuddling her, playing peek a boo with her fingers, making her smile. Now the little girl had drifted into a gentle sleep.

He watched them both and as he did, finally, *finally* things seemed to settle.

And if they were settled, if he were to do this thing, if he was to say what he needed to say, he had to do it now.

'If we were to go for a walk,' Angus asked the nurse,

feeling as though he was treading on egg shells, but also feeling, for the first time, like a man with a plan… 'If I take Misty out for a bit, could you promise to ring us the moment Lily wakes?'

And the nurse beamed. She'd been on duty every daytime shift of Lily's admission and she'd seen how Misty had hardly moved from Lily's side.

'Of course,' she said. 'Your little girl's so settled and you need a break. I'm thinking you have two or three hours before she wakes. But I'll leave the curtains open and I promise I'll ring the moment she does. I'm thinking a walk would be what you most need.'

'Misty?' he said, and Misty turned from the cot. She looked a bit dazed.

Her world had changed, too, Angus thought. In these last weeks, since her decision to hand Lily over, she'd now… fallen in love?

Of course she had. Love seemed to be a Misty specialty.

Could it be his? Could he find the courage?

She was rising now, looking doubtfully at him, but she allowed herself to be ushered out, into the lifts, out of the hospital and down to the river.

Brisbane's river was bordered by a swathe of parkland. At some time in the past a marshy floodplain had turned into a gorgeous oasis of trees and grasses and sand and water, and it was an obvious destination.

They didn't talk as they made their way towards the huge lagoon which was its centrepiece. There seemed no words.

Being outside seemed strange, almost wrong. Their whole centre for the last three days had been one cubicle in a massive hospital. Now Misty seemed almost numb.

He steered her to a bench shaded by a massive Moreton Bay fig tree and went across to a coffee cart to buy coffee. She took it gratefully—well, she would, hospital coffee was disgusting—sipped a couple of times, then and sat and cradled her cup in both hands.

Time to speak?

Dear heaven, he needed courage to say what he needed to say. What if she refused?

Say it, he ordered himself. Say it, say it, say it.

'Misty.' His voice came out as a croak and he had to try again. 'Misty?'

'Mmm?' She turned and faced him, still with that dazed expression.

And the way she looked… His heart twisted and twisted again, then finally his world settled. What he needed to say was right. It was the only thing he could say. If she refused…well, that was her right and he wouldn't blame her, but he had to try.

He lifted her coffee cup from her hands and placed it on the ground. She made a tiny mew of protest, but he smiled.

'If it gets cold, I'll buy you another. I promise.'

'So…this is more important than coffee?'

'I think it is,' he said gently and took her hands in his. 'Misty, I've fallen in love.'

She gazed at him, uncomprehending. 'With Lily?'

'Yes,' he said and his heart was hammering in his chest, because how could he express the way he was feeling? He'd spent the last few days questioning his emotions, pushing himself down dark alleys he'd had no wish to explore, facing emotions he'd blocked for long, wasted years. But finally, he'd accepted what his heart had been trying to tell him from the moment he'd seen Misty in his clinic's waiting room almost a month before.

'I do love Lily,' he said, slowly, sounding out each word as if it might be loaded. 'I thought I couldn't, as… Misty, as I thought I couldn't love you. I was wrong. Stupidly, blindly wrong. It was cowardice, leftover damage from my family's deaths. But the idea that I could hold myself away from loving, that I could protect myself from pain was just plain dumb. If I hadn't been here these last days…if I'd been in Melbourne… It was bad enough that I was surfing when Lily needed me. It was bad enough that I wasn't able to hold you while you needed me.'

'Me…'

'Because I love you, Misty,' he said, growing surer of his words now. 'I never thought I'd be able to say it—I never thought I'd want to. But your courage, your strength, your honour… Misty, every time I look at you I love you more.'

Silence. She didn't say a word. She simply sat, her hands in his, an expression on her face that was unreadable.

'It doesn't matter,' he said, too fast now, struggling again to get the words out. 'I mean…if you don't want… I know you love Lily and if you want, I'll back away. Know, though, that I'll support you in every way I can. I'll pay every expense Lily incurs and that also means supporting you while you care for her. I'll pay locum wages so you can get help on the island. Jodie might even stay on—she loves it and if I pay… No matter, I swear you won't be under financial pressure again, that you'll have help. But, Misty, there is an alternative.'

'Which…which is?'

'That I stay on.' There, it was said, and he'd never felt so exposed, so open, so raw. This woman… It was impossible that she'd take him. He didn't deserve it. How could she…

'I… I could stay on the island,' he said. 'Maybe we could buy Sapphire Seas, or maybe we can just do up the doctors' quarters. We could share the medical needs of the island. We could love Lily and we could love Forrest and Alice. Maybe we could have a dog of our own. Maybe…' He faltered, but the thing had to be said… 'Maybe we could even try for a baby ourselves. But all these things…'

He stopped then because tears were tracking down her cheeks. He'd made her cry? Dammit, he'd cut his heart out before he'd do such a thing. He felt ill.

'Misty, don't,' he begged. 'I won't say another word. You and Lily and Forrest can go home to your happy ever after, knowing that you'll be supported by me at a distance. I'll go back to Melbourne. I won't ask again…'

'Stop it,' she managed. 'Angus, where's your handkerchief?'

He felt in his pocket, but no. 'I didn't bring one,' he said blankly.

'Oh, for heaven's sake, what sort of hero are you?' she demanded, swiping her sleeve across her face. 'And what are you saying, go home to my happy ever after without you? What sort of heroine does that make me?'

'Do you think…?' he said. 'Does this mean…? Misty, could you possibly love me?'

'I think I already do,' she told him as he gathered her into his arms. As he kissed her and kissed her again. As he held her against his heart and felt that here at last was his home.

And when finally, finally she emerged for long enough to speak, her words confirmed it.

'Angus Firth, if you really want us—all of us,' she said, cradling his face, loving him with her smile, 'then prepare to be loved for a very long time.'

CHAPTER THIRTEEN

'YOU HAVE TO come and see. Tomorrow at Boardrider's Beach. All the learners' mums and dads are coming. *Please?*'

Of course they were coming. So now, on a balmy Saturday morning, Angus and Misty were watching Forrest try to surf. It had taken time and patience to teach him to trust the water—indeed, to trust the world—but bit by bit his confidence was building. Surely today he'd ride his very first wave to the shore?

He missed the first couple of waves. The third he caught, but barely got to his feet before he wobbled and toppled, though it didn't seem to dent that fragile confidence. 'Wipe out,' he yelled, and headed out again.

There were five other kids waiting at the back of the waves, all aching to catch a curler. Forrest was surely the most eager of them all.

Angus and Misty stood together on the beach, their hearts in their mouths, their fingers crossed, hoping desperately that this would come off.

'Well done, Forrest, great stand, but get that leg further back.' It was a yell from their surfing tutor, out the back of the waves, on her own board. Jodie.

For Jodie had returned. She'd come back for Misty and Angus's wedding, but afterwards she'd stayed.

'If you can figure out a way for the island to afford me, I'd love to work here,' she'd said and Angus and Misty had spent a part—a very small part—of their honeymoon working on a plan for a health resort. It was a place for rehabilitation, for healing…for happy ever after?

'We should call it Happy Ever After.' That was Cath and Alice's idea, but Jodie had howled them down. 'It's too soppy for words,' she'd said. 'We have enough of that every time we look at Misty and Angus.'

So their health resort had taken the name of the place they'd bought to build it. Angus's magnificent Melbourne home had been sold to fund Sapphire Seas Healing and that gorgeous horizon pool was now being enjoyed by many.

Including the island medics.

There were now three doctors on the island, which meant there was enough time for playing in the surf, in the pool, with the kids.

With each other.

It was a gift beyond price, Angus thought, as he and Misty held hands, held their breaths, and watched Forrest wait for his perfect wave.

At their feet two-year-old Lily was filling in a hole—or trying to. Biggles, their five-month-old beagle pup, was intent on digging to China. He dug, Lily filled—ad infinitum. Cath and Alice were watching from a distance, with Doozy hovering between. Doozy was helping the digging, but Cath had sandwiches. How was a dog to decide? Doozy's leg was still a bit weak, but you'd never know it by the speed he gained when a sandwich was on offer.

He was healed.

And so am I, Angus thought. The sun was on his face. Lily was at his feet and Misty, the woman he loved with all his heart, was by his side. As she'd sworn to be until death do us part.

And that would happen one day, hopefully in fifty years, or even more. He accepted the risk and that acceptance was part of his healing. He'd figured it out. Love was finite—and yet infinite.

One day the little girl at his feet would grow up, leave home, do what? Become a surfing instructor in Hawaii? And Forrest? Lately he'd been reading everything he could find about whales in Antarctica. Hawaii seemed a much warmer bet.

And what of the others he'd learned to love? Alice's heart was getting weaker. Doozy was getting old.

So there'd be loss, but he couldn't protect himself from pain by not loving. The trick was that he just had to love more.

And he'd learned it from Misty, his beautiful, huge-hearted wife, who'd opened her heart to the world and somehow included him. He still couldn't believe she'd said yes. Every morning he woke to find her body spooned against his and he couldn't believe his luck. How had he ever thought he could live without loving? Right now he felt like the luckiest man alive.

And then there was a whoop, a yell from Jodie. 'Coming in now, Forrest, this is your wave.'

And Angus stopped thinking about luck, he stopped thinking about anything, because he was struggling to breathe. The swell was building. Forrest was paddling his hardest, glancing behind him, watching the water build, paddling faster.

Misty's hand was digging into his. He glanced down and saw her face and he thought, Forrest's not riding this by himself. And it wasn't just Misty. A quick glance told him every heart on the beach was riding with this damaged kid, this little boy the island had taken as their own.

And then the wave crested and somehow Forrest was on his feet. He staggered, there was a collective gasp, but then he steadied.

And he rode.

The wave was perfect. It swept in, a long line of cresting foam, breaking at just the right angle. And Forrest had found his centre and everything came together.

In he came, confidence building, enough for him to look towards the beach and give a grin so wide it enveloped his face. He'd done it.

And Angus was hugging Misty and she was hugging him, then Forrest was off the board, tearing out of the water to get his share of the hug, and Lily was grinning up from her hole because she knew this was exciting—except she did have to get back to her hole because Biggles was winning.

And Angus thought, how perfect is this?

He'd take it. Love, family, kids, dogs, islanders, weddings, funerals, catastrophes, celebrations, the whole kaleidoscope of emotions he could possibly feel.

Forrest was racing back into the shallows. He'd managed one perfect wave, now he wanted another.

And why not, Angus thought, as his embrace of Misty turned into a kiss of pure triumph. Why not aim for more?

He'd thought love could be destroyed. How wonderful to be proved so wrong.

How wonderful to know that love, in all its forms, could last for ever.

* * * * *

COMING SOON!

We really hope you enjoyed reading this book.
If you're looking for more romance
be sure to head to the shops when
new books are available on

Thursday 21st December

To see which titles are coming soon, please visit
millsandboon.co.uk/nextmonth

MILLS & BOON

MILLS & BOON®

Coming next month

SURGEON PRINCE'S FAKE FIANCÉE
Karin Baine

'In that case, we'll announce the engagement as soon as possible. I know you want time to let your family know what's happening, but I think the truth is going to come out sooner or later.'

He watched Soraya's face contort into a puzzled frown as none of that would have made any sense to her whatsoever.

'What on earth—?'

The second she made it obvious she had no idea what he was talking about the game was over. He would never recover if he was exposed as a liar in the press even if it had been done with the best of intentions. There was only one way he could think of temporarily stopping her from breaking their cover, and, though it might earn him a slap, he had to take the chance. It would be easier to explain things to her later than to the entire country.

Raed grabbed her face in his hands and kissed her hard. He expected the resistance, her attempt to push him away. What he hadn't been prepared for was the way she began to lean into him, her body pressed against his, her mouth softening and accepting his kiss. All notions of the press and what had or hadn't been captured seemed to float out of his brain, replaced only with thoughts about Soraya and how good it felt to have his lips on hers.

She tasted exactly how he'd imagined, sweet and spicy, and infinitely moreish. He couldn't get enough. Soraya's hands, which had been a barrier between their bodies at first, were now wrapped around his neck, her soft breasts cushioned against his chest in the embrace. Every part of him wanted more of her and if they'd been anywhere but in the middle of a car park he might have been tempted to act on that need. It had been a long time since he'd felt this fire in his veins, this passion capable of obliterating all common sense.

He knew this had gone beyond a distraction for any nearby journalists but he didn't want to stop kissing her, touching her, tasting her. Once this stopped and reality came rushing in, he knew he'd never get to do this again.

Continue reading
SURGEON PRINCE'S FAKE FIANCÉE
Karin Baine

Available next month
www.millsandboon.co.uk